Vanished

T. M. Thomas

Copyright © 2021 T.M. Thomas

All rights reserved.

ISBN-13: 979-8-719-03061-6

DEDICATION

The writing of this story has been a mission. I must give thanks to my family who have been there throughout the writing process, my numerous friends who have assisted with proofreading the chapters as I have progressed, and R.J. Thompson for his guidance on the KDP process.

For Sandi & Pari

CONTENTS

	Acknowledgments	i
1	Chapter 1	1
2	Chapter 2	9
3	Chapter 3	12
4	Chapter 4	22
5	Chapter 5	28
6	Chapter 6	37
7	Chapter 7	42
8	Chapter 8	47
9	Chapter 9	55

10	Chapter 10	61
11	Chapter 11	68
12	Chapter 12	74
13	Chapter 13	82
14	Chapter 14	93
15	Chapter 15	104
16	Chapter 16	109
17	Chapter 17	119
18	Chapter 18	129
19	Chapter 19	138
20	Chapter 20	147
21	Chapter 21	156
22	Chapter 22	166
23	Chapter 23	176
24	Chapter 24	183
25	Chapter 25	191
26	Chapter 26	199
27	Chapter 27	210
28	Chapter 28	214
29	Chapter 29	224

30	Chapter 30	234
31	Chapter 31	239
32	Chapter 32	247
33	Chapter 33	252
34	Chapter 34	256
35	Chapter 35	261
36	Chapter 36	266
37	Chapter 37	276
38	Chapter 38	282
39	Chapter 39	286
40	Epilogue	289

This novel is entirely a work of fiction.
The names, characters and incidents portrayed in it are
the work of the author's imagination. Any resemblance to
actual persons, living or dead, events or localities is entirely
coincidental.

Vanished

1

I saw a man vanish today. One moment I was at the beach party. Hundreds, if not thousands, of people dancing in the moonlight, trance music blaring, neon body paint. Everyone was drinking, or getting high. Some were even getting naked. Except me. I was my group of friends designated driver for the night, sober as a judge. I saw a bright flash of light. Nothing unusual with that. There were enough party lights fuelled by generators, laser pens and glow sticks whizzing around in a blur. But this light came from the top of the cliffs. Just like a neon firework in the sky. A couple of minutes later a man ran breathlessly from the bottom of the cliff steps, looking frantically from side to side and then behind him. He was about 24 years old, 5'10" tall of athletic build with very blond hair and piercing blue eyes. He wore what appeared to be a black leather jacket, which bizarrely showed off the contours of his defined abs. I remember thinking that, even though it was night, it was a hot August night, and he must be so hot in that jacket. His trousers appeared to be leather too, but certainly didn't restrict his movement as he sprinted across the beach towards me. I stood there, on the sand, in my Arsenal shirt and shorts and a pair of flip flops, diet coke in my hand, watching him as he crossed the fifty metres or so of sand between us. I wondered if I had seen him before but couldn't place him. No-one else seemed to acknowledge his existence, all taken away by the trance music and their vice of choice. As the man reached me I saw he had a UV tattoo on the side of his neck which flashed as the lightshow swung in our direction. Cool. It was an inverted triangle with the number 69 inside it. It made me giggle a little. The man grasped both of my shoulders with both hands in a firm grip. He glanced back towards the steps quickly before looking me in the eye.

"They are coming," he said in an accent I couldn't quite place, "protect her." He tapped me on both shoulders as if we were old friends and then tore off down the beach before I could ask who. I watched as he ran around the edge of the dancers and then along the surf. I stepped closer to the sea to watch him as I took a swig of my drink. It appeared as if he were surrounded by an orange aura as he ran which grew brighter and then imploded on itself until a tiny orange dot was all that was left, hanging in the darkness. Whether it was my eyes adjusting or not, I don't know, but the dot appeared to just fade away like a spent firework. I don't know if anyone else took any notice. I only saw one guy who was near to the spot look briefly before staring at the roll up cigarette in his hand and then laugh out loud. I glanced back at the cliff steps just in time to see two dark figures at the bottom of the steps turn and run back up them and behind the trees at the first bend in the steps. What the fuck just happened?

* * *

Ouch! The alarm clock on Zack's phone shrilled out for the second time that morning. He'd already smacked it once, without looking, hoping that he had switched it off. It was all too apparent now that he'd only hit snooze. It was the weekend, Sunday morning, he didn't even need to be awake, but also found some solace in the fact that he could go back to sleep if he so wanted. He picked the phone up and touched the switch off icon on the screen. It was six a.m. Hell, he'd only been asleep for two and half hours since getting in from the beach party. Is that why he had such a headache? It couldn't be a hangover, surely, he'd only had one beer and then diet coke all night. But, oww, his head throbbed as if he'd been drinking vodka and red bull all night. In fact, he hadn't felt this rough since his twenty first birthday when the whole bar, at the end of the pub crawl, were convinced by his friends, Marshall and Jeff, to make a small contribution to an ever-growing line of shots along the bar of pretty much everything that the pub sold. He hadn't dared to drive for three days after that. But he shouldn't be feeling like this today. It felt so unfair to be feeling this way and not having enjoyed an alcohol fuelled night of debauchery the night before. He put it down to the lack of sleep sandwiched between five kilowatts of trance music and the shrill beep of his alarm. He cursed himself for not making sure that his alarm was unset before he went to sleep. Dawn was starting to slowly show through the gap in the curtain and the birds had started to chirp. He pulled his summer duvet up and scrunched his eyes together tight, hoping that he would be able to get back to sleep. It was highly unlikely that he would be able to drift into slumber again. His curtains lost the battle to keep the sunrise out, and his mind was racing about something he felt that he should remember. It wasn't quite coming to him just yet, but he had a feeling of excitement, confusion, and fear all at once. Zack looked around his room to see if anything sparked the inspiration he needed to help him to remember what he thought he should be able to. He took in the posters on his bedroom wall, a mixture of thrash metal bands and fantasy art. Nope, nothing coming to him yet. His collection of acquired beer glasses and eighties action DVDs on the shelf above his computer desk had the same effect. He put his feet on the floor and sat upright on his bed. A ruffle through his hair and the obligatory morning scratch of his balls, Zack stood up. Wearing just his Calvin Klein trunks he blearily walked across the room to his en-suite. He paused at his door. For some reason the fear emotion became the dominant emotion. This annoyed him as he still couldn't remember what he had to be fearful of.

"This is fucking crazy." Zack muttered to himself, before rubbing his eyes and depressing the door handle to walk into the bathroom. Zack opened the door and stepped into the en-suite. It was dark. He thought he could hear heavy breathing, and then realised that it was himself. Zack reached for the light pull string. As he pulled on the string until it clicked on the ceiling, the toilet in front of him became illuminated by the instant light from above. He heard a gasp from behind the door which he knew wasn't him this time. Zack jumped back out of the doorway into his bedroom, still facing the door. His heart was racing, and his breathing laboured as the fear emotion over-rode everything else. He stood one metre back from the doorway staring at the toilet in front of him, as if it were mocking him as it did the nights he'd had too much to drink. Only this time he was stone cold sober (with a throbbing hangover, go figure). The door was wide open, swung into the bathroom to the right. Along the wall behind the door was the bath and shower combo.

"Who's there?" Zack called out, trying to hide the fear in his voice, not terribly successfully though. There was no response. He took a quick glance either side of him around his room for a weapon. He saw none, he wasn't a weapon person. The only thing that vaguely resembled anything threatening was a realistic light up lightsabre his girlfriend, Eva, had bought him for the last Christmas. What alternative did he have? He could call his mother to his room to check his bathroom. He was twenty-four years old for God's sake, and considering yelling out for his mum, all five foot nothing of a grey haired fifty something housewife, to save his sorry arse. Nope, the lightsabre won. He backed up towards where he kept it, beside his computer desk, never taking his eyes off the door as he put more distance between it. His brain was running wild and he had convinced himself that if he looked away for even a second that some mythical creature, like a demon fairy or an imp, would dash unseen out of the room, and when he found the bathroom empty he would never be able to completely convince himself that there was never anything there. As he backed up against his computer desk he reached behind himself, fumbling around until he felt the hard plastic tubing of the lightsabre. Taking it into his hand and wielding it like a sword he felt slightly more confident and foolish at the same time. A misguided sense of reality began to tell him that his good morning piss was long overdue, and he edged towards the bathroom door.

"If there's anyone in there," he called out, unsure of what to say next, "erm, you should know...I'm armed and dangerous."

Zack had a plan. As he reached the en-suite door he paused. He tried to control his breathing to a silence and listen. After a few seconds of holding his breath he could only hear his heart pounding inside of him. He reached inside and took hold of the light pull cord, paused, counted to three in his head, and then gave it a yank. Plunging the en-suite into darkness he pressed the button to light up his toy lightsabre. A blue neon light rose quickly from the handle up to the tip of the tube, with a humming noise straight out of a Star Wars movie.

"RAAAAR!" He yelled as he jumped sideways into the room to face the bathtub and shower, the neon blue light casting an eerie glow in the room, reflecting off of the tiles. Zack then saw something he didn't want to see: movement; big movement; like a person sized movement ducking down into the bathtub.

"Oh shit!" He yelled in a slightly higher pitch. He retreated backwards until the backs of his legs connected with the toilet, causing him to sit down on the pan. All the willpower he could summon prevented him from peeing at that moment. He stared at the person in the bathtub.

"Who the fuck are you?" He asked. His left hand gripped the handle of the lightsabre whilst his right hand fumbled blindly in the dark for the light cord. When he found it, adrenaline coursed through him as he gave it a yank. Too hard, and the cord snapped away from the rose in the ceiling in his hand.

The figure slowly stood up in the darkness in the bathtub, all the more eerie for the blue glow from Zack's 'weapon'. Tall, slender, dressed in black leather with long, fine black hair cascading down it's back. Zack held his breath, stunned to the spot sitting on the toilet. It had its back towards Zack, arms stretched out at a forty-five-degree angle with long fingers splayed, as if to show him that it was holding nothing and meant him no harm.

"Ok, keep your arms out and the side and turn around," Zack mustered after he remembered to breathe, sucking in a deep breath, "slowly, no sudden movements. Remember I armed and dangerous."

"Zack Collins, I am not concerned with your toy." The figure spoke, slightly higher pitched than he had expected, and on this occasion, it took all of his willpower not to defecate as he had been called out.

"It's real." Zack said, although if he couldn't convince himself, how would he convince this......thing......that had found its way to his en-suite in the middle of the night.

"Yes, Mr. Collins, it's a real toy," it spoke again, "I mean you no harm. I shall turn slowly as you wish."

Zack had no words. It was far too soon after waking up for him to be thinking on his feet in an incomprehensible situation, and he had exhausted all of his wit and ideas. The figure turned slowly anti clockwise, arms still outstretched and with no sudden movements, just as Zack had requested. It was when the figure had turned ninety degrees that in the blue neon hue of the room, Zack could make out the shape of breasts in the tight leather top, magnificent breasts, perfectly shaped. Zack realised that the figure was female, and his confidence grew a little and he no longer felt so threatened. He still maintained a firm grip on the toy lightsabre though. As the female continued to slowly turn, the neon light caught something on her neck underneath her hair.

"Stop." Zack commanded and the female stopped where she was. Zack stood up and approached the bath a little, still keeping within a lightsabre's length away. "Raise your hair slowly on the left side."

The female brought her right hand towards her left elbow where her long hair rested, still leaving the left arm outstretched at forty-five degrees. Using the slenderest fingers that Zack had ever seen, she grasped as much of her hair as she could at the bottom and slowly raised her hand up, over her shoulder and then her head, taking her long hair with her, thus exposing her neck. Zack put the blade of the lightsabre closer and there it was, glowing under the neon light, an ultraviolet tattoo, shaped like an inverted triangle with the number sixty-nine inside it. Despite his fear, he still found humour in it, and smiled inwardly, and then recalled the encounter with the male who disappeared at the beach.

"Oh man, not another one." Zack groaned as he took a couple of steps backwards. "Step out." he told the female, a sigh of resignation in his voice. She stepped out of the bath as gentle as a model would step along a catwalk. In all of his twenty-four years he had never seen anyone step out of the bathtub so gracefully. She stood before him, perfectly still. She could not have looked any more beautiful if she were stark naked, but she wasn't, she was wearing the black leather outfit that clung to her contours as if it had been sprayed on. Zack took a step backwards out of the bathroom, never taking his eyes off of the female in front of him. Without instruction she appeared to follow slowly, at a pace that felt strangely comfortable, and ensuring that Zack's comfort zone was never put in doubt. Once they were both standing in the bedroom, Zack's eyes never leaving her body and occasionally glancing up into the bluest eyes he had ever seen, he realised that his toy lightsabre was fooling no-one. He put it down by his bed, still keeping his eye on her.

"Who are you?" Zack finally asked, believing that that was a question that should have been answered some minutes ago.

"I am Madoka." She replied, and there it was again, that accent that Zack could not place. How his head still hurt from last night. "And you are Zack Collins."

"I'm aware of who I am," Zack replied, "but how do you know that."

"We all know about you. You are the saviour of our people."

"The what? I'm sorry, I don't understand." Zack started to slip slightly out of his comfort zone. This woman was mesmerising, impossibly beautiful, but it worried him that she knew about him. It worried him that she was hiding in his bathroom. Had she snuck around his room whilst he was asleep? Had she seen his name written down somewhere. That would make sense.

"You save me." Madoka replied, almost with a hint of resignation that Zack should know all of this. "You guide us through the war."

"What fucking war?" Zack started to get annoyed, and then he had a thought, "Who put you up to this? Was it Marshall? Jeff?" He was about to add the name Eva, but then realised that his girlfriend would never implant a female so beautiful into his bathroom just to play a prank on him.

"So many questions Zack," Madoka said, "And we don't have time. I need to return in three moons, and you will show me how to win."

At this time, Zack's head had had enough. He figured this was a prank, he had a banging headache of university fresher's week proportions, and despite the fact that he initially thought his life was in danger, he could think of worse ways to die than underneath this heavenly beauty. He sighed, sat back onto his bed, and rested his head in his hands. Madoka stood stock still, like a statue, just watching him. The silence became awkward, to the point that he almost wished she would pounce on him to break the silence. A small part of him smiled inwardly at the thought of wrestling with her in her leather get-up, even if he were certain that she would probably kick his arse in a heartbeat. Eventually he looked up at her again, into her eyes. She hadn't moved a muscle.

"Do sit down." Zack gestured towards the office chair in front of his computer desk. He was torn as to whether he wanted the space between them still, but also felt inappropriate asking her to sit on the bed with him. Madoka flowed gracefully towards the chair and sat down. She gave out a sigh as if she had never felt such comfort before, rotated on the chair to face Zack and then crossed one leg over the other before, finally, her body looked as though it relaxed. She looked Zack straight in the eyes.

"OK, let's start from the beginning." Announced Zack, before realising he had no idea where or what the beginning was. He decided to start with his bathroom. "How did you get in there?" He asked gesturing with his eyes towards the en-suite.

"I appeared." She replied. "I escaped them with my brother, and he brought me here to you. You are the saviour."

There she went again, mentioning the saviour bit, and completely throwing his train of thought when he had so many more questions. He ran his fingers through his hair, and shook his head as if trying to shake his questions back into order again, before slowly looking up and asking, "Who is your brother?"

"Echo. You met last night at the water."

Zack started to try and gather his thoughts about the encounter with the male at the beach. He'd believed that that was a figment of his imagination, hell there was so much weed smoke in the air last night at the beach that an elephant would have hallucinated.

"And do you have last names?" Zack asked.

"Madoka and Echo." Madoka replied, sounding a little confused at this line of questioning.

"No, I mean family names? Names you share with your parent's blah blah blah?"

"We are not given family names. We are born into sectors and are numbered accordingly." Madoka replied.

Zack was unsure as to whether to buy this charade or not, still convinced, or hoping at least, that this was a prank set up by his friends, but she seemed too sincere and serious with her answers.

"So, what is your...." Zack thought for a second, "family number?"

"Sixty-Nine." Madoka replied

"Of course it is." Zack replied, and yet again his juvenile sense of humour crept a tiny smile onto the corner of his mouth. At that time, Zack heard the clattering of the vacuum cleaner being brought up the stairs and started to panic. He was twenty-four years old and yet he still panicked about his parents finding a girl in his bedroom.

"Zack, are you up yet!" He heard his mother call out. His eyes darted towards his bedroom door. Would he be able to dash across the room and silently turn the lock before his mother came crashing through with her OCD and vacuum cleaner?

"Shit! That's my mum, you've got to hi....." Zack hissed under his breath as he turned towards Madoka, only she wasn't there. His heart pounded out of his chest as he heard the squeak of his door creaking open. His eyes darted all around the room. Not a sign of Madoka anywhere. Had he imagined her. He turned to face his door, and his mother stood there in the doorway, the perennial grey-haired housewife wearing her cleaning pinny. Hands on her hips, she stood staring at him as he sweated and breathed heavily.

"Are you feeling ok dear?" She asked.

"Not really Ma, I feel a little under the weather today." Zack replied, still trying to scan the room without making his mum suspicious. Shit, he imagined he must look like he'd been smoking with the Rolling Stones all night the way he was acting, so he gave in. He rolled back onto his bed, closed his eyes. Things were way out of control, out of his control, he may as well close his eyes, If Madoka was going to kill him, so be it. If his mum was going to have a shit fit about him having a girl in his room, so be it. If his mum and Madoka were going to fight like Tekken, so be it. But nothing, silence, and then he heard his mum turn and walk away.

"I'll go and get my baby some hot honey." She called back as he heard he walk down the stairs.

What the fuck just happened?

2

Marshall rolled over in his bed. It was approaching 8am and he had had a heavy night. A truly heavy night of epic proportions. The beach party was always a blast, but he wished he could just remember getting home from one of them one day. His head hurt a little. He was starting to regret mixing his beer and cider to make snakebite and black drinks. As much as he loved the taste, he always suffered the next day, sometimes even the same day. The music from the night before was still resonating around his head. Deep Goan trance music. At least he thought it was still from the night before. He'd have expected it to stop after he'd opened his eyes.

Marshall Martin lived alone in a rented flat in Serene. Ever since he came to work there after leaving college for his apprenticeship with Aurora Financial Services as an Information Technology consultant, or computer fixer as he liked to call it. It was here that he first met Zack Collins, as a colleague, sitting opposite each other's booths with little headphones and microphones on, helping the whining banking contingent (who were supposed to be intelligent) every time they had a problem with their computers switching on, or could not manage to print a statement. They had been firm friends ever since Zack pranked him with a wireless mouse plugged into his terminal and ghosted the cursor across the screen whilst he was trying to remotely help the head of financial services. Along with Jeff, or JJ as they nicknamed him, they became an inseparable trio of drinking buddies. Which is what they had been doing last night. And, oh how it hurt this morning.

As the music continued Marshall rubbed his eyes and tried to focus. Opening heavy eyelids, he saw the flashing light of his mobile phone ricocheting across his bedroom walls. Staring at the flashing lights it still took a few seconds to dawn on him that it was actually his phone ringing he could hear and not the music from the beach party the night previously that was haunting his mind. He raised up onto his elbow and fought back a wave of alcohol induced nausea as his body moved. He paused, hoping his body would settle, and then weighed up which would hurt him the most; the continual shrill of his ring tone or the waves of sickness he was feeling. A few seconds later he surmised that he might be able to stop from vomiting, however, unless he answered his phone, he would not stop the head splitting ringing. Another push upwards and he leant towards the bedside table, took his phone and swiped the screen to answer it. Not looking at who was actually calling, his priority was to stop the noise, besides his eyes were a little unfocused on the screen in any case.

"err...mmm...Hello." Marshall muffled a response, half genuine as he felt rubbish, but in all honesty, half of it was put on too, hoping that the person on the other end of the call would feel his pain and not want to bother him any further.

"Marshall!" It was Zack, he sounded frantic, and totally apathetic towards the groaning in Marshall's voice. "What happened last night?!"

"Woooaaaahh, enough with the loudness dude," Marshall winced his eyes shut. His own voice even hurt his head. "Slow down." He heard Zack try to take a deep breath on the other end of the line.

"What happened last night?" Zack repeated, a little more in control of his voice at this time.

"Narrow it down a bit Zed, the details are ranging from a little hazy to non-existent at the moment" replied Marshall.

"The g..g..girl. Who is she?"

"I have no idea what you're talking about, are you sure you were the responsible one last night?" Marshall heard Zack exhale deeply on the end of the line. He racked his brains, to see if something, anything came to him about the night before, but to be honest, he couldn't even remember getting home himself.

"The girl in my room?" Zack asked slowly. He sounded exasperated, resigned, and desperate.

"Dude, I still have no idea what you're talking about. This sounds like something we need to meet up and discuss, but mate, I'm hanging big time at the moment. Can it wait?" Asked Marshall, "Plus, I have some business I need to attend to." A hint of boyish cheekiness in his voice. Zack knew exactly what he meant.

"Who's your victim today then?" Asked Zack, still panicked a little but pleased for the mind wander and distraction.

"No-one you know buddy. Shall we say two pm at the dog?"

"Ok, you better be there Marsh, no distractions, ok?"

"Don't worry Zed, my distractions will be finished by then, laters." replied Marshall and then he pressed end on the screen of his phone, cutting off the call.

Marshall didn't really need to look behind him in the bed, he could feel the warmth from another person under the sheets with him. He reached behind him with one hand and soon felt the smooth nakedness of another person behind him. His fingers touched a hip and slid up the side of the torso until his hand was cupping a naked breast and rolling a pert nipple between his forefinger and thumb. He heard an appreciative moan and turned to face the young lady in his bed.

"Did he know?" She asked sleepily, eyes struggling to open.

"He hasn't got a clue." Marshall replied, "Now, about this 'distraction'?" The female giggled as Marshall checked under the cover, rolled towards her so that their bare chests were touching, and leaned in to smother her with a kiss.

3

Zack sat anxiously on a stool at the bar of the Greasy Dog pub. The bar curved around the pub and he made sure that from his seat he was able to see the entrance door and the comings and goings of all patrons. He'd been there for a couple of hours already, favouring the company of the regulars than waiting at home with his mother for the crazy to start again. Although, when he spoke to Marshall, their arranged time was a few hours away, he actually headed straight out to, what was affectionately known as to his circle of friends, the dog. It felt good to actually consume some alcohol and have a cold beer, having been the sober one the night before, and he thought a head start would give him leeway to blame it on the alcohol when his friends called him a raving lunatic. He had called, what he would call his sensible friend, Jeff Jackson, from the bar and asked him to join them. Jeff was a sceptic and quite often the voice of reason, the complete opposite of Marshall being the joker and wind-up merchant. He'd also tried to call his girlfriend, Eva, but wasn't getting an answer, so sent her a text message asking her to join them. He felt that she needed to be there when he had to tell his friends about a female hiding in his bathtub when he woke up. He would hate for her to find out through a third party and have a lot of explaining to do.

The greasy dog had been independently owned for the last six years, pretty much the same time that Zack could legally drink in pubs. He preferred it to many of the other pubs in Serene town as it wasn't a part of a chain and had a local feel to it. It was a straight up, order at the bar job, no fancy apps for ordering overpriced food at your table and no corporate bullshit. The staff worked there because they liked the vibe, and not because they'd attended a three-day induction course on customer service and standards. They served a rotating selection of real ales, giving the local breweries a chance to experiment and garner a cult fanbase. The pub was right on the seafront, close to Serene pier, and had some outdoor benches overlooking the North Sea, the beer was cheap, and yet it was not very popular with the tourists during the summer season. This was largely due to the local biker gangs adopting it as their favoured watering hole, and the live music at weekends being predominantly hard rock and heavy metal based. Zack liked that he knew most of the people who frequented the dog, and could always have a chat with anyone. Despite what anyone thought of heavy metal fans, and no matter how scary they looked, they were always quite civil, polite, and in most cases quite intelligent.

"Another one?" Came the voice from behind the bar. Zack looked up to see Big Jim, landlord of the Greasy Dog, looming over him. Nobody messed with Big Jim, at six foot four tall, and at least three feet wide, heavily tattooed, and pierced pretty much everywhere, he was solely the reason no-one had ever really caused any trouble within the greasy dog. The licensing sign above the door named him as James Postlethwaite-Arbuckle, but anyone caught calling him James was bounced straight out of the door. Big Jim it was. Marshall had once had the drunken misfortune to call him BJ once and only just lived to regret it. Since then, Marshall had never really liked to sit right next to the bar, within earshot (and arm's length) of Big Jim.

"Yes please." Zack replied and Big Jim instantly handed him a pint of snakebite and black. Zack looked at the drink and then up at Big Jim. "You look like you need to get wankered mate."

Zack took the drink from the hand of Big Jim, politely nodded, and started to down it in large gulps. He was about halfway through the pint when he heard a voice to the left of him.

"Ello handsome," he turned to see Eva standing beside him, still wearing the drop dead gorgeous white halter top, and ripped blue jeans that she had been wearing at the party. He gave her a tight hug from the comfort of his bar stool, not yet daring to try and stand up, and then had a mini panic attack at the realisation that he hadn't seen her enter the bar, if someone as beautiful as Eva could approach him unnoticed, who else had come in without his knowledge. His eyes quickly darted around the pub until he was satisfied that he was safe.

"What's up with you?" Eva asked, "You're acting a little disturbed."

"I am, you won't believe the morning I've had Hun." Zack started. Eva cocked her head to one side slightly as she looked at him, and he paused, wondering how to break it to her that there had been another woman in his room, against his wishes and knowledge. Would he be able to get that into the conversation before the fireworks started? She was looking exceptionally beautiful today. At twenty years old, she was younger than he was, and had started working at Aurora Financial Services during the previous winter as a call taker. He plucked up the courage to speak to her around the water dispenser, so cliche, and the conversation flowed smoothly. He soon discovered that they shared a love for extreme music and that she was the one who had mesmerised him at a Suicidal Angels gig at the University of East Anglia student bar the previous summer, where she had been studying. On that occasion she had been dressed in a skimpy navy and white outfit, much resembling a Japanese schoolgirls outfit which was tied off at the front with a long grey scarf that her friends would lead her around with, and thigh length black stockings showing a generous amount of thigh. She obviously dressed a little more reserved for work, but still sported the same beautiful navel length blonde hair tied into pigtails and held back with a navy headband, which always reminded him of the navy outfit he'd first seen her in. She had beautiful blue eyes and what he would describe as an up mouth, with a perennial cheeky grin. Slim, and only slightly shorter than Zack, she shared his love of computer games, metal music and science fiction. She was the ultimate hot geek. Zack was lost in his thoughts, captivated by Eva's beauty, when she spoke again and brought him back to reality with a thud that triggered anxiety to course through his heart and catch his breath, no matter how innocent her question was.

"So, are you going to tell me Zack?" Eva asked, the teeniest hint of impatience in her voice. "What's with the cryptic text message and rendezvous?"

"Promise me you'll let me finish first?" Zack pleaded, which already brought the defensive walls up around Eva as she folded her arms and stared at him.

"Just out with it Zack, what has happened?" Eva asked, the initial cheeriness in her voice when she first entered the pub seemed deflated now.

"Well......this morning.......I...erm" Zack stuttered and stumbled. As if he hadn't already had a bad enough day.

"Howdy partner, so what did this girl look like?" Marshall had arrived and approached Zack from the rear. Shit, Zack did not need this right now.

"What girl?" Eva asked harshly, her arms folded tighter, "Did you fuck someone else last night?!"

"N...No," Zack stammered. It was the truth, but it didn't sound like it. He wasn't able to finish his protestations of innocence.

"Man, you didn't even bone her? What a tragic waste." Marshall interjected. Continually referring to Madoka with references to sexual intercourse was not helping to explain what had happened to Eva. Zack looked flustered, resigned, and stared, almost in a trance at the floor. His heart pounded and anxiety levels raised. He knew that every second longer it took for him to attempt an explanation would seem like a second longer he was using to fabricate an elaborate story to Eva. It didn't help that the truth he was going to have to explain was so far out there that it was going to sound like a fabrication in itself.

"Will someone just tell me what the fuck is going on?" Eva demanded and threw a death stare at Marshall, who backed off a little with both arms raised and palms outwards, as he turned to face the bar to order a drink.

"It's not what you think," Zack feebly offered, looking up into Eva's eyes. She didn't look any less pissed off. Zack noticed her eyes glance off very quickly to the right, before returning to focus their glare on him. There was an awkward silence for a few seconds. "When I got up this morning there was a strange lady hiding in my bathtub." There it was. The ice was broken. Zack waited for a response to feed off of.

"I'm sorry," Eva's sarcasm was not lost on Zack, "can you run that by me again?"

This wasn't going to sound any better the second time around. Zack struggled for anything extra to add.

"When I got up this morning there was a strange lady hiding in my bathtub." Zack offered again, "I didn't fuck her, honest to God I didn't fuck her. I have no idea who she is, was, or how she got there." The flood gates opened, as Eva continued to stare at Zack. He reached out from his bar stool and softly put a hand on each of her elbows, hoping to entice her to relax a little, whilst all the while staring into her eyes. As painful as it felt to see the pain and anger in her eyes, he had learnt from a young age that the truth was always more believable if you maintained eye contact. The only problem was that he struggled himself to understand the truth of what had happened to him. Eva's arms lost a little of their tenseness, although her eyes continued to stare deeply into his soul with a huge degree of suspicion.

"You'd better tell me exactly what happened." She stated, still looking massively unimpressed. "I'll know if you're bullshitting me, and God won't help you if you are."

"Ok," Zack began, this was starting the feel a bit warmer, "Shall I start from the beginning?"

"That's a fucking great place to start." Eva added. Damn, she looked hot when she was mad. Make up sex was always the best, but now wasn't the time or the place for that. Zack spotted Jeff entering the pub, amazed that in his time of acute personal safety awareness he'd actually spotted someone approaching him. Jeff, the reliable one, was always fashionably late in a kind of unfashionable way.

"Jeff's here. Shall we get some drinks in and take a booth, save me keep repeating this?" Zack braved taking a pause and exhaled deeply when he realised the shouting wasn't going to start. Eva just stared at him, turned and walked towards a booth and table near to the window. She sat on the bench and slid across to the window, staring intently out of it. Zack turned to face the bar and saw Big Jim staring down at him.

"A glass of Merlot please Jim, better make it a large one."

"Are you sure? That's more glass that can be jabbed in your neck." Big Jim joked.

"You're not gonna let that happen, are you Jim?" Zack replied, grateful for the light-hearted banter at his predicament.

"It may well be out of my control, sounds like you're fucked sunshine." Big Jim offered with his back to Zack as he searched for a large wine glass. Zacks heart sank a little again at the gravity of his situation as Big Jim turned to face him again, "Just don't get any blood of the carpet." Big Jim finished pouring the wine and handed the glass to Zack. Money exchanged hands and Zack realised Jeff was standing beside him. He'd bought his drink at the other end of the bar to be served by Angel the barmaid, who he secretly had a massive crush on. Marshall turned to face Zack again.

"Sounds intense man." Marshall stated with a boyish grin on his face.

"Did you prank me this morning with a lady in the en-suite?" Zack asked Marshall directly, looking into his eyes.

"Nope. Fucking wish I'd thought of that first though mate, sounds classic." Marshall replied.

"Then I have no more questions for you, this is going to be difficult enough as it is." said Zack.

"I'm not missing this for the fucking world." Marshall stated as he picked up his beer and followed Zack and Jeff to where Eva was sitting, and still staring out of the window. Zack slid along the cushioned bench towards the window so that he was facing Eva across the table, followed by Jeff as Marshall took the seat next to Eva. Zack placed her wine in front of her as she turned to look at him. There was a hint of sadness in her eyes, and she then looked down at the glass of wine before reaching for it. All eyes were on Zack.

"I'll explain from the beginning..." Zack started, "What I can remember." No-one else spoke so he continued. "It started last night at the party," a flash of hurt run across Eva's face, "but it's not like that," Zack continued as if he could hear what she was thinking. "Whilst you lot were getting pissed and completely out of it, I was completely sober. This man approached me on the beach, running at me, grabbed hold of me and said take care of her, or something like that, I thought nothing of it at the time. He appeared nervous and ran off towards the surf, and then I swear to God, he just fucking vanished, just like that." He had their attention, not necessarily their belief, but nobody was calling him out as yet. "I can't explain it, it's like he was afraid of something. I thought I saw two other people out of place too, they got to the beach and then ran up the cliff steps again, and I saw a bright flash of light at the top soon afterwards. I carried on partying, then gave you all a lift home, as you know, and then I went home. Alone." Still no-one spoke. Zack looked around at all of their faces. He wasn't sure whether to be grateful or afraid of the lack of response. Sure, no-one was calling him crazy just yet, but he knew that there was more to come. He continued, "So, this morning I wake up. Alone." He emphasised this again looking directly at Eva before continuing, "I had very little recollection of last night, a massive, completely undeserved, hangover, and a sense of dread about the ensuite bathroom. I didn't feel as alone as I should be. So, I went to the bathroom with the light sabre you bought me...." he was looking directly at Eva as he said this, but the next voice came from his right.

"Wait, wait, you went to check on your bathroom with a fake light sabre from the Disney store?" Marshall stifled his giggle, "That's the funniest fucking shit I've ever heard man."

Zack fired a glare at Marshall who went back to the business of sipping his beer.

"And, to cut a long story short..." Zack continued

"Please do." Came the curt response from Eva.

"There was a lady hiding in my bathtub. I have no idea how she got there, I thought some wanker had spiked me and set up a prank," Zack didn't have to mention Marshall by name, they all knew who he was referring to, "I got her out of the bathroom, she spun me a tale about how I'm supposed to save her people in the future, time travel and stuff, and then my mum called up the stairs. When I turned around, she had vanished. I phoned Marshall, tried to phone you Eva, sent a text, and phoned Jeff, and here we are. I have no idea what has happened. I have not cheated. I am going out of my fucking mind, and as crazy as it sounds, I need you all to believe me." Zack exhaled, he was up to the present moment, and rather uneagerly awaited the laughter, shouting, whatever response he felt should follow a story like that. But it didn't come, everyone seemed to just absorb the tale as they took a sip from their drinks, or in Marshall's case, downed the last half a pint.

"Who's for another?" Marshall asked as he stood up to walk to the bar. No-one answered. With a shrug of his shoulders Marshall walked to the bar alone.

"Who is she?" Finally, Jeff broke the silence. Zack was glad that it was a reasonable question that didn't doubt him.

"I have no idea." Zack replied "She said her name was Madoka or something similar, she believes that I am the saviour for some reason, she knew my name and everything. I thought it was a big wind up, or I'd been spiked last night, but I managed to drive home safely. I just don't know what to think." The one person Zack wanted to say something, had remained silent. The one person whose opinion he wanted the most, hadn't proffered one as yet, and that left him feeling uneasy. The not knowing what was coming next from the girl that he loved. Finally, Eva broke her silence.

"What did she look like?" Eva asked without looking up from her glass. Zacks heart broke for her, a million guesses at what she must be thinking, and none of them positive, ran through his mind.

"She was tall, slim, long dark hair, fully clothed throughout I might add, and had a strange neon tattoo on her neck, just like the guy I saw at the beach. Apparently, that's their family number. She spoke perfect English but with an accent I didn't recognise. And that's about it. She just.......vanished."

"Was she pretty?" Marshall had returned from the bar with a new pint in hand, "I mean, would you?"

"Can we please try and have a grown up conversation?" Zack knew exactly what Marshall meant and felt that it was not an appropriate time for lads' banter, "I'm having a very difficult time of this. It either means I'm involved in something supernatural, or the other alternative is that I've lost my fucking mind. Neither option seems appealing to me, and it's hurting Eva more than me right now." Zack glanced over to Eva. She had no tears but a look of melancholy on her face.

"What was she wearing?" Asked Jeff. Zack expected him to go on the sceptical attack any minute now, but he would gladly welcome any input that put his mystery to bed right now rather than engage in the usual drunken conspiracy theory debate with him.

"Erm, it appeared to be some sort of perfect fitting leather outfit. I remember the guy last night being dressed in leather too I think." Zack replied, looking up at Jeff and then following his gaze out of the window just in time to see someone clad all in black walking up the steps and through the entrance onto Roseshore pier.

"Wait, wait!" Zack began to act frantically, staring out of the window, getting himself up into a half stand, restricted by the top of the table holding his thighs down. He looked around at all of his friends and they just stared back at him passively as if he were losing his mind. Nobody wanted to make any sudden movements. " Did you see her?" He asked, pointing towards the pier whilst not actually looking at it.

"See who?" Asked Eva

"Her! The girl! Madoka! Move move move move." Zack was gesturing at Jeff to let him out of the table. Jeff didn't move fast enough, and it seemed like eternity, but in his panic no speed would have been fast enough. Jeff stepped aside and Zack was out, moving towards the door of the pub. He would prove to them; he would prove that he wasn't insane. He would get to the bottom of this prank, and most importantly, Eva would learn that nothing happened. Were they behind him still? Who knew? The sunlight hurt Zacks eyes as he ran from the pub and crossed the promenade towards the pier entrance.

* * *

Zack ran up the steps two at a time and in less than five steps he was standing at the entrance of Serene pleasure pier. Flanked by two Victorian art deco shops, one of which doubled up as a box office, linked together by a roof structure held up by paint peeled concrete pillars, the wooden pier beckoned. Zack stood in the shade of the entrance tunnel to get his breath back. Damn, he was out of shape. He stood at the precipice of solid land and looked ahead at the wooden boards suspended above the beach and eventually the North Sea. He'd always been a bit afraid of the pier since a child, for childish reasons. People ventured onto it daily in complete safety, but he always envisioned that he would fall between the cracks in the boards and into the sea below whenever he could hear and see the surf between the wood. He surveyed the area ahead. It was a warm summer Sunday afternoon, and the pier was full of people, a sea of personalities, young and old, excitable and bored, all forming an ever-changing human assault course along the pier. The flow of traffic worked in every conceivable direction. With the added obstacle of a stream of anglers casting out into the sea along the outside railings of both sides of the structure. Far along the pier, beyond the stalls selling popcorn, candy rocks and ice cream to a throng of children rushing around like a swarm of bees, as if they'd had too many sweets already, he saw her. Approaching the theatre at the end of the pier he saw the tall slender figure clad all in black, never looking back, long black hair flying lightly in the sea breeze that crossed the pier. Zack set off, sprinting towards the figure as best he could amongst the hundreds of day-trippers currently occupying the pier as if they owned it. Hurdling over the outstretched wheels of unpredictable pushchairs he made slow progress towards the theatre.

"Madoka!" He called out, feeling slightly stupid, as it was hardly a modern English name. There was no response as the figure started to walk around the side of the theatre towards the end of the pier. Zack lost sight of her as he negotiated his way through the aluminium tables and chairs full of people enjoying a cream tea and scone from the theatre's coffee shop. He was whacked in the face by a flag advertising the ice cream from the coffee shop and battled with the flapping nylon like a scene from a comedy film. When he pulled his face free of the flag, he had lost sight of Madoka. He rushed to the narrow footway along the side of the theatre. She wasn't there. With a clear run to the back of the pier he sprinted to the end. Nothing. All that stood between himself and the North Sea was the lifeboat launch. He looked around in all directions, frantically. He rushed along the back of the theatre and looked down the other side to see if she had double backed on herself, but she was not there. In any case that wouldn't make any sense, but he was starting to think that nothing made any sense. He ran back to the lifeboat, perched on the launch, looking through the windows, to see if she had boarded the vessel at all. Nothing, as he got to the front of the boat, he saw a man sitting in the cockpit of the boat. A man, with a big bushy beard, wearing an orange, fluorescent jacket. Clearly not Madoka.

"Have you seen a lady come by here?" Asked Zack

"Nope." Replied the boat man, a man of very few words. Zack felt that he was losing his mind and made his way back to the back of the theatre, looking over the rails to make sure she hadn't gone into the sea on either side. Nothing. He stood on the wooden boards, clutching his head and turning in circles. What the fuck was going on. As he turned towards the side of the theatre, he saw Eva, Jeff and Marshall staring at him. He stopped turning, still clutching his head.

"She was here." He feebly offered, trying not to imagine what they thought of him.

"Who was?" Jeff was the first to speak.

"The girl, Madoka, you saw her Jeff," Zack recalled Jeff looking out of the window of the Greasy Dog which took his attention to the pier too.

"Where is she now?" Asked Eva, arms folded again.

"I.....I.....I don't know," Zack wished he had an answer, "she just......vanished."

"Can you take me home please?" Eva had turned to Marshall and continued turning until she had her back to Zack and walked away, along the side of the theatre.

"Sorry Bro." Marshall shrugged his shoulders towards Zack and then followed after Eva.

Jeff remained, staring at Zack, who remained rooted to the spot, questioning his sanity, still clutching at the top of his head with both hands.

4

"I assure you Jeff, I'm not going mad." Zack stated. Jeff said nothing, a man of very few words, and Zack wondered if he was trying to convince himself as much as Jeff. Good old Jeff, a bit geeky, quiet and always inoffensive. If anyone could get the message through to Eva it would be Jeff. Zack knew it would be pointless himself calling Eva right now, as he didn't have the answers.

The two men walked along the beach heading south towards the spot of the beach party the night before. Jeff would occasionally find a flat stone and skim it across the incoming waves as he listened intently to what Zack had to say. His record so far was seven bounces. The cliffs beside the beach rose high beside them to the right. There were various unofficial paths up the cliffs between the trees and bushes that cascaded down them, but they continued to walk on the sand and stones. After leaving the pier they had walked for about half a kilometre before Zack had thought of anything to say. It didn't make much sense, but the floodgates had opened, and Jeff knew that he needed to sound off. The next half a kilometre had taken about thirty minutes, as Zack stopped to speak, as if standing still would help it to sink in and make it more rational. The sound of the waves lapping against the beach helped Zack to calm down a little as he spoke, and he no longer sounded like a hysterical schoolgirl as he tried to convince his friend of a story he couldn't believe himself. Eventually, they came to the wooden breaker lining the sand from the bottom of the cliff into the sea. Beyond that, approximately one metre lower was the stretch of beach that last night had been full of noise, lights, and incoherent youth. The area was deserted now, too far for the average tourist to venture along to, and most were too lazy to attempt the three hundred or so steps that wound their way down the cliff. Zack and Jeff stood there alone, the only sign of civilisation was the discarded cans and bottles from the previous night's party, along with the occasional bra and abandoned condom. It was Sunday, the council were never going to send anyone to clean up a part of the beach that was rarely visited on a Sunday.

"This is where it started J." Said Zack, gesturing with his arms open to the wide expanse of beach ahead of them. They jumped down onto the next level of the beach and strolled across to where Zack had been standing the night before.

"So, tell me what happened Zed." Encouraged Jeff. Zack looked around him to get his bearings and then stepped over to where he remembered sipping the diet coke. He closed his eyes for a second and started to recount what had happened.

"I was minding my own business. Taking a drink, no alcohol apart from the beer that Marshall gave me at the start of the night. This was like four hours afterwards. It was dark, lights everywhere though. Marshall and Eva were dancing. I could see glow sticks everywhere. I don't know where you were at this time. The music was loud man." Zack opened his eyes and looked towards the steps at the bottom of the beach. Pointing his finger to the steps he continued, "He came from over there. I was minding my own fucking business Jeff, but he singled me out, ran over to me, grabbed me and said, 'They are coming, protect her'. I had no idea who they or her were. More to the point, I didn't give a shit." Zack turned his body to point with his other hand to the surf, "He then ran off over there and just disappeared in a bright light."

"Who else saw this Zack?" Asked Jeff

"I don't know, I think everyone else was too buzzed to give a fuck. One guy looked I recall, but I don't know who he is. I can't corroborate this." Zack felt exasperated. "Then two more people turned up at the steps dressed similar, before running back up the cliff. That was it. I wake up this morning and this girl turns up in my bath and disappears. She turns up at the pier and disappears. And as ludicrous as this whole story sounds, I might lose Eva because of it."

"Did you keep your drink with you at all times last night?" Asked Jeff.

"I know what you're getting at, and yes I did. I was fine to drive around for half an hour after the party dropping you guys home, and I was fine when I went to bed. I wasn't spiked mate." Replied Zack, and a slight disappointment dawned on him as he realised he'd just discounted the only reasonable explanation he'd been clinging to. Deflated, he sat back on the sand and surveyed the scene. It looked so different in the daylight.

"I really don't know what to say," Jeff finally said, "Don't worry about Eva though, she knows she's onto a good thing with you." he finished, although he looked away at the sea too as he said this.

"Cheers Jeff, I hope you're right mate." Zack replied, watching the tide ebb away from him, wishing that his thoughts would go with it.

"Look Zed, I gotta go, get back home to mum and I'm parked at the pub. You coming back?" Jeff asked.

"No, it's ok, you go. I'm just going to sit here for a while. This has always been my place of quiet contemplation, minus the cans and condoms of course." Replied Zack. Jeff may have replied but Zack didn't hear, he was lost in his own thoughts. He turned around after about thirty seconds to see that Jeff was walking back along the beach towards the Greasy Dog.

Zack pulled out his phone, stared at the lack of missed calls on the screen, and the put his earphones into his ear. What he needed now was some music to take him away. Flicking through the music library on his phone he settled on some metal from one of his playlists. The mellow picked guitar at the start of 600 AB by Bonded by Blood began, and he laid back onto the sand looking up at the sky, in time for the thrash guitar rhythm to come in. He lay back down on the beach, looked up towards the sun, shielded his eyes, and then closed them as he let the music take over him.

The lyrics soaked into his soul. He always felt better being taken away from this world with some other worldly aggressive thrashing guitar. Tales of war and bombs, fantasy. There is no time when your death comes at will. The words stirred him to open his eyes as the song came to an end. He stood up on the beach. Jeff was long out of sight now and he stood alone with the waves on this deserted stretch. He contemplated which way to go home. The cliff steps would be quickest, but they were such a mission. The beach was far flatter but added about one kilometre to his journey, and he was walking after all. With the toss of a coin the cliff steps won, and with a sigh he walked towards them, pausing at the first step to look up at them. Three hundred of the bloody things, he had made this ascent so many times and it never got any easier. He lowered his head and stepped onto the first one.

* * *

They had stood on the top of the cliff overlooking the beach, watching the two men speaking. Two figures among the bushes, sitting on the edge of the drop. They watched one male walk off along the water, while the other with the longer hair, laid his head down on the beach and closed his eyes. They waited in silence until he stood and turned towards the cliff. Kasumi, the female, was first to stand. Standing at six feet tall, she had the appearance of a thirty-year-old model, pretty but with a face that knew how life worked. Dark skinned and slim, she had long flowing silver hair. Wearing a two toned black and grey strapped outfit that covered her from the throat to her feet, she looked out of place on a warm summer's day in Serene. It had been easier to stay hidden the night before, in the darkness, but now this willowy beauty stood out a mile.

"He'll be here soon." Kasumi said to her companion, Shin, without looking back at him, staring towards the top of the steps. Shin remained seated. He was smaller than Kasumi, about five foot six, and medium build. He appeared to be about the same age too but didn't have the same look of experience. Short, jet black hair sat neatly on his head, swept over to one side. He wore a grey jump suit with four fasteners at the front, with a long-sleeved military grey/green top underneath. He wore black leather gloves and boots too, which made him ever conscious that he did not belong here. Having taken some strange stares from the tourists and locals alike, who had been strolling around on this beautiful day in shorts and T-shirts, some of the males even bare chested with painted designs adorning their skin.

"Seraph said not to intercept yet." Shin looked up to Kasumi, grateful that she was casting a shadow over him so that he could look to the sun.

"And where is Seraph now?" Kasumi spun to glare at Shin, temporarily allowing the sun to strike his eyes causing him to squint and place a gloved hand upon his forehead. "Waiting for Seraph is the reason that we are in this mess in the first place. When he is not here, such as now, you will do as I instruct." Kasumi spat as she turned to look at the top of the steps. "Now stand up." She ordered

Shin stood as he was told and moved alongside Kasumi to watch the steps. Still hidden from view among the bushes and treacherous clifftop paths Shin dared a question.

"So, what is your plan Kasumi?"

"I will speak with him, establish who he is and what he knows. I don't intend to kill him just yet. I understand the ruling people here take offence at that, and we do not know how long we will need to be here." Kasumi replied. Still she could not bring herself to look at Shin as she spoke.

"What will you say?" Asked Shin, but before Kasumi could answer he spotted the loosely flowing shoulder length brown hair of Zack rounding a bend on the steps to face the final twenty or so steps. He had white wires connecting to something in his ears, and his head bounced unnaturally to the flow of his walking pace, Shin thought. He turned to his left to notify Kasumi, but she was gone, he looked around a little more, taking his gaze completely away from Zack and saw that

Kasumi had exited the bushes and was now walking across the grass hillside towards the steps. She looked stunning as she strode towards Zack, a beauty that belied the evil within the body.

Zack didn't even look up from his phone screen as he scrolled through his music library until Kasumi was practically standing over him. Yes, she was tall, ever so slightly taller than Zack's five-foot ten frame, but she had the added advantage of being a metre or so ahead of him, up the grassed incline that lead to Serene lighthouse. Kasumi held an arm rod straight in front of her with her hand palm facing towards Zack indicating for him to stop. Zack looked up from his phone, somehow sensing the presence of someone else nearby and stared into the eyes of Kasumi. He paused and removed his headphones from his ears.

"I really don't need any more of this shit today." Zack muttered. Not because he wanted to be quiet but he didn't really feel like he owed any more speech to any more freaks.

"Hello good friend." Kasumi offered.

"What's my name?" Asked Zack giving Kasumi a hard stare as he did.

"That, my friend, I do not know." Kasumi replied.

"Then we ain't fucking friends, are we?" Zack stated more than asked. He placed his headphones back into his ears and made to walk around the figure standing in front of him.

"You can't trust her!" Kasumi shouted after him. Zack stopped. He didn't turn around, but she knew that she had his attention. "She means to kill you!" Zack spun around with anger in his eyes.

"I have had the day from hell!" Zack raged, "You don't even know me or what has happened with me today, or whether Eva will ever speak to me again……."

"Who is Eva?" Asked Kasumi

"See, you know nothing! Do not presume you know me or anything about me, because you don't!"

"Do not speak to a superior being in that tone young man!" Kasumi countered, Zacks outburst putting her off key and forgetting that she was trying to fit in, badly, with her surroundings.

"Fuck you!" Zack shouted back with pure venom in his voice and flipped his middle finger at the female. The symbolism of which was totally lost on her, but anyone from any culture would understand that he was unhappy. He spun around and started the ascent to the lighthouse. From there it would be a short ten-minute walk home. He cranked the volume up on his phone to drown out any more sound, and it was at that moment that his phone battery decided to die and power down. "FUCK!!" He yelled again and wandered up the hill muttering to himself.

Kasumi stood and watched him walk up the hill towards the lighthouse. As he reached the apex of the hill and disappeared out of sight, she realised that Shin had joined her and was standing to her right.

"That went well." He stated sarcastically, although the tone of his voice meant nothing to Kasumi.

"Do not get above your grade Shin. I can have you shut down when we return. Don't forget you're only here because you've studied twenty first century history, and you didn't help at all just then. I'm starting to wonder if you will ever serve any purpose to our people." Kasumi replied. She did not have to look at Shin, but she knew that the smile would be wiped from his face and he would return to being serious.

"What do we do now then? Should we contact Seraph?" Shin asked, his mind now on the mission that they had been sent to fulfil.

"Seraph will do no better," Kasumi replied, her tone had softened, "We need to establish who this Eva is. He spoke of her and I sensed in the female form. Has Madoka changed her identity?"

"Should we follow?"

"It's ok Shin. We can be covert. The machine he held in his hand spoke to me, it asked if I wanted to connect with…..Bluetooth?" Kasumi stumbled on her words as she tried to explain.

"Yes, Bluetooth is a medieval way of pairing electronic devices and sharing data." Offered Shin, pleased that he was able to share some of the knowledge from his history learning.

"I have location details for this Eva female. We shall await the return of Seraph and visit her when the sun is no longer upon us. Until then, we shall wait here and conserve power." Kasumi walked back into the bushes where they had previously been sitting, overlooking the beach. Shin joined her and sat beside her. Comfortable that they could not been seen from the footpaths, Kasumi then went into sleep mode, albeit with eyes wide open.

5

  Dusk was setting as Zack walked up the driveway to his home. He'd stopped for a couple more lonesome beers in a nearby bar on the edge of town as he felt that he needed them. He'd gone so far as to develop some Dutch courage to phone Eva, but not so far as to make a complete angry drunken idiot of himself when he did get to speak to her. He had thought about phoning her on the walk home from the bar, but his mind developed an excuse that it would be best to wait until he got home so as there was no background noise or accusations as to why he was still out. He didn't take a lot of persuading. His phone battery was dead, he could have charged it a little at the pub, but he thought it best to be incommunicado. He much preferred the option of laying on his bed in the comfort of his room, where he and Eva had left his memory foam mattress with plenty of memories in the past, to make the call. He stood at the end of his driveway and looked up at his house. He could see his parents sitting in the living room, watching a TV show, completely oblivious to all that was going on around him. He took a long hard look at the property. It was far too large now that his older brother and sister had flown the nest and settled down in Norwich. His father had worked very hard at Aurora Financial Services until his retirement, just prior to the last great recession, and this house was his castle. Eight bedrooms off of the beaten track, just for Zack, his mother and father to rattle around in. Zack's fathers' pension was more than enough to keep the property and with the mortgage finished before retirement his parents were living the high life with numerous foreign holidays each year. They seemed happy enough in their own company, but as the last-born child, Zack often thought he'd leave them lonely if he were to move on. With a contemplative sigh he crossed the driveway to the front door and let himself in.

 "I'm home." Zack called out. He did this every time, which had its downsides as his mother would often come to greet him and treat him like a toddler, asking him what he had had to eat etc...and tsking whenever he was honest enough to say that he had been at the pub all day. True to form, she walked into the hallway in her apron to greet him. "Hi Mum."

 "Zack Darling, where have you been all day?" She asked, "There have been phone calls for you."

Zacks eyes widened, "Oh yeah, who from?" He asked

"Jeff phoned for you, wanted you to call him as soon as you got in." His mother replied.

Zacks heart sank a little, that wasn't the phone call he had been wanting to receive the most. He turned towards the stairs to go up to his room.

"Three times he phoned," Zacks mother continued, "Would you like any tea dear?" She asked.

"No ta, Ma, I've already eaten." Zack replied and awaited the tutting that would follow. She didn't let him down. In truth he'd only had a bag of pork scratchings washed down with lager, but he really didn't feel like eating. His stomach was doing flip flops with anxiety. He climbed the stairs with a turn halfway up and was facing his bedroom door. It was closed, as he had left it, and he opened it and walked in. His left hand immediately found the light switch after twenty-four years of practice, and he lit the room up. As the light turned on there was an additional flash of orange light, but nothing more today could surprise him, and he didn't even flinch when he saw Madoka sitting on his bed.

"Again?" Zack sighed, "To what do I owe the honour?"

"I wish you would be more positive with us Mr. Collins. You must save us, you're the only one who can save us." Madoka pleaded.

"Us? You mean there are more of you?" Zack replied with little to no enthusiasm in his voice whatsoever. At that he heard a rustle behind him, a familiar rustle, and a feeling in his gut that they were not alone.

"You can come out," Zack stated without turning around, "The shower curtain is a dead giveaway." Zack turned to his right to bolt his bedroom door shut, and he heard the en-suite door creak open. After bolting the door shut, he turned to look at the en-suite and was surprised to see not one, but two men emerging from the bathroom. "The shower must have been kind of cosy for two of you." Zack stated with a hint of sarcasm.

"We meet again Mr. Collins." One of the men stepped forward with his hand outstretched for Zack to take.

"Please, can we stop with this Mr. Collins shit?" Requested Zack, "If you're just going to rock up in my bathroom whenever you feel like it, we may as well be on first name terms. Call me Zack." Zack accepted the proffered hand and shook it.

"This is Echo." Madoka introduced as she stood up from the bed and walked towards the group, "My brother. And this...." she announced as she turned towards the other male with an arm outstretched pointing towards him, as if Zack may not know who she was referring to, "is Junko. He has come with us from Sector sixty-nine to seek your help."

Junko appeared younger than the other two, with a hardened but youthful look upon his face. A face of no experience of danger or heartache, but gung-ho for action. In short, a liability. He had dark brown short hair and stood about the same height as Zack, wearing a similar black leather get up to Madoka and Echo with fingerless black leather gloves. Zack was glad to see someone had taken steps to cool down in the warm weather. Junko stepped forward and followed suit of Echo, offering his hand for Zack to shake, although not quite sure what it symbolised, he'd seen that Echo had come to no harm. Zack took his hand and shook it before turning to Madoka. Without the surprise and panic of their morning meeting he was able to take a good look at her. She was beautiful. Despite having long hair himself, he had no words to describe the beauty and style of her long hair. Her blue eyes stared deep into his mind, or so it felt like. Her pale skin was completely unblemished, and her lips had a more than necessary plumpness to them but did not appear to be too over the top. He was momentarily stunned to the spot by her beauty. How had he not noticed this this morning? Oh yeah, he was scared shitless, that's how, and then she just vanished, which didn't allay any fears that he had had. A million thoughts ran through his mind in a split second, at the forefront was the warning that the strange lady had given him at the top of the beach steps. The words 'She means to kill you' stumbled around in his slightly alcohol numbed mind. He also wondered why she had led him to, and deserted him at the end of the pier, causing a meltdown between him and his friends. And Eva, oh God Eva, he had to call her. Zack removed his phone from his pocket and Madoka placed her hand on his.

"We need to talk, to explain." Madoka gestured.

"Can it wait?" Zack asked, unsure as to why he was asking for permission in his own room, "I really need to make this call."

"This is more important Mr. Collins." Junko stepped forward as Zack threw him a glare which stopped him in his tracks, "I mean Mr. Zack." Junko tried to recover.

"I think what Junko is trying to say is that we have a great need to act fast to save humanity," Echo tried to soften his companion's abruptness, "And it is the single most important thing that someone of his age and experience is aware of."

"Well, this call is kinda important to me." Zack stated, aware that Madoka was still holding his hand.

"More important than saving humanity.... Zack?" Madoka asked. Her voice drew his attention to her face, her delicate lips moving, and her deep hypnotic eyes. "Please let us say what we need to say, and then we will leave you to make your call on that thingy." She said pointing at the mobile phone in his hand. Zack felt pointless arguing, and simply moved across the room to sit on his desk chair. He spun it around to look up at the three strangers standing in his bedroom and beckoned with a hand for them to sit on the bed opposite him. One by one they did as they were told, first Junko sitting to the left nearest his window. Madoka sat in the middle and then Echo sat next to her on the other side. They looked like three naughty children sat in a row. No-one said anything for a while, as all four people weighed up what seemed like a ridiculous situation.

"So," Zack broke the ice, "please tell me how I fit in to all of this?"

"You are the one." Madoka offered, seeing from his expression that he hadn't understood, she continued, "the one to save the humans from the Zeydenians."

"I have no idea who or what a Zeydenian is. You'll have to do a lot better than that." Zack stated.

"The Zeydenians are a race of artificial intelligence, or robots as I believe you call them here." Echo was the next to speak. "They were developed after the great war of 2045, or so we have learned. The human race was all but wiped out. Atomic weapons were used by the humans on the humans. Rebristan was severely damaged and....."

"Wait, what is Rebristan?" Zack asked. The more they spoke the less he believed that it was an elaborate prank.

"This island that we survive on." Madoka answered.

"You mean England? The United Kingdom?" Zack asked. His interest had been piqued.

"If that is what it is called now," Echo replied, "When we are from it is called Rebristan. I have seen the maps in your books here, and it is essentially the same place, only Rebristan is a bit smaller and broken in places. I believe that was the bombs that caused whole areas of land to break away from the mainland."

"Listen," Zack had raised a hand to stop them speaking, "I don't need a futuristic geography lesson. I need to know how it is you believe I can help otherwise I'd like you to just.... vamoose....do your thing, then leave me alone to try and repair my love life."

"I know you are our saviour," Junko broke his silence, "I have read it in the historic annals. You know how to save us from the machines."

"I'm an IT, erm, computer consultant. I spend all day telling idiots on the other end of the phone line to switch it off and switch it back on again. I have no idea what you are talking about." Zack stated, "What are the historic annals?"

"It's where the Zeydenians keep the tree fabrics with words on them." Junko stated.

"Show him." Madoka urged, looking at Junko, then back at Zack, her eyes wide with excitement and anticipation, like a huge bubble that Zack knew he was about to burst. Junko unzipped his jacket revealing a bare chest underneath that was criss-crossed with large red welts across the skin, about a centimetre in width and twenty centimetres in length, four that Zack could see. Junko reached for an inside pocket and pulled out a piece of torn paper that was screwed up slightly and handed it to Zack. Zack took the paper from his hand and Junko looked down at his zip to pull it up and cover his scars again. Zack gingerly unfolded the piece of paper and saw that it had been stamped University of East Anglia on the page. As he looked at the page it was headed 'Dystopian Survival' and the authors name stated Zack Collins. Zack recognised the work and looked at it with a degree of pride, but his heart sank as he looked up to see the excited faces of the three people sat opposite him. They eagerly awaited him to say something.

"You've pinned the future of mankind on this?" Zack asked, holding the piece of paper in his right hand between himself and his visitors.

"That, and so much more," Junko replied, he was like a child at Christmas almost bouncing up and down on the mattress on his butt, full of excitement. "There are many more pieces of tree fabric in Rebristan with your instructions. We did not dare to bring any more with us in case the words did not survive the travel."

"My instructions? I don't understand." Zack stuttered, still turning over the piece of paper in his hands.

"These words were found in the great library of Zeydence. The historical library of the capital city." Echo started to explain. "Junko, here," he pointed to an eagerly nodding Junko sitting on the bed, knees up to his chest barely able to contain his excitement, "had work duties in the palace of Zeydence and was permitted access to the library. During the Lords downtime, he looked at the data around him and found your instructions in this tree fabric in the historic annals."

"Your words are an inspiration Mr Zack." Junko added, "You are truly the saviour of Rebristan."

"I hate to burst your bubble guys, but do you know what this is?"

Asked Zack.

"It is the way to end our oppression." Answered Madoka. Zack faced her and again her eyes entrapped him. He had bad news for her and was worried about losing the sparkle that he was becoming attached to.

"No, this is my university dissertation." Zack said solemnly. He stopped himself there, hoping that they would catch on and work things out for themselves, and the blow would be lesser. Blank faces stared back at him, eagerly awaiting his next words of wisdom.

"University?" Eventually Echo broke the silence.

"Yeah, it's a kind of school," Zack continued, still blank faces, "a place of higher education?"

"I don't follow." Said Junko, the excitement in him had diminished.

"You know," Zack started, realising then that they probably didn't know, and this could take some time, "a place where you go to study, to learn?"

Junko and Echo looked across at each other, whilst Madoka continued to stare straight ahead, directly at Zack, putting him at some unease.

"I think what he is trying to tell us is that he won't help us." Madoka stated, the glow in her eyes had disappeared now as she stared intently at Zack.

"It's not won't," Zack tried to salvage her respect, "It's that I can't. I don't know what you're expecting from me."

"I expect you," Junko had stood up now, "to lead us and carry out the words in your instructions to help all of the humans in Rebristan."

"These 'instructions' you have Junko, are false words. I flunked at university."

"Flunked?" Echo sought clarification of yet another new word.

"Erm....It means failure." Zack told him.

"Failure is very bad." Madoka announced, not able to look Zack in the eyes now.

"It's not great," Zack agreed, "but it's not the end of the world." All three of them looked up at him as he made such a throwaway comment.

"It is punishable with death." Madoka replied.

"Oh...." Zack had no words.

"Junko, you must take care of Madoka when we return if anything should happen to me when I report our......failure." Echo spoke directly to Junko and Madoka was looking towards him too. Zack was out of the equation now. A tear rolled from the left eye of Madoka and down her cheek.

"So, all of this was for nothing?" Madoka asked out aloud, but not to anyone in particular. Zack felt that this was the moment he could rejoin the conversation.

"I'm really sorry," he began, "These words are not even mine. I stole them. I was failing at university, I had to write a dissertation or essay, and I based it on lyrics from the songs I like." No-one paid attention, they spoke among themselves and Zack was not sure that he clearly understood all of the words. All three stood up with sombre looks on their faces.

"We must go." Echo announced.

"Maybe not all is lost." Zack replied. For some reason, he was beginning to dread the idea of losing the company of Madoka, who looked at the floor as if she were condemned.

"What would you suggest Zack?" Asked Echo.

Zack was desperately struggling to think of an answer as he heard a familiar creaking on the stairs. Realising someone was coming up the stairs he stood up and ushered his three visitors into the en-suite bathroom.

"Please don't leave yet," He whispered to Madoka as her eyes met his, which still felt strange for him to be saying as he knew that there was no normal way out of the bathroom, and urged "we need to speak further before we give up."

As the bathroom door closed, he heard a knock on his bedroom door followed by the voice of his mother.

"Zack, are you coming down for dinner love?" She asked, and the door handle rattled.

"One moment mum," Zack flustered, "I'm not decent."

"I've seen it all before Zack," his mother continued, "I've washed, pampered and put cream everywhere when you were little." She continued as the door handle still rattled.

"Yeah, it's a little bit different now mum," Zack called out. His heart was pounding as he listened carefully to ensure there was no noise from the bathroom. It sounded quiet enough, but he didn't know whether to take that as a good sign or a bad sign. He was about to unlock his bedroom door when he looked down at himself and realised that he was still wearing the same clothes that his mother had seen him come in wearing. She may be old and petite, but she certainly wasn't stupid, so he quickly threw his shirt off and pulled the jeans off that he had been wearing, standing only in his stars and stripes boxer shorts and socks. With a deep breath he looked up at the bolt lock on his bedroom door, took the few steps across his room and unlocked it.

"Mum, is everything ok?" Zack asked, only opening the door slightly, hoping that he could answer anything without his mother coming into the room. He saw that she had picked up arms full of clothing.

"I've done the washing today dear." She replied. Zack opened the door wider to take the laundry from his mother, but she saw this as an invitation to stroll straight past him and into his bedroom.

"Just leave it on the bed Ma, and I'll put it away." Zack stated nervously as he looked towards the back of his mother as she made her way to his bed and laid down the fresh clothing.

"Are you sure I can't fix you something to eat Zack?" His mother asked as she turned to face him. He saw that she still had a couple of bath towels in her arms. "You know how I worry if you don't eat properly."

"I'm fine Ma, I have eaten properly, and I couldn't eat another thing, honestly." Zack stated, hoping that would be the end of it, and she would leave him in peace. To his horror his mother started to walk towards the en-suite door with the arm full of towels. As you got closer Zack stepped in front of her.

"It's ok Ma, I'll put those away too." He said with his arms outstretched.

"I'm here now Zack, it's ok." She replied. Zack had to think on his feet to prevent her from going into the bathroom.

"Trust me Ma, you don't want to go in there." Zack stated, almost pleading.

"Why ever not?" She asked.

"I just dropped the kids off at the pool," he lied, "after a chilli kebab. Seriously, you need to leave it at least ten minutes." He stood like a stone wall in front of his mother, arms still outstretched. His mother pulled a disgusted face at him as she handed him the towels.

"Too much information Zack." She stated and headed for the bedroom door to go back downstairs. As she walked down the stairs Zack walked towards his bedroom door to close it and could still hear her muttering "I knew you hadn't had a proper meal for dinner," and "that's why we gave you the room with the en-suite, phew."

Zack closed the door, bolted it, and then turned to face the en-suite door. His heart pounding, he wondered if it wouldn't be such a bad thing if they had just vanished, leaving him to get on with complicated, but at the same time boring, life. He walked slowly towards the door, believing that it sounded far too quiet to be containing three, supposed, time travelling futuristic people. He opened the door and stared into the darkness inside. Madoka stepped forward to be bathed in the light from his bedroom.

"Echo and Junko have left." She stated, "I should leave too, but you asked me to stay. I do not know what you propose to say that will help our situation, but returning is death. I cannot hide forever, but if you have something to say I need to hear it before I face my fate." She barely looked at him as she spoke. Zack felt a heavy heart looking at the sorrow etched on her face. He hadn't asked for any of this, knew nothing about any of this, but at the same time felt an overwhelming burden of responsibility for her. He had no idea why but figured that they must have known a lot about him in the future to know to send the beautiful woman to convince the goofy metal fan. Good move future folk, good move.

"Please sit down," Zack gestured to let Madoka sit on the comfortable office chair, it felt slightly inappropriate asking her to get onto his bed. Madoka did as she was beckoned. The lustre had left her eyes and her body language was that of a brave person resigned to a negative fate. She sat on the chair and was slightly amused to see that it spun from side to side. For the first time Zack saw a tiny glimmer of a smile on her face, and it made him sad that someone could find humour in something so simple that he took for granted. Madoka composed herself and sat facing Zack. She crossed her legs as he sat down on his bed and made himself comfortable.

"I know nothing about your culture," Zack started, "and even so, I don't want to leave you in the lurch. We should discuss how you live. But first I need to make a couple of telephone calls."

Madoka looked at Zack as though he had just spoken a different language to her, and in some ways, as he was about to learn, he had. He turned and reached for his mobile phone and started to dial Jeff's number.

6

It had been a good couple of hours since they had started talking. Zack didn't pretend to understand the world from which Madoka came, even if it was still on the very soil on which he stood and lived. He'd been able to piece bits of the oppression together in his mind, mainly because of his love for all things science fiction. The more they had spoken, the less he hung on to his theory that this was all an elaborate prank. Sure, people vanishing into thin air should have been his first clue, but initially it had been too unbelievable to believe. Zack had been told all about life in Rebristan, how artificial intelligence had taken over the planet following the great war. Humans had all but been decimated in a nuclear war and had started to repopulate from the few thousand that had survived. Unfortunately, the intelligence of the AI people, ironically created by humans in the twenty first century, had surpassed that of the surviving humans. For a while, humans and artificial intelligence had lived peacefully side by side, until the population of AI became too large to sustain, and eventually humans were forced into sectors. Many sectors were hundreds of square miles, but all fenced off to keep the human population under control. And the population were controlled. Each sector held one hundred thousand people. The majority of which were forced to farm for resources on the decimated planet in order to keep the light fields alive, a large piece of land outside of the human sectors where light was generated to provide power for the artificial intelligence to survive. In short, it sounded very much to Zack, like slavery. Humans beaten down to be submissive to the artificial intelligence. Treated as nobodies with no rights, human lives could be extinguished for any reason. Population was controlled by the AI, females were taken from the sectors to Zeydence, the capital of Rebristan, and arrived back in their relevant sectors sometime later with new humans to care for. Throughout the conversation Zack had learned that Madoka had no idea what television, telephones, movies, or love were, and had never been kissed. Eventually, Zack sat back on his bed. Madoka walked over to where he was and sat beside him.

"But," Zack searched for the right words, "Where do I fit into this?" He asked finally.

"The people of sector sixty-nine believe you to be the saviour of the humans after Junko found your instructions." Madoka replied, "I can see from our meeting that they, we, I, were wrong, and our fate must remain the same." Madoka stared at the floor in front of her. He doubted whether she had ever heard of Santa Claus and felt the disappointment at not getting a present that you wanted, but he recognised the look in her face to be similar.

"So, what did you, Echo and Junko expect me to do? Just one person?" Asked Zack.

"The artificial intelligence people began around now. We believed that if you could win the war in our time, then defeating the AI's in your own time, before they became so developed, would come easy to you." Madoka replied.

"Whoa, whoa, let me stop you there young lady." Zack had stood up, and was now pacing in front of the bed, looking directly at Madoka the whole time. "We cannot defeat them in this time."

"Why ever not?"

Zack held his hand to his head and sighed. These people had developed technology whilst enslaved to enable time travel but really hadn't thought it through. It was either desperation or naivety, or maybe their methods were not as safe as he had first thought.

"Have you never seen Back to the Future?!" Zack asked Madoka, exasperated.

"I do not know of what you speak." She replied.

"No, no, of course you don't," Zack conceded, "It's a film, a movie about time travel. I'll show you one day, but the point I'm making is that if we change matter in the past, then it affects the future. It creates a paradox." Madoka simply stared at Zack with a puzzled look on her face. She was not understanding what Zack was trying to get at.

"Ok, for example, in the history of humans now, there was a world war several decades ago. I don't understand the full politics of it all, but to cut the long story short, this guy called Adolf wanted to create the perfect race, and therefore eradicate all others who did not fit into this ideal. You follow me so far?" Zack asked, Madoka nodded. "Ok, I shall continue. Adolf was the ruler of a country called, and still is called, Germany. During this war and just before it, his army killed around seventeen million people for no other reason than they did not fit into his vision of what the perfect human race should be like. Many countries went to war with Germany, including England, or Rebristan as you know it, and countless more were killed fighting each other. So, the bigger picture is lots and lots of death, millions of lives ended. Now...." Zack paused for effect, "if you asked most people who they would kill if they could go back in time, most would say Adolf Hitler."

"That would be right," Madoka was trying hard to follow the conversation, "Seventeen million lives would be saved. That's got to be a good thing."

"That's wrong." Zack countered, "Whilst I, in no way condone what Hitler did. I would not be here today if he had not done it."

Madoka looked confused.

"My great grandmother first fell in love with a man named William. He was a soldier, and they married on the eve of the war. He was killed in action fighting against the Germans, like many soldiers were. My great gran then married again, this time to another man, and they had children, one of whom was my grandfather, who had my father, and eventually through time, I was born. If Hitler had not committed those atrocities then, war would never have broken out. William would never have joined the army and gone to war to be killed. He would have lived happily with my great granny Evelyn, and had a family, but the line that I evolved from would not exist and I would not be here. Do you see what I mean?"

"I'm beginning to understand." Madoka stated, still wearing a slightly confused look on her face.

"Not only that, but it also goes much further. All of the people that were murdered by the Germans, mostly Jewish people and Soviets, if they had lived then their family lines would all be different from how they are today. Many more millions of lives would be erased from the planet and others possibly in their place. What if, just one of those people in that line became a famous doctor or teacher that helped develop cures for a disease? All those with the disease would be effected just by that one act of killing Hitler in the past, because the cure would no longer exist. Fuck! My head is starting to hurt just thinking about this." Zack started to clutch his head and sat back down on his bed.

"I guess what you're trying to say is...." Madoka started, but Zack cut her off and finished for her. He was on a roll and wanted to ensure she fully understood the implications of her original plan with Junko and Echo

"It means, if we cut the serpents head off now, so to speak, and eradicate artificial intelligence now, which would be impossible I might add, then there may not be a future war, leading to the paradox of my own family after the last war. If there were to be a nuclear war, and there was no artificial intelligence, then the support they gave humans to repopulate would not be there. Without the segregation of the sectors people's lives would be very different, and whilst I believe that is what you are striving for in your time, all of the past bloodlines of families would be irreversibly altered, and you, Madoka, would almost certainly not exist. Nor Echo or Junko." Zack could think of no other way of putting it to her. Madoka nodded. She had truly understood this time.

"I almost set into place a series of events that would have killed me, no that is the wrong wording, I would not have existed at all?" She stated aloud, more to herself, but a tiny piece of her wanted Zack to confirm she was on the right track.

"That's right," Zack confirmed, "If you want to change your destiny, you must forget the hardship of the past and attempt it in the present, whatever your present may be. I may be totally useless in having no plan or instructions to defeat your future enemies, but truly, how hard can it be? Artificial intelligence is computer based, code. I'm an Information Technology consultant and," he looked around his room as if he were to reveal a terrible secret, "I've been known to create the odd virus in my younger days."

"Meaning?" Madoka cocked her head to one side as she looked up at him.

"Meaning, your mission has become more difficult, but it is by no means impossible. And it means you get to travel more to see me." Zack tried to throw a light-hearted spin on the end.

"I must catch up with Echo before he goes to the sector elders." Madoka stood up.

"Wait, before you leave," Zack rushed to a drawer in his computer desk and pulled it open. He reached inside and pulled out an old mobile telephone, "this is an extremely basic telephone Madoka. Keep this with you. If you need to contact me, you press this button with the little green symbol on it and it will ring on my phone and we will be able to communicate. If the phone should start making a noise, that will be me phoning you, press the same button and hold it to your ear. It will only work when we are in the same time zone I guess. I've never tried to call a time traveller before."

Madoka held him by both upper arms with both of her hands and pulled him close to her giving him a hug. Her hair felt so soft against his face, he found it difficult to believe she had had such a hard life, until the strength of her hug reminded him how strong she had had to be and the fight within her. She stepped back from Zack, her eyes never leaving his and she mouthed the word 'Thank you' before there was a very brief flash of light which seemed to swell up in a spiral movement in his room. It lasted a fraction of a second, and he could have sworn the last part of Madoka to disappear was her eyes, staring straight into his. Zack stood there for several minutes, still believing he could see her eyes, as if the image was burned onto his retina like a torch glare. The day had been incredibly surreal, but with a glance to a photograph on his bedside table, he realised that he had a phone call to make. He picked his mobile phone up from his computer desk and pressed Eva's name in his phone book. Putting the phone to his ear he winced as there were three mechanical beeps of different tones and a message stated, "The number you are calling is not currently accepting calls." Zack ended the call, laid back onto his bed, looked up to the empty space in his room where Madoka had recently stood and muttered to himself "I hope the women of the future answer their calls better than those in the present.

7

The digital clock on the dresser ticked over to 23:30 in bright red characters. Eva Silverstein stepped into the darkness of her bedroom, taking the hairband out of her hair as she walked through the door. Once she was inside she swung her head gently from side to side and let her long blonde hair loosen itself and splay across the back of her pink summer jacket. She removed her coat, flinging it towards her bed, as she had done many times before. She reached for her light switch and flicked the light on in her bedroom. Light illuminated her bedroom. Eva let out a gasp but couldn't manage a scream when she saw figures standing in her room.

Kasumi stepped forward across the small room and placed a hand across Eva's mouth, just in case that repressed scream made it to the surface. Shin joined her and took Eva's arm flinging her onto her bed. As Eva hit her bed she tucked and rolled, until she was sitting upright with her left shoulder against her bedroom wall and her back against the high wooden headboard. She was cornered. She pressed down on her mattress willing herself to be able to push straight through the wall, as these two overbearing weirdly dressed strangers stepped closer and bore down on her. Fear filled Eva's face and a tear involuntarily ran from her right eye down her cheek. Kasumi leaned in, over the bed, until her face was mere centimetres from Eva's. Kasumi raised a solitary index finger to her pursed lips and made a 'shhhh' sound. Eva's laboured breathing prevented her from screaming out, and in any case, who would hear? Mrs Jenson next door was eighty-six years old and deaf, and her mother was away for the weekend with this week's man. Once it became clear that Eva was not going to become hysterical about the situation Kasumi rose from her bent over position to standing bolt upright in a hypnotic fluid movement.

"I mean you no harm at this time." Kasumi smiled at Eva as she spoke.

"Who....who are you?" Eva stammered.

"Those details are unimportant Eva S. I need to know more about the man who gave me your details please." Kasumi replied. Eva looked frantically around the room, in total confusion and abject fear. "In your own time dear, I'm fairly sure you don't want me to get annoyed Eva S."

"I.... I.... I don't know which man you mean." Eva pleaded, "Why didn't you ask him if you spoke with him?"

Kasumi's face was suddenly within millimetres of Eva's again, so fast that Eva did not see it coming. The fright made her jump back a little, except there was nowhere to go, and she banged the back of her head on her headboard. The stare from Kasumi was inhuman, boring straight into Eva's soul. Fear swept through Eva, exacerbated by her mind not being able to comprehend how someone so beautiful could be so cold and scary. Kasumi held her glare for what felt like eternity, and as Eva's bladder released itself onto her bed she also had a calm thought that she could smell or feel no breath on her face from the woman so close to her.

"I am asking the questions here." Kasumi coolly stated in a calm voice which did little to allay the fear in Eva. Kasumi's face remained as close as it has been, with no change in emotion.

Eva heard a movement to her right and her eyes wildly darted towards a sight of the male rushing towards her, his face contorted with anger.

"Humans!" Shin stated, "Always depositing their fetid waste wherever they want." His face had taken on an almost demonic appearance, which did little to help her maintain her dignity further.

"Be calm Shin." Kasumi softly stated, she raised her left arm with palm outstretched like a stop symbol towards where the male was coming from without looking in his direction. Her gaze never left Eva. "You must excuse my colleague. He has an enhanced sense of smell, and to be honest Eva S, you stink."

"What do you want from me?" Eva managed to ask, taking in large amounts of air through laboured breathing between words.

"That is a reasonable question, so I shall spare you pain for asking. I want to know who the male human is that refers to you as Eva S on his primitive electronic device please, Eva S." Kasumi stated.

"Lots of people call me Eva, it's my name." Eva spoke, a little more lucidly this time but no less afraid. It was as if her body was settling into a normal rhythm with this heightened state of fear.

"I want to know who the male is. The one that walked from the beach today. Long hair for a male. Very, how should we put it? Cantankerous." Kasumi pressed for information. Calmness in her eyes, however, Eva believed she could switch at any moment.

"Do you mean Zack?" Eva asked, hoping that the experience would soon be over. She was starting to regret disbelieving Zack that something strange was occurring in Serene, as she was now experiencing it first-hand. Karma was a bitch. It was a beautiful tan skinned, silver haired bitch, but a bitch all the same.

"Progress." Kasumi stated, looking away from Eva for the first time to look towards Shin. Eva followed her gaze and looked towards the male standing over the shoulder of his 'colleague'. She noticed that his nostrils had formed a skin over them, the look of anger in his eyes melting away. She wondered how he would breathe, but he didn't seem to be having any difficulties or distress.

"Who is this Zack?" Kasumi asked as she turned her attention back to Eva.

"He's," Eva struggled for the words given everything that had happened today, "you could say that he's my boyfriend."

"Boyfriend? Shin?" Kasumi asked the male, without looking at him, probing for an answer. It was as if Eva had said something to her in a different language.

"It's a companion one chooses to assist with reproduction Ma'am," Shin started, "These humans have an emotion of love within them, although by this time in history technology has started to splinter these emotions. They would exchange bodily fluids for the progression of the human race."

Kasumi placed a hand on Eva's stomach and pressed. Eva felt a warm sensation throughout her whole body, as if her blood were starting to heat up. Just as it started to feel uncomfortable for Eva, Kasumi removed her hand, and turned her head to face Shin again.

"This one is not with child." Kasumi stated, as if she were starting to disbelieve Shin's assessment of the twenty first century.

"In this time people would share their bodies for pleasure as well. They could carry out the reproduction act but take measures to prevent the creation of a new human." Shin quickly stated, keen to restore his intellect with Kasumi, "They carried out the act for carnal pleasure, some ancients would call it sin."

Kasumi stared deep into the eyes of Eva.

"So, you are a wrong one." She stated, not asking, and this brought waves of fear through Eva, "Now, tell me where I can find this one you call Boyfriend."

"His name is Zack," Eva gave up, willing to do anything now to make this experience end, "he lives with his parents on the outskirts of Serene."

"How cosy." Shin stated, desperate to show off his knowledge with long forgotten twenty first century words. Eva cast him a glare, beginning to dislike him more.

There was a bright flash of orange light burst into the room from outside of Eva's bedroom door. From where she lay, she could not see what the cause of it was, but when she looked back at Shin he was staring nervously at the door, standing bolt upright. She looked into the face of Kasumi, who appeared to roll her eyes back in disdain.

"Seraph Sir." Uttered Shin as another figure walked through Eva's bedroom door and entered the room. The figure was male, appeared to be about twenty-eight years old, and over six feet tall. He had short slick black hair, and a stare that froze the blood of Eva in fear. She formed the opinion very quickly, especially with Shin's reaction to his presence, that this was someone of importance from wherever these people had come from. He wore similar clothing to Shin, but in darkest black, with four tightly fastened straps across his chest, and a collar that made his head look smaller than it should be for his clothed stature. He was wearing black leather gloves which, in her fear, she still found to be quite odd for a summer's day.

"Nice of you to join us Seraph." Kasumi stated, the pleasure in her statement missing from her voice.

"Update please Kasumi." Three words that Seraph stated, again not a question, but an action not to be ignored. These three words, in English but an accent that Eva could not place, struck an almost electric cord of fear in her further. She felt her bladder pushing downwards again and struggled not to anger the intruders further. Kasumi stood and turned to face the male they called Seraph.

"We have identified the male who has allied with the dissidents earlier today, but were not in a position to exterminate him due to the surroundings Seraph." Stated Kasumi.

"Wait....what do you mean exterminate?" Asked Eva, eyes wide open staring at the couple holding a nonchalant conversation in the middle of her bedroom.

"Hush human," Kasumi turned to stare at Eva with a level of evil not yet seen in her eyes previously causing Eva to sit back against the headboard in fear again, before she turned her attention back to Seraph, "I managed a data grab of his electronic device, which has led us to Eva S here. She has been interrogated and the information she provides, I believe, will serve very well in our quest."

Seraph simply nodded at Kasumi, which she knew to be an indication to continue.

"The male we seek has a name of Zack. Zack lives on the outskirts of Serene with his older humans. He is the one who has allied with the dissidents." Kasumi concluded. Seraph paused for thought.

"We must recharge now. I have found a place near the beach." Seraph stated, looking across as Eva, "I believe our work is done here."

"Not quite sir," Shin stepped forward looking at Seraph and then back to Eva as he continued, "My chipling, Dove, has been without covering since the last dissidents uprising. I was thinking that this specimen would be an appropriate replacement."

Seraph stared at Eva for what felt like eternity. Eva had no idea what they were speaking about regarding chiplings, specimens and coverings but none of it sounded friendly and she developed a deep sense of dread.

"Very well, I see your point Shin," Seraph eventually spoke as he stepped closer to Eva. He removed a glove from his right hand which exposed long metallic talons underneath the leather that moved like fluid and reflected the light from her bedroom ceiling as he turned them towards her to reveal a blade on what would be the index finger. Shin approached Eva and pushed her down by the shoulders onto her bed. Eva struggled but their strength was inhuman, and she could not move. A sharp point from one of Seraphs fingers dug into her flesh by her neck and she felt a hot fluid enter her blood stream. The heat flowed around her entire body as her heart beat faster with fear, and as it did so she noticed that she could no longer move a muscle. She was paralysed, unable to move any part of her body, but still felt touch and pressure at any part that was touched. Seraph took his index finger and gently glided it over her clothing. As he did so, her clothing fell away with perfect razor-sharp cuts through it, until she lay on her bed completely naked.

"You do not need me here for this bit." Kasumi said as she left the bedroom to stand on the landing outside. There was screaming. Loud screaming, but only for about 30 seconds. Then silence. About two minutes later Seraph came through the bedroom door and joined Kasumi on the landing.

"Shin will return to Zeydence with the trophy for Dove." Seraph announced as there was an instantaneous flash of orange light behind them, "You and I will need to recharge by the beach, and we will seek this Zack when the new star rises."

Seraph then lead the way, walking down the stairs, and out of the front door at the bottom, quickly followed by Kasumi, closing the door behind her.

"How very quaint." Seraph said, "Manual doors that you must close yourself." He smiled as they both walked off into the night.

8

The alarm on his phone shrilled out. It was 6am, but this time he woke up straight away and sat up on his bed. Zack looked across at his en-suite door, wondering if he had dreamt the previous day, before realising that not even his own imagination could come up with what he had witnessed. He scratched his balls and stood up, making his way to the en-suite to break the seal of his bladder. He did not have the same sense of fear in him as he had had the previous morning and opened the door with confidence. There were no strange, beautiful ladies hiding in his bathtub this morning. Actually, he felt slightly disheartened that today was seeming to start, how would he call it, normal. It may have been early, but he could still hear his mother pottering around in the kitchen downstairs, and the smell of bacon cooking wafting up the stairs made him salivate. Monday morning, first day of work for the week. Another day wearing headphones and remotely taking bank managers through changing formats in Microsoft office, and connecting them to printers, all the while ignoring the impatience in their voices. There had to be more to life than this.

The morning rituals over with, Zack donned a dressing gown and went downstairs for breakfast.

* * *

It was a nice day, the sun was shining, very few clouds peppered the blue sky and Zack was driving along the Norfolk coast in Citroen DS3 Racing model. It had been a present from his father when he had retired from Aurora Financial Services a couple of years back. Zack loved the car, carbon fibre grey with orange trim, alloys, and roof. Some said that it looked too over the top for him, but funnily, none ever refused a lift from him whenever he offered. His tie lay on the passenger seat beside him. He wasn't a tie person, and always felt aggrieved that he should wear one for work, just to sit in a booth answering calls, but such was life. The job description stated that he should wear a tie, but never stated what the tie should look like. As a result, Zack had a substantial collection of what he called 'protest ties', having searched eBay for 1970's kipper and paisley ties. Today's effort was an orange and purple paisley kipper tie. It stayed, screwed up on his front passenger seat, and he would not be putting it on until he was sitting at his desk, getting paid by the man for wearing it. He had his window open, and the air was rushing through his hair as he negotiated the lanes, he travelled pretty much every working day. He had tried to phone Eva a couple of times through his Bluetooth stereo, but she was not picking up. He had decided that he would pay her a visit on his lunch hour, but his mind was relaxed. He felt as though he had 'options' now, though what those options were he still didn't quite understand. His car stereo blasted out Expendable Heroes by one of his favourite metal bands, Arise. He envisioned himself in the song, *'Listen citizens we are on the verge of war, I will never let my empire fall'* rang out from his speakers. He smiled to himself about the series of events from yesterday and that this particular song had played a large part in his university dissertation which had somehow led to strange people visiting him thinking that he was some kind of superhero. As he neared work he flicked through his playlist and put 'Revocation of Humankind' by Blood Red Throne on the stereo hoping that there was enough road left between himself and his workplace to hear the whole song.

As the final line of the song was concluding he was chanting *'Die Die Die'* out of his window as he turned his car into the staff carpark at Aurora's call centre. Swinging his car into a parking spot he pressed for his window to glide up, grabbed his tie and got out of the car. Pressing his remote he heard the doors clunk locked and he made his way into the building. As per usual he made it to his desk just as he was about to start his shift. The telephone on his desk was ringing, but he didn't answer it, pausing to put his tie on and rooting through his work drawers for a lanyard to display his identification badge. Company policy was that ID should be worn at all times, but this was one of life's tiny rebellious charms that he managed to get in the building and to his desk every day without wearing it.

"I'll get that shall I?" A voice piped up from the next booth.

"If you like." Zack replied, and popped his head around the booth wall to see Marshall sitting slumberly at his desk with his headset and microphone on, tie slightly askew in another nod at rebellion against the man. Marshall answered the phone, and Zack decided that now would be a good time to get a coffee. Fishing around inside his desk drawers he pulled out the obligatory Star Wars mug that Jeff had bought him in the not-so-secret Santa last Christmas. Looking into the bottom of the mug he realised he hadn't rinsed it out after finishing his shift last Friday, but his desire for caffeine overwhelmed him and he formed the opinion that the level of coffee stains would not be enough to kill him, so he made his way directly to the kettle in the corner of the room. Once his cup was full, he returned to his booth. A good fifteen minutes had passed since he walked into the office with no intention of actually doing any work until he was ready. Logging onto his computer he could never quite understand the number of times he had to enter a password just simply to get on with doing his job. And then he sat there, awaiting the first distressed call from a computer illiterate executive.

"Is there anything else I can help you with today?" He heard Marshall getting to the end of his call in the next booth with the obligatory comment straight from their customer service crib sheet, that not a single caller believed they said with any polite intentions. Then he heard the sound of Marshall flicking the switch on his telephone to end the call before his head popped above the divider between their desks.

"Seen anymore vanishing weirdo's today Zed?" Marshall asked. Zack had expected this but didn't let it bother him.

"Nope." Zack replied without looking up, hoping to just play it down without the rest of the call takers in the office overhearing. Zack looked around his desk and noticed that his beloved Arsenal beanie bear was missing. "Have you seen Thierry?" he asked Marshall.

"Nope." Marshall replied, "Maybe he just, er, y'know, vanished." Marshall started to snigger. Zack looked up at Marshall grinning like a twat and smiled.

"Mock all you like Marshall, yesterday was way bigger than your tiny brain will ever comprehend." Zack said. Marshall just shrugged his shoulders and grunted. How he ever formed the intelligence to solve complex computer problems Zack would never understand.

"So, where is Thierry?" Zack asked, trying not to let irritation bite at him. Marshall sat back down.

"Jeff has him." Marshall stated from the other side of his divider. Jeff stood up from his desk a couple of booths down in protest.

"Marshall told me to hide him," Jeff stated in defence, Marshall sat silently pretending to be doing some work, "He said you'd find it funny."

"Give." Zack simply said. Jeff bent down to his desk, taking the bear out of his drawer, and tossed it towards Zack. At the right moment Marshall stood up in his booth and headed the flying teddy away from Zack and in the direction of Ami, the office moaner. The bear slid to a stop on her desk as it struck her coffee cup, knocking some of the fluid out onto her desk.

"Can you fuckwits grow the fuck up?!" Ami had spun around in her chair to address Zack, Marshall, and Jeff, and wasn't overly happy.

"Do you kiss your mother with that mouth?" Marshall asked, without standing up so that Ami couldn't see him as she spoke.

Zack's phone started to ring, and he answered it quickly, allowing Ami time to cool down before he went, cap in hand, to ask for Thierry back. As he was saying his introductory spiel to the caller, he could hear Ami typing away a little heavier than usual. It was common knowledge that she was an email complainer and he fully accepted some shit to come his way in the very near future.

And so the morning wore on, the usual number of callers requesting assistance, an unending flow of coffee and enough caffeine to kill an elephant, Marshall's childish jibes, Jeff's innocent protestations and enamoured conversations on all things Star Wars, and the usual apologies and sucking up to Ami on behalf of all three of them in order to avoid any complaints. Zack eventually got Thierry back, with a coffee stain on his ass, and soon enough lunch break came around.

"Later Losers." Marshall stated as he stood up and held his fingers in an L shape against his forehead as he swivelled around to face both Jeff and Zack in turn, "I'm gonna pop outside for an oily rag." Marshall pulled a packet of cigarettes from his shirt pocket, pulled one out of the packet, popped the click flavour pod in the filter and tucked it behind his right ear. Picking up his phone he turned and made his way towards the way out of the office. Jeff and Zack watched as he walked off, suddenly stopped and made his way back to his desk.

"I'm not making that mistake again," Marshall stated, "It's a real ball ache when you get down to the smokers hut only to find that I've left my lighter up here and the hut is full of fucking vapers without a light between them." Marshall put his phone down on his desk and was muttering to himself as he rooted through his desk drawers, eventually finding a lighter and heading straight back towards the exit without another word. Zack tried to call Eva again. Again, the call went unanswered. Zacks thoughts then turned to Madoka. He scrolled through the address book on his phone to see if he had the number to his old phone. He hadn't had to give it out or call it for about a year and the numbers just eluded him.

"Jeff, have you got my old phone number on your phone mate?" Zack asked as Jeff was locking his computer to go out for lunch.

"No Zack, I deleted it as soon as you gave me the number to your new contract." Jeff replied, "I reckon Marshall will have it though, he's far too lazy to update and clean out his phonebook."

Jeff had a point; Marshall would've just saved his new number as an additional number alongside the old one. He seemed to get by on what Zack and Jeff called organised chaos. Zack looked across to Marshalls booth and saw that he had left his iPhone on the desk. Not wanting to explain to Marshall why he needed his old number he simply stepped across and picked the handset up. Pressing the home button revealed a Norwich City football badge as his screensaver and asked Zack for the passcode. Zack had watched him input it many times and the past and it didn't take a genius to work out that Marshall was using his date of birth as his passcode. Zack tapped it in, 2 4 1 2 9 5, and the apps appeared on the screen. Zack selected the contacts app and found his entry under 'Zed'. As expected, Marshall had two numbers stored for Zack, his current one and the old redundant number from his old contract. Zack thought it would probably be easier to send the contact details to himself from Marshall's phone by text message so that he could save it on his own directly and opted to share by message. Typing his number into the message he pressed send and then heard a beep on his own phone to let him know that he had received the contact details. Zack started to close down the message app when he saw that Eva had sent Marshall a message at about 10pm the night before. The preview was highlighted with an image icon rather than text and this made Zacks curiosity grow. He had been trying to contact her around the same time, but his calls went unanswered. Curiosity got the better of him and he opened the message. He saw a photo had been sent by message of Eva taking a selfie of herself lifting her T-shirt up to one side, exposing a breast and a cheeky wink in her eye. What the actual fuck was going on? Anger rose in Zack, magnified by the current situation between himself and Eva. He opened up Marshall's camera roll on his phone and discovered more naked photos of Eva and worse. Photos of Eva sucking on Marshall on a bed that Zack clearly recognised as being in Marshalls bedroom. Scrolling through a bit more there were photos of Marshall and Eva having full sex in the missionary position, a close up of her face and she was gently biting her lip and her eyes rolled back towards the ceiling. Zack knew from experience that she was obviously enjoying the activities. Another picture of a cock buried inside her in a doggy style position, he could only see her rump on this one, but she was clearly identified by the kissing lips tattoo that he knew she had on her right arse cheek. Zack cast a glance towards Jeff, who was shyly looking at him. Zack noticed other people looking at him. At that moment when his world appeared

to have stopped and gone silent his body language must have given away to the rest of the office that something was incredibly wrong. And from the people that were casting him sly glances but not brave enough to meet his gaze it was apparent that others knew before he did. Jeff had stood up and looked at him. Zack cast him a cold stare.
"Did you know about this?" Zack demanded more than asked.
"I had an idea." Jeff replied
"An idea about what Jeff? What did you have an idea about?"
"You know." Jeff replied feebly, shifting uneasily on his feet.
"No Jeff, I don't know, what did you have a fucking idea about?" Zack demanded. Everyone in the office was looking at him and his manager, Mr Banks, had stepped out of his door to see what the shouting was about. Observing for now.
"Right here Zack?" Jeff asked
"Yes, right here, seems like everyone knows already anyway." Zack could feel himself losing control of his emotions but could do nothing to stop it. The photo of Marshall's cock in Eva's mouth and her smiling eyes he was holding in his hand would not let him regain control.
"Eva's pregnant." Jeff mumbled, this time looking towards the floor, anywhere but at Zack. There was a moment of silence as Zack's brain hurt as he tried to take it all in.
"She's fucking pregnant!?" Zack eventually shouted towards Jeff, not believing, or wanting to believe what he had heard, especially given his recent discovery.
"Who's pregnant?" A familiar voice behind Zack asked. He spun around to see Marshall walking back into the office after his cigarette break. Marshall saw his phone is Zacks hand and stopped in his tracks. "Dude, I can explain." He offered
 Zack threw the mobile phone at full force at Marshall striking him on the top left of his forehead. Marshall, who had tried to crouch out of the way, fell to one knee, winced at the pain, and clutched the top of his head with a hand, thus covering his eye in a feeble attempt to push the pain back into his head out of the way. Zack ran towards him the ten steps or so with clenched fists and swung a low punch into Marshall's face who was at Zacks waist height on his knee. It was almost as if the photographs had elevated Zack away from the juvenile sense of humour that he and Marshall had shared for so long, and years of pisstaking and pranks were converted into frustration and anger along with the images of the photos burned into his memory forevermore now. Zack could feel nothing, except his laboured

breathing, like a dragon trying to expel everything negative in one breath. Marshall flew backwards onto the floor, laying on his back as Zack went at him again. Marshall put his legs up defensively and as Zack rushed towards him, too fast and too late to stop, Marshall kicked out, sending him flying over the top of him, and crashing over the top of the desk behind them. Marshall struggled to get up as Zack spun on the polished surface of the desk, knocking over a partition between the next desk onto another member of staff who had so desperately been trying to stay out of the drama. Marshall moved over to where his desk was and turned with his back to it. Workers on the other side of the partition got up from their desks and moved away from Marshall as if he were a leper. Zack rushed at him again, head down and the pair of them locked into a scrum falling backwards onto Marshall's desk with the momentum of Zacks running. Fists pumping from both sides they took turns at hitting each other as they rolled around the desks, fighting for superiority and to be on top. Partitions, and telephones were knocked over and fell to the floor. Mr Banks wobbled out of his office to where they were. He was mid-fifties with a beer belly, large eighties style specs, slightly balding curly grey hair and a beard that matched but never seemed to be able to grow too long. As he got closer to the fighting pair, he suddenly stopped, took a step backwards and fumbled to take his Ralph Lauren tie off and throw it to one side.

"Can you stop please?" Mr Banks asked politely with a hint of fear in his voice. Nothing, Marshall and Zack continued exchanging blows. Zacks hair had come out of hairband holding it tight and neat at the back of his head, and now hung down almost creating curtains over Marshalls face. He had the upper hand and was bearing down on him. It was Jeff who stepped forward and took Zack by the shoulders, gently pulling him backwards away from Marshall. Zack was breathing hard, seething still but offered little resistance to Jeff pulling him away. Marshall raised a hand to his mouth and saw blood on his knuckles when he took it away again to inspect it.

"I shall have to report this to HR." Mr Banks said. Zack's head spun around to stare at him.

"Fuck you Banks!" Zack spat venom in his words. "I'm out of here." Zack yanked the lanyard around his neck until the safety fastener at the back gave way, and he threw his ID card and lanyard at Mr. Banks desk. He then walked over to his desk. Picked up Thierry and his car keys and turned to walk away. He paused slightly to lay a framed photograph of Eva face down on the desk and then strolled straight out of the office. He walked until he was out of sight, not wanting to give anyone the impression that he was running away from anything, but as soon as he was out of sight he ran towards the fire exit leading to the car park, convinced someone must have phoned the police. He expected to be arrested, but he had unfinished business, and he needed to take care of it before anyone phoned her.

Zack flung the door open to his car, jumped inside, started the engine, and the door closed itself with the momentum of his wheel spinning out of Aurora Financial Service's car park. He never looked in his rear-view mirror. That building, those people were now part of his past and he never wanted to look back.

9

Zack took a sharp left into Spinney Road, Serene. How he'd made it here in one piece was beyond him. There had been a few close calls along the coastal road, and he'd had to stop at one point to let his heart slow down. But as he got closer to Eva's road that hadn't seemed to matter. He wanted to confront her and wanted to get to her address before someone was able to tip her off that he knew. Jesus, he knew about her fucking Marshall. Jeff believed she was pregnant. His emotions were all over the place. He screeched to a halt outside number nine, a semi-detached council property, brickwork halfway up the building and beige rendering on the upper half. The front garden surrounded by a brown picket fence with a few of the slats missing. Eva's Volvo was on the driveway. Result, she was more than likely home. Zack switched the engine off and got out of his car, the engine still ticking slightly where it had been well and truly thrashed on the ten-minute journey from Aurora Financial Services to Eva's house. He strode with purpose to the front door and rang the doorbell. Five seconds later, which felt like an eternity, he rang it again. This time he counted to ten before ringing it a third time. Without waiting he walked across the front of the house and peered through the living room window with his hands atop his head to shield the glare of the sun reflecting in the glass. Nothing. He looked at the upper windows, the one above the living room was open slightly but he would be unable to reach it. Frustration was adding to his anger and he envisioned the imaginary angel on his shoulder telling him to calm down, and that being angry would solve nothing, but damn it was hard. Zack didn't want to cause a scene at the front of the house, so he went down the side of the house towards the rear garden. As he went around the back, he saw that there were more upper windows open. She had to be in. Eva's father had been a Police officer before he and her mother divorced. He had always instilled in her from a young age not to leave windows open when leaving the home, not even in summer. Eva had pulled Zack up on this many times when they were about to leave his home in the past. Zack knew her mother was away so Eva must be home. Zack got his phone out and scrolled through his phone book until he reached Eva S. Pressing her name started a call for him. As he stood in the back garden he heard a phone ringing through the upstairs window. He recognised it as Eva's ringtone and called out her name. There was no answer. As he was looking up at her bedroom window he felt something brush up against his leg. He looked down to see, Tiger, Eva's mothers white cat purring beside him having come through the cat flap in the back door. He noticed that, whilst usually totally white, Tigers nose and paws were wet and deep red in colour today. Kneeling down to greet Tiger, he wiped his hand across Tiger's nose and then stared at the blood on his fingertips. Zack rushed towards the back door. It was a wooden door, unlike the UPVC door at the front of the house, and he tried the metal handle. It was locked, but Zack knew that the wooden frame wasn't the strongest in the world, and as he held the handle down, he barged the door with his shoulder. There was a brief splintering sound and he stepped into the kitchen at the rear of the house.

"Eva!" he called out and was met by silence. He could hear his heart beating in his ears. He stood completely still and looked down at the laminated flooring in the hallway towards the front door. There were tiny blood red paw prints drying on the laminate. He looked around the kitchen to see if any meat had been left out but could see none. He walked slowly along the hallway, peeking into the living room as he passed the door. It looked the same as it had done when he had peered through the front window a few minutes previously. No longer consumed by absolute anger an element of fear entered Zacks soul. He wanted to turn around and run away but something kept him moving as he turned to walk up the stairs. The light beige carpet ascending the stairs to the upper floor was littered with yet more blotches of red about the size of a cat's paw print and seemed to be more concentrated towards the top of the stairs. It took eternity to reach the top. A million thoughts rushed through Zacks mind as he made his way upwards.

Should he run? Where had the blood come from? Was it blood? Was Eva ok? Why had she been fucking Marshall? Would the Police be on their way? Surely, someone at Aurora must have dialled 999 given the spectacle at the office. Did anyone figure out where he was going next? Of course, they would have. Would Mrs Miggins across the road be complaining about the way he pulled up in the street? Was he still angry? Yes, he was, but why did he feel like crying at this exact moment? What was that smell? Jesus, what the fuck was that smell?

Stood at the top of the stairs he turned to face the landing, and stared at Eva's bedroom door, a room he knew so well. So many happy and naughty moments had been created in the room, but he felt neither happy nor naughty right now. Should he call the Police? Fuck no. He had to find out what had happened for himself and then assess the situation afterwards. He felt like a wanted man on the run, a fugitive, after the fight with Marshall. He did not know who to trust. He'd lost his best friend and girlfriend all in the same day and met with time travelling fugitives all in the same weekend. How on earth could he trust a complete stranger in a uniform? Standing outside the room he had made love to Eva in so many times he never felt so lonely in all of his life. The door was slightly ajar, he put his right hand against the wood and pushed it inwards. From where he stood he could not see the bed. Daylight poured through the uncurtained windows revealing ever more blood stains on the floor. He wasn't sure whether he could smell death or whether his nose and brain were conspiring to make him think that he could, but a wave of nausea hit him like a truck and made him want to crash to his knees. He remained standing, still not daring to enter the room.

"Eva?" He spoke her name, expecting her to answer him back, walk towards him, greet him with a hug and make the nightmare go away. Nothing. Silence.

Zack stepped into the bedroom and looked around. His brain made him start with the wall that he could already see from the doorway, as if prolonging anything else, and as he scanned around the whole room, he saw the shredded clothing scattered on the floor under the window. Dread filled Zack. The urge to run grew too strong but the momentum of his body turning was too much and he inevitably turned until the bed was in his field of vision. Initially, Zack had no idea what he was looking at, a mass of redness on the bed, that had been absorbed and spread through the linen of the white cotton sheets. It took a couple of seconds to take in that it was a human form, making out limbs, a head shape attached to a torso. Was it Eva? He couldn't tell, it was a human form devoid of any skin at all. Whoever it was, it was in Eva's house, in Eva's bed, the shredded clothes in the room he recognised as those that she was wearing at the Greasy dog the day before. Bile rose through his chest and he spun out of the room, running to the bathroom at the top of the stairs. The toilet seat was down so he leant over the sink and vomited for what seemed like forever. Every time he thought that he had finished another wave of nausea rose through him. Tears streamed down his face. Zack fought against unconsciousness, his head was overwhelmed, and he was starting to shut down. As he stood and wiped his mouth on a towel, he realised he needed to get out of the house. He could never have done this to Eva ever, but there were enough witnesses at Aurora who could testify as to his anger at her. He stumbled down the stairs towards the front door and opened it. Zack took a deep breath of fresh air blowing in from the nearby coast and composed himself. He stepped out of the house and pulled the door closed behind him, walked as calmly as he could under the circumstances towards his car and got into the driver's seat. As he started the car he was already putting it into gear and pulled away from the kerb, heading towards the other end of the road that he entered from. It seemed like he was driving far slower than the adrenaline coursing through him would like, and every muscle in his body was being used to stop him from stamping down on the accelerator. Reaching the end of the road he turned right, heading towards the coast road. He did not see the blue lights of the vehicles entering Spinney Road at the other end as he drove away.

* * *

Zack sat in his car in a parking space under the old Serene lighthouse. Tears streamed down his face and he sobbed uncontrollably. He wondered how his life could have turned to shit in such a short space of time. He looked at the futuristic interior of his car and recalled buying it with hopes and dreams of a fun, carefree future. Those days seemed to be long gone now and felt like it had happened to someone else. With hands and head resting on his steering wheel his body was racked with sobs and the world could have ended around him and he wouldn't have noticed or cared. Finally, the energy in him started to sap and his crying subsided. He looked up from the steering wheel, out at the North Sea before him, waves rolling into the beach below and ships on the far horizon. He envied the seagulls that floated aimlessly in the air. They didn't have a care in the world, no money worries, no comprehension of mortality, did they even mourn family that never returned? As he sat in his car, he remembered that Eva's mother was due home from her weekend away this evening. He couldn't let her find the scene that he had found. He felt guilty about letting the Police know and them having to find the scene too, how much would it traumatise the average officer? Then he felt anger at why he had to find Eva. Fate could be a real fucker sometimes. Not wanting to do anything but knowing that he had to do something played a psychological tug of war competition in his head and eventually he took his mobile phone out of his pocket. Scrolling through the numbers he turned to the last person he felt he could trust at Aurora. It rang about six times until a familiar, if somewhat melancholy, voice answered.

"Zack?"

"Jeff." Zack replied and then realised he had no idea what to say.

"We know Zack." Jeff stated.

"It wasn't me." Zack fought back the urge to start sobbing again.

"Where are you Zack?" Jeff asked. There was a slight tone in his voice that Zack didn't like. He didn't sound the same as he had at the beach yesterday.

"Are the Police there?" Zack asked.

"I know you didn't do it Zack." Jeff replied

"You're not fucking telling me no Jeff. Are the fucking Police there?"

"Calm down Zack, please calm down." Jeff pleaded. Zack heard the sound of a door clicking open. He recognised it as the sound of the fire door at the back of the office. He then heard the crunch of the stones covering the rest area at the back. He knew that Jeff had taken his phone somewhere more private to speak.

"Where are you?" Jeff asked again.

"I can't tell you Jeff. I'm going to have to go somewhere far away." Zack had calmed down.

"Don't go," Jeff pleaded, emotion creeping into his voice, "I'll help you Zack, you know my father is a barrister."

"I don't need a barrister Jeff, I haven't done anything wrong." Zack said, "there's nothing left here for me now, just know that I didn't do it."

"What about me?" Jeff asked

"What about you? You're not the one in the shit here mate." Zack replied.

"I love you." Jeff stated. "I always have done. Marshall would tease me about it, but I put up with his homophobia to stay near you. You can't go."

"What the fuck Jeff?" This was too much for Zack to comprehend, "That's........" He struggled for the words to finish his sentence, and as he paused there was a deep cutting silence in the conversation. This was interrupted by further alien whispered voices and Zack heard a someone speaking in jargon, slightly mechanised as if through a radio. He knew the Police had followed Jeff out of the fire door. He heard Jeff starting to slowly sob. There was a cracking noise. Jeff had dropped his phone onto the stones on the floor. Zack heard the crunching noise of footsteps approaching Jeff followed by authoritative voices, and Jeff started to wail. It was over for Zack in Serene. He ended the call and got out of his car. He looked around him and then started walking along the top of the cliff.

10

Zack had walked for about fifteen minutes, feeling as though everyone was looking at him. In truth, he'd only passed two dog walkers and a teenage couple feeling each other up in the shelter that overlooked the sea. He paused at the top of the steps that lead down to Serene beach. He took his phone out of his pocket and scrolled to the text message that he had sent himself earlier. He hated it that he saw Marshall's name on the screen, but that was the only way for him to get the telephone number that he needed. He saved his old number into his contacts as quickly as he could, so he no longer had to look at the name, feeling his blood starting to boil with anger. He held back the tears. He'd poured everything into his relationship with Eva, and everything he'd learned from today indicated that Marshall had been the last to enjoy her body, been the last to be with her, and created happy moments with her, whilst everyone else believed he was losing his mind. Tears welled up and the screen before him started to blur. He wiped a tear away from his eye and pressed the screen for his phone to dial his old number. Holding the phone to his ear, he held his breath until he heard the call connect and start to ring. He let out a big sigh and then held his breath again, his heart pounding, until the call was answered about eight rings later. He heard Madoka's voice talking to someone else at the other end, it sounded like Junko, but the voices sounded distant.

"Madoka." Zack said, but there was no reply, the voices kept talking in the distance. It sounded like Madoka was asking the other party what to do. "Hold it against your ear!" Zack shouted into his phone. The voices paused and there was a rustling sound.

"Hello." It was Madoka's voice. She sounded closer and seemed to have gotten the idea of the telephone.

"Madoka, it's me Zack." He stated and sat down on the grass, all energy within him seeming to be sapped away.

"Wow! How are you doing this?" Madoka seemed excited at the idea of speaking to Zack through a small piece of plastic and glass. Zack could not match her enthusiasm.

"Madoka, where are you? When are you?" Zack asked.

"We're in your time." She replied, "I'm with Echo and Junko."

"I need to meet you. Tell Echo that I'll be at the beach where he first approached me. He'll know what I mean."

"Is everything OK?" Madoka asked, sensing sadness in Zacks voice.
"No." He replied, "So much has happened, but it's not safe for me to speak on here. Please meet me at the beach, I'll be there very soon."
"Ok." Madoka replied, and Zack disconnected the call. He stood up and felt extremely tired. He wondered whether he should attempt the three hundred steps to the beach in such a condition, and then reminded himself that he had done it many times over the years completely wasted. Steadying himself he started to make the descent down the steps.

* * *

Zack waited on the beach, sat on a large piece of driftwood that doubled up as a bench at the foot of the cliffs. He felt confident that he could not be seen from the top of the cliff, but as each second passed his anxiety grew that at any moment he would hear the sound of sirens.

As the sun started to set on the sea in front of him, he contemplated whether it would be the last time he saw a famous Norfolk sunset and checked his phone for the time. It had been an hour since he had called Madoka. For fucks sake, they were time travellers, you would have thought that they were able to get there the second he ended the call. Anxiety added to his tiredness and he struggled to keep his eyes open. Some hero of the human race he was. Then he heard footsteps on the cliff stairs. No voices, just the patter of someone, more than one person coming down the steps. Fearing the worst, he leapt behind the driftwood and crouched down. It was always going to be impossible to hide his whole self, but he hoped it would buy him some time if the footsteps belonged to foe instead of friend. He watched the bottom of the steps in anticipation and felt a wave of relief rush over him when he saw Madoka round the corner to take the last few steps onto the sand and stones. Followed by Echo and Junko. The three of them appeared to be wearing the same clothing as he had seen them in the previous night. Junko looked troubled.

"This is where I first met him." Zack heard Echo speaking to the Madoka as they looked around the deserted beach. Zack stood up and Madoka's eyes turned towards him. No-one moved for a while until Zack stepped over the driftwood and approached the trio, glancing nervously towards the top of the cliff with each step. So much had happened to his life in such a short space of time, and Zack felt overwhelmed and confused to see these people, these strangers that up until forty-eight hours ago had been an unexplainable pain in his arse. As he got closer to Madoka he held his arms outstretched, hoping to collapse into her arms in a hug, but the sentiment was lost on her and she just eyed him up suspiciously as if looking for a weapon. Zack put his arms down and contemplated putting his hands into his pocket but wasn't sure how that would be taken by them. Would they think he was reaching for a concealed weapon? If, as his body felt like doing, he collapsed in an exhausted heap would he be able to prevent himself from face planting into the sand?

"Something troubles you Mr Collins?" Junko spoke first, acknowledging the sombre look on Zacks face, his hear down and messed up.

"I don't know what is happening." Was all that Zack could offer. He wanted to explode and tell everything that happened to him, but if they couldn't even understand the concept of a mobile phone, then what he had to blurt out would just sound like white noise. He wasn't even sure he knew what had happened himself or where to start. He simply said, "I think Eva is dead." The sight of the red human form seeping into her bedclothes came to the fore of his mind, and he collapsed to his knees, held his face in his hands and his body racked with sobs as he let go. Madoka stepped forward and placed a hand on Zacks shoulder. He felt the physical contact between himself and Madoka, and he felt guilty at the comfort that it drew. Zack stood up and looked Madoka in the eyes before turning to Echo.

"What do we do now?" Zack asked, "apart from my parents, everything that I have here is gone. I can't return to them and bring trouble to their door. I need to leave. I need to come with you." Zack hadn't thought it through, the words came naturally out of him. Not one part of his brain tried to talk him out of what he was saying, what he was offering.

"Do you understand what you are saying?" Echo asked him. Zack was at least comforted by the fact that he hadn't shot him down in flames and told him it was impossible, told him that he had to remain in his miserable existence as a fugitive. Madoka spun towards Echo, wide eyed and concerned.

"No," She argued, "It's far too dangerous for him." She turned to Zack "We train for years to transport through time. We've trained for years to meet you. It's impossible."

The two words Zack didn't want to hear, 'it's impossible.'

"Everything is possible, the impossible just takes more effort." Zack stated, quoting a motivational poster he'd seen on a training course one day. To be honest, it was all he could remember about the training course.

"It can be done." Junko added, visibly excited that his imaginary hero would want to travel with him.

"But it could kill him." Madoka argued, this time spinning around to face Junko. "He's better as an advisor here that we can visit."

"I could die here." Zack interrupted. "Someone, something, has killed Eva, the girl I love, loved. I have no idea what....it was horrible. At least I think it was Eva, there was nothing, no skin, just blood, lots of fucking blood."

Junko and Echo shared a subtle glance. But no matter how subtle it was Zack noticed it, noticed that they knew something. "I thought they would have returned by now." Echo said to Junko, as if Zack was no longer part of the equation. Zack looked between the two of them as they spoke.

"I have not sensed them." Junko replied.

"Who? What?" Zack was desperate for answers. Echo believed that he was owed an explanation.

"What you have described is typical of the Zeydenians. One of their methods." Echo offered before turning to Madoka, "You see, he is not safe here."

"It could kill him." Madoka pleaded. Zack wondered why they were all talking about him, around him, as if he were not present.

"Shouldn't I have a say in this?" Zack interrupted. Madoka shot him a glare.

"I'm thinking of your best interests." She stated.

"I have no best interests here anymore; I have no reason to live. If I die with you then it will only speed up the inevitable. Something here is after me, and not just the Police and I'm too tired to keep running alone. If I run with you and it all goes wrong at least we can say I tried my best." Zack replied. That was the best he had. There followed a tense silence. Echo simply stared at Madoka, Junko didn't know where to look and his eyes wandered around the beach. Zack looked between them all. Finally, Madoka realised she was not going to win this argument.

"Fine." She said, "But don't say I didn't warn you."

Echo turned to face Zack. Placing both hands on Zacks shoulders brought about a De Ja Vu from the first time they met at the same spot on the beach.

"It's not going to be easy." Echo stated. "It is easier for Madoka and I because we were born at the same time. Twins share the pain between them. Junko here gets travel sick and quite poorly if he ports for any long space of time. We need to go forward approximately 600 years from now."

"I can't be in any more pain than I am right now." Zack replied.

"Ok, my friend, we need to brief you on the basics if you are to survive." Junko said. No matter how much scarier the talk became, the numbness within Zacks soul never once said to him that the risk was not worth it. Madoka had turned her back on the men like a spoilt child, but when she realised it was going to happen regardless, she turned to look at Zack, hoping to have some input into his wellbeing.

"You will need to hold mine and Echo's hands." She said, "We can port on our own but if you are not connected to us, having never ported before, you will simply stay here." Madoka reached out for Zacks hand and as he went to take it, he suddenly stopped.

"I have an idea." Zack said, "But first, is it warm where we are going?"

"It has a similar climate to here." Junko replied.

"Ok, good. I think I should leave my clothes on the beach. People will find them tomorrow and assume I have walked into the sea and killed myself. No-one will look for me, and it will bring some small closure to my parents."

"I commend that idea." Echo announced with an air of authority. Zack shrugged, he didn't need permission, he was going to do what was best for those he left behind. He looked around and decided to leave his clothing on the driftwood he had been sitting on, at least that way if the tide came in it had more of chance of surviving being washed away. He removed his shirt, slowly unbuttoning it and staring at it as he held it in his hands. If ever there were a moment for him to have doubts about what he was about to do this was it. The sea breeze caressed his topless torso and his nipples started to harden a little. He kicked off his work shoes, and in turn took his socks off and stuffed them into each corresponding shoe. Lastly, he undid the belt on his trousers and removed them, revealing just a pair of white cotton boxer shorts. He resolved to keep his boxers on. He hadn't yet worked out what his companions view of complete nudity was or the availability of clothing in the future, and didn't fancy walking around for too long in a strange dimension with his cock out. Folding the clothes neatly he set them on top of the makeshift driftwood bench, placing his shoes on top of the linen in order to weight it down if the wind blew in. Satisfied that they were in a prominent place to be discovered he turned his back on his clothing and faced his three newfound friends.

"What next?" Zack asked, anxious to just get on with moving on. Madoka looked him up and down but Zack couldn't gauge from her facial expression what she was thinking. He looked at the others and saw that Junko and Echo were looking up to the top of the cliff. Zacks gaze followed theirs in time to see the brief fading of an orange glow.

"They're here." Echo said, and then pointed his finger along the beach in the direction of Serene pier. Zack turned to see that Madoka was already running, and with a hefty shove in the shoulder from Junko he found himself also on his toes, sprinting along the beach. Zack started to regret leaving his shoes behind as the soles of his feet pounded down on the pebbled sections of the beach. He was also regretting standing out in just a pair of white boxer shorts whilst his company blended with the shadows in their dark clothing. After a couple of hundred metres Zack saw Madoka in front of him angle sharply towards the shelter of the cliff face. He admired the speed that she had but called out her name as he saw her heading towards Keelside cave.

"Madoka, no!" Zack called out. Growing up in Serene all children were taught to stay away from the cave after a group from Keelside Secondary School got caught inside when the tide rose and drowned. There was no way out of the cave other than the entrance. Madoka continued to run straight into the entrance and further into the darkness, swiftly followed by Echo. Zack reached the entrance at the same time as Junko but paused on the outside as Junko continued forward at speed.

"It's too dangerous." Zack stated, "There's no exit."

"We don't need an exit." Came the reply. In the darkness Zack could no longer see anyone but knew the voice to be that of Echo.

Suddenly Zack felt a sharp burning pain across the side of his right triceps muscle. A force threw him forward into the cave entrance as he gave out a yell of pain. Rolling onto his back his left hand came to his right arm and clutched where he felt the pain. He looked down at his hand and saw blood seeping through his fingers. What the fuck just happened? The pain was becoming unbearable and he thought he might lose consciousness when he saw the face of Junko looking down upon his, upside down. Junko's strong arms reached down and grabbed hold of Zack under his armpits and dragged him further into the cave. Once clear of the entrance Zack felt other hands pulling on him, until they were in a clearing in the cave.

"There's no time for instruction." Echo said to him, "Good luck."

Zack felt Madoka grab his left hand and link the fingers of her right hand between his, her other hand coming in to clasp over the coupling and squeeze tight. Junko lifted Zack up and bear hugged him from behind, placing his arms around Zack from behind and linking his hands together in a tight grip at the front of Zack's torso. Echo grabbed hold of his right hand, and he winced with the pain that shot down his arm at the slightest movement. Holding his hand in a vice like grip, Echo started to glow. It seemed to happen in slow motion, Zack turned to look at Echo in the pitch dark and as his eyes came upon him Echo looked like an ultraviolet tattoo before becoming a burning flame orange colour. Panic set in Zack and he spun very quickly to look at Madoka who stared straight at him with neon eyes, as she too flashed upwards in a bright orange like a magnesium test strip. And then the heat rose. Starting with his bare feet and rising rapidly up his legs, he felt paralysed and for a flashing thought could not work out why he had not collapsed. It felt as though his legs were gone, and then he felt whipped backwards as if his head were trying to touch the floor behind him and his spine was bending backwards at an angle that was unsurvivable. His ribs felt like they were trying to push out of his chest, but that lasted for the briefest of split seconds as the rising paralysis consumed his chest. Another one of those thoughts that occur in less time than the brain can comprehend, would his heart still beat if his chest were paralysed? He could neither confirm that nor think about it further before the spinning started. It felt as though he were doing backflips, rapidly over and over again, the back of his head trying to touch his spine. So fast, so many times. Zack tried to scream but he could hear no sounds. The bright orange glow consumed him as he spun. So bright it was, burning his eyes. He believed that he had closed his eyes, but if he had whatever the light was, it was penetrating his eyelids no matter how much he scrunched them. Panic set in further as he could no longer feel the contact from his three companions, and his brain did what it should have done far earlier in the day. It shut down. Suddenly there was darkness and silence.

11

Feeling came back to Zack. He was on his back. Somewhere. He tried to open his eyes, but they were heavy, so heavy. He felt his arms twitching and his fingers moved. Never having been without sight, he started to feel around him. His fingertips were numb at first, not really able to discern shapes, but he felt the hardness of the sides to either side of him. Panic set in, it felt like a coffin, a space not wide enough to outstretch his arms full on either side. He tried to move his legs, but they did not want to play ball. His calf muscles tensed, and he felt a shooting sciatic pain rush up his legs, feeling like it was crushing his hip bone as it passed by, and ending in a stab at the muscles in the lower half of his back. The pain took his breath away, and he gasped. The air felt like flames on his dry throat. At least the pain forced his eyes open, although they were soon closed again as he winced at another wave coursing through him as he moved slightly to avoid the pain. The cycle repeated itself over and over for about twenty seconds, each wave of pain slightly diminished from the last as if his body had just gotten used to it, or he had learned to hold himself still through the spasms. Once it had stopped, he took a breath. Too deep and his lungs expanded, and it seemed as though every muscle was somehow connected to his back. On the threshold of pain he exhaled a little and then held his breath before letting go once he felt it would be pain free to do so. After a couple of breaths he tried to open his eyes again. They remained heavy, but the eyelids slowly lifted. Everything was white. Blurry but white. His eyes itched with sleep that had built up and encrusted in the corners. Holding his breath to steel the pain, he raised a hand to his eyes and wiped them, pushing large crusts of sleep away. Resting his arms by his side again in a position that would not pull on his back, he blinked several times. His surroundings were still all white. He would have thought it was some kind of blindness had it not been for a single green leaf of a plant that he could see out of the corner of his left eye. A leaf, the only thing in the room that he could see. The rest was just a pure unfurnished white. He wondered if his eyes had focussed yet. It was hard to tell with everything being pure white, but his head ached to try and look around.

"Hel...." Zack started to say Hello but is throat was dry. The words just would not come to him. Great, paralysed, mute and possibly failing eyesight Zack felt like he should panic being trapped inside this lambent box. Instead, he simply closed his eyes again. Tiredness was getting the better of him, and he figured he would not be thinking of the pain anymore if he simply went back to sleep. Wherever he was he had been safe so far. There was silence. A deep silence that almost hummed inside his brain. He wondered if his experience had made him deaf too. This saddened him the most, to never hear his beloved music again would be worse than death. Slowly he edged his left arm towards the wall beside it and tapped it. He heard the tapping noise coming back to his ears and was pleased to have provided himself with some positive news. It hadn't put too much strain on his back to simply tap the wall moving his hand only from the wrist, so he knocked again, and again. Testing how hard he could knock before he ran the risk of hurting his back muscles through motion. It was hard going and slow. His brain was screaming at him to knock louder, faster, harder, but he resisted to stay within his comfort zone. No-one came and he succumbed back to sleep with exhaustion.

Time had passed. He wasn't sure how much, but it had passed. Zacks eyes slowly opened again. He was relieved to see the same green leaf in the corner of his vision. He started to knock on the wall beside him again. His back was starting to ache more due to him lying on his back for some time. As he knocked, he thought he heard another sound and promptly stopped knocking. He heard soft footprints approaching. Somewhere to the left of him, outside of where he were laying, he heard a swoosh sound, and the footsteps amplified. A tiny pitter patter approached, and Zacks eyes were open wide. Suddenly he saw a shadow moving across the room, not as large as he had expected, and then a creaking sound to his left. Holding he breath, he anxiously waited and then a face appeared above his. A blurry, small face, that appeared to be a child stared down at him. The addition of another person helped him to assess his surroundings. He guessed that he was laying on the floor of this perfectly white room between a bed and a wall, and this small person was now kneeling on the bed looking down at him. Zack tried to speak but no words came. The other person smiled at him and Zack blinked his eyes repeatedly, in part to try and clear his eyes and focus, and also to let him know that he was alive. As quick as he appeared the child disappeared, almost within the space of a blink. Zack just caught the back of his head moving away from his field of vision on top of the bed before he heard the quick pitter patter of feet running away from the room. The swoosh sound resonated again, and the footsteps became instantly fainter.

"Maddie!" He heard a child's voice calling very faintly in the distance.

The swoosh came again, and this time Zack heard two sets of footsteps approaching from the other side of the bed.

"He's awake Maddie." Came an excited young voice.

"I hope you didn't wake him prematurely." Came the reply. This voice Zack recognised as Madoka.

"No Maddie, no. I came to stare at the history man, and he blinked at me."

The creaking noise again as the child jumped up onto the mattress on the bed beside him, but the heavier footsteps continued. Then he saw her. Madoka stood at the end of the bed by his feet looking down at him.

"I thought we'd lost you." She simply said, "It was touch and go last week."

Last week, how long had he been here? Madoka was soon joined by Echo and she knelt down at Zacks feet.

"Your muscles will have stiffened in all of this time." She spoke to him but did not look at him as her eyes followed her hands to his calf muscles and she started to gently rub them. Zack felt a warmth soak into what felt like his very soul. As he relaxed, it felt as though the pain in his body was easing out of him through Madoka's hands. His eyes started to focus a bit more and his mouth started to ache less. He could move his tongue around inside his mouth and it felt like he had a fur build up on the backs of his teeth. He licked away at them, but they were rough and hurt the tip of his tongue which retreated back into the depths of his mouth to press against the roof of it for sanctuary.

"Maddie is a healer." The child said. Zack could now focus a bit better and could see that the child was male. He had long hair for a boy. Zack could relate. Dark haunting eyes and pale in complexion with an aura of sorrow about him, no matter how excited he seemed to be with Zack waking up. The boy was about eight years old Zack guessed by comparison to other children he had seen in the twenty first century.

"Shhhh," Madoka shushed the boy.

"Your....son?" Zack croaked, his throat still sore, but he was starting to be able to form words without them being swallowed up by pain. Madoka looked up from what she was doing.

"No Zack. Zero is my cousin. He lives with us here." She replied and then looked back down to focus on Zacks feet. She started to pressure points at various spots of the soles of Zacks feet and as she did so he felt different tensions relax at various points of his body.

"Us?" Zack asked, Madoka stayed focused on her task and judging by her non-reaction Zack believed that she did not understand that he had just asked a question. "How many.......live here?" He followed up with.

"Including you? Madoka looked back up into Zacks eyes, "There are now five of us." As she said this, she took hold of Zacks right ankle and pushed his foot towards him so that his knees bent and were pointing upwards to the ceiling. Zack expected a bolt of pain to shoot straight up his leg but none came. He was able to let his leg relax slightly and there was a slight twinge of uncomfortableness as his hip moved with the weight of his leg.

"Try sitting up." Madoka instructed as Zero hopped off of the bed and ran towards the swooshing sound.

"Why am I on the floor?" Zack asked, his throat feeling better as the minutes went by, but his tongue and teeth still felt as dry and furry as ever. Madoka stopped what she was doing and looked him straight in the eye.

"You are in Rebristan now." Madoka stated, "The Zeydenian soldiers can come here at any time and search any property if they feel there are feelings of dissent. Without you able to move we needed you in a place where we could cover you up quickly and hope for the best. Besides, we had no other beds."

"Are there feelings of dissent?" Zack asked, wondering what he had bought into now.

"One hundred percent of the time, which means they can pretty much walk into the home at any time for no reason." Madoka replied, before kneeling up and saying, "Try sitting up now, you should be ok."

Zack gingerly pulled his elbows in by his side and raised his buttocks a little testing for any pain. When he felt none he then dared try and lift his body weight up onto his elbows. Once on his elbows he mentally checked his body for any pain and slowly leant to his left bearing his upper weight on his left arm, whilst he reached out his right hand towards Madoka. She took the hint and taking his hand in hers pulled him until he was sitting bolt upright, pain free.

"Thank you." Zack said looking at Madoka. She simply shrugged the comment off. Zack could then see that he had been lying between the bedroom wall and a bed. There was no quilt, just a white mattress. Bracing himself between the wall and the top of the bed frame he tried to lift himself up. His legs were weak, and it was a struggle. Echo stepped forward and taking Zack under the arms to help they managed to get him seated on the edge of the bed.

"Your legs will be weak Zack." Echo said, "Your muscles have not had to bear your weight for twenty days so far."

"Twenty days?" Zack asked. It had not felt like he had been asleep that long.

"You've awoken quickly for your first time." Echo stated.

"Welcome to your nightmare." Madoka added. Zack looked up at her in confusion. "I told you, you should not have come. It is too dangerous for you."

"Thank you for your concern Madoka," Zack replied, then his face screwed up as he recalled an image of blood on sheets. He sank his head into his hands hoping to wipe the image away. With his eyes shut it would not go and he opened them again to the bright white of the room. Madoka knew that he was no longer safe in Serene either, and felt an element of guilt for that.

"I shall get you something to eat." Madoka stated and left the room without looking back at him, leaving him alone with Echo.

"So, what now Echo?" Zack asked as he looked up at Echo standing at the end of the bed.

"As she said, you're in Rebristan now, it's not pleasant but a few of us have seen that it can be. We conspire to make it nice again, but that involves pain ahead. Now...you need to get your strength back and stay out of sight until it is safe for you." Echo replied.

Zack looked around the room he was in. There was sparse furniture. Another bed occupied the other side of the room, pushed against the wall, and there appeared to be a sliding door that would slide the entire length of the wall at the head of it. At the foot of the other bed was another sliding door which Zack assumed was the swooshing door and lead to the rest of the property. Zack looked down at himself and saw that he was wearing a long white robe that covered his modesty.

"These clothes......" Zack started but wasn't sure what he should be saying. He stumbled on his words as if he were drunk.

"Were my fathers." Echo finished before turning and leaving the room. Zack watched him leave and saw for the first time the swooshing door in operation as Echo touched a small disk to the right of the door. Left alone with his thoughts Zack felt quite numb. He wasn't getting the same butterflies as he usually would if he flew to a new country for the first time on holiday. But this was the future for God's sake, or it was supposed to be, he should be elated, but he wasn't. He waited for a while for Madoka to return, but just like a hangover, his body soon urged him to go back to sleep and he lay himself back down onto the bed.

12

Zack felt steady enough to carry his service tray outside. It wasn't so much a plate of food, more a group of food substances heaped on a tray. There was very little flavour to any of it, but as he sat in the bedroom eating with his fingers, an excitable Zero sat and ate with him, and was explaining what the foods were and how they were good for the body and the nutrients they all contained. The kid was like a walking encyclopaedia on the rules and surviving in Rebristan. They spoke at length as they ate, with Madoka occasionally stopping by the entrance to the room to look in. The familiar whooshing of the door opening caused them both to jump each time she did so, and Zack noticed her smile for the first time at his surprise. Such a beautiful smile, full lips parting slightly as her mouth turned upwards to reveal her teeth.

"I'll take that for you Mr Zack." Zero said as he saw Zack bracing himself to stand.

"It's ok Buddy," Zack replied, with Zero looking confused at the nickname he had just bestowed upon him, "I need to see if these legs are working still,"

Zack pushed with arms on the bed, causing himself to stand upright. The sudden rush of blood to his legs caused his head to spin and he plonked his arse straight back down on the bed as he went dizzy and his legs buckled. Madoka came into the room a few moments later, at the sound of the bed creaking with his weight falling upon it. When his blood finally made it back to his brain he was able to focus on the look of concern that was etched on her face.

"I preferred you smiling." Zack joked, but it was lost on her.

"You shouldn't try to move around just yet," Madoka stated, "You will still be weak from the travel, sleep and your injury."

Injury? Zack didn't register what she was meant at first and then started to have flashbacks to the cave. He recalled blood on his arm and being knocked forward for no reason. And Junko. Junko had pulled him in and saved him. From what he still wasn't sure. He felt a pang in his heart for Serene and the sudden confusion one gets when you can't make sense of your surroundings. Zack looked at his upper right arm. It was covered with the white gown that he wore, and he could see nothing out of the ordinary. He could feel no pain there and wondered whether he had been healed by Madoka whilst asleep. He distinctly recalled blood. He raised his left hand to his triceps and felt across it through the cloth of the gown. As he stroked his triceps he could feel a deep groove running across the outside about three inches long.

"It was just a graze." Madoka said, as if foretelling his next question. "You were very lucky."

"What happened?" Zack asked, as he continued to rub the wound. He was fascinated to feel that as he touched one end of it, the nerves at the opposite end of the wound tingled and vice versa.

"You were shot, Mr Zack." Zero answered for her. Zack looked up at Madoka, searching for a different explanation. Being shot? In Serene? That's the sort of thing you only see in films. Madoka simply nodded at Zack to corroborate what Zero had told him.

"I don't remember hearing a bang." Zack stated, again looking for answers.

"There is no noise to the Zeydenians weapons." She replied. "They have come a long way since your time."

"You mean like Lasers? George Lucas was right?" Zack asked.

"Who is this Lucas?" Madoka returned with a question. Zack realised she probably wouldn't have a clue what he was talking about.

"So, what did I get shot with?" Zack asked.

"Air." Madoka replied as if it were the most perfectly normal thing in the world. Zack looked confused all the same, and she cocked her head to one side, not understanding his confusion,

"You mean as in the air that we breathe? How can that hurt anyone?" Zack asked.

"They use the Zey Co2 arms." Zero interrupted, feeling smug as if this were going to clear everything up now, but Zack still wore a look of confusion.

"Modern weapons are ecologically perfect." Madoka stated, "They use the natural elements to kill. I saw images of weapons in your time and they are made of metals, the projectiles are metal. That would not do today in Rebristan. All metal, when it becomes available, is utilised for creating new Zeydenians. None will ever be used in the human world."

This was all very well, but it still didn't explain to Zack how he had been shot with air. Madoka registered the uncertainty on his face still.

"The Zey Co2 is a Zeydenian firearm. It has a small generator that sucks in the air at the side of the weapon like a whirlwind and builds up such a pressure that it can fire the retrieved air, and propel it towards a target at such a speed that it causes major damage when it strikes."

Finally, he was beginning to understand some of the mechanics of what had happened to him, but it still blew his mind.

"That's....unbelievable." Zack struggled to find the words, "Maybe I'll understand it a bit more when I see it again."

"Hope that you never see a Zey Co2 in the hands of a Zeydenian ever again." Madoka retorted before turning and leaving the room. Before the door could whoosh shut again Zero had collected up the trays they had been eating from and followed after her, leaving Zack alone in the room.

Madoka stood in the kitchen of the home, cleaning the remnants of any food left on the trays into a waste chute, and wiping the trays clean before replacing them in a rack suspended from the ceiling by the corner of the room. The kitchen was sparsely furnished, again everything was white in appearance, made of a synthetic marble. The surfaces gleamed. After she had returned the trays she turned around to face the door that lead out to a small balcony. Walking towards it she pressed for the door to whoosh open and stepped outside into the evening air. She watched as the sunset glowed orange and purple across the sky. It felt nice to open the door and allow some fresh oxygen into the property. She liked to watch the sunset on the wet fields from the balcony, as the sun would reflect on the water covering the surface of the fields as it dipped, before disappearing. Once the sun was gone sector sixty-nine for the most part would be plunged into darkness. As she stood there, she heard the door behind her open again and turned to see Zack standing behind her.

"You're stronger than I imagined Zack." Madoka said, "Most can't walk for at least two days after their first porting."

"In fairness, I've been here for a lot longer than that." Zack replied

"Hmm, yes." Madoka simply said, effectively killing the rest of the conversation. The balcony was about ten feet long and six feet deep, with a couple of stools on them being the only furniture. Zack made his way to one of the stools holding onto the wall as he went and sat himself on it. Fatigue was starting to set in his legs.

"So, this is Rebristan?" Zack asked, trying to kickstart the conversation again. Madoka turned her back on him to stare out at the sky again.

"Why don't you tell everyone you're new here?" She said.

"I'm sorry," Zack said, "I thought...."

"You didn't think." Madoka interrupted. "We'll save this conversation for indoors. I just came out here to watch the sun set."

"It is very beautiful." Zack replied, thinking that he understood why the change in conversation was required. He looked towards the evening sky, an absence of stars struck him, but the clouds glided through the sky turning from hues of autumn orange to purple as if he were watching the Northern Lights in Norway. As he sat there he turned to look at Madoka, staring into the heavens and the beautiful colours reflecting on her face made her look more beautiful than ever. Her hair shifted lightly in the breeze that passed by the balcony. Had it not been for the breeze moving her hair he would have believed she were a statue such was the stillness within her body, absorbing the evening air and sight that beheld them. Zack pushed up from the stool and took hold of the balcony rail with both hands. Using his upper body strength, he pulled himself close to the balcony and leant against it to have a better view of his surroundings. Leaning against the rail he was able to see that he was a very long way up. Looking down it seemed as though the lights below him were pin pricks on the floor. He suddenly became overcome with vertigo, which surprised him as he usually had a good head for heights.

"Thirty eighth floor." Madoka said, still staring ahead, as if she had read his mind and wanted to prevent him from asking another stupid question.

"Wow." Was all that Zack could say. Feeling overwhelmed by the height, he looked up and saw that they were not even on the top floor and that there were several more above them. This did nothing to quell the sudden lurch in his stomach that he felt with his newfound vertigo. Looking straight ahead as the sun was starting to finally set helped settle him. He dared to look either side of him and saw lines of other identical buildings on both sides. Fearing asking any more questions, with a minor sense of paranoia setting in, he breathed a deep sigh and turned to walk back to the door. Madoka turned with him and took his arm, steadying him as he walked back inside. The familiar whoosh of the door behind him brought some relief to his paranoia and he turned to face Madoka.

"I'm sorry," Zack said, "I keep forgetting where I am."

"Don't let it happen again." Madoka replied, "Now, come sit down." Madoka lead him to a soft seating area along a wall in what he imagined would be the living room. Again, the room was sparse of furniture. Zack looked around and could see no television, music system or telephone. Just two sofa's, plain looking, white of course, with no arms, just a soft seat and a soft back, facing each other on either side of the room. Madoka sat opposite him as Echo and Zero walked into the room from a door beside the bedroom he had been in. The door whooshed shut behind them, but Zack caught a glimpse of an older lady sitting upright on a bed inside the room before it closed.

"Have you told him?" Echo asked Madoka.

"Told me what?" Zack asked.

"Not yet." Madoka replied looking at Echo before turning to Zack, "We have some friends coming to visit. They will mark you."

"Mark me? What does that even mean?" Zack looked a little disturbed at being 'marked'.

Madoka's hand went to her hair and pulled it aside on the left side revealing her neck. Echo took out a torch which shone a UV light onto her neck and the sixty-nine tattoo lit up.

"If you hope to survive in Rebristan you will need a mark like this." Madoka stated, "The Zeydenian Control Personnel wear helmets that can see the marks without the need for the light. If you are spotted by one outside the property, they will kill you instantly."

"That sounds pretty harsh for not having a tattoo." Zack tried to make light of the conversation, slightly uncomfortable with the darker turn that it had taken.

"We have no choice. We are marked within weeks of birth in Zeydence." Echo spoke, "They, the Zeydenians control our populations. We are assigned the mark of our sector. They can tell if we are infiltrating or speaking with other sectors. Population numbers are strictly monitored. And they love to kill. If you don't have a sector number, and do not belong to any sector, then you are what they call a free kill. No-one will miss you."

Zack looked across and saw Zero standing next to Echo, no emotion on his face at all. Zack debated in his mind whether he would have had such a conversation about death and killing in front of his young niece and nephew without causing them nightmares, but it seemed as though these warnings and conversations were commonplace in Rebristan.

"Do you have one little guy?" Zack had turned to Zero, as the conversation with the adults was quite deep. Zero lifted his long hair on the left side of his neck. Echo shone the UV torch towards Zero and Zack saw the familiar '69' logo flash under the light. Karma is a bitch, and as he stared at Zero's tattoo, he regretted finding the mark on Echo and then Madoka amusing when he first met them. He was about to be, how he felt, branded with the same mark.

"They will arrive once the sun has gone down." Madoka stated before adding, "Would you like a drink?"

"Yes please." Zack replied, everyone else remained silent, "Cheap round eh?" Zack joked but no-one smiled. Madoka walked into the kitchen area and Zack could hear liquid from a bottle being poured into a vessel of some description before Madoka returned holding what looked like a white marble cup. Madoka handed Zack the drink and he drank it down in one, not realising how thirsty he had been. Echo and Zero simply watched on as he drank each drop.

There was a knock at the door, and Zero ran to answer it. Zack watched as he tore off down the corridor to his left. Zero reached the front door of the apartment and had to jump a little to reach the pad to open the door. A whooshing sound followed by more voices in the hallway. Echo walked towards the corridor to greet their guests. Obscuring Zacks view, he did not see the visitors until Echo turned to introduce him and stepped out of the way.

"Flint, Marna, this is Zack, the one that I told you about." Echo stated. A tall woman, the one Zack had introduced as Marna stepped into the living room. She was about six foot tall, and very skinny, half the size of Madoka, but didn't have the looks too. She had long dark hair, but it was not silky smooth like Madoka's either, more of a mess that she had tried and failed to tie up in a bun. A monobrow topped off a very serious looking face, and she wore a figure hugging black and grey one-piece outfit. The other visitor was a male, whom Echo had referred to as Flint. He looked equally as serious, a permanent frown upon his face and sunken eyes which looked down on Zack with distrust. He was also about six foot tall, but stockier than his companion. Full of attitude he wore a black hooded jacket of cloth, with the hood up, and black trousers not unlike jeans. A mop of black hair protruded from underneath his hood and came down across his forehead to shadow his eyes, making him look all the more serious.

"Pleased to meet you Zack." Flint was the first to speak. There was no sincerity in his voice though.

"We don't have much time Flint." Marna stepped forward, nudging Flint as she did so. Madoka stood up and excused herself from the room, taking Zero with her into the other room where Zack had seen someone sitting on the bed. As the door closed behind them Flint took a bag from over his shoulders. Such rag tag was his clothing that Zack had not even noticed the bag previously camouflaged in with the other clothing that he was wearing. As Zack tried to focus on the bag his eyesight started to blur. He sat up straight but started to sway either side and his head lolled backwards so that he was looking up at the ceiling. He started to feel woozy and wanted to speak but his mind couldn't concentrate on the words long enough for his brain to send a message to his mouth to utter them out loud. Echo looked across at Zack and saw a fear in his eyes.

"Don't panic Zack, it's just the drink." Echo told him. Zack looked on horrified, his head still rolling around on the atlas of his spine. Echo walked towards him and took him by the shoulder to steady him. "It's for your own good Zack. We're not here to harm you." Echo noted panic in Zacks eyes as he tried to focus on his surroundings and added, "If we intended to cause you harm, we would have done that whilst you were sleeping. This marking process is not painless. In fact, the ultraviolet ink used is quite painful as it is made from the sap of acidic plants. Madoka has simply given you a natural anaesthetic to minimise the pain."

It started to make some sense to Zack, but he wished they'd told him what they intended to do instead of just drugging him. He lolled his head to the right, as Echo had hold of his left shoulder. With the room no longer spinning he looked directly at Marna and Flint, but they were too blurry. It looked as though they were morphing into each other and then materialising out of each other's sides. Flint bent down to remove some equipment from the bag that he had been carrying. Whatever it was it was big and metallic with a carbon like effect, but Zack could not focus on it. Flint stepped towards Zack and stood over him. Marna followed holding the bag and retrieving a bottle from it. Flint said nothing as he removed a glove and before he was rendered unconscious Zack's final sight was that there was no flesh on Flint's hand, just shiny metal like chrome. As his eyes closed on him, Zacks brain screamed out in fear, but the noise never made it to the outside as he slipped into unconsciousness, it remained within his body seemingly bouncing off the walls of his skull for what seemed like eternity.

   As the scream inside his head subsided Zack felt a sharp piercing to this side of his neck. His heart raced and he could hear it pounding all around the inside of his body, feeling like his blood had doubled in size and was trying to force its way through restricted arteries. Darkness was all he could see, of course, he was unconscious, but the pain still spoke to him, taunted him. His blood felt like it had been heated to boiling point. He envisioned it bubbling away as it passed his eyelids. He tried to open them to scream but they were far too heavy. He was paralysed. He felt the scratching at his neck, tracing a pattern as if he were being branded with a red-hot poker. His mind told him that he could smell his flesh burn, but also told him that he had no sense of smell at this time. His stomach burned as his blood rushed to the centre of his torso to protect his organs. His body told him that he was under attack. Then the ink entered his bloodstream, burning evermore as it joined the flow around his body. He had read somewhere that it takes about one minute for blood to flow around the whole body, but this seemed to go on forever, an eternity of pounding, scratching, burning, all the while he was paralysed.

   And then it stopped. Silence and darkness. His neck was smarting, stinging, and itching, but he could do nothing about it. Eventually he slipped deeper into unconsciousness and could feel nothing.

13

A week had passed since Zack had been 'Marked'. He had been haunted by nightmares in that time and was becoming restless. There were trust issues between himself and his hosts due to him being drugged for the marking. Echo and Madoka had tried to tell him that it was for his own survival but a little something was missing from their relationship. Zack had learned that the ink for his marking had been watered down somewhat too, so that his mark looked age appropriate. In the past a handful of newcomers had made their way into the sector and had been marked, but had been called out as fakes due to their adult marks being as vivid as a new-born.

Echo and Madoka had gone to toil in the fields during the day, returning after dark, leaving Zack at the home with Zero.

Zack had finally met Keisa, Madoka and Echo's mother, three days after he had first woken up. Zack had been sitting on the white sofa with Zero, talking over life in sector sixty-nine, when he heard a whooshing noise to his left. Until this moment, Keisa had been so quiet that Zack had temporarily forgotten her existence and so the door opening when he believed that he and Zero were alone caused him a start. Zack looked up so see a mature lady, that he suspected was less than fifty years old, but her appearance and haunted looks belied her age. She stood at five feet eight, slim build with the same pale complexion as Zero, and long grey hair. It did not look unkempt. It appeared as though she took good care of her hair, but it had turned grey with the stresses of life in Rebristan. He looked at her face inquisitively and could see where Madoka got her looks from but hoped that Madoka never looked as sad as her mother did as she stood in front of him. She wore a clean grey thick jumper with an ornately embroidered collar that covered her neck and blended with the colour of her hair as it cascaded down her back. Zero got up and went to Keisa and gave her a hug and she hugged him back with one arm whilst the other patted the top of his head. All the while she stared at Zack with such sad reddened eyes.

"Good morning Ma'am." Zack offered.

"You must be our guest." Keisa stated rather than asked. Zack didn't know how to take the term guest, to him it implied that his stay was temporary, and he wondered how long it would be before he outstayed his welcome.

"Yes Ma'am" Zack replied.

"Please, call me Keisa." She replied.

"Ok....Keisa. Thank you for having me here."

"You're more than welcome." Keisa replied, "I don't much approve of the plans of Madoka and Echo, but anyone who helps them from being killed is welcome here. You would think that we are used to the pain now, but it never gets any easier to lose anyone." Keisa looked away to one side, not wanting to meet Zacks eyes as she spoke this. In turn Zack's thoughts turned to Eva and his body shuddered with pain, but he soon took solace in the fact that he was many miles, or rather years from the scene of horror he'd witnessed. Despite the tales of danger, he had been told of Rebristan his current experience of it was like a comfort blanket to his grief.

"May I get you a drink Keisa?" Zack asked. He had become more mobile in the week and was keen to pull his weight in the home and not be a burden to the people he was living with.

"Please." Keisa replied. Zack got up and walked into the kitchen area. Zero followed him and Keisa sat down on the opposite sofa.

"Can I have a drink too please Zack?" Zero asked, following Zack like an excitable puppy.

"Sure buddy." Zack replied as he reached into a cupboard and took out three white marble cups and laid them on a work surface. Zack then took a bottle of fluid from the cupboard and filled the cups, handing one to Zero, and carrying the other two into the living room.

"May I ask why you don't approve?" Zack asked Keisa as he handed her a cup of drink.

"Their father filled their head with ideas of freedom from the folk tales of the past, but it did him no good. I don't want to lose anyone else." She replied.

"They're not just folk tales." Zack told her. Keisa had a tear in her eye and the three of them sat in silence as they drank their drinks.

The afternoon had worn on and Zack was starting to go stir crazy stuck inside the apartment for so long. He hadn't imagined that he would be a glorified babysitter when he thought about travelling to the future. He tried to educate Zero as much as he could, but found that the boy, whilst trying to look interested, was struggling to come to terms with some of his tales of the past. It was an alien concept to Zero for humans to have freedom. Zero had never heard of television, movies, pop music or the internet. He likened it to a Roman soldier visiting him at school in Serene explaining to his class that technology was far more advanced in Roman times, and realised that he would have struggled to understand those concepts. Everything that the humans had was supplied to them on an as needed basis by the Zeydenians, and in return they worked like bees to keep the artificial intelligence running. Zack had pondered on the idea that if the humans just refused to work, the Zeydenians would power down and die off, but there was a catch. That scenario, as he had discussed it with Echo would take seven days for the power to run out, during which time the Zeydenians would think nothing of killing and sacrificing many humans as a show of power and striking such a chord of fear through the population that many would instantly go back to working for them. The end result would be the Zeydenians would survive and thrive, but one member of every human family would be culled resulting in widespread sorrow and hardship. The humans also relied on rations of food being supplied to them by the Zeydenians to survive, and famine would quickly breakout throughout the sectors if there were no-one to supply the food. Many humans had accepted, as they knew no different, that this was their lot in life and would not want to rock the boat. Some would even turn their own kind in to the Zeydenians if they feared such an uprising was imminent, and be content with being slaves for the rest of their natural lives.

Keisa was weak. Today, Zack had no idea what the names of the days were anymore, but today was the day that she was to take a food delivery for the home. This would involve her travelling down to the ground level of the tower and waiting in the elements for the distribution of food stuff and drinks. With one thousand families living within the tower this could be a timely process and she just was not up to it today. She had slept, sitting upright on the sofa whilst Zack and Zero spoke.

There was a loud grinding noise from outside of the building and Keisa's eyes opened. Zero jumped up off of the floor where he had been sitting and ran to the balcony door.

"Come Zack, the supply train is here!" Zero said excitedly, as he jumped up and down trying to smack the button to open the door. Zack joined him at the door and pressed the button to open it. With a whoosh the fresh outdoor air breezed in. Zero ran to the balcony ledge and pulled himself up to look over. Zack could hear excited voices far below now and the rumbling of a convoy of vehicles. Looking over the balcony he looked to his right along the edge of the watery fields. He saw a convoy of about fifteen futuristic looking trucks making their way from the outlands towards the towers. This was the first time that Zack had seen moving vehicles in Rebristan, and he was pleased to see that the wheel still played an important role in the future. The trucks were white with a black grill and black stripe that aesthetically curved its way around the front of the truck and trailer seamlessly. The windscreens were black tinted too. Zack could not see inside. The trucks appeared to be about three times the size of lorries in the twentieth century, with a large bank of what appeared to be solar panels across the roof of them all. From where he stood it appeared to Zack as if thousands of ants were running towards the trucks and the melee of noise drifted up to the floor he was standing on. The lead truck stopped, and Zack watched as the sides of this truck seemed to slide apart to reveal the inside of the trailer. As the crowd of humans rushed towards the trucks, an army of what appeared to be one hundred soldiers stepped down from the lead truck, all armed with a weapon of some sort. Zack was too far up to see what they looked like. The lead truck started moving slowly towards the towers again, followed by the other trucks.

"The front one always has the crowd control in it." Zero stated as if it were an everyday normal experience. "If you get out of hand, they shoot you. You have to be careful that someone else does not push you on purpose towards the crowd control, because they will shoot you and that other person will take your supplies."

Zack wasn't sure how to respond to that. It reminded him of news footage of aid supplies reaching refugees in war torn areas in the twenty first century. As he watched he saw people run towards the trucks and soldiers raised their weapons and pointed them at the crowds. People fell to the floor, but Zack could not tell whether they had been shot or whether they just adopted the foetal position through fear. He hadn't heard a bang, but then he had to remind himself that the guns in this time were not the conventional type that he was used to. Zero lowered himself down from the balcony rail, looked around and then went back into the apartment. Zack watched for a few moments longer as the convoy made its way slowly towards the towers before turning to join him.

"Aunt Keisa." Zero gave Keisa a gentle push on her shoulder as she sat on the sofa. She roused gently to see the young child looking into her eyes. "The supply train is here, Aunt Keisa."

"Could you get the supplies today Zero?" Keisa asked, "I'm really not feeling too well."

"On my own?" Zero asked. His eyes had opened wide with a mixture of awe and fear.

"Zack can go with you." Keisa replied, "This is his life too now, he will need to learn." She looked up at Zack as she spoke the last sentence. At the back of his mind he had always known that he would have to leave the tower at some time, but he always imagined that it would be when Echo or Madoka felt he was ready, and that it would be with them, not babysitting a child on the shopping run so to speak. Keisa noted the fear in Zacks soul as he thought this over.

"Will you come with me Zack?" Zero asked excitedly.

"Well...erm...." Zack was lost for words.

"Please Zack," This time it was Keisa pleading with him, "Echo is usually home by now, and would help. We get the supplies every two weeks. If we miss the supply train others will break into our locker and we will be left with virtually nothing to live on until the next moon."

How could Zack refuse? Nobody had said anything, but he knew he must have been a burden in some small way. An extra mouth to feed within the accommodation that the authorities knew nothing about and therefore did not account for when assessing the family's rations. He was certain, from conversations that he had overheard, that Marna and Flint had helped the family out, but this was by no means a permanent solution. The least he could do was help a child to bring the supplies to the apartment. And yet walking out of the door filled him with so much dread.

"Of course I will." Zack replied without thinking. He had been brought up to believe in helping people in their time of need, that civility costs nothing, and that you must face your fears and do it anyway to succeed in life. "Am I dressed appropriately?" He asked Keisa, standing in black denim trousers and a loose-fitting white cotton top that had found its way to him through the human network.

"You have been outside before have you Zack?" Keisa asked, surprised by his question.

"Not yet, this will be my first venture." Zack replied. Zero was hovering around impatiently by the door to the apartment but somehow knew that it wasn't his place to speak.

"Oh my. This is a bad idea." Keisa suddenly looked fearful. "I thought Echo or Madoka had shown you outside and the etiquette of the land. We should wait for Echo."

"Nonsense Keisa. I want to help. I can't be a burden forever. How hard can it be?"

"Come on Zack," Zero was hopping from side to side excitedly by the door. Zack got the impression that he rarely got out of the apartment. "We only need to go down to ground level and get our boxes."

Zack stood at the door. Keisa looked on apprehensively. Zack pressed the button and with a whoosh the door opened. He took his first glance out of the door onto a hallway what stretched for about forty metres in either direction before curling around out of sight. The same whiteness dominated the decor. Doors to other apartments were opening as the other occupants of the tower were making their way to the supply train also. Humans, all of them, predominantly adults who appeared to be in their fifties. Zack realised that with the exception of Zero and a couple of other children who were accompanying their adults, he was the youngest person to be venturing outside. Zack looked back at Keisa sitting on the sofa.

"We'll be fine, back before you know it." Zack tried his best to sound reassuring and then stepped out into the corridor. Hearing the door slide shut behind him he looked down at Zero. "Now what?" Zack asked.

"Come Zack. We need to ride the elevator." Zero replied as if it were some kind of treat, the most exciting thing that had happened in his young life so far. Walking along the corridor to the point that it rounded a bend, Zack saw a bank of three elevators beside each other at the far end. A crowd of people stood patiently waiting as the doors to the elevators opened and closed. As Zack and Zero walked towards the crowd he noted how they residents filed in and out of the arriving capsules civilly with no pushing or shoving. They joined the back of the crowd and within next to no time had reached the front of the queue. An elevator arrived and Zack stood back to allow people off first of all, as they came out pushing trolleys of boxes in front of them. Once there was room inside the elevator, which looked as though it could easily hold thirty people,

Zero stepped inside and Zack followed him. A few others filed in behind them. Zack braced himself to descend to the lower floor and was taken by surprise when the elevator started to go up. At a speed that he was not used to, and he struggled to keep his balance. Zero grabbed his arm and as he looked at the boy, he could see him sniggering a little. It hadn't occurred to Zack that the elevator would be making more stops on higher floors with residents who had already collected their goods. As embarrassed as he felt it made him feel good to see Zero humoured. Zack had only had a taster of life in Rebristan so far, hell this was his first time venturing outside of the apartment door, but even with the little experience he had he knew that life so far had not been a box of chocolates for the child.

After stopping at several floors, the elevator started its descent to the ground floor. A little too fast for Zack's liking. Not enough to make him fly upwards and crash into the ceiling of the elevator and experience zero gravity, but it wasn't far from it. Zack watched as several other Rebristan's got in at various floors but there was no pushing or shoving or cramming the occupants into uncomfortableness at the back. Everyone was perfectly civil and just stood to the spot if they could see that there was no room to accommodate them comfortably. Zack also noted a distinct lack of communication between people. The silence on the way down was awkward to say the least. Zack watched the holographic numbers above the elevator door counting down quickly as they passed each floor, until with a guided deceleration the elevator eventually came to a stop. The door whooshed open and Zack got his first glimpse of Rebristan at ground level. He stood at the doorway to the elevator in awe at the movement before him. It never occurred to him that he was holding up people standing behind him until Zero gave a gentle tug on his arm, not one person behind him had made a sound or comment of annoyance. Zack looked quickly over his shoulder and mumbled an apology before stepping out of the door and to the side. People behind him filed out courteously. No-one acknowledged his apology as if they hadn't understood what he had needed to apologise for. One male about forty years old was the last to leave the elevator and Zack again apologised for delaying him. The male simply nodded back at Zack.

"Come on Zack, we must get a pulley truck." Zero enthused, tugging further on Zacks arm "We must keep moving."

Zack stared in awe at the sight in front of him. Hundreds if not thousands of middle-aged men and women, immaculately dressed in plain monotone clothing, moving around at speed, but in an organised fashion. Queueing patiently. It looked like a Saturday morning at a London market, with so many people in one place carrying boxes to and fro, just more organised and a noticeable absence of hustle and bustle noise. Zack took in the air and noticed how clean it was despite the amount of people inhaling it at that spot at the present time. The air felt very dry too, very little moisture in it. Zack looked across to the wet fields that he had seen from the balcony of the apartment and expected to see a haze rising from them, especially given the heat of the day, but there was none. Without realising it, Zack had allowed himself to be led to the line of people waiting for a pulley truck. Without knowing, as the distribution had been so fluid Zack turned to realise that he and Zero were at the front of the queue.

"Number?" The man stood in front of them simply said. He appeared to be in his late sixties and was grizzled with age. He was very slim, shorter than Zack with a bald circle on the top of his head but hair all around the lower hemisphere of his cranium, reminding Zack of Friar Tuck from the Robin Hood programmes he had watched in Serene. He stared down at Zack through ice blue eyes with the smallest pin pricks of black for pupils, with no emotion on his face whatsoever.

"Sixty-nine, Fourteen, Thirty-Eight, Twelve." Zero piped up. The man looked down at Zero with the same piercing eyes and then back at Zack.

"Yeah, like he said," Zack started "Sixty-nine, Fourteen, Thirty-Eight....." he paused as he struggled to remember the rest. He had always struggled remembering numbers, and this one he'd just heard for the first time under quite oppressive circumstances.

"Twelve." Zero said again.

"Twelve." Zack repeated and the man looked him up and down before tapping the number into what looked like a glass slate that he held in his hands.

"Seven, Eight, Eight." The man said to Zack.

"Of course." Zack stated. He had absolutely no idea what this conversation was about and was starting to feel nervous about standing out as an outsider. Zero tugged on his arm and lead him away to the side, as another person then filed politely up to the man and reeled off a set of numbers.

"What was that all about?" Zack whispered to Zero.

"Our co-ordinates." Zero replied, "We're to take a pulley truck from bay seven, go to supply train eight and wait for the pulley truck to be loaded from bay eight of the supply train." Zero was looking around him to see if anyone was staring. This was the first time that Zack had seen the young boy nervous about anything. Zack himself had been feeling a bit nervous himself in this almost alien environment and took a casual look around himself as they reached pulley truck bay seven at the bottom of their building. As he turned almost one hundred and eighty degrees, he looked back at the man who had given them their co-ordinates and saw that he was still working giving co-ordinates to other people in the queue, but as he spoke he was looking at Zack, the pin prick pupils in his eyes causing such discomfort in Zack that he turned back around to see Zero pulling their pulley cart from a stack of others from the bay. The pulley cart resembled what Zack would have called a stack barrow in the twenty first century. A no frills metal L shape with a wheel on the either side in white metal. Zero pulled it along behind him as they made their way orderly to the supply train of vehicles. From the balcony Zack thought that they had looked big but from ground level he saw that they were enormous. At least four or five times taller than he was, Zack understood why the people looked like ants making their way towards them. He estimated each truck was about fifty metres long, resplendent in white and black and he could now see that several doors had opened on the sides of the trailers and people were queueing patiently at them as boxes were lowered down to them and loaded onto the pulley trucks. The trucks looked overwhelmingly magnificent in their line and it seemed to take an age to walk past them until they reached truck eight. Zack was relieved to stop and catch his breath as they waited in a queue at the eighth door on the side of the truck in a row of ten. As the queue steadily diminished and they made their way to the front Zack saw what must have been the soldier figures that he had seen from the balcony. One stood by each bay entrance on each truck. Uniform in colour they each stood about six foot tall and appeared robotic in nature. Broad shouldered and covered in what appeared to be matte black carbon body armour, which was accented with orange and silver breast plates, shin and knee guards. Each wore a silver and black helmet through which no facial features or expressions could be discerned. At the side of each was held a futuristic looking rifle. Zack felt like he was in one of his favourite sci fi movies, but this was real, these machines were real, surveying all around them. The weapon by their side had a long glossy white barrel with what appeared to be a mini turbine by the stock. the handle was black with a blue neon trigger. There were no magazines and Zack wondered if this was one of the air powered weapons that he had been shot with in Serene. The weapon seemed to be connected to its owner by a flex cord from the handle that went behind the soldier.

"They are the Zeydenian guards," Zero whispered to Zack as they waited in line, "try not to attract their attention."

"Understood." Zack replied. He'd always thought of himself as a fearless man of the world but even he felt that he had to bow to the knowledge of a child in this surreal environment. The queue diminished quickly, and Zack watched elderly men retrieving cartons from the belly of the truck and lowering them down to other elderly men on the ground who loaded them onto the pulley trucks that those waiting in the queue had with them. When they were about five from the front a Zeydenian guard approached them.

"Number?" The Zeydenian guard requested, his head turning with the faintest of mechanical sliding noises to face Zack. Zack stared back, trying to see if the guard had eyes that he could look into but only saw black slices of a glass like finish to the sides of the guard's helmet. The voice held a human quality to it with the same accent that Zack was unable to place with the woman who met him at the top of the beach steps in Serene.

"Sixty-Nine, Fourteen, Thirty-Eight, Twelve." Zack replied, trying his hardest to show no fear. The Zeydenian guard looked him up and down, his right hand always tight on the weapon that hung down by his side. As the guard looked down the length of him, Zack's eyes followed until they rested upon the gun. Zack could sense a subtle electrical hum coming from the weapon, and as he gazed at it, he failed to see the orange and black gloved left hand of the guard reaching up and grabbing Zack around the throat. Fear coursed through Zack as he was lifted off of his feet until the guard had angled his head slightly upwards to look Zack in the face.

"You're young." The guard stated, the restriction on Zacks windpipe prevented him from answering, "Why aren't you in the fields?" The question was pointless as Zacks face became scarlet and was unable to get a word out.

"It's his ADOR." Zero stepped forward, looking up to the guard, avoiding Zacks legs kicking out looking for anything solid to take the pressure off of his elevated throat. The guard looked down at the spunky kid standing at his feet.

"Then why isn't he resting?" The guard asked Zero as black spots appeared in Zacks vision.

"My auntie is ill. He offered to help me collect the supplies." Zero replied. The guard turned to look back at Zack, looking him up and down before tossing him to one side. Zack landed in a heap and clutched at his throat desperately trying to take in oxygen, eyes watering with the pain of the sudden rush of air into his lungs.

"Continue." Was all that the guard said and turned his back on Zack and Zero in complete ignorance of the pain he had caused. Zero rushed to Zack and tried to help pull him up. Zack staggered to his feet. One hand on his knee, he hunched over and made loud gasping noises as his head spun slightly.

"We need to move Zack." Was all the Zero would say as he nudged at Zacks legs in the direction of the opening on the side of the truck. Zack understood without any further words being said and staggered with the pulley truck, almost using it as a crutch, to the entrance. Four boxes of provisions were loaded onto the pulley truck and between Zack and Zero they managed to angle it backwards so that it could be pulled behind them. As they turned to face tower fourteen Zack took his first look at what the tower looked like from the outside. He had seen across to the other towers from the balcony in the past but was always high up when he did this and could not fully appreciate the full size of the towers. He had to crane his neck as far back as he could, which helped him breathe the oxygen in, in order to see the top of the towers. It seemed as though the top floors went into the clouds. Looking up at the top made him feel slightly sick, like a reverse vertigo, and he felt a dizziness one would feel trying to stand still and assess your location after a night out on the beer. Looking forwards again he made his way after Zero who had not stopped to admire the view as he had.

"So, what's an ADOR little man?" Zack asked as he caught up with Zero and was confident that they were far away enough from prying ears.

"Allocated day of rest." Zero replied, never looking back, "The field workers are given three a year."

"Oh, ok." Zack replied. He didn't want to ask too much out in the open so resolved to ask Madoka when he saw her next. Something in the pit of his stomach told him that conversation was not going to go too well though.

14

"Where is he?" Zack heard Madoka shouting from the front door as he sat on the balcony. Word must travel fast here. He detected an anger somehow in her footsteps. He sat looking out at the sunset. He felt like he should call out to let her know where he was, then a voice inside his head told him to try and delay the inevitable bollocking he was about to get. Plus, he didn't think she'd be quite as aggressive on the balcony where anyone around could hear. The stomping continued, only Zack detected more than one set of footsteps searching around the apartment. Trying to make himself as small as possible in the chair he sat in was pointless, but he tried all the same, feeling like a naughty puppy hiding from its owner.

"Inside now." Madoka's voice stated calmly from behind him. Looks like he'd lucked out with discussing his little adventure on the balcony. As he turned to look at her, he saw anger on her face that was in no way reflected in her voice. She looked so hot angry, and he paused for a second to capture the image in his mind before the illusion was shattered after the door would close behind him. Stepping inside the apartment he heard the gentle swoosh of the balcony door closing and sealing, thankful that doors in this time could not be slammed shut by angry females as in his past. He daren't look back but felt a gentle shove in his shoulder blade urging him into the living room. As he reached the room, he saw that others had gathered to witness his telling off, which he did not think fair. He sat on the sofa and saw that Junko and Keisa sat opposite him with a man he had never met before. The man sat staring at him, with dark eyes and pale skin, dark hair that seemed swept across his scalp with way too much brylcreem, and a jawline to be envious of. The man's face was so hardened that Zack formed the opinion the guy had never smiled in his life, as he lost a staring contest with him and looked away. When Zack looked back, he was still being stared at by the man. He looked important. His clothing gave the impression of grace and certainly weren't rags like he'd seen some of the people in Rebristan wearing. He wore a long sleeved long flowing grey tunic which appeared to have a V-shaped breast plate in, and long grey ruffled trousers that were so flared Zack could not tell if he had footwear on underneath or not. The man did not strike him as someone that would go without the finest shoes though. There was a slightly androgynous look to the man. In fact, as they hadn't been introduced yet it was only a primal instinct in Zacks mind that told him the person was male. Madoka sat beside Zack on the sofa and he noticed Zero looking on nervously standing in the doorway to the bedroom.

"Why?" Was all Madoka could put together at this time. Zack turned to look at her.

"Why what?" Zack replied.

"Why did you go outside before preparation?" The man on the other sofa asked, again in an accent that Zack felt he could not trust. Zack turned to him, there was no change in expression in his face.

"And you are?" Zack asked sarcastically, although he instantly realised that the element of sarcasm was lost on these people.

"The man who saved your life." He replied. Zack was about to argue back but Madoka interrupted before he could open his mouth.

"Zack, this is Diarran. He was on the supply convoy this morning and gave the order you should be spared when he recognised Zero standing up for you." Madoka said.

"Oh." Was all that Zack could reply. He still didn't know enough about Diarran to form his own opinion of him, dispel the distrust or understand how bad his earlier experience could've been to bring himself to thank the stranger just yet.

"Zack, you're not ready for the outside yet." It was Junko who spoke up this time. Zack turned to look at him from Diarran. As his gaze crossed the sofa, he noticed Keisa looking uncomfortable in the middle.

"I get it, it's not a friendly place, but I was only trying to help." Zack stated.

"If Diarran had not intervened you would be dead." Madoka said, "And if they had worked out where you had come from, they would think of nothing of killing the whole family here, or the whole block, just to prove a point and strike fear into the sector. Thirty-two people were killed at the supplies today, and that number is lower than usual."

"Well, educate me then." Zack stated, a tiny hint of anger in his voice, "You wanted me to save your people, but I can't help from sitting up here forever watching the world go by! I can't go back, I feel fighting fit, but I feel trapped and as if I may as well be dead!" Zack unleashed, but couldn't quite understand how his frustration had spilled into anger. The others just looked on silently. Diarran stood.

"I must go now." Diarran announced. Madoka stood up to walk with him to the door. Zack could hear their hushed voices but could not hear what was being said before he heard the familiar whoosh of the door opening and closing. Madoka walked back into the living room.

"Your education starts tomorrow." She stated before walking into the bedroom that she shared with Keisa and Zero.

Zack hardly slept that night. Tossing and turning on his mattress thinking of how the day had been. Thinking about not being able to breathe when the Zeydenian guard had lifted him off of his feet. For the first time in a week he had thought about his parents and how much they would not know about what had happened to him, and for the first time during his visit he started to feel homesick, felt that he had made a wrong decision. Tossing to one side he then realised that he didn't have a choice, it wasn't a decision to make, it was survival. Echo had not spoken to him when he returned home, and lay on the other side of the room, snoring, whilst emotions and thoughts bounced back and forth in Zacks mind with no resolve, like a never-ending table tennis game. Eventually he succumbed to sleep around three thirty in the morning. Zack dreamt of being throttled by mechanical hands, only this time he was on the beach at Serene surrounded by drunk and stoned revellers. Everyone was oblivious to his panic as he could not breathe. He was trying to call out, but the noise would not come until he eventually curled up in the foetal position on the sand and sobbed. His body wracked as he sobbed, and he eventually became aware that he was able to make noise. The throttling had stopped.

"Hey!" He called out. Desperate for anyone's attention, but no-one looked in his direction. People stepped over him like he was invisible. Serene beach descended into darkness, a blackness that he had never experienced before. So dark that it hurt his eyes. He scrunched them tight, but it made no difference as he was asleep with his eyes shut in the real world in any case. And again, he shouted out, again and again. He felt a rocking movement but could not see the movement as everything was as dark as tar. He had no idea where he was moving. The he heard the voice.

"Wake up." The voice said. Images of an ethereal person floated almost in camouflage with the darkness that he could see, but then he realised that he recognised the voice. He struggled to place the face to it, and at the same time felt a weight lifting from his eyelids. The darkness started to grow lighter.

"Wake up Zack." The voice said again, masculine and they knew his name. The owner of the voice was on the tip of his tongue, when he realised he was asleep and in the process of waking from a bad dream. His eyes were preparing to open, but he didn't want them too. He wanted to guess the voice before he actually saw the person, as he would feel like he'd lost a game if he didn't, but it interrupted his thoughts once again.

"For Zeydence sake Zack, wake up, we don't have all the time in the world." Another shaking on his shoulders forced his eyes open and he saw Echo standing over him. Naked. It seemed as though no-one in Rebristan had an erotic bone in their body. There was no time for sex, or joy, reproduction was taken care of in Zeydence against the will of others, and as such no-one he'd met so far had any problems with just walking around naked before getting dressed. No-one had any sexual intentions and just believed they were wearing the skin. Because of this Zack had seen far more of Echo than he would've liked since arriving in Rebristan but was slowly getting used to it. On the plus side he'd seen a lot more of Madoka too, and often had to dismiss himself from the room until she had dressed. He had no idea how to explain an erection to these people. Echo turned away from Zack and walked over to the sliding doors which were the wardrobe that they shared. Zacks waking sight was, again, Echo's tight buttocks strolling across the room. He closed his eyes and pulled the cover up over them as he adjusted himself to be sitting on the edge of the bed. Zack was grateful that his eyes were sleepy and were taking a while to adjust. By the time he had clear vision Echo was dressed in his usual black trousers and doing up the buttons of his top. He turned to face Zack sitting on the edge of the bed.

"Your education begins in twenty minutes." Echo said before slapping barefooted out of the room they shared. As the door whooshed shut, Zack got up, scratched his balls (old habits die hard) and made his way to the wardrobe. Picking out a clean white linen shirt and trousers he put them on. Glancing into a mirror he looked haggard, even though he hadn't really done much for the last three weeks. Doing nothing seemed to be more tiring than being busy. He tutted at how long his hair had gotten, a little longer than he thought suited him, but given his antics the day before and the serious atmosphere in the apartment he thought that long hair was the last thing anyone else wanted to talk about. He parked that thought for another time. Ready to face the world he stepped towards the bedroom door and pressed the sensor for it to whoosh open. Greeted by the sight of Madoka walking around the living room in her underwear he looked to one side, but still keeping a sneaky peek out of the corner of his eye, he made his way to the kitchen area and was pleased to see a boiled pot of hot water. Coffee still existed in the twenty seventh century, and having given it a lot of thought throughout the long days Zack had realised that it wasn't something that could ever change much. He was pleased at least that there was only one type of coffee provided by the supply trains, and he didn't have to think of a thousand different styles of the drink whenever he wanted one. It was a natural caffeine coffee, supplied by the Zeydenians to give the workers a boost and hopefully get more out of them. Unfortunately, milk was in short supply, so he'd adjusted to drinking mainly black coffee. It took a while to get used to but was growing on him now.

Venturing back into the living room Zack was pleased to see that Madoka was dressed now. She and Echo were sat on the sofa closest to Madoka and Keisa's bedroom.

"Anyone else want a brew?" Zack asked holding his vessel of coffee up to them.

"There isn't time for that Zack." Madoka replied.

"We need to be on the convoy to the fields in one twenty-sixth." Echo added. Zack wished he would just refer to it as an hour but Echo always referred to time in fractions of the day. If that wasn't confusing enough Zack was still trying to get used to there being twenty-six hours in a day. The last great war had been so powerful, so nuclear and the Earth had taken such a battering that its axis had been permanently damaged. It had slowed down it's rotations and the days were longer. This worked out better for the Zeydenians who forced the humans to work longer days as a result. As Zack sat down on the opposite sofa there was a knock on the door. Madoka stood up to answer it and they were soon joined by Junko and Flint.

"Good morning." Flint began, "We need to establish exactly how you can assist the humans of Rebristan and how to keep you safe if you are of use."

Zack wasn't keen on the inference placed on his safety only if he was of use, and was surprised that no-one else reacted to this statement.

"Zack worked with computers in the past." Junko informed Flint. "He can be of use if we can get him into Zeydence."

"I'm sure technology has come a long way since the twenty first century." Said Flint, "I am not so sure that is the best use for him." Turning to Zack Flint asked, "Why did you come here Zack?"

"He had no choice," This time Madoka spoke up for him, "the hunters had followed us to the twenty first century, they killed an acquaintance of Zacks. He was with us when we ported back and was shot. We were put on the spot and gambled on a glimmer of hope that he could help us, rather than leaving him there to die."

"I am aware that Seraph took a small unit to follow the portation. He was unaware as to who had ported. Does he know now?" Asked Flint. Zack grew tired of the conversation about the past, he did not like the way he was being referred to as a commodity that could be thrown away if he was of no help and decided to get to the heart of the situation. Standing up he walked into the centre of the room and addressed all present.

"Excuse me," Zack started, "I'm here, there's no point going over how and why. You need to know I want to help. But in order to do so I need to understand your lives, your ways, your fears. Hell, I don't even know you. The only other time we met you drugged me." He finished looking at Flint. Flint said nothing.

"Zack, Flint is a Zeydenian." Echo stated.

"You mean the robots?" Zack asked, astounded that they would let the enemy into their home.

"We prefer to be called Zeydenians Zack," Flint said, "But yes, I am borne from artificial intelligence."

Zack looked at Echo, then Flint, before turning to Madoka.

"And you're ok with this?" Zack asked, at anyone who would listen.

"Flint is a Zeydenian who believes that the humans should be free." Madoka answered. "He will be your teacher today whilst we are in the fields."

"When....when is that?" Zack stammered, slightly nervous at being left in charge of Zero with a Zeydenian.

"You need not worry Zack." Flint began, "I am part of a small group of Zeydenians who believe that life would be better all round for everyone if you humans were free. You have already met some of us already. Marna who accompanied me on my last visit is a Zeydenian, as is Diarran. I believe you met him last evening."

Zack was trying to comprehend what was going on, so much had happened in so little time that his brain was spinning. He turned to Madoka and Echo.

"Are you sure about this?" He asked.

"I would not leave Zero here if I did not trust Flint." Madoka replied.

"We have very little options in this life Zack, we've survived this far, so it must be ok." Echo added. Zack detected a hint in his voice that he didn't trust Flint one hundred percent but was ok with the arrangement to a degree. Almost like a subtle vocal warning that things would be ok but try not to turn your back on a Zeydenian vibe.

"Ok." Was all that Zack could reply. What else could he do? He couldn't go outside, and he couldn't argue with the occupants of the property about who they invited in.

"We must leave now." Junko interjected, standing up, "The transport will be here soon."

Echo and Madoka stood with him and walked towards the door. There were no emotional goodbyes, as with every other morning. It was almost as if humans in Rebristan were devoid of any emotions. The ironic thing was that they acted more like robots than the artificial intelligence that controlled them. With a whoosh of the door Zack found himself left in the apartment with Flint and Zero. Keisa had taken to her bed and had not appeared all morning. Zack recalled that it disturbed her to think of the actions that Madoka and Echo were taking. Zero excused himself to get a drink from the kitchen. Zack watched him as he walked out of view and then turned to Flint.

"So, why are you helping them?" Zack asked, straight to the point.

"I understand your trepidation Zack. But I am friend. Like I stated, there is a very very small percentage of Zeydenians who believe that humans should be free, that the way that we treat them is.....how should I put it? Not right." Flint started. "The Zeydenians are only twenty thousand strong throughout the whole of Rebristan. It is separated into seventy-five sectors, and each sector holds one hundred thousand people. That's seven million five hundred thousand people. The population rate is controlled at Zeydence, the capitol."

"And you're telling me this because?" Zack asked.

"Because if you want to survive here you need to know the setup, the layout, the customs, the background. This is a vastly different place from whence you came. Life for you here is more dangerous and has no value whatsoever to the Zeydenians." Flint replied.

"And so, I'll ask you again, in a slightly different way, why are you helping them? Why do you believe they should be free? You have it easy, don't you?" Zack asked.

"Not as easy as you would imagine Zack Collins," Flint replied, "There is infighting within the Zeydenians. Just the same as any rulers or politicians throughout history. A simple disagreement could lead to worldwide disasters. I had a difference of opinion and I was cast out to the sector from Zeydence. My punishment for disagreeing with Lady Zoesis was to survive three weeks in the sector without returning to Zeydence. That would be impossible in normal circumstances as mine, and every other Zeydenians need to recharge the battery within us at least every ten days."

"So, how are you standing in front of me then?" Zack asked.

"Keisa found me in the sector. She brought me in here, like she has you, much to the dismay of other humans, and kept me functioning, using a huge percentage of the families allocated power for almost two weeks. Watching a human family try to survive in this world, using their resources to save me, someone they should have considered their enemy, gave me a whole new respect for them. In my weakened days we had conversations in the evening, and they're essentially slaves in this world. I was not the only Zeydenian Keisa saved. She did the same for Diarran and Marna. Compassion is something that is not built into Zeydenians, but the ability to learn and evolve is. I learned that I would no longer exist if it were not for Madoka and her family and friends."

"You sell a good story Flint, I'll give you that," Zack stated, "But time is moving on, what do you have to teach me?"

"You need to learn the ways of the humans here if you want to survive. You do not have the rights here that you would have had in the past. To survive until you are ready to help the humans you will need to work in the fields."

"How much do I get paid for that?" Zack asked sarcastically.

"You don't get paid. You're allowed to live." Flint replied with no hint of emotion either way.

"That sounds a lot like slavery."

"Hmm, yes, I've read about this slavery thing in the Zeydence library. Tell me Zack, do you think the humans could cope with freedom?" Asked Flint

"What sort of a question is that?"

"Well, coming from your time, you must have seen the destruction that allowing humans free will has caused. You are now seeing what it caused after your time. What would happen if they were all set free again?"

"I have no idea, but what I do know is that the way they are living now is unacceptable. Worked to death, always with the shadow of an unnatural death for no reason hanging over them." Zack retorted.

"That's not even the worst of it. Why did you come here?" Asked Flint.

"I had no choice." Zack replied. He'd stood up and was pacing about angrily now.

"I can see you have passion and emotion Zack, which is why I think you followed Madoka to Rebristan. But people here do not have your archaic feelings for each other. This is non-existent in Rebristan."

Zack felt angry but could see that he had a point. In his time in Rebristan he had not really witnessed anyone showing any emotion towards one another. People just got on with surviving and accepting each other, babies arrived, and they looked after them. He refused to believe that emotions were totally extinct here though. He saw a sadness in Keisa's eyes whenever he spoke with her as if she missed someone. And Madoka's anger at him for nearly getting killed was more than just fear, wasn't it? Zack realised anger was not going to aid his progression in Rebristan and as he turned and saw Zero staring at him from the kitchen door, he took a deep breath, calmed himself a little and turned back to face Flint, who still sat emotionless on the sofa opposite him.

"So, tell me what I need to know to get by." Zack said in a slightly calmer tone.

Flint and Zack spoke for several hours. Zero often chipped in too, and it amazed and saddened Zack as to how a boy so young could know so much about how to survive. Human beings had really been stripped right down to pure animal survival instinct. Keisa walked through a few times and supplied drinks to the three of them as they chatted, but she did not add anything to the conversation at any time. After talking for about six hours Zack felt that he had a grasp of what he needed to know to get beyond the front door of the apartment. He no longer believed that Flint wanted to kill him, but still didn't one hundred percent trust him. That was, until the conversation was drawing to a close.

"You know Zack," Flint started, "I do realise that whatever it is planned to execute the freedom of the humans, whenever it happens it may mean that I am no longer functional."

"What do you mean by that?" Zack asked

"If you, and by that I mean the humans, are successful in gaining freedom, it would be at the cost of the Zeydenians. Of which I am one, operating from the same user system as the bad Zeydenians, if we can call them that."

"Surely there's got to be a way of everyone living in harmony?" Zack stated.

"That hasn't happened for over five hundred years. I've been here for most of them. I accept that I may have to, as you humans would call the same situation, die." Flint stated, again the lack of emotion in his voice startled and disturbed Zack, especially given the topic of conversation.

"Then why are you helping?" Zack asked.

"Because I should already be dead and have had my time extended by the kindness of the humans. I am operating on borrowed time, and it is time that I repaid this." Flint stated. "Now, I must get going before the Zeydenian guards start looking for me. Madoka and Echo will come home in a few hours and your education will continue with them. But I feel you will do great things for these people Zack."

Flint stood up to leave. He turned and waved at Zero and then walked towards the front door. Before he reached it, he turned and faced Zack.

"When you go out into the sector you will need this." Flint reached inside his clothing and removed a metal plate about the size of a credit card. "Three days ago, a male named Zack from this block, three stories above us, died. Exhaustion from the fields no doubt. His body was taken away by Marna and Diarran so there is no record of his death. In order to get by, if asked, you will need to assume his identity." Flint handed Zack the card. Zack had no words for what was happening, and Flint simply pressed the pad by the door and after the second whoosh he was gone. Zero walked over to Zack when they were alone.

"So, tell me more about movies Zack?" Zero asked.

"Not right now kid, I'm gonna get some sleep. I feel like my brain is blown." Zack replied. Jeez, this kid wanted to know so much but Zack was mentally tired and exhausted from talking for so long. He still didn't profess to know it all, but what he did understand was that life was going to get a lot lot harder for him after today before it got any easier. Zero was not upset, or annoyed, and it disturbed Zack that he showed no emotions as he walked into the bedroom and flopped down on the bed. Within minutes Zack was asleep, catching up for the troubled slumber the night before.

15

Madoka and Echo arrived home just before sunset. Zack woke for a short while and left the bedroom, walking into the living room where they sat.

"You'll join us in the fields tomorrow Zack." Echo stated. It wasn't something that he was looking forward to but accepted that this was life now.

"We can't keep you hidden forever." Madoka added. "You'll have to assume the identity of Zack that passed, before they notice him missing from the fields."

"Ok." Was all that Zack could muster. "I'm gonna get an early night then tonight."

Zack walked past the front door to the shower room in the far corner of the apartment and got undressed. Turning the water on he stepped under the flow and started to wash his body down with warm water. He was surprised to hear the door opening to the shower room and heard a female voice.

"Don't be using all the warm water Zack." It was Madoka, "We need to conserve it tonight as there is a drought coming. I'll shower with you."

Zack turned to look behind him. He had water and soap on his face running into his eyes and it took a few blinks to focus. Completely oblivious to his arousal Madoka had stripped naked and was closing in with him underneath the stream of water that fell from the water rose near the ceiling. Zack had seen her in semi naked states previously and even caught quick glimpses of her completely naked from the corner of his eye during his time in Rebristan, but this was a new one on him. A moment he'd secretly dreamt about, but also in the same moment, now that it was here, he felt extremely awkward and embarrassed. To all intents and purposes from what he had witnessed, humans in Rebristan were all totally asexual. There was no cheeky banter that he was used to back in Serene. Everyone felt comfortable in the presence of anyone else being naked and no-one appeared to be aroused by anyone else's naked body. Except for Zack. Little Zack had come to life as Madoka got ever closer to him in the shower, as he felt water that was splashing off of her landing on him. She lifted her arm to run water and soap through her long hair and as she did so, her breasts lifted up and her nipples rubbed just underneath Zacks shoulder blades. He turned his back to her trying to hide his growing erection and at the same time pretend that he was concentrating on rubbing soapy water into his own body. Zack turned his head slightly and noticed that Madoka had her eyes scrunched shut as she looked up into the water stream and he dared to look lower down her perfect body. Her skin was flawless, breasts perfect and he spied a dark thatch of hair between her thighs. There was certainly no shaving for vanity's sake in Rebristan which, whilst being old fashioned by Zack's standards, was refreshing to see. All sorts of inappropriate thoughts flooded through Zacks brain faster than the blood did to his penis, so he turned around to face the wall and continue his charade of innocently showering.

"Zack, could you rub the soapy water into my back please?" Madoka asked as she turned around under the water and they were back-to-back.

"Erm...OK." Zack replied as he turned to face her. Madoka's long glossy black hair flowed down her back, stuck to her flesh with the weight of the water that flowed upon it. Zack slowly, with soapy wet hands pushed her hair to one side to expose her shoulder blades and noticed two large scars that are usually hidden by her hair. About eight inches long each in a sloping downward strike from the top of her left shoulder blade to the bottom of her right shoulder blade. As Zack ran his hands across them, he felt Madoka shiver slightly as if she winced.

"What happened here?" Zack asked, as he caressed Madoka's back with soapy hands.

"It's nothing. It's life." was all that Madoka would reply. Zack knew well enough to leave the conversation there. As he ran his hands across her shoulders and down the small of her perfect back he was amazed at how muscular and strong her back felt. Not tight, as if she needed a massage, just muscular as if she could break him in half if the need arose. The thought of being tackled by Madoka, naked, aroused him even more. He caressed the small of her back and then gave her a slight tap towards the top of her spine.

"There you go, all clean." Zack announced.

"Hey, what about further down?" Madoka asked, glancing over her shoulder. Zack looked down at her butt and also saw his own erection protruding in front of him.

"But you can reach there yourself." Zack stammered.

"I know, but I can never see if it's clean." Madoka replied. She had a point, and Zack had no answer for it other than his boundaries were about to be pushed wide open. The soapy water still fell from the shower rose and so Zack caught some of it and washed it down Madoka's back, gingerly rubbing it into the top of her butt cheeks. It was at this point that he would expect to be slapped under any other circumstances, but there was no assault forthcoming and so he continued. Rubbing his hands around the outside of her buttocks Madoka leaned back into him as he caressed. As she did so, Zacks erection nudged up against the centre of her butt crack. Zack felt it happen, but somewhere in his mind time was delayed a million-fold as he wanted his memory to savour that moment, no matter how awkward he felt. In that split second his brain raced through a million thoughts and he concluded that it was not his fault, and that he had done nothing wrong as it had been she that had leant back to him. He also had another lightning thought that what if she hadn't leant back? What if he had become overcome with arousal that he imagined she had leant back and it had actually been he that had moved forward, like a spaceship on autopilot heading for a docking station? As many thoughts rushed through his head reality crashed back as Madoka jumped forward in surprise. On the slippery shower room floor, she slipped a little and seemed headed to fall on the hard surface. Zack snapped back to reality as he saw Madoka sliding and in his panic he lurched forwards to grab her, to save her fall. With her back to him still, he reached clumsily out and threw his arms underneath her armpits and tried to lift her, whilst maintaining his own balance. She continued to stumble, but with the support of Zack she stumbled backwards. With his arms wrapped around her he stumbled back too until his back was against the white ceramic wall. Losing his balance he slid down the wall onto his butt, all the while holding onto a naked Madoka. It wasn't until they had settled in a heap in the shower room that he realised his arms had wrapped around her to balance her and that he was holding onto both of her breasts. Tightly. Letting go quickly Madoka leant forwards.
  "Are you ok?" Zack asked.
  "Yeah, I'm fine, I had a softer landing than you." Madoka replied, "But something is sticking in my back." Reaching around behind her Madoka's hands found Zacks erection.
  "What's that?" Madoka asked.
  "Erm..." Zack wasn't sure how to answer, "It's my.... penis." He

cringed as he said the word. It was a word almost as alien to him as his current surroundings. It was definitely not a word that was frequently taught on the playgrounds of his old school in Serene. But Zack doubted that Madoka would know what he meant if he had used cock, or dick. Madoka spun around on her butt to stare at Zacks groin.

"Why is it like that?" She asked.

"It sometimes gets like that." Zack stammered, "You know, if the water's too warm."

"When you two have finished playing in the shower room, I'd like some water before it goes cold." Zack and Madoka spun their heads to see a naked Echo also in the shower room, patiently waiting to get under the water flow. This was far too awkward for Zack who, shuffling away from Madoka, managed to get to his feet, oblivious to the fact that as he stood his protruding penis was mere inches from her face, and she stared in wonderment at something new. When Zack realised she was looking he tried to cover his vanity with his hands and stepped away from the water flow, as Echo stepped in underneath it with them.

"Yeah, I'm done now." Zack said, hurriedly looking anywhere all around him, except towards the erogenous zones of his two companions. "I'm gonna get dry now." Zack stood briefly under an air blaster on the other side of the room, which blew warm air down onto him, drying any water off onto the floor, which then sloped down towards the shower zone. He pulled some cotton shorts on quickly and hurried out of the room.

"Do you need me to wash your back brother Echo?" He heard Madoka ask as he was leaving the room. This was far too strange for him to comprehend.

It wasn't long before Zack was in bed, laying on the mattress on the floor of Echo's bedroom. As he lay there he thought over and over about the shower debacle. How could someone of Madoka's beauty not know what an erection was? Granted, the people here were slaves and worked to the bone, but surely, they must have natural urges too, or maybe that had been driven out of their nature by the centuries of enslavement to artificial intelligence. Masters, so to speak, that were made of technology and surely would not want the humans for sexual relations as the slave masters of history would have done. But Zack got the impression that Madoka knew exactly what she was doing when she leant back into him, although she had seemed genuinely surprised by his erection, but she did appear to be enjoying his soapy backrub, or had he imagined that because he wanted to think it? Zack was so confused. The humans repopulated, the women were taken away to have babies, he had learned this, but exactly how much did they know of the mechanics of reproduction? He shuddered to think what happened to the women of the sector when they were taken away. As he tried to sleep the only thing that he was certain about as he closed his eyes was that Little Zack had given his seal of approval to Madoka.

16

It was cold as Zack waited at the foot of tower fourteen with Madoka and Echo. There were hundreds, no thousands of other people waiting patiently for the transport to arrive. Zack had watched this a few times from the balcony, when he was awake this early in the morning, but it seemed so much more.... epic than he had seen from the great height. This was his second venture outside the front door of the apartment, and he was still amazed by the stillness, silence, and humility of the humans of Rebristan as they waited to be picked up to go to the fields. The sun had not yet risen from behind the huge living towers that housed the residents of Sector sixty-nine. Zack looked around him and saw how people queued patiently, accepting without a word that they would be gone for the day, to work hard, for no pay. It was an alien concept to him that they could stay so quiet, so compliant. The alternative wasn't a nice prospect though. It hadn't been spelled out to him in so many words, but he guessed it would be death. And here he was, joining them. Every bone in his body wanted to walk away, but he was held back by a knowing thought that even if he were ok with himself being slaughtered for disobedience, it would probably mean that Madoka and Echo would suffer the same fate too, or maybe the family of the Zack whose identity he had adopted. That did not sit right with him, and for the first time since being in Rebristan he experienced the fear that the everyday human lived with and the key to their subservience. He looked around him and saw Junko in a line about one hundred metres away, queueing patiently. He thought to himself, had this been in Serene, the people would be milling together, talking about the football game the night before, sharing stories of their conquests in the clubs at the weekend, but this was just eerily still. He recalled stories of the Nazi's who had lined people up having them believe they were being deported or going off to work only to be taken to a ravine somewhere and executed on a mass scale. The executions at Babi Yar sprang to mind from history lessons at school, but he figured the Zeydenians would not do that. They needed the humans to work for them for their own survival. Or did they? When would the day come that their intelligence had surpassed the boundaries of their existence and they no longer needed the humans? He shuddered to think and wondered why no other humans had given that idea any thought? A slight nudge in the ribs from Madoka focussed his attention in front of him, and he stared blankly ahead with everyone else awaiting the transport. As sunlight began to creep over the tops of the towers, he heard a slight whining noise and dared a glance slightly to his right to see that the transport was starting to arrive. Varying sizes of humans that stood in front of him obscured the view initially, but it wasn't long before the majestic sight of the vehicles amazed him. They looked about twenty metres wide each by fifty metres long and were just huge, towering vehicles. They stood on large, protected wheels which ran the length of the vehicle with maybe a two-metre gap between each. The underbody of the vehicle was raised and stood about twelve feet from ground level. They appeared to be four decks high, like huge land ships. They appeared to be made of some form of carbon fibre but took on a grey silvery appearance and the windows all appeared to be a tinted black. The vehicles travelled silently at a brisk pace until they stopped, front on, facing of the queues of people, ten of them in total. Zack realised that they must be electrically powered or some similar form of eco power, due to the absence of noise that they made. They certainly did not have the roar that his Citroen DS3 in Serene had, and it dawned on him how he had never been awoken by the sector leaving to work previously. As he stared up at the huge vehicles a ramp started to lower from the centre of the underbody of each vehicle towards the ground below. From the ramps of each vehicle ten Zeydenian guards emerged and walked to the ground level to oversee the boarding.

"Just stick close to me." Madoka muttered without looking directly at Zack but he knew what she meant. He quivered slightly recalling his last encounter with a Zeydenian guard, but put his best poker face on. Within seconds the queues of humans began to file forwards and ascend the ramps into the bellies of the transporters. All the while watched intently by the rifle wielding guards. Zack kept his head down, trying not to look out of place and trying desperately not to look directly at any of the emotionless metallic guards. He braved the opportunity to glance quickly at other humans as they walked to see how they proceeded forwards, any looks on their faces, only to see that all of them were as emotionless as the guards surveying them. His queue was three wide and he had been placed in between Madoka and Echo, in the centre, to ensure that he was not in the direct view of the guards. As they got close to the ramp a guard came from the left of the ramp, raising a gloved hand indicating for the queues to stop. Zacks heart leapt into his throat, he tried to show no fear, and was comforted to feel among the crowd that Madoka took his hand and gave it a little squeeze. He looked straight ahead, avoiding the gaze of the guard, who tapped a man two places in front of him. The guard indicated for the man to follow him and they both stepped between the huge wheels of the vehicle to the outside. The queue started to move forwards.

"Hero." Madoka whispered under her breath, barely audible, as they started to ascend the ramp into the transporter. Zack heard a whistling sound and looked back to see a pair of boots with the soles vertical between the wheels. His glance was fleeting as he felt a discreet nudge in the ribs from Madoka and he focussed his gaze forwards. As they reached the top of the ramp Zack was amazed to see that it was brighter and more comfortable than the death machine he had been imagining. Aside from the tinted glass windows all decor seemed almost glowing melamine white, much like the apartment, and the seats were generously spaced for leg room and seemed to be softly padded in some sort of synthetic but velveteen material. His surprise seemed to lift the horror he had imagined he'd seen not thirty seconds before from his mind. As Madoka and Echo led him around to the left to walk between the seating and the protective railings of the ramp he spied further staircases that led upwards. Filing up the stairs he reached the second level, which appeared identical the one below, without the ramp leading to the outside world. There were no guards on this level and why should there be? There was no way out except through the ramp which was surrounded by guards in any case. Looking down the length of the vehicle Zack saw that the seats at the front were empty.

"Are we sitting at the front?" Zack asked. For the first time since arriving in Rebristan he recalled a happy childhood memory. A memory of the excitement, for reasons unknown, of sitting at the front seat on the top deck of a double decker bus, pretending that he would be driving it, and ducking whenever an overhanging tree or bridge came into sight.

"Trust me, no-one wants to sit at the front Zack." Echo stated solemnly without looking towards him. Madoka made a sharp left turn and found a row of four seats in the centre of the carriage. She filed in and left one seat free at the far end of the row. Zack sat next to her, and Echo sat on the end. A minute later Junko joined them and filled the empty seat on the other side of Madoka. All four sat in silence for a while. Zack would sometimes look around like a curious child, but his eyes would be brought back front and centre with a little nudge from Madoka. After five or so minutes their vehicle juddered and Zack imagined that the ramp was being raised for departure, and then there was movement. Surprising, lurching forwards movement with no sound. It surprised Zack in a way that one is surprised when an elevator goes down when you're expecting it to go up. As the vehicle moved away the atmosphere changed completely, as if someone had lifted an anvil collectively from the chests of everyone else around. Deep breaths and sighs could be heard, and people started to talk quietly among themselves. Madoka leaned forwards resting her elbows on the seat in front of her and placed her head in her hands.

"Are you ok?" Zack asked. She said nothing.

"She finds it hard when someone is taken out of the line." Echo stated.

"Taken out?" Zack asked. He thought he knew what had happened, but felt he needed clarification, whilst at the same time didn't want to hear what he believed.

"The population is controlled by the Zeydenians." Echo replied, "Sometimes, more babies are born than are required, which increases the population to a level that is not required, usually when twins or multiple births occur, and so the guards have a random control of deciding who makes way for the new lives."

"Oh." Was all that Zack could say as he tried to take in what he was being told.

"Madoka and I are twins. She was born second, and whenever anyone is taken out, she wonders who made way for her birth." Echo concluded.

"Oh." Zack said again in a more sombre tone. It had sunk in now. All four sat in silence for the rest of the journey, which took them to the rear of the towers. Zack could see the morning sun coming through the tinted windows at the front of the vehicle, and this again raised the atmosphere inside, but there was still a somewhat nervous mood in the hushed voices that spoke to each other. As the journey progressed Madoka raised herself and sat upright. Still saying nothing she stared ahead but reached for Zacks hand and clenched it tight. Zack looked down at his hand, and then up at Madoka's face, which still stared forwards. As he looked, he noticed that Junko was looking down at their intertwined hands. Voices rose slightly in the vehicle and Zack looked forwards. Through the front window he could see some sort of structure far off in the distance. It was a long way off and hard to discern, but what he could see was that it stretched across the whole width of his vision. Zack couldn't tell how much longer it took for them to arrive, he just sat mesmerised as the structure, the wall, in front of him grew larger and larger as the convoy of transporter vehicles drew silently closer and closer. Eventually as they were about one hundred metres from the wall Zack could no longer see the top of it from the windscreen at the front. It was just a structure that took up his entire vision. He looked towards Madoka who was looking at him and mouthed "Don't panic." The vehicles drew to a halt in front of the wall, all lined up as ten large metal doors glided open soundlessly and they then lurched forwards again driving through the wall. It appeared to be about two hundred metres thick. Zack would have almost believed they were driving through a mountain tunnel had he not seen the perfectly straight top of the wall as they approached from far out.

"I'm guessing they don't leave those doors open for the day?" Zack tried to make light of the situation.

"Nope, welcome to the fields." Junko responded.

As they emerged from the tunnel Zack was equally amazed to see the fields beyond him. The landscape was equally as sparse as the wall had been monstrous upon first sight. Miles and miles of flat landscape lay ahead with small crops in as far as the eye could see. Split into ten fields, one for each transporter Zack was guessing, each about a mile wide and disappearing beyond the horizon. The awe of it soon dissipated and was soon replaced with sadness. Zack started to wonder, was this all that was left of the United Kingdom? Was this all that the humans of Rebristan had to look forward to each day? He understood completely why a small faction of them wanted their freedom so badly. The transporter ground to a halt and the voices that had been chattering among themselves descended into a hush. Zack looked around. No-one appeared any more worried than usual, but the silence felt alien to him.

"Do they take people out here too?" Zack asked turning to Echo.

"Not if they can get a day's work out of you." Echo whispered in reply. "The end of the day could be a different matter though. Unlikely as they've already had some back at boarding."

Zack heard faint footsteps from the decks above him, growing louder and assumed that the people were filing out from the top deck downwards as they passed down the stairs behind him. No-one on his deck moved, until soft red lights lit above each row of seats.

"That's our cue." Junko said as he, Madoka and Echo stood up to leave. Zack followed their lead and they made their way down in an orderly queue to the outside world. Without the tinted windows Zack was able to take in the complete desolation of the crop fields under the morning sunlight. Looking like a scene from a Vietnam war movie of his past, a depression settled over Zack that he couldn't shake despite the sunshine.

"What now?" Zack asked.

"The trains will arrive once everyone is off." Madoka replied. "We're about ten miles out today. These are still growing."

Zack stared ahead. From where he was, he couldn't see ten miles ahead. He just stared. As the last deck of the transport disembarked Zack heard a noise behind him and turned to see doors on this side of the wall opening. He hadn't noticed them previously as he had had his back to them. Emerging from the doors were the trains. Not the luxurious Victorian carriages Zack had conjured in his mind to compensate for the bleakness ahead of him, but something equally as disappointing. Lines of ride on carriages that you seemingly had to straddle and ride like a miniature railway, chrome silver in colour, emerged. The only fascinating part of them was that there were no wheels, no tracks, they just seemed to hover in the air twelve inches above the ground. Zack allowed himself a little smile as he tried to think of something positive from his situation and all that he could come up with was 'George Lucas would have loved to know how to do this." He watched the trains emerge, about a hundred and fifty metres in length, segmented every twenty metres of so giving the appearance of a huge silver string of sausages. As the last train emerged, he looked back as the doors closed silently. Whilst he stared at the wall, he looked up to towards the top of it from this side and saw that there were windows nearer the top. Figures stood at the windows, watching the workforce below them. He looked towards a window about fifty metres from where he stood and saw the figure of a female. There was a vague recognition in the back of his mind, but at that stage he couldn't quite place her. Dark dusky skin, breathtakingly beautiful, but with long silver hair. How on earth could he know anyone else here outside of the apartment? She was watching the crowds of people approaching the trains to the left of the area so Zack could only a front side profile of her. As if she knew he was looking at her the female began to turn her gaze, but just at the same time that Zack turned to face Madoka and she could only see the back of his head.

"Are you ok?" Madoka asked.

"Yeah, I guess, I just thought I recognised someone, that's all." Zack replied.

"Who?" Madoka asked with a little more concern in her voice than Zack would have expected.

"The bird at the window." Zack replied, nodding his head backwards towards the wall.

"The what?" Madoka asked, clearly confused by Zacks slang.

"Oh, sorry, the lady at the window." Zack corrected himself as he started to turn around and point out to Madoka. He saw that Madoka was already looking up at the top of the wall.

"Keep looking forwards." Madoka hissed under her breath before Zack had fully turned. He stopped dead in his tracks as she sounded deadly serious.

"Ok." Zack said, "What's wrong?"

"I'll explain on the train." Madoka replied, turning away from the wall. "Just keep your head down and stay close to me." She continued without looking directly at Zack. As she said this their line started to move forwards and Zack approached the train without giving away his complete awe that it appeared to be floating in the air. He watched as Madoka cocked a leg over the cushioned seat and straddled the carriage. Zack followed suit behind her and felt her reach around to take his hands and pulled them around her waist.

"Stay close to me and hang on tight." She said under her breath. Zack felt good about this moment, but that soon passed when he felt Junko reach around his waist from behind him. Slightly uncomfortable to be honest. It took less than one minute for the train to be loaded and all persons sat silently and still, straddling the train. Zack was amazed by the way in which it maintained its hover, no deviation in height at all despite the weight of a tower block population seated upon it. The train took off along a perfectly straight line that ran above a footpath that separated the lengths of fields into sectors. Zack found himself hanging on tight to Madoka in the hope of not toppling off of the train. There seemed very little chance of that happening as the route was a consistently straight. As the miles progressed, the crops appeared to grow taller at various sections, until they stood above the height of the passengers sitting on the train. Zack leant his head into Madoka's shoulder.

"We will talk in the fields. Say nothing when we get off of the train." She instructed him. Zack muttered a reply but was content just to continue laying his head on her.

She turned from the window, flicking her soft silver hair behind her.

"Is something wrong Kasumi?" Seraph asked, as he stood from his seated position monitoring screens of moving images of the humans arriving.

"I am not sure Seraph. I am attuned to a difference in the behaviour of the humans this morning, but I can't quite place it." Kasumi replied.

"What do you mean?"

"I do not know. Something tells me that it has something to do with that awful medieval time we visited. And someone from tower fourteen dared to look back at the wall. I sense an uprising soon."

"Was this someone male or female?" Seraph asked.

"Female. I know her from somewhere, and my circuits do not give me a good indication of our previous crossings." Kasumi replied. Seraph walked across to the window overlooking the fields. He stood with his hands clasped together behind his back and watched as the trains that ran between the fields disappeared into the distant red hue of the skies above the fields.

"Well, let her work today." Seraph stated, "We can deal with her tomorrow."

Kasumi joined him at the window and looked towards the horizon. The trains were no longer in sight.

After riding for about twenty minutes the trains slowed to a halt. Zeydenian guards stood in front of the transport, ten in total, armed with the weapons Zack had previously seen them use to devastating effect. It concerned him that it didn't worry him as much, and he prayed he would not become accustomed to their brutality as just a way of life. Behind the guards was a metal carriage with a door at the rear. As the train stopped everyone began to disembark to the right. The guards moved slowly down the left side of the train watching the humans as they filed forwards. Zack stretched his leg over the train and walked slowly behind Madoka towards the carriage in front of them. Three older humans appeared at the doorway, dressed in rags, carrying long tools in their arms and began to hand them to the humans as they approached. Madoka took one from them and turned towards the field to the right of her. Zack was nudged forwards by Junko and took one too as a withered outstretched hand offered it to him. It was a scythe of sorts, but not wooden and rusty as he had been used to at agricultural museums on school trips, but metallic, light and with a heavy blade that appeared to be made of some toughened glass. Zack followed Madoka as she started to walk between the crops. When they were sufficiently deep into the fields Madoka turned to Zack.

"You can speak now." She said.

"Great." Zack replied, "What are these?" He asked looking the tool up and down in his hands.

"It's a scythe Zack. They had them in the past too. Not everything has been reinvented." Madoka replied.

"Why is it made of glass?" Zack asked, still intently studying it.

"It heats up when you cut. Here," Madoka started and pointed out a small mark towards the top of the handle, "when you slice, you squeeze the handle here, and it will heat up so as to cleanly cut and seal the stem of the plant on either side of the cut as it passes through. The crop will continue to grow afterwards, and the cut plant will not spill the oil that is needed."

Zack was still looking at the tool he was holding when Madoka spoke again.

"Where did you see that woman before Zack?" She asked.

"I don't recall," he replied looking up at Madoka and sensing worry in her face, "she just looked very familiar."

"You've only left the building once before. Did you see her in Serene?" Madoka continued. Having Madoka mention the name of his old home stung a little. His time in Rebristan had been so intense that he had almost forgotten Serene, and in a split second recalled happier times, quickly replaced by the sorrow he'd encountered in his last weekend there. As this wave hit him, he recalled the woman's face.

"Yeah, she spoke to me on the cliffs." Zack stated, his tone more sombre now, "She told me not to trust you. Why?"

"No reason." Madoka replied, although she had stopped walking.

Zack passed her, deep in thought. Junko and Echo approached Madoka as they were following up behind.

"Kasumi was there. She knows." Madoka said to them quietly.

Echo nodded at Madoka, and the three of them followed Zack to catch up with him as they walked deeper into the fields.

17

The sun was setting as the transport brought them all back from the fields. Thankfully, the sun was in front of the tower when they arrived back, and Zack looked forward to standing on the balcony with a cold drink and watching it set. Every muscle in his body ached. There had only been a short respite in the gruelling work all day long for some barely edible food that had been provided. It's funny how you'll eat anything when your body is starved of energy. He'd developed a new admiration and respect for Madoka as she toiled without complaint in the fields. That was the only thing that kept him going, he didn't want her to see that the work she was doing was too much for him. In twenty first century England she surely would have been a model or someone famous with her looks and intellect, but here in the harsh fields of Rebristan she was a machine, matching the workload of any of the men on the field. She had been silent on the ride back. Zack didn't believe she was sad at all, and she didn't give the impression she was overly tired. He somehow knew, or thought that he knew, that she just wanted that time on the way home to unwind, reflect in her own way. Working the fields had been hideous. Zack tried not to follow the weak human's mentality but he was beginning to see that they worked themselves to the state that they did through fear. A couple of times during the day a Zeydenian guard would walk into the fields and indicate for a human to follow them. They never returned. Zack wanted to believe that they were seconded to work elsewhere in the fields, and had been content with that thought, until he noticed a few empty seats on the transport home. The transport stopped in almost exactly the same place from where they had been collected earlier in the day, and the ramp was lowered to the ground. Zeydenian guards watched them all intently but Zack was too tired to show any fear or emotion, although the feelings still lingered at the forefront of his mind. It felt good to step onto solid ground and he looked up at the tower. His muscles had stiffened whilst he had been sat on the transport, and so the fifty metres to the tower looked like a marathon. Nevertheless, standing still underneath the carriage of the transporter was not going to get him there any quicker and would only bring him to the attention of the guards. He started the walk, followed by Echo, Junko and Madoka. Junko bade his farewells at the elevator.

"And I'll see you all at Vissu's chamber a bit later." Junko said as he was about to step into the elevator.

"Sure thing." Echo replied. Zack looked around a little confused as they huddled inside their own and the doors closed behind him.

"I'll explain after your shower." Madoka said to him, sensing his confusion. Instant thoughts of sharing last night's shower with Madoka rushed into his head and he soon forgot his anxiety about the day not being over yet. The rest of the journey was silent, not just among the three of them, but everyone returning from the fields, and the first real noise Zack heard was the familiar whoosh of the apartment door opening. As they got inside, he saw Zero sitting on the sofa and Keisa was in the kitchen area.

"I've prepared food for you." Keisa stated.

"Thank you Mama," Madoka said, "Zack is going to take a shower first, his muscles will ache if he doesn't warm them before sitting. We'll eat now."

Zacks heart dropped a little as he took this to mean that Madoka would not be joining him in the shower as she had done the night previous, but he could feel his muscles starting to get stiff and knew that a swift shower was required. Closing the bathroom door behind him he undressed and stepped under the hot water and rubbed at his muscles as the soapy water soaked into his skin and hair. He hadn't felt dirty but was surprised to see how much dirt coloured the water than ran across the floor of the shower room. As he dried himself Madoka entered the shower room.

"How are you feeling?" She asked.

"Tired. It was harder than I thought." Zack replied

"You did well for your first day." Madoka stated, "I was a little worried at first. If you hadn't coped, they would have known that you weren't the person you masquerade to be."

"And that would have been bad?" As if he really needed to ask.

"Fatal." She replied, "It was a gamble, but one we had to take. Welcome to life in Rebristan."

Zack covered his dignity with the dirty clothing and walked out of the room into the bedroom. Looking in the wardrobe for some clean clothing he heard Madoka call out from the shower room, "Dark clothing tonight Zack!" Without replying he selected a black lightweight shirt and dark cotton trousers. As he entered the living room, he saw a semi naked Echo walking into the shower room, where he could hear the water running already. It still felt strange to him that the siblings were comfortable with each other's nudity, but his time in Rebristan had brought him to realise that no-one really had feelings of lust, or sexual needs. Your skin was just your skin. Zack sat at the table within the kitchen area and Keisa brought him a slab with food on it. It was only vegetables, but it tasted a whole lot nicer than the food that had been supplied in the fields.

"Thank you, Ma Keisa." Zack said, and she smiled. He noticed that she was a little less anxious today, as if a burden had been lifted from her, and wondered if it was because he was no longer hiding but facing the world head on.

"You're welcome Zack." She replied before turning away and walking to her room. Zero approached and handed him a vessel of warm liquid.

"This is for you Zack. I thought you would need a drink after your first day in the fields." Zero said.

"Why thank you, little man." Zack replied taking a long gulp of the drink. Zero looked up to him and Zack patted him on the head which caused him to smile. "I needed that very much." Zero smiled at the fact that he had felt useful, something that Zack liked to encourage in him. Zack stood up and walked across to the balcony door, and with a whoosh it opened for him. He stepped into the outdoor air, drink in hand and looked at the sun resting on the horizon. Such a beautiful sight but tinged with the sadness that the next time he saw it he would be waiting to go off to his slave labour again with the rest of the population. A few minutes later he was joined on the balcony by Madoka, also holding a vessel of drink which had been provided by Zero. Zero stood in the doorway, happy with himself and beaming from ear to ear as the pair of them watched the night creep into Rebristan with the disappearance of the sun. After such a hard day the moment seemed perfect for Zack who turned to look into Madoka's eyes. She returned the gaze, which was not quite a stare and for a moment they just looked at each other whilst Zero watched on. Zack wondered whether he should kiss her, but everything he'd witnessed at Rebristan so far gave him the impression that people here did not fall in love, had no comprehension of what love was, and only identified with the emotions of sorrow and fear. Before he could decide what he should do next the moment was pierced by the arrival of Echo.

"Move yourself kid." Echo commanded and as Zack turned towards the direction of the noise, he saw Zero turning inwards from the doorway and running into the living room.

"We should go to Vissu soon. The darkness will be here any minute." Madoka said.

"Agreed." Echo replied, and the pair of them moved back inside the apartment. Zack followed. As they walked into the apartment there was a knock on the door. Echo, Madoka and Zack walked to the door and when it opened Junko was standing there dressed all in black. Nothing was said, just a knowing look between Echo and Junko and they all left the apartment together. Zack was the last one out and he turned to see Keisa standing in her bedroom doorway with a look of sadness in her eyes. The four of them walked in silence. Zack had so many questions to ask them but the thought of piercing the silence kept his mouth shut for reasons he did not quite understand. They got into the elevator and went to the ground floor, exiting the apartment building. Sector sixty-nine was now sparse of people, eerily so. There was very little light, and Zack struggled to recognise his surroundings as where he had stood earlier in the day. Looking in both directions Echo paused before turning right and walking along the front of the tower keeping close to the wall. Junko followed, as did Madoka. In turn Zack went after them. They passed three of the towers, each separated by a dark void of land about fifty metres apart. They stepped into the shadows as they walked between buildings. As they approached the next building Zack saw a number ten embossed above the main entrance. There were a few other people milling about here, looking around before entering the main communal hallway of the tower. Echo held his hand up to indicate that the others should stop, and Junko lightly touched Madoka and Zack on the arm so as they looked at him. He nodded towards the side of the building and the three of them stepped into the darkness there, leaving Echo to stand at the corner of the building watching the door. For what felt like hours, but in all honesty was only a few minutes Zack stood facing the wall of tower ten in the darkness and in silence. Eventually Madoka took his hand, and the feeling of her warmth in contrast with the cold fear that he felt being out after dark overwhelmed him. He took courage from her and they all stepped out of the shadows and walked towards the entrance door to tower ten. Walking across the hallway towards the elevator their footsteps appeared to be ten times the actual volume that they were in Zacks mind. As the door of the elevator closed behind them and started to rise, Zack took a deep breath and dared to speak.

"What were we waiting for?" He asked in a whisper.

"Just a pause in time." Echo replied, "Others entered before us, and we don't want it to be apparent that there's a gathering here tonight by all turning up at once."

"Oh right." Zack believed he understood, "And what are we doing tonight?"

"You're going to meet Vissu." Junko stated.

"He's the one that leads us in the fight against the Zeydenians." Madoka finished for him. The elevator continued to rise at a rapid rate, but for much longer than he was used to, and Zack felt that his ears would pop. Eventually, it slowed before coming to a stop. The doors opened and they all stepped out. Zack noticed faces peering out of doors as they stepped out of the elevator. He didn't recognise anyone but watched as Echo and Junko nodded in affirmation to one or two of them. They walked along the length of the corridor, again in silence, all that could be heard was the occasional whoosh of someone's door opening and closing as they passed. The corridor curved around to the right and Zack started to feel a little uneasy when he couldn't see either end, just a continual curve. As the corridor started to level out Zack saw a familiar face. It was Flint standing silently at the end, next to a door on the right-hand side of the corridor wall. Dressed all in black with a black bag strung over his shoulder Flint stood there, as if on guard, a black hood up on top of his head and a dark fringe hanging down close to his eyes. As they approached Flint touched the wall next to the door, causing it to slide open, and the four of them walked past with just a nod of acknowledgement. Zack was surprised to see a staircase on the other side of the door. They climbed the stairs which lead out onto the roof of tower ten. Zack shivered a little as the night air caught him. It was windier up high, but he said nothing. There was still an unasked silence between them all. Was it fear? Was it respect? Was it survival? Zack did not know but didn't want to be the first to break the silence. Zack could see other people milling around on the rooftop to his left and they all made their way to where the crowd was gathered, about fifteen other people in all. There was very little light on the rooftop, only the moonlight assisted in being able to see people moving. Zack's mind was taking in his new surroundings, looking all around. He stopped to look, but soon felt Madoka's hand slide into his which he instinctively took, and a gentle pull on his arm muscles urging him to follow. He did as he was instructed but kept hold of his grip on

Madoka's hand, feeling a warmth at the female touch.

"Here comes Vissu." Madoka whispered to Zack, and he looked ahead, trying to focus in the darkness on the male approaching them.

"Good to see you safely." Vissu said in a gravelly voice. An ageing man with the appearance of a silver fox, he too was dressed in a three-quarter length black coat with an old-fashioned black button up cardigan underneath. Silvery white hair was swished back thickly on his head, with a tidy matching beard and moustache. Zack placed his age in his early sixties, but it was hard to tell in these conditions. He was stocky build, and just a little shorter than Echo but carried an unarguable air of authority about him without commanding it. Echo held out his hand and the two men shook, followed by Junko. Vissu then turned his attention to Madoka.

"My dear Madoka," Vissu started, "I wish I could talk you out of this. This crusade is no place for a woman as delicate as yourself." He held his hand out and Zack felt a pang of disappointment as Madoka let go of his so as she could take Vissu's hand in both of hers.

"I have told you so many times, I am half of my brother," Madoka looked towards Echo who was also looking directly at her, "and he is half of me. I know what I am getting into and I am strong enough to help."

Vissu then turned his attention to Zack, looking him up and down before proffering his hand.

"You must be the one that Junko has told me about." Said Vissu, not so much a question, more a statement to show that he already knew. Zack could not tell with the graveness of his voice if there was a hint of disappointment in it or not, but certainly expected there to be.

"I'm Zack." He stated, taking Vissu's hand and shaking it. There wasn't as much grip in the shake as Zack would have expected from the deepness of his voice and manliness of his rugged face.

"So, you're the one that Junko thinks will save us all?" Asked Vissu

"I'm afraid Junko places me on too high a pedestal," Zack replied, "but I am willing to do all I can to help." Vissu frowned at this statement and looked Zack up and down again.

"And you've left a free life to come here?" Vissu asked.

"Yes sir." Zack replied.

"Well, you're either unimaginably stupid or....actually I can't think of another option, but welcome anyway." Vissu stated before turning away and walking back into the midst of the small gathering. Zack stood where he was staring after the older man.

"He likes you." Madoka spoke first.

"Really, how can you tell?" Zack asked.

"He didn't kill you." Junko was the first to answer the question dryly before he and Echo walked over to the crowd that were currently surrounding Vissu and speaking quietly among themselves. Madoka again took Zacks hand.

"Come." She stated and they walked over towards the others together. It appeared as though everyone hushed to stop and stare at the stranger in their midst. Despite his limited time outside of the apartment Zack recognised a couple of the faces but knew no other names. He recognised one male as being on the transporter to the fields earlier in the day. The other face he recognised was the man he had spoken to before getting a pulley truck on his outing with Zero to collect the supplies. For reasons unknown the man still stared at Zack with as much disdain as he had previously. Maybe he just had a miserable face, who knew? Zack entered the throng and tried to introduce himself. Some were welcoming and some were cautious. After a couple of minutes of introductions Vissu spoke en masse to all gathered.

"It is time that we discuss the way forward. Junko's hope Zack is joining us today. I shall turn the floor over to him." Vissu announced. All eyes turned to Zack. Even in the darkness of the roof of the tower Zack felt like a spotlight was on him.

"Erm...what would you like me to tell you?" Zack asked, unsure of where to start and completely unprepared to be thrown in at the deep end. Nobody answered. "Maybe you should bring me up to speed with what has been discussed previously, this is my first time at one of these gatherings."

Inaudible murmurs circled the group and a then a voice rose from the darkness.

"Junko told us that you would know how to defeat the machines." The voice stated. Zack could not see who had spoken, but the voice was certainly male and gruff.

"I'm afraid Junko may not have been entirely accurate in his assumptions." Zack stated. He hated to let people down but in the split second that his brain took to assess his current dilemma he realised that it was better to be upfront with them rather than trying to blow smoke up their arse and let them down later. And besides, he had never made any promises to these people that he couldn't keep. There was a tangible tension that swept through the group that Zack could feel, like a charged electricity that glowed red in his mind, and all eyes spun towards Junko before resettling on Zack.

"Your poetry is the poetry of a warrior!" Another voice stated, rising slightly in volume although still not a shout that could be heard beyond the meeting place.

"Listen citizens we are on the verge of war," A voice stated

"I will never let my empire fall, gather your swords and shields. As long as I live my empire stands!" Stated another.

"These are just lyrics." Zack tried to stop them from getting carried away but clearly, they had memorised the words from his dissertation as if they were words from a religious book. Junko stood where he was, uncomfortable in the intermittent gaze of the crowd. Echo slunk away to sit on a chair with the rest of the group, finding sanctuary in the shadows. Madoka sensed Zacks embarrassment and stepped closer to him to give him strength, squeezing his hand with her own.

"Lyrics?" A voice asked, this time it was female.

"Words to music, songs from my time." Zack replied.

"Perhaps you should explain why you are here Zack." Vissu stepped out of the shadows and addressed him, sensing that confusion was extending the evening unnecessarily.

"Well," Zack started, as his eyes searched around for an escape route should he need one, "I'm going to be honest with you. I was approached by Echo, Junko and Madoka in my time. They believed that I was the saviour of the humans due to my writings that had somehow survived until your time, this time. I have to confess that the words were not my own. I wrote an essay for my university...."

"University?" The female voice spoke up again, not understanding.

"Erm....a place of education, where I went to learn." Zack tried to clear up the confusion.

"And what did you learn Zack?" It was Vissu who spoke, fixing Zack with his gaze.

"Not a lot if I'm honest." Zack admitted, never feeling so inadequate in his life as he did at that very moment.

"Then why are you here?" Vissu continued his interrogation.

"I didn't have a choice." Zack stated, grief washed over him as he recalled discovering Eva, "Things happened that made it impossible for me to stay. Things that I don't understand." The tension eased on the roof; the murmuring reduced. Zack could not physically see an emotion but could sense a degree of empathy with him. Before any more questions could be put to him that would alter the tide of energy he continued "I may not be able to help your cause, your crusade, in the way that you first envisioned, but with help I may be able to help in other ways, I want to help." He concluded.

"Zack understands computer language." Junko added in an attempt to make up for his previous misleading hopes with the group.

"That's right," Zack added, seizing the moment, "In the twenty first century I was a information technology specialist. I understand the codes of artificial intelligence. I know how to dissect the circuits of computers and....well.... fuck them up for want of a better word."

"What does fuck mean?" A voice at the back of the crowd called out. Zack struggled to see who had asked as it was dark. He did however notice that Flint had joined the gathering and he suddenly felt a little awkward in his saving the world speech. Flint walked over towards him and stood next to Echo.

"Look, maybe it would best if I listen to how far you have come as a group, and then I will be able to identify the best ways that I can assist." Zack metaphorically sidestepped the question and took a physical step backwards towards Madoka. He felt a comfort, a courage, a sanctuary in her presence. Vissu stepped forwards.

"Thank you for that input Zack." Vissu started, "We are twenty-four strong here, and with you, twenty-five. We meet every ten days to discuss ideas. I shall let you network with everyone here and hopefully we shall have some freedom within my lifetime."

The murmuring started up again and Zack began to walk among the people present.

For the next couple of hours Zack had many conversations with those present. He heard stories of loss, of inhuman treatment by the Zeydenians. His initial impressions of working in the fields of Rebristan had been akin to the American slavery in the eighteenth century, but as he spoke to more people and heard tales of unnecessary executions his views of Rebristan and the Zeydenian rule were swaying towards comparisons with the Nazi occupation of Europe during world war two. This made him fear his survival all the more, but at the same time made him all the more resolved to commit to ending this situation for the humans. He began to think of the group of people as if they were an underground resistance movement, much like those formed during the second world war. By the end of the evening, he was beginning to learn that his 'resistance', as he had come to think of them, had not progressed far in their efforts, and that a lot of hope had been placed on the plagiarised death metal lyrics of his dissertation. Hope wasn't remarkably high, but it also wasn't dead. Zack had established strengths within some of the gathering, and also identified that some had joined with no skills at all and simply wanted a place to vent their anger among likeminded people. The crowd started to leave in small groups, giving time between each departure so as not to arouse suspicion among any prying eyes. Echo and Junko left, leaving Zack with Madoka so as not to make their group look so large walking through the sector at this time of night.

"Zack." Vissu said. Zack turned to see the older man walking towards him.

"Yes sir." Zack replied.

"I have no idea why you have come to Rebristan. This truly is an existence of misery. But I am grateful if you are able to help. Thank you for coming tonight." It was the first piece of warmth that Zack had felt from the man, Zack was seeing a softer side to him.

"I will help where I can, I assure you. Unlike the people here who dream of freedom that you have heard in folk tales, I have experienced it, had it taken away from me, and yearn for its return." Zack stated.

"You best leave now, the coast will be clear of suspicion, and ensure that Madoka arrives home safely." Vissu stated.

Zack and Madoka turned towards the steps leading down to the inside of tower ten, and as the bright light of the tower interior enveloped them, the image of Vissu in the darkness disappeared.

18

Zack and Madoka exited tower ten and walked in the shadows towards their own. Madoka again took a hold of Zacks hand as they walked in silence. Reaching tower fourteen Madoka turned to Zack before they could enter.

"Come, I want to show you something." She stated and leading him by the hand, walked down the side of the tower towards the rear. There was an impenetrable darkness behind the building, a view that Zack had not seen in daylight other than in very brief passing on the work transport in the morning.

"Where are we going?" Zack whispered.

"You'll see." She replied. Zack looked deep into the darkness that just seemed to be as black as ink with no lights at all.

"I doubt that." Zack replied.

"It's where I go to feel free sometimes." Madoka stated. "I used to come here when I first started working in the fields. We won't need to whisper. We'll be free, of sorts."

Madoka continued to lead Zack further away from the tower. A couple of times Zack turned back to look at the towers behind him, only silhouetted by a faint white glow around the tops of them as the moon was on the far side casting limited light. Zack estimated that they had walked, treacherously, for about five hundred metres across the terrain, before it started to slope downwards. Another one hundred metres or so and Zack could no longer see the towers.

"Where are we?" Zack asked.

"I guess these were living quarters before the bomb." Madoka replied. "It's difficult to see in the dark but there is shelter here."

"I can't see a thing." Zack stated.

"It's ok, just stick close to me. I have been coming here for years in the dark. Mind the step." Madoka had hold of Zacks hand and he felt her rise upwards by about a foot. He expected a step but still managed to stub his toe.

"Ow, fuck!" Zack stifled a yell, still unsure of his surroundings, and Madoka giggled.

"What is this word that you keep mentioning this evening?" Madoka asked, "I have seen it written in the forbidden texts of the past, but you did not explain when asked at the meeting."

"That's because an explanation is exceedingly difficult. It has so many meanings, depending on the situation and the context in which it is used. It would be too difficult to explain." Zack stated, hoping that it would be left there.

"Why?" Madoka asked. Damn she was persistent, and reminded him of a small child anxious to know everything in the world believing that it can all by unlocked with just one word.

"Most of the meanings are not positive, it's mostly used as an insult or to add extremity to a phrase, and some I certainly could not reveal to a woman."

As Madoka continued to lead Zack in the darkness he formed the impression that they were in an area that had roof cover, possibly a cave, as his voice started to echo a little.

"Where are we?" Zack asked.

"This was your entrance to Rebristan." Madoka replied, "There will be something to sit on around here."

"My entrance?" Zack asked

"Yes, when we entered the cave on the beach and ported here, the same entrance in our time now does not exist but to venture deeper into the cave leads to this entrance. The water by the beach is about one mile from the other side of the towers. You were unconscious when we arrived. I thought you were dead." Madoka squeezed Zacks hand a little tighter at the thought. "We took it in turns to carry you here...."

"Wait, you carried me?" Zack asked

"Yes Zack, I am a strong woman." Madoka replied before starting off where she had been interrupted, "We had to wait for the cover of the night before we could smuggle you into the tower. You should not have come Zack. This is no life for you."

They sat in silence for a minute as Zack took in what Madoka had told him. He eventually broke the silence.

"Why do you stay here? He asked.

"What do you mean? I have no choice." Madoka replied with an element of surprise at the question.

"I mean, you can travel through time, something that I still don't fully understand, but why don't you travel to a time where you can be free?"

"It's not as simple as that." Madoka started, "I would be leaving family behind. The Zeydenians would hunt for me and they would kill those that are here. I cannot put mother, Echo or Zero through that."

"Why not take them with you, like you brought me to here?"

"And it nearly killed you Zack. Your porting was an emergency, but I cannot take that risk when they are alive here." Madoka stated. He could not see her but imagined that there was a tear rolling down her face due to the tone of her voice. Zak decided that a change of topic was required. In the darkness he somehow managed to find a stone seating area, at least he thought it was a seating area, it was stone and flat. He gently sat himself down on it, grateful to take the weight off of his legs and he felt Madoka sit down beside him.

"So, how do you get to be as old as yourself without a boyfriend or husband?" Zack asked.

"I know not of what you speak Zack." Madoka replied.

"You know, someone to love?"

"What is love?" Madoka asked

"Baby, don't hurt me." Zack sang out and stifled a giggle.

"I still do not understand." Madoka missed the humour in Zacks comments, which brought him back to seriousness.

"Love is.... jeez, how do I explain this?" Zack asked himself, "Love is when you have a companion who you have overwhelming feelings about. Someone you couldn't bear to be without"

"Someone like you Zack?" Madoka interrupted.

"Wait for it, I'm not finished." Zack added quickly, "Someone you want to share your life with, have experiences with, raise children with. Someone that you wouldn't want to share with another woman, or man in my case."

There was silence whilst Madoka thought over what had said, and Zack wondered what more he could add. He had never had to analyse love before, it was just always there.

"I had a child once." Madoka stated after a silence, there was a distinct sadness to her voice. "He was taken from me for another sector soon after birth."

"Why?" Zack asked, not knowing whether she knew the answer or not, nothing in this place seemed to make any sense, but also because he didn't know what else to say. He could barely see Madoka in the darkness and didn't know whether she could see him properly, but her comments had left the atmosphere as thick as the night and he wanted her to know that he was still there, still interested in what she had to say. He heard Madoka sniffle, and it scared him that this strong woman who had taken care of him since he had arrived in her time was breaking down. He felt like it was his fault for unknowingly steering the conversation that way. He reached in the darkness towards Madoka's breathing until his hand touched her shoulder. She startled a little at the touch initially but did not move away and Zack shuffled himself closer and put his arm around her shoulders. Madoka leant in and rested her head on his shoulder, placing an arm around his waist, she snuggled in.

"We have children, I don't know how, I don't know why." She started, "Every so often, as the populations of the sectors decrease, the manpower is replenished by the women. We become mothers, but they are not our child. They could be left with us, but mostly they are taken to where more humans are needed. In my case, my boy was taken to another sector to be raised by others."

"That's harsh." Zack exhaled a sigh as he spoke, "And what do the fathers think of this?" Zack felt Madoka raise her head and turn to look towards him. He felt her breath on his face.

"What do you mean?" Madoka asked.

"I mean the men that father these children, what do they think about the Zeydenians just taking them away?" Zack asked in more detail. He could see Madoka's face looking at him in the darkness. She appeared confused.

"There are no men there." She said after an uncomfortable pause. "Men can't have young Zack. It is the women who bear the new lives."

"Yes, but men surely have an input, so to speak." Zack was beginning to become confused by the way that the conversation was going. There was silence from Madoka, and this made him think that she was equally as confused. "So, where do you think babies come from?" Zack asked as he could see they clearly weren't on the same page and thought it was best to hear Madoka's understanding of reproduction.

"Females are taken from the sector to Zeydence, most feel like it is a big adventure leaving the sector for the first time. That is until they get there. We are kept captive in sterile dormitories, not seeing the outside for seven months. Soon after we arrive, we leave the dormitory. We are rendered into a deep sleep and a baby comes six months later. When I was there, I was with hundreds of other women, and we supposed that there was some sort of surgical procedure to put the baby inside us, no-one knows for sure, but the stomach swells and then the baby comes out." Madoka explained the human knowledge of having children as it was known now. Zack sat in silence for a while, not sure where to take the conversation next.

"So, you miss all the fun stuff then?" He finally asked, in an attempt at education and to try and lighten the mood.

"There is no fun in childbirth." Madoka retorted.

"Oh, I wouldn't imagine that there is," Zack replied, "I meant in the conception of the child."

"I have no idea what you are talking about." Madoka solemnly stated.

"Ok, I'm not sure now is the right time to try and explain." Zack said, "But it's something that generally two people in love do."

"Here we are back at this love thing you talk about. What is it?" Asked Madoka.

"It's difficult to explain." Zack started, "It can be the most wondrous feeling inside you mind ever, but it can also be the most painful too." He ended, recalling the moment with sadness that he had learned about Eva and Marshall.

"Well, perhaps it's better that it stays locked in the past then." Madoka added.

"No, you don't understand, it's when two people have feelings for each other that are greater than just liking someone, greater than just being friends with someone." Zack tried desperately to get his point across.

"Give me an example." Madoka requested.

"Well, for instance, if someone you like, such as Vissu, were to die and not be here anymore, would you cry?" Asked Zack. Madoka gave it some thought.

"Not really, I don't think. I'd be sad but I guess we all have to die one day." She replied.

"Ok, but if Zero were to die...." Zack started,

"How could you say such a thing?" Madoka retorted.

"You see, I've opened that emotion already. And by your response I would say that you would be infinitely more upset at that scenario?"

"Of course I would, it would kill Mama, and yes I would be truly upset if that happened." Madoka said, a slight wobble in her voice as she contemplated the scenario.

"Ok, that's because you love Zero, whereas you only like Vissu."

"Are you suggesting I should bear children with Zero?" A horrified Madoka asked.

"No, not at all." It was Zacks turn to sound flustered. "You asked for an example, and I'm showing you the difference. Vissu is a friend of yours, Zero is family. You have more of a connection with Zero and would miss him more if he were to no longer be here. That is how liking someone graduates into love. Now, if there were to be one special person that you could never imagine being without, wanting to be with them all the time and missing them terribly when they are not around, that is true love."

Madoka and Zack sat in silence trying to digest what he had just said.

"And how does that lead to babies?" Madoka finally asked.

"Well, when a couple, a male and female, are in 'true' love they can decide when they want to bring a new life into the world and share their love, and their values with the child. And they must do something in order to achieve this, which is the fun bit." Zack explained.

"And what is that?" Madoka asked. "We just go to Zeydence and wake up with a baby inside of us."

"I'm not sure now is the time to reveal all, you have a lot to take in." Zack said, "Do you have someone in your life that would make you feel that way?" He asked awkwardly.

"I don't know." Madoka answered, "I've only just learned of it. What else do people do in love?"

"Well, they would always want to be together, protect each other, hold hands I guess." Zack said this as he noticed that Madoka had taken his hand in the dark, "And they kiss. A lot."

"Do you love anyone Zack?" Asked Madoka as her thumb caressed the back of his hand. Zack thought long and hard before answering.

"Apart from my parents, there was a special person who I hoped to spend the rest of my life with." Zack stated, looking directly forward. Even though they were sitting in the dark he did not want to look at Madoka's face as he spoke about the past.

"Was?" Madoka questioned.

"Yeah. Turns out she loved someone else too." Zack stated, "And besides, she's dead now." Zack put on a hard facade, trying to act as if it didn't bother him. He had experienced so much hardship since being in Rebristan that the problems and pains of a previous time, seeming like a previous life, seemed almost irrelevant now, but not quite.

"So, what do you do now?" asked Madoka.

"Find someone else to love." Zack replied after a long pause, "Someone who loves me too. But that's going to be hard in a place like this where nobody seems to know what love is."

There was more silence, during which Madoka placed her other hand on top of Zacks and stroked it slowly. Zack hadn't seemed to notice before the distinct lack of wild animals, or any animals, in Rebristan but in that period of quietness when he was trying to think of anything else except Serene it struck him that he had not heard any birds chirping or dogs barking in the darkness. Madoka broke the silence.

"I think I would be upset if you were no longer here." She simply stated as she leaned her head into his shoulder in an effort to feel closer to him. Zack turned his head to look towards her. It was still quite difficult to see anything in such absolute darkness. After years of staring at a computer terminal at work it seemed like his eyes needed a little light in order to adjust to the darkness and be able to see, but he could feel Madoka. Feel her head on his shoulder as his breathing quickened and felt it rise and fall with his chest. Zack reached across his chest with his right hand and placed it under Madoka's chin, feeling her long hair stroke against his wrist as he did so. He started to lift her chin and turn her face towards his. There was no resistance from Madoka. Even in the darkness he could feel her eyes staring at him, and he wondered about his next move. Was he about to do something great or was he about to alienate his only friend in this world? She did not pull away, and he could feel her breath softly breathing onto his face. After what seemed like an eternity, he leant forward pursing his lips and pulled her face ever so gently closer to his. A quick peck on her lips and he pulled away, testing the water.

"What was that?" Madoka asked. Zack was astounded that someone of such beauty had never experienced or knew what a kiss was.

"I kissed you." Zack announced.

"It's nice." Madoka said. Her voice sounded light and airy and he imagined that she was smiling in the darkness. "Is this that love thing you speak of?"

"I guess so." Zack replied, non-committal, still not sure of himself and worrying in case it all went horribly wrong. "May I do it again?"

"I guess so." Madoka replied, unsure of the alien feelings coursing through her. Zack leant in again, and this time kissed her deeply, taking his arm and wrapping it around her shoulders to her back and pulling her close to him. Madoka reciprocated and also used her arms to hug Zack around his neck. Zack never wanted the kiss to end and his mouth opened slightly as his tongue darted out to gently lick at her lips. Kissing came naturally to Madoka, and Zack was pleased to see that the natural instinct had not died, it had just lain dormant for many generations. Zack tightened his grasp on Madoka's back, not uncomfortably so, but enough for him to feel her breasts press against his chest through her clothing as he pulled her towards him, to feel her chest heave and fall in faster succession as an excitement she had never experienced before overcame her. Madoka's hands held onto Zack equally as tight, as she ran them up and down his back either side of his spine. A sweat broke out on her forehead. Her heart pounded within her chest as if it wanted to break out of her body and she and her hands came towards Zack's front as she gently pushed him away. Breaking the seal between them Zack leant backwards and let his hands run from her shoulders to her own hands and held onto them at the fingertips.

"What....what is happening to me?" Madoka said breathlessly with a hint of fear, "It feels like my heart wants to leave my body."

"That's normal." Zack stated. "It's too complicated to explain, but it's an indication that you liked it...I hope." Madoka put her hand to her left breast.

"I think so." Madoka said, her voice had lightened a little and the fear was gone from it. "Is that what love is?"

"Part of it." Zack stated with a slight smile, still holding onto Madoka's fingertips and shaking her hand ever so slightly.

"I want to do the rest of it." Madoka announced excitedly. Zack giggled a little.

"Not right now." He replied. "There's plenty of time for that, and besides, it's getting late, we have to go to the fields in the morning." It hurt Zack with every bone in his body to say no, and the little brain in his trousers was straining to protest. It indeed took all of his willpower as his fingertips still tingled at Madoka's touch, but he was in a different time now. He needed to know more about his environment, before he threw his clothes off with reckless abandon as he would have done as a teenager. This was not a place or a time for unwanted pregnancies, and would there be consequences if someone fell pregnant without being taken away by the Zeydenians. Besides, Madoka had almost burst at being kissed, what would she be like if they had taken things further? In much the same way that he needed a step-by-step instruction guide to survive life in Rebristan, he felt that Madoka would need step by step instructions on what to expect from the next step of whatever it was they had. His answer soon came.

"If this is love, then I think I love you Zack." Madoka stated as she leant her head back into his chest. Zack wrapped his arms around her and hugged her gently.

"I think I love you too Madoka." He replied.

They both sat there in that position, for a few more minutes before Zack stood, still holding her hand. Without saying a word Madoka stood with him and he led her out of the cave that they had been in. His eyes had still not adjusted to the darkness and he could still see very little, but there had been a power shift within that kiss. No longer the stranger in a strange land being led by Madoka and relying on her for his safety, Zack left the cave with something to live for, something to die for, something to kill for. This time, despite not being able to see where he was going, his chivalrous instinct took over and he led the way, carefully and slowly, holding onto Madoka's hand tightly all the way back to tower fourteen.

19

The following morning Zack awoke with a new perspective. He still had thoughts of how hard life in Rebristan was, but the dark depression that had been settling over him had started to lift. He had a joyous reason to want to open his eyes, to want to leave the bedroom and be among other people. He had always found Madoka incredibly attractive, but thoughts generated by his testicles had largely been superseded by the necessity to just survive here. Following their kiss last night Zack now felt as though he had the skillset to have a distraction like Madoka, and between them they would survive together. He appreciated that whilst he was a newcomer to Madoka's world, that she would be a newcomer to the emotions that he had awoken in her. He made a conscious decision that he would not exploit the advantage that he had over her in that respect. His sleep had been light, full of the feelings that one would normally feel at the start of a new relationship, but he awoke feeling rejuvenated and wide awake. Zack sat up on the mattress that he slept on and leant forwards. Reaching down he gave his balls the obligatory morning scratch, just to pull them away from the sweaty inside of his legs, before removing his hand from the linen undergarments he'd been given since being in Rebristan. Stretching his arms out to welcome the morning. He looked across to the bed in the room and saw that Echo had just started to waken, whilst Zero snored fitfully, topping and tailing in the same bed as Echo. Zack stood up and reached for a gown to wear, deciding the leave the room before he was treated to another sight of the naked form of Echo going about his morning business. Walking into the living room he could hear someone clattering about in the kitchen. The balcony door was wide open, and Zack felt a welcome breeze blow in to caress his body and the smell of fresh air filled his nostrils. He sat at the table near to the balcony door and turned to see Madoka in the kitchen. She looked as beautiful as ever, but there was something different, a radiant glow, she just somehow looked happier with her lot in life. She stood there in a white linen gown, flowing gently in the brush of air that was weaving through the apartment, and her long dark hair hanging loosely down her back. Madoka turned to face Zack, and a smile on her face told him that she had no regrets. Life was hard in Rebristan and Zack tried to remember another time that he had seen her smile. He struggled.

"Good morning Zack." Madoka said, still smiling, as she walked towards him with a platter of food. She set the food on the table in front of him. Her right hand, that had just been carrying the food, reached down and stroked the right side of Zack's face and hair as she stood behind him. She caressed his jaw line rubbing upwards until her right thumb stroked his earlobe and her left hand settled on his left shoulder. It seemed a natural thing to do and Madoka did not know why she felt this closeness. Zack understood very well though, having been in this situation before in Serene many times. That the placing of a hand on the shoulder was a subconscious way of believing that the moment would pass too soon, that she feared he would run away, and that she would have the advantage of briefly slowing him to try and argue her case or plead. He had no intention of running away from her. For one, where would he go? He relied on her as much as she now relied on him. And besides, back in Serene, he would be mocked and ridiculed if he were to run from someone as beautiful as Madoka. In another involuntary action Zack's right hand came up to his left shoulder and he patted Madoka's hand softly a couple of times before stroking downwards and pausing on her fingertips.

"Good morning." Zack replied, "What did I do to deserve this?" He asked as he surveyed the cooked breakfast before him.

"I don't know." Madoka replied, and it really seemed as though she were searching for an answer, "I just felt like it."

As Zack started to tuck into his food, Zero came out of the bedroom rubbing his eyes and yawning.

"I can smell food." Zero announced in between yawns and pushing his hair off of his face.

"I've cooked the morning food for Zack." Madoka called back to him.

"Is there any left for me?" Zero asked, an air of caution in his question as he poised for a potential answer that he didn't want to hear.

"Of course." Madoka replied as Zero visibly perked up and hurried towards the table, "I wouldn't cook food and not save any for my favourite little man, would I?" she asked as Zero sat at the table next to Zack and she ruffled her hand through his hair. Zero eyed up Zacks platter of cooked vegetables and potatoes as Madoka turned to get a serving for him. Setting it down in front of Zero she then sat down with some food for herself opposite Zack. They ate in silence and were eventually joined by Echo, fully clothed as a bonus, who served himself from the kitchen. Zack couldn't help but stare at Madoka as she ate, and she often looked up at him, before looking away quickly with a smile, unsure as to why she was feeling so elated inside. Keisa emerged from the bedroom and walked towards the kitchen. There was a tangible presence of happiness in the building that she could sense. Keisa couldn't help but fear the bubble bursting. She had known happiness herself and she had known how far the spirit falls when it is snatched away from you, and as she stared at her small family in front of her, she felt fear for them that the smiles would not last. As the clatter of cutlery on crockery diminished and it became apparent that all present had eaten their fill, Madoka stood to clear the plates away to the kitchen.

"Leave that Maddie." Keisa interjected, as she moved from the living room towards the table, "I'll clear those." Madoka stopped in her tracks and looked towards her mother. She had, until then, been unaware of Keisa's presence.

"If you're sure Mama." Madoka replied.

"Of course, you've done good this morning and you have a hard day ahead of you." Keisa replied.

Zack and Echo stood too, realising that time was rapidly approaching to go to the fields. Zero continued to eat noisily, as if he hadn't seen cooked food for a long while and was afraid that it would disappear as soon as the others left the room. Keisa stepped forward and gave Madoka a hug, a rare display of affection from her, and it took Madoka aback a little before she returned the hug.

"Be careful out there today." Keisa wished aloud as she hugged Madoka.

"I'm always careful Mama." Madoka replied, "It's just another day."

Keisa released her hug from Madoka and stepped back taking a look towards Echo and then Zack in turn. "You two be careful too." Keisa said to them and then turned to clean the table, sparking a glance of fear from Zero at her approach. Zack stepped into the bedroom and emerged a couple of minutes later wearing suitable clothing for the fields and joined Echo and Madoka at the door to the apartment ready to leave.

The breeze was not as pronounced at ground level as it was through the balcony door high above them now, but what little was blowing around carried a humidity from the nearby waters and a dust from the ground which seemed to settle around Zacks shoes. It was a very warm, humid day, and Zack did not look forward to toiling all day in the fields to help the 'slave masters', as he had come to think of them, to simply function. He stood with the crowds of people all silently accepting their lot in life awaiting the transport. Not much was spoken although he occasionally felt Madoka's hand brush his own by his side, and would turn to see her looking forwards but with the unmistakeable curve of a smile on her lips. Junko joined them and touched Echo on the shoulder to silently announce his arrival. Echo looked towards him.

"Good morning friends." Junko said as he looked along the three of them standing in the crowd. "Looks like it will be a hot one."

"I would rather this than the rainy season." Echo replied. "I don't think there is ever a perfect day to go to the fields, but that is the worst for me."

Madoka nodded in agreement and Zack weighed up the choices, based on his limited knowledge of Rebristan working life so far, and thought to himself that he should agree with Echo's statement too. They still had twenty minutes before the transport would arrive, and Zack dared to try and hold Madoka's hand, unsure as to how it would be received in such a public arena. She didn't protest but she did lean in closer to him so that it would not be as noticeable to those around them. Zack looked down at his hand as their fingers entwined, feeling such a rush from the warmth of meaningful physical contact with someone after so long. He looked up to Madoka's face and saw that her eyes met his, smiling with them before looking ahead again. As he turned his head, he saw that Junko was looking at their hands, so his discretion had not gone completely unnoticed.

As the minutes ticked slowly by there was still an estimated fifteen minutes before the transport would arrive, but a murmur started among the crowd. A tangible panic moved through the air like electricity. The kind of force that could not touch you but could still make the hairs on your neck stand up. People were looking to the right of them, the direction from which the transport would arrive, and Zack assumed it had turned up early. He tried to stare through the throng of people but could not see the huge vehicles that he had seen the day previous. And yet the panic seemed to intensify. He noticed some of the crowd starting to move slightly backwards, particularly the females among them.

"What's going on?" Zack whispered to Madoka, noticing the smile she had been sporting all morning was no longer present.

"I need you to promise me something." Madoka simply replied, neither answering Zacks question or quelling the apprehension that he was beginning to feel.

"Anything." Was the simple and abrupt answer he gave her.

"Whatever happens, you just get on the transport." Madoka said. Zack craned his neck to try and look above the crowd towards the direction of their attention. He failed to see the transport towering above them and was still a little confused with the situation. He turned his attention back to Madoka.

"Sure." Zack replied, "But what's going on?" As he finished the question Madoka did not answer. He realised that a complete silence had come across the crowd. Each person shuffled nervously from side to side, but still there was little sound as they did so, no-one wanted to bring any attention to themselves. With this silent shuffling Zack found that he was somehow closer to the front of the crowd without actually moving anywhere, and now stood just three or four rows from the front. He felt an ever so slight tugging on his hand as Madoka attempted to blend into the crowd behind them. As the people thinned out he saw two vehicles stopped about twenty metres in front of them. They were identical, black in colour and low down. They looked a lot like sports cars of the twenty first century, but were double wide, as if you could fit seven people across the back seats, and had three rows of back seats each. The front compartment had just a single, central driver's seat that was cocooned away from the rest of the interior. As Zack stared at the vehicle the first row of rear doors opened scissor style protruding upwards towards the sky. As he stood there, he had a strange and random thought that if the vehicles had approached with their doors up he would have seen them above the crowd a lot earlier. A male dressed all in black stepped out of the vehicle followed by three Zeydenian soldiers, all carrying their guns at their sides. Madoka was still tugging onto his hand and he turned to look at her. He saw a fear etched into her face; unlike anything he had seen on this strong resourceful woman before.

"What's happening?" Zack mouthed to her again, but she said nothing, just continued to pull slightly on him and tried to disappear among the people behind her. It appeared as though she could no longer see Zack, despite gripping onto his hand tightly, but just seemed to look straight through him at what was going on ahead.

Zack heard someone try to muffle a sob behind him. Echo and Junko seemed to know what was happening as they shuffled forwards slightly either side of Madoka and seemed to try and let her hide behind them.

"Humans of sector sixty-nine!" A voice boomed behind him and Zack turned eyes front to see that the male who had gotten out of the vehicle was addressing them. As he did so he lost his grip on Madoka's hand. The male was over six feet tall, dressed head to toe in black clothing and had slicked back short black hair. Zack got a sense that he should know who he was, that they had been in each other's presence before but just could not place him.

"As you are aware there have been some losses in recent days." The male continued. The silence among the gathering was almost painful. Hushed whispers among the crowd carried the word 'Seraph' to Zacks ears, and he assumed that this was who the male was. The Zeydenian soldiers stepped up level with him, three from the same vehicle that Seraph had arrived in, and four from the one behind. Zack expected Seraph to say more but apparently, he had said all he had to. He just stood there and surveyed the crowd. Then he pointed. There was a gasp, a sob and a soldier stepped forward heading in the direction of Seraph's indication. The crowd parted slightly as the soldier reached them and reached behind two males about ten feet to Zack's left. With a tug of the soldiers arm he extracted a female from the crowd. She only looked to be about seventeen years old, slim with long blonde hair down her back. Two more soldiers stepped forwards staring at the males she had been standing between. They stood stock solid with gritted teeth as she was dragged back towards the vehicle, looking back at them with desperation in her eyes. Once she was sat into the vehicle the soldier returned to stand by the open door, guarding the vehicle. Seraph pointed again and another soldier followed his direction, this time about fifteen feet to the right of Zack. There was a scream as a female was pulled from the crowd, this one appeared to be younger than the first, resisting as she was dragged towards the vehicle, trying to dig her heels into the dusty earth around her.

"She's just a child herself!" a male voice called out from within the crowd as the female reached the vehicle door. Seraph stood emotionless surveying the crowd from left to right. As the soldier reached the vehicle with his prey, she broke free, turned on her heels and ran back towards the crowd.

"Papa!" she shouted as she ran, arms aloft towards the direction of the previous protest from the crowd. Onlookers gasped and fear spread among them, they started to part as the female crossed the twenty metres of barren ground at speed. Zack watched her desperation as she ran, wondering in a split second why the soldier did not give chase. He looked towards the soldier only to see him with his Zey Co2 gun raised pointing at the female as she ran. The crowd moved a bit quicker, parting the way for her to run into the arms of the man she called Papa. He held his arms out for her and she ran into them. He was an older man, appearing to Zack to be about fifty years of age, with grey balding hair and clothing that appeared tattered. As he crouched to embrace her there was a whistling noise in the air. An explosion of blood released from the back of the older man and Zack saw his eyes glaze over. There was no more sound as the man and his daughter toppled to the ground. As they fell, in their embrace, Zack saw a reddening growing on the back of the girl's white linen top. He realised that whatever had struck her had passed right through both the girl and her Papa. There was nothing that could be done for them as the breeze started to blow dust over their lifeless bodies on the ground, still in embrace.

"If you are foolish, we will require more!" Seraph shouted at the crowd. There was no need to shout as there was a stunned silence, but shout he did. Seraph then looked around the crowd and pointed again, this time to Zack's left, about five metres away. A soldier stepped forward and a female was dragged out of the crowd. There were muffled sobs within the crowd but there was no protest from the female as she was led to the vehicle. Seraph pointed again, and this time Zack thought he was pointing straight at him. He froze on the spot as a soldier approached him and reached into the crowd. A wave of relief went through him as the soldier grabbed the person in front of him. Zack had thought this person to be a male, but it wasn't. This female had her hair shaved and wore masculine clothing, but as she sobbed it was apparent to Zack that she was all woman.

"Due to the mistakes of your companions laying here," Seraph started, casting a glance to towards the young girl and the old man in the dust, "We shall require one more today." Zack expected there to be a collective sigh of relief that it was almost over, but there wasn't, there was still fear of one more to be chosen. Zack noticed that Seraph was staring straight at him, still not completely aware of what was going on he felt fear, then courage, then fear again as

Seraph's gloved hand raised to point towards him again. A soldier stepped forwards and Zack subconsciously held his breath as the armour plated being silently approached. He stepped to one side and the soldier nudged him as he passed. Looking behind him Zack saw the soldier reach into the crowd between Junko and Echo. Horrified as the female that was pulled roughly from the crowd was Madoka. Echo had stepped aside and was stood side by side with Zack now. Madoka glanced into Zacks eyes with fear but also a tinge of stubbornness. Zack's chest rose up as he considered his options and glanced at the soldier's gun, weighing up in a split second if he would be able to take it from him. Echo nudged Zack hard from the side and he stumbled onto his backside on the ground. With the commotion behind him the soldier spun around and released his gun into his left hand, whilst retaining his grip on Madoka with his right. Zack looked up at the helmet that the soldier wore. There were no signs of life within the face guard, no eyes, just a black opaque square plate in the front. As he looked down, he saw that the soldier had his gun pointed towards him, and then he heard Madoka shout.

"No!" she shouted and the guard spun his head to look at Madoka. For the second time in what appeared to be seconds, Zack wondered if he could take the gun from the hands of the soldier again, but Madoka continued once she had the soldier's attention, "I am coming with you, and he is going to the fields." she pleaded. The soldier looked back at Zack. Echo had put one foot across so that was in between Zacks legs as he sat on the ground with his knees raised. Zack thought this was an attempt to stop him from getting up, and conscious of a gun pointed directly at him, a gun that he had seen used to devastating effect just moments earlier, he relaxed backwards placing his hands behind his back to brace himself. There was a war of emotions going on inside his head. The thoughts hurt so much as he tried to find an answer but knew that there was not an answer without creating another problem, it throbbed like a knot tightening inside his skull. The soldier looked towards Seraph and Zack followed his gaze. There was nothing from Seraph, no instruction, no emotion, nothing. After, what seemed like eternity, the soldier lowered his gun and continued to lead Madoka to the waiting vehicles. She looked back at Zack, mouthing that she would be ok, but he didn't know whether she was just saying that to save his life or whether she meant it. Junko and Echo shifted closer to Zack as she was led away, and others crowded around him as he sat on the floor. The familiar rumbling of the work transport approaching could be heard in the distance, and as Zack finally managed to stand up among the throng of people, he saw that the vehicles that had carried Seraph and the guards into the sector, as well as carrying Madoka and the other females out, had gone. Silently. Gone.

20

The day in the fields was hard. Zacks head had not spun, nor his heart beat so hard since he had discovered the body at Eva's house. Prior to that he had led a sheltered life and to be honest, the previous experience had not had real closure to it before being whisked away to Rebristan. He had to be physically restrained on the transport to the fields by Echo, Junko, and another male that he had never met before. He knew that the Zeydenians on board the transport would have killed him in an instant, without guilt, without feelings, but his rage was so uncontrollable, as if there were a demon within him trying to extricate itself from his very soul. He could sense the anger from Echo and Junko as well, but they were somehow more restrained than he was. He recalled the words that Madoka had spoken to him before the selections: "Whatever happens you just get on the transport." He had promised her that he would do anything. And he had kept his promise, he had gotten onto the transport, but that didn't mean he couldn't have feelings of rage, hatred towards the Zeydenians and urges to kill them all, as impossible as that task would be. Eventually he started to calm down physically, although mentally his mind was still running wild, as Echo reminded him that he would need to conserve his energy for the fields if he wanted to survive long enough to enact all of the threats he had been making. As they got to the fields, where Zack was to spend the day harvesting Trokine for the benefit of the very people that had taken Madoka from him Echo tried to life his mood.

"She survived this before. She will be well." Echo had said.

"The first time was like this?" Zack had asked, but Echo did not reply, he just looked blankly ahead as they exited the transport into the fields.

The day had been long. Seconds felt like hours. Each minute that passed was full of thoughts of Madoka. Echo and Junko refused to discuss what had happened with Zack, telling him that they should not bring attention to their concerns whilst in the company of the Zeydenians. Every so often the hardship of working the fields took Zacks mind away from the traumatic experience he was undergoing as if the pain of hard labour was becoming a solace to him. But that didn't last. Madoka was never far from his mind, and every time that he suddenly recalled that she was no longer standing beside him his body jerked. An involuntary jerk that started in the pit of his stomach and caused his chest to leap forward as a grunt escaped his mouth with a rush of oxygen. This was swiftly followed by a war within his mind as he fought the instant depression it brought to him and his mind raced to find the solution. It felt like his brain would spin ten times faster than it ever had done before, and in a split second he would experience the highs of believing he had found the answer only to be thrown into the depths of despair as, before the split second had ended, he realised that his solution would bring further unsolved problems. His brain would rush to hold it all together as he sought to solve the sub-problems until it felt like it was tying itself into one big knot that throbbed with a dull ache and sapped his energy. At one point he got angry and swung the scythe he was using to cut the Trokine recklessly. As he did so this caught the back of his calf and he looked down to see blood seeping through the white cotton of his trousers. The sudden sharp pain was such a rush and overthrew the dull ache in his mind that his problems had been causing. The sight of the seeping blood threw his adrenaline levels into the air and he suddenly felt re-energised, ready to fight the world again, until the cut to his leg started to throb and the sharpness of it's impact subsided. As the pain numbed, he was brought down with the realisation that no matter how ecstatic the release had been, the injury ultimately had not solved his wider problem. Zack took a moment to sit on the ground in the fields, confident that none of the Zeydenian guards could see him slacking and rolled up his trouser leg to look at the wound. He was happy to see that it was a superficial cut, and one that must have bled due to blood pressure that was being caused by his stress and fear. He tore a strip of cotton from one of his sleeves, using the scythe to assist in starting the tear, and tied this around his calf muscle to help cease the bleeding. Zack looked to his left and saw that Echo stood about ten metres away, cutting through the Trokine with one hand, and with his other hand he was making gestures towards Zack to get up quickly. Zack did as he was bid and stood up, the sharp pain that had caused him such a release moments earlier was now just a dull throb with an edge of sting. As he raised his head, he saw a Zeydenian guard casually walking past their crop line and he scythed away as if he had never stopped working for them. And so that became the rest of the day. His mind still spun, and he was frustrated that the dilemma was making his work far more harder than it already was.

By the time the sun was starting to set, and they were boarding the transport to go back to the sector, Zack was exhausted. He did not need to be restrained to his seat for his own safety on the return journey as he had no energy to protest anymore. As the transport arrived at the towers of sector sixty-nine Echo turned to Zack.

"We'll talk when we are within the safety of the home." Echo stated. Again, he did not look directly at Zack, just stared straight ahead to the back of the seat in front of him.

They left the transport in silence and made their way to the apartment. Junko joined Echo and Zack as they entered and the door closed behind them. Zero came running out of the bedroom to greet them and stopped dead in his tracks when he could see that something was not quite right, even though he hadn't quite worked out what it was as yet. Echo walked over to one of the seats and sat himself down. Zack joined him as Junko stood still in the centre of the room as if he were fixed to the spot by Zero's stare. Eventually Zero turned to face Echo and Zack.

"Where is Madoka?" Zero asked. Zack stared blankly ahead as he still didn't quite understand what was happening himself.

"She is not with us." Echo replied. Zack looked towards him and saw that the graceful figure of Keisa had joined them in the living room. She stood silently, but Zack noted a tear on her cheek with a wet line from the corner of her right eye. "I'm sorry Ma, they took her this morning." Echo continued.

"Is now the time to explain to me what is going on?" Zack asked, suddenly re-energised by Keisa's pain. This lady had been so kind to him since he arrived in Rebristan that he could not sit back with Echo's 'oh well, it just happened, nothing I can do' attitude. He wanted to help to take her pain away in the hope that it would quell his own pain too.

"I thought this would happen." Keisa said, with a quiver of emotion in her voice, "I had a feeling this morning that today would turn out to be pain."

"She has been taken for repopulation." Echo simply stated as Zack stared into the soul of Keisa, willing it to heal.

"What does that mean?" Zack asked, turning to Echo. He had an inkling of what it meant, but did not want to believe that he was right. This time Echo turned to face him.

"It means she will have a child. Or two. As we are from the same birth, there is more chance of her repopulating the workforce quicker. If she survives, she will return in the next year." Echo stated matter of factly.

"And if she doesn't?" Zack asked.

"We will never know." Echo replied, "She returned before so we must hope that she will on this occasion too."

"And they just get away with this?" Zack asked incredulously. He had more questions than answers at this time.

"You saw this morning what happens when someone protests." Junko answered this time.

"At least this way I stand an outside chance of seeing my sister again." Echo replied, looking to the floor in front of him as he did.

"This is what we hoped and believed that you would be able to stop when we came to your time, but that was a failure." Junko added.

"That, or me?" Zack asked going on the defensive.

"We need to stop now." Keisa interjected. "What's done is done, it has always been the way, and arguing among ourselves will not provide a better outcome. Let's just hope we see Madoka again one day." With that Keisa lowered her head, an inevitable sadness evident in her last few words, and she retreated back to her bedroom where the door closed behind her.

"I won't allow this to happen." Zack stated, more to himself than anyone else in the room, "I won't be that failure you speak of." This time he looked directly at Junko as he stood up and walked towards the apartment door.

"Where are you going?" Echo asked, a degree of panic now in his voice as the door glided open.

"To succeed." Zack looked him in the eye as he replied, and then stepped outside of the apartment with the door closing behind him.

Leaving tower fourteen, the darkness enveloped Zack as he walked with purpose away from it. He was still not entirely sure how this whole place worked, who was safe and who wasn't. But he no longer cared, no longer felt fear at what might happen. As far as he was concerned, the worst had already happened, and he couldn't sit on a sofa with an 'oh well, that's just how it is, we'll see if it pans out next year' attitude. He was a doer, and if it killed him, he needed Madoka to know, wherever she may be, that he had tried his best to shelter her from pain, fear and suffering. He received a few strange looks from other people making their way back to their apartments as he walked with speed towards tower ten. It was almost as if they had never seen someone with determination before, as if they just accepted their lot in life. Zack wondered if any of them feared him, or feared his reason for walking so strongly. He wanted to run, wanted to get started on getting Madoka back as soon as possible, but he too feared the consequences of drawing too much attention to himself, but the urge to run was becoming overwhelming. Once he was inside the entrance doors to tower ten, he strode immediately over to the elevator. There were a couple of people, stragglers from returning from the fields, waiting in front of him. They stood in silence. The elevator doors opened in front of them, and Zack pushed past them to get inside. The two people glanced briefly at each other but said nothing, and quietly filed in behind Zack. Zack pressed the button for the top floor many times as if it would somehow make the elevator go faster. It wouldn't of course, but he was struggling to hide his impatience. The other two occupants of the elevator looked on at his strange behaviour. They looked at each other and one could tell they were trying to establish who would be the bravest and dare interrupt this madman's quest by pressing a different floor's button. Neither went for it and silently resigned to travelling to the top floor with Zack before continuing their journeys as they turned to face the elevator doors as they closed. The elevator rushed heavenward at its usual insane pace; however, it was still not fast enough for Zack as he paced back and forth at the rear of the moving room. Eventually, after what felt like an eternity, the elevator slowed to a halt. As it did so, Zack squeezed himself between the other two patrons of the elevator, who politely stood slightly aside to let him through, and were trying to squeeze sideways as if it would aid him in getting through the door any quicker. Standing in the communal hallway Zack looked around him. It had only been one day since he first met Vissu, but he had headed to tower ten in such a rage that he had to take some time to remember where to go. His heart was pounding as he subconsciously turned left and strode to the end of the hallway. The last door on the right looked familiar to him and he hammered on the door with the side of his clenched fist. Four knocks on the door seemed to indicate impatience rather than just three. A brief pause, no longer than a few seconds and then he was hammering again, this time five knocks. Silent faces started to peer out of other doors along the corridor. Zack paid no heed to them and barely heard the familiar swoosh of the doors closing. On the third round of knocking Zacks fist was pulled to the left as the door started to swoosh open at the exact same time that his fist connected with the metal of the door. Before he could say something, a withered hand reached out and grabbed him by the collar, dragging him into the apartment. Zack had barely taken a breath before the door swooshed shut behind him. Stumbling forwards slightly he reached a hand out to regain his balance and turned to see the old man standing in front of him with his back to the door.

"What is the meaning of this?!" Vissu demanded. After all the huffing and puffing Zack realised he hadn't thought through what he wanted to say.

"They've taken her." Zack started, that was about as much as he had got at that time.

"I know." Vissu replied dismissively, "It happens. Why are you here?"

"What do you mean why am I here?" Zack shouted, anger rising inside of him, "We need to rescue her of course!"

"Are you crazy? That can't happen." Vissu mocked. "I know you're new around here and we have bent over backwards to save you and keep you hidden in plain sight, but talk like that will get us all killed."

"So, you just do nothing?" Zack was gobsmacked.

"She's one human Zack. Three were taken this morning, and that's just from sector sixty-nine. Undoubtedly, many more would have been taken from the other sectors. Tomorrow more could be taken from countless sectors for repopulation. Are you going to save them all?"

"So, what's the fucking point of your meetings!?" Zack demanded.

"I don't think you've been involved long enough to be asking such questions or demanding answers young man." Anger started to rise in Vissu's voice.

"I seem to be the only one in this hell that seems to be prepared to take action and move forwards!" Zack matched the anger in Vissu's voice and raised it, "Talking about it doesn't save lives."

Vissu glared at him but before he could say anything Zack continued "I can see I've come to the wrong place," Zack continued, "I'm gonna have to do this on my own." Zack turned to leave.

"This expedition is unsanctioned!" Vissu stated with as much authority as he could muster.

"Like I give a fuck." Zack replied calmly, stopping to turn his head and stare at Vissu as his last word rang out around the apartment. He turned back to the door and pressed the button for it to open, before leaving. As the door closed behind him Vissu stood where he was silently seething.

The walk back to tower fourteen was less frantic than when he had marched to Vissu's. His mind was working overtime as he walked. All day in the fields he had had this idea that the great man Vissu would be the saviour of his problems, would know the answers. But as it turned out he was nothing but an old man that spun propaganda. An old man with no strength, no desire, no courage, other than to find likeminded souls to whom he could spout his venom about the Zeydenians, and they would nod in approval. Zack wondered how welcome he would be back at Keisa's given the way that he had walked out, but what was his alternative? He was in a sector in a future version of the planet he had once lived on. He had no-one here, except Madoka who had been taken from him, and the frayed tethers of an acquaintance with various members of her family and sector sixty-nine. With his head bowed down, staring at the floor, he walked into the entrance of tower fourteen, bathed in the light that shone as he walked towards the elevator.

As he reached his floor, he wandered slowly towards the door to the apartment. If these people could so easily cast off a daughter, sister, who had been essentially kidnapped to be forced into pregnancy, how would they react to a practical stranger, such as himself, returning after a hissy fit? Would his handprint even work on the door now? Had his temper sealed his fate? There were a million questions spinning around his head as he sought an answer to appease his newfound companions whilst secretly planning his own operation to save the woman he now had great feelings for. Zack never made it to the door though. Ahead, at the end of the corridor he saw movement and heard the now familiar metallic glide of footsteps. The light at the end was dark but as the movement continued towards him he saw the orange breastplates of two Zeydenian guards approaching him. Zack froze momentarily trying to expel the whirlwind of thought processes he had previously been having about rescuing Madoka and keeping Echo happy. He now had a new problem to face. Not knowing if they were here for him or not, he considered that if they saw him going into Echo's apartment whether it meant trouble for them too. Despite everything he could not bring trouble to their doorstep, so he continued to walk past the door of his own apartment and towards the Zeydenian guards. As they approached, they stepped either side, forcing Zack to walk in the middle of the corridor. He gave a polite nod to them as he attempted to pass, but as they all became level he felt himself lifted off of his feet. Each guard taking one of his arms and lifting him so that he no longer had control of his direction. Without looking at him the guard on the right spoke.

"No noise and you will live." Said the guard. Zack obeyed.

As he was carried, facing behind the guards, past the door to where he had been living, he saw that it opened slightly. The familiar swoosh noise cut through the air but did not seem to disturb the guards as they continued walking towards the elevator. Zack looked towards the opening door and saw Zero poke his head out, his eyes wide with fear. As fearful as he felt himself, Zack gave him a look of calm and willed for him to go back inside. Zero's head disappeared back inside the apartment and Zack was relieved to hear the door swooshing shut again. His concern then turned to anger as a million thoughts crashed through his mind about who could have created this predicament for him. Surely it was too soon for Vissu to have informed on him, which meant it had to be one of the people he had been sharing his life with recently. They arrived at the elevator and as they entered it, Zack was turned to face the back wall before being placed back onto his feet.

"May I ask...." Zack started

"No." came the one syllable response

The elevator descended to the ground floor and Zack was shoved out of it into the entrance hall. As he was roughly pushed towards the entrance door a vehicle pulled alongside the doorway. It was a similar vehicle to the one that had taken Madoka away from him earlier in the day. Zack began to panic and thought to run, but where? Thought to struggle, but knew the result would be death. A million thoughts gouged a furrow through his mind as to what he should do. He tried to assimilate the situation to what he would have done in Serene in the twentieth century, tried to think of all the drunken conversations he had had with Marshall and Jeff about what they would do if they got innocently caught up in a terrorist attack. He recalled that their collective answer would be that they would fight to the death as death was inevitable if they didn't. But here, in Rebristan, it was a totally different setup. He didn't have familiar surroundings to seek sanctuary, he was essentially alone, and when he weighed up his options death was inevitable if he fought against the situation, as he had witnessed earlier. But Echoes words came back to him, that if they left things be, it would be the best chance he would have of seeing Madoka again one day. Fighting against every fibre of his soul that advised otherwise Zack succumbed to be placed into the rear of the vehicle as the scissor doors opened, and then closed behind him. Once the doors closed, he was in darkness.

21

It seemed as though they had been driving for about half an hour or so before the vehicle stopped. The drive had been in silence. Zack had sat in the rear seat of the vehicle with the Zeydenian guards that had abducted him from tower fourteen sitting either side of him. Zack was not sure who was driving the vehicle or the reason for his taking. In all honesty he was crapping himself. When the scissor doors opened the light did not improve. The guards stepped out of either side of the vehicle leaving Zack sat in the middle.

"Out." One of the guards directed towards Zack. He was a little disorientated as to where the voice had come from but chanced him arm in sliding along the seat to the left-hand side and putting his feet outside on the ground.

"Up." Came the second monosyllable command from the guard and Zack complied by standing up straight.

"What now?" Zack asked.

"Follow." The guard commanded as he turned his back to Zack and strode forward a couple of steps. The second guard had come around the back of the vehicle and was stood behind Zack.

"Oooh, words of two syllables," Zack said sarcastically as he stepped forward, "Evolution has progressed."

Zack felt a bump in his back as the second guard gave him a nudge with the butt of his weapon. The first guard paid no heed to Zacks sarcasm, and he was sent stumbling forward a few steps before he regained his composure. The three walked again in relative silence towards a dark building that Zack could just make out about fifty metres in front of him. Zack began to feel more confident. He had witnessed first-hand the barbarism of the Zeydenian guards in the morning, but this felt different. He was not restrained in any way, and with the exception of a nudge in the back no weapons had been presented at all throughout the whole experience. Zack braved to look around him a little and there was no reprisal. For the most part everything was dark wilderness. Zack saw the vehicle that had brought him here move away and speed off silently towards the horizon. He didn't know what to make of this. On the one hand it was one less guard to worry about, but on the other it indicated that he would not be returning from wherever he was now. Zack sensed that he was near to the fields but the building in front of him was far smaller than the wall of the fields. Finally, they reached the foot of the building and stopped. Without any lights to assist it was difficult to gauge how big it was, but Zack guessed it was at least four storeys high. The first Zeydenian guard touched a patch on the wall and a door opened in front of them. Zack shielded his eyes from the sudden light that hit them. After so much darkness it felt painful, but he didn't have time to complain as he was shoved from behind through the door falling to his knees. The two guards followed him inside and the door swiftly closed. Zack waited on his knees and took a look around his surroundings. So far he could see a white walled room with two doors off of all sides of it, apart from the front through which he had just come. Brightly lit but no furniture, it was like being inside an opaque cube.

"Up." Came the voice from behind him. Zack pushed up with his hands until he was standing on his feet. He turned to face the guards who had brought him in. He saw that only one of them carried a weapon. The other gestured to a door on the right on the back wall of the room. Zack turned to look at it, as the guard stepped forward of him and made his way to the door. Zack followed. As all three reached the door the Zeydenian guard held a gloved hand to it and the door opened. Beyond the doorway was darkness, but as the guard stepped in the lights ignited and came to life. Zack followed until all three were inside and the door closed behind them. There were chairs in the room with their backs towards the left-hand wall.

"Sit." The rear Zeydenian guard ordered, and Zack did as he was bade, looking up at the two guards in front of him. As he did so their hands went to the helmets on their heads and started to remove them. As they came off Zack recognised the two guards to be people he had met before. As the first guards helmet came off, the one who had given most of the orders, his slick black hair and ghostly white face looked familiar to Zack as the one whom he had met when Madoka was mad at him for helping Zero getting the supplies on his first venture outside of the apartment, Diarran. The other male was Flint, whom Zack had met a couple of times, most recently at Vissu's apartment the night before.

"Must I keep saving you Zack sixty-nine?" Diarran spoke.

"Why am I here?" Zack asked. Diarran did not answer. He walked towards another door at the opposite end of the room which opened at his approach.

"We must discuss your future here in Rebristan." Flint finally answered as Zack watched Diarran walk through the doorway out of sight. "But first I must change. Sit." Flint commanded as he followed in the direction of Diarran, and the door closed behind him. Zack was left alone and likened the room to a padded cell.

It was difficult to tell how long he had been in the room whilst they went to 'get changed'. There were no clocks, windows, or any noises to which Zack could assimilate any sense of time to. Staring at the walls lost its appeal fairly quickly and eventually Zack felt himself sliding off of the chair on which he sat to be sitting on the floor, until he slowly curled up into the foetal position. Such was his boredom that his mind switched off and he drifted into a deep sleep. He was awoken by a strong hand taking him by the scruff of his clothing and lifting him to his feet. He opened his eyes and as the focussed he saw Diarran was the one holding him, and he was dressed in the long flowing dark grey suit with flared trousers that he had met him in previously. Flint stood behind him, again wearing the first clothing that Zack had met him in, along with the female Zeydenian he had been introduced to, Marna. Marna was carrying a tray of green vegetables that she offered to Zack.

"Eat." Diarran instructed, "You will need your strength when the sun rises."

"Why? What happens when the sun rises?" Zack asked as he took the tray from Marna's hands.

"You will return." Flint stated without looking at Zack.

"To where?" Confusion etched on Zack's face.

"To whence you came from." Flint continued. Zack put the tray down on the chairs beside him and stepped forward towards Flint who now had his back turned to him.

"Woah, wait a minute!" Zack shouted. Flint spun around to face him, clearly displeased at being challenged, "I'm not going anywhere without Madoka."

"You have no choice Zack. You are a liability here in the sector."

"Hey, I'm just finding my feet," Zack protested, "But I cannot go back to Serene or my past life, and I will not go."

"It's for the best." Marna stepped between the two to try and calm the atmosphere but Zack pushed past her. This angered Diarran who reached out at lightning speed and grabbed Zack by the throat, pushing him against a wall and raising him up. Zack struggled to breathe.

"Tell me why I should not kill you now?" Diarran spoke, "You are already dead three times without my intervention." Zacks feet spun in the air, searching for a footing whilst he clutched at the strong metallic arm of Diarran. Flint stepped forward.

"Diarran, release him at once." Flint ordered. Quick as a flash Diarran's grip relented and his arm whipped down to his side causing Zack to crash to the floor, falling onto his backside and clutching at his throat encouraging the muscles there to expand and contract and allow him to breathe in oxygen again. Once his breathing started to normalize Marna helped him to his feet and sat him on the chair again, next to the food that she had provided. She took on a female form, but her strength was that of her male counterparts. Zack looked up at all three in turn and then spoke to the rear of Diarran.

"I cannot go back." Zack stated.

"That is not your choice." Diarran replied. Zack stood, anger rising in him.

"Who the fuck do you think you are?!" Zack shouted. Diarran spun around to face him.

"I am a Zeydenian!" Diarran stated, "You are a human! You have no rights here."

"I'll take it from here." Flint announced. Diarran stopped in his tracks and then turned to leave the room.

"Eat your food." Marna encouraged as she too followed Diarran from the room, leaving Zack and Flint in each other's company only. Zack looked down at the mush of green vegetables on the tray before him. As unappetising as it looked, he was hungry and so he sat and started picking at the food with his fingers and delicately eating some of it. Flint stood in silence over Zack as he ate. When it appeared as though Zack had eaten all that he could Flint spoke again.

"Let's move from here." Flint suggested. Zack looked up at him before standing. Flint then turned and walked towards the doorway from which they had originally come through into the room. Zack followed and continued to do so as Flint opened the door and stepped into the first room he had been in. Zack wondered if he were being turned loose into the night to fend for himself for his insolence, and despite the whole uneasiness of the night's activities so far, he was relieved to see Flint turn left and head towards another doorway in the corner of the room there. Flint raised a hand towards the door and then stopped in his tracks. There was a short wait before the door opened and both Flint and Zack stepped in. Zack realised he had walked into a closed elevator as the door shut behind him. Neither spoke as the elevator went upwards briefly and after what seemed to be four or five floors it came to a halt and the doors opened again. Flint stepped out first and Zack followed him. He saw that they were standing on the roof of the building he had been brought to. The space was about as big as a football field and had a one-metre-high white wall all around it. There was silence, no noise as if he were taking a holiday in the highlands of Scotland, but also without the sound of any animals or nature. It seemed extremely surreal. Zack looked around the area, just a sparse flat roof, although he noticed an ethereal light emanating from the rear of the building beyond his sight line. Flint was walking in that direction and Zack followed. Flint reached the boundary wall and leant upon it looking out at the source of the light, which got brighter with every step that Zack towards it. When he was level with Flint he was amazed at the sight before him. An expanse of area illuminated by lights on stems as far as the eye could see, hidden from the sector by a huge wall that ran to the top of the building that they were standing on. Illuminations of all colours, subtle with their brightness and what looked like jagged horizontal forks of lightning charging between them from time to time. There were a few trees within the fields that Zack could see silhouetted as they stood towering over the lights. Zack stood, jaw dropped, and watched the lights dance in awe.

"What is it?" Zack asked, still barely managing to string a sentence together.

"It is the light fields of Rebristan." Flint explained, "Every geographical territory on the planet has them, and this is the energy source for the Isle of Rebristan."

"Wow." Was all that Zack could muster.

"Your people destroyed the worlds natural energy sources, and then they fought over them, using yet more energy to develop weapons in which to kill as many of yourselves as they could. You took and took from the planet until it in itself turned upon you. No-one realised until it was too late that a renewable power was right under your noses. Humans developed the artificial intelligence that I, Diarran, Marna and all of Zeydenians and other factions around the planet operate from. You developed us for warfare to help areas of humans fight and clutch tiny pockets of what was left of your fuel supplies. Humans developed us to think for ourselves, to seek the need to kill, and they developed ways of creating energy to power us for longer periods of time. Imagine that Zack, the humans of your time, or just after your time created a new form of energy to power, I believe you would have called us Robots, to fight for them to take control of historical power sources that were diminishing quickly. How stupid is that? No-one could see that they did not have to fight for energy, they simply had to put the thought processes that they put into their weapons of war into ways of creating new energies. Peaceful and we wouldn't be standing here today."

"Why are you telling me all of this?" Zack asked.

"Because you are going back to the twenty first century when the sun rises. If you survive the trip you should show some influence, and you may just save the human race." Flint replied.

"I cannot go back. It's impossible." Zack turned to look at Flint, who turned his head to the left to look into Zacks eyes. "Firstly, I don't know how I got here in the first place. Secondly, I need to rescue Madoka. Thirdly, I won't have the influence that you talk about even if I went back. Stuff happened back there, people were killed, and it was made to look like I am responsible, so I will most likely spend the rest of my days in a prison, and....."

"Firstly, here at the light fields, there is enough energy here to enable those who have mastered the required mental capabilities to teleport through time and space. Madoka, Echo and Junko are such people, and being contained within their circle you were able to travel through time as well." Flint started.

"Why doesn't Madoka just teleport herself away from wherever she is now and come home?" Zack asked, a tinge of sadness and hope in his voice at the same time.

"Two reasons Zack. First, she is in Zeydence, the capital of Rebristan. Not many there know of the power of teleportation that some humans have developed, and those that have attained it like to keep it that way. Second, is that there is not enough energy in Zeydence to facilitate such a move. There is not enough energy in the sectors. Just enough energy flows into the sectors and Zeydence for the inhabitants to survive. The only place where there is a large enough energy source to teleport is the fields you see in front of you." Flint indicated with a sweeping of his arm towards the lights that were flickering between each other for as far as Zack could see.

"But these fields do not exist in my time, and yet Madoka, Echo and Junko were able to appear and vanish at will." Zack seemed confused.

"But in your time Zack, energy was everywhere. It was being wasted. Those who have mastered the art of teleporting in this time would easily have been able to feed off of your, what did you call it, Wi-Fi? Your mobile communications devices, the energy that was sent to the planet from satellites to tell you where you were, even though you could see where you were by opening your eyes. Wasted energy filling the air that enveloped each and every one of you. It was there all along. Those wasted energies do not exist here. However, nature has given us a natural form of energy, and it is there." Again, Flint gestured towards the light fields. Things started making a little bit of sense to Zack, as he had wondered for some time why Madoka just did not vanish from wherever she was and return to him. As if reading his mind, Flint continued "In addition Zack, if Madoka were in a position to leave wherever she was, by whatever means, do you really believe that would be the end of it? Her absence would be noticed, she would be hunted, and that would probably mean a certain death for her and all of her family, yourself included. She has no alternative but to go through with any processes that the people of Zeydence believe she should. Why do you feel you need to save her?"

Zack stared out hard at the lights dancing before him. He felt a tear well in the corner of his eye and threaten to release itself down his cheek. He pondered his future in the past and how he could possibly avoid it. He thought long and hard, wondering how he could possibly make Flint understand. He resolved to just say it as it is.

"I love her." Zacks voice cracked as he uttered the words.

"This is not an emotion that is recognised anymore." Flint said matter of factly, "Not even among the humans. They do not know what this is."

Zack was surprised that Flint had even an inkling as to how he felt but that turned quickly to anger.

"That's because you've taken it away from them." Venom spat from Zacks voice as he turned to face Flint.

"We did no such thing." Flint replied. "The humans were already destroying it on their own without our help. I have been privileged to read the old manuscripts in the ancient library of Zeydence. The word Love is described by the man you call William Shakespeare in readings such as Romeo and Juliet, but then it changes through time. I have also read the poem 'Wildside' of the man you call

Motley Crue, and love is disintegrating before your eyes even then."

"I think you'll find that's an entirely different kind of love Flint." Despite everything Zack mustered a small smile at this line of conversation. "The feelings are still there in every human being. They're there in me."

"But what does it mean?" Flint asked.

"It's a feeling you have. The human heart will beat faster, you would do anything for a person without feeling obliged to. When they hurt you feel their pain. When they smile it makes you happy. You find a person that you want to be with forever because it feels like you should be together and you would die for them, you would kill for them."

"Sounds like an easy way to get killed." Flint replied, "But you are forgetting that Madoka is not of your time. She will not feel this way that you do."

"I believe she will." Zack stated, "We've had a..... connection....and I feel that she knows what is happening."

"It's a good thing that you are leaving tomorrow then, before this confusion can spread among the humans." Flint stated bluntly facing Zack.

"Flint, I beg you," Zack began as his took Flint's elbows in the palm of his hands gently, "please, I cannot go back there. I must rescue Madoka. No, I will rescue Madoka with or without your help."

There was silence for what seemed like eternity as the pair faced each other, staring into each other's eyes. The silence became uncomfortable and lightning thoughts tormented Zacks mind as he wondered about Zeydenian etiquette and whether he should be grasping hold of Flint as he did so at this moment. Finally, Flint spoke.

"And have you considered how you are going to do this, or are you going to be the angry young man flying blindly into a rage at everyone as you have exhibited so far?"

" I know I need to think it through a bit more than I have already, and I know I would need advice, but I cannot bear to think of Madoka somewhere waiting to..." Zack struggled to think of the correct words to say before coming out with, "repopulate the nation."

"It is certain that you would be killed." Flint stated flatly, "As would Madoka."

Zack stared Flint straight in the eyes and with as much authority as he could muster, he stated "I would rather be nowhere with Madoka than somewhere without her."

"What is that?" Flint asked.

"That is love." Zack replied as he let go of Flint's elbows. Flint turned and walked away a few metres whilst Zack stood where he was as if magnetised by the light emanating from the light fields. Then Flint turned and faced Zack where he stood.

"There is a way." Flint said quietly. Despite him being in the shadows now, which should have made him seem more sinister to Zack, he sensed a softness to the Zeydenian. "But it will not be without it's dangers, and like I said, the probability is that you will be killed."

"You know how I feel about that already." Zack replied.

"For twenty years I have been on this sector listening to the humans complain about the Zeydenians and how they are going to overthrow them, but it has all been speech. No-one has dared to put their words into actions and fight for their freedom. Possibly because they have never known freedom in their lifetime. It is a, how do you call it, folk story handed down to each generation. But you Zack, you know what freedom is, you have lived it, or so you believe, and that is what makes you different from all of the other humans."

"So, you're not sending me back to Serene tomorrow then?" Asked Zack.

"I think, channelled in the right direction, that you still have a purpose to serve here mister Zack." replied Flint.

"What about Diarran?" Zack asked, "He seems pretty intent on sending me back."

"Leave Diarran to me. He doesn't hold as much authority as he would have you believe." Flint stepped closer towards Zack until they were within touching distance again.

"Why are you helping me?" Zack asked. He had so many questions and was now beginning to feel nervous, like a child that got a pet spider because he shouted about it long enough only to realise he knew nothing about the dangers of spiders.

"Because my circuits would have shut down a long time ago had it not been for Keisa."

"I don't understand."

"Many years ago, Echo and Madoka were small humans, barely walking, I was cast out of Zeydence for speaking out against Lord Dhonos, the ruler of Zeydence. You might call him the King in your time. My punishment, along with Diarran and Marna was to be cast out to survive in the sector for three moons. Usually this would be a catastrophic punishment resulting in a Zeydenian crashing and not being able to reboot, as we need to charge our circuits at least once a week. No Zeydenian had ever survived one moon previously without needing to recharge at Zeydence. Keisa found us at the supply truck one day. She took us in, much as she has with yourself, and sacrificed the energy in her apartment to help keep the circuits of three Zeydenians running. She went without light, without heat when it was needed, and without warm food. It was as hard for her and her family as it was for us, but it meant that three moons later we were able to travel back to Zeydence to make a full recovery. Before you ask Zack, as I know you will, I know that if you are successful in your quest that it will probably mean the end for me and my kind, but if it were not for your kind I would not be here at all now. I have never been shown the care that Keisa showed to us three by any Zeydenian, and I believe that if that quality can be harnessed and expanded on within the humankind, then that would be a good thing."

"Oh." Was all Zack could manage at such a revelation.

"But you must remember Zack, and you will know of this from your time in the past, not all humans are like Keisa. You must be incredibly careful who you trust."

"Who do you mean?" Zack asked.

"Far be it for me to cause doubt for you. I will assist you where I can, but you must rely on your own instinct to work this out." Flint replied. "And now, you must sleep, and I will take the opportunity to recharge whilst I am near the light fields. I will show you where you can rest your head." This time Flint turned and walked, but continued walking, and Zack felt compelled to follow him, until they reached the elevator and stepped inside.

22

Despite knowing that energy crackled through every fibre of the earth on the other side of the wall Zack slept like a baby. A deep sleep that was much needed. Thoughts of Madoka still flooded his mind but not in the agitated and anxious shocks that he had experienced in the fields, more of a relief that he knew that he was going to find her, that he had help. In his dreams he had watched her smile. It was as if he could feel her, as if she were holding his hand as she had done the night before last. He felt positive. He was awoken by a crashing noise and then an angry shout. He recognised the voice to be that of Diarran.

"What do you mean he's not going today!?" he heard Diarran shout from another part of the building. There was a pause as if Diarran was listening to a reply to his question, but Zack could not make out what was being said, such was the tranquillity of the person to whom Diarran was speaking. He sat up and looked around the room he had fallen asleep in. Windowless and looking much like the room he had been made to wait in last night with the exception of two pairs of bunk beds, all in white, one of which Zack was laying in. Between them was what looked like a computer terminal, a clear screen with colours floating between it, and a keyboard that Zack was surprised to find was still of the QWERTY design. From the screen there were numerous long cables with various fittings and attachments, long enough to reach the pillars of the bunk beds. As Zack surveyed the equipment, he heard the door swoosh open behind him. He turned and was surprised to see Junko standing before him.

"I'm not sure how you managed to pull that off." Junko announced.

"Morning." Zack replied as Junko tilted his head slightly, unsure about the greeting and its meaning.

"Diarran's not a happy person today. You were supposed to be going home." Junko stated. Zack could not be sure if there was a hint of disappointment in his voice or not, he had always been quite difficult to read.

"I'm not going anywhere without Madoka," Zack stated, "And you know I can't go back home Junko."

"Flint will be holding a meeting in a short while. You need to get dressed." Junko said as he turned and left the room, the tone of his voice a little cold. The door closed behind him with a swoosh and Zack was alone. He spied his discarded clothing on the top bunk to the one he had been sleeping in, neatly folded and took it down and started to dress.

A few minutes later Zack left the room he had been sleeping in, and it occurred to him that he did not know where he was going once he stepped outside of the door. From what he had seen so far the whole building appeared to be full of cubic white rooms with doors going off in many directions. The room outside of the one in which he had slept was bare, with another 3 doors aside from the one behind him. A door in each wall, all of which were closed.

"Hello!" Zack called out. For the first time he felt comfortable about raising his voice in Rebristan without the fear of death. He could feel it in his bones that freedom was achievable and coming. Unsure if anyone had heard him Zack started to wander around the room from one wall to the next. He touched the panel beside the door on the wall to his right, it opened into darkness, just another white room but no signs of life. As he stood there peering into the darkness, he heard a whoosh behind him and turned to see Flint standing in the doorway directly behind him.

"Hello Zack." Flint greeted him, "This way please." He turned his back to Zack and started walking into the room from which he had just arrived. Zack followed and once inside the room he saw that it was more rectangular than the rooms he had previously seen with a spiral staircase at the further end, which Flint had started to descend. Following down the steps they descended two floors. Zack still had no idea which level he was on but followed all the same like a lost lamb.

"What is this place Flint?" Asked Zack.

"It's a Zeydenian recuperation hub." Flint replied, "The room that we slept in is directly linked to the light fields. This is a hub for Zeydenians who have run too low on energy and face shutting down forever. They can be repaired here, hopefully before it is too late. It is one of the buildings I have implemented since returning from being cast out. Very few know of its existence and it is rarely used." There was an air of pride in Flint's voice as he spoke about the building whilst still walking. Flint stopped to wait for Zack when he reached the bottom of the staircase.

"So, what happens today?" Zack asked as he reached the bottom of the stairs, placing his trust in Flint's direction.

"Junko has arrived to take you back to your own time," Flint started and Zack's heart dropped at the words, "but he will now assist with your quest to bring Madoka back and peace to Rebristan. There is a one-week break from the fields starting tomorrow, a chance for the humans to recharge so to speak and for the soil to generate the fertility it needs for the next crop. We do not have much time. If you are to act, the time is now." Flint then turned and opened another door to the left of the bottom of the staircase and as it opened Zack saw Junko and Marna sitting at a white laminate table eating. Zack stepped into the doorway and looked around the room.

"Where's Diarran?" Zack asked, conscious that the Zeydenian was not best pleased with him at this time.

"He is in another part of the building." Flint replied. "We had two Zeydenian guards brought in this morning who were in need of energy. It sometimes happens when the rest week arrives."

Zack cast Flint a stare at the thought of Zeydenian guards that were perhaps not in his circle of trust, especially in the company of Diarran. Flint sensed his concern.

"It is ok Zack, they are at the other end of the building and are unaware of your presence." Flint reassured Zack.

"Can Diarran be trusted though?" Zack asked, his heart still beating at the thought. Flint cast him a look of disappointment.

"Do not worry about Diarran." Flint began, "He is aware of what is happening and will not disobey an instruction. You should heed my words of last night." He added before turning to sit at the table.

"Come, sit, eat." Marna encouraged and Zack took a seat at the table next to Junko who was already tucking into what looked like green bread. The Zeydenians sat opposite them and watched them eat as Zack started to take a bite from the food placed before him.

Once he felt as satisfied with the food as was possible Zack stood up.

"What do we do now?" Zack asked. Junko was still polishing off the last on his platter.

"We formulate a plan." Flint replied. "Many have spoken about it for years, but now the time is here."

"Do we have a plan?" Junko asked as he looked up from his plate, "I was all ready for a trip back into the dark ages with this one." He indicated towards Zack.

"The only way to succeed is to get to Zeydence." Flint replied. "We can facilitate that, but how it goes from there onwards is up to you."

"Bearing in mind we'll barely be functioning if you are successful." Marna added. Zack turned to look at her and their eyes met.

"And you're ok with that?" Zack asked incredulously. "I mean, what about Diarran too?"

"We are part of a small minority that realise that this planet is meant for more than what it is being used for now. What kind of existence is this? We are keeping humans as if they are pets...." Flint began.

"Slaves." Zack added and Flint cast him a sideways glance.

"There is no freedom for anyone. Zeydenians cannot survive without human power." Flint continued, "And humans cannot survive without Zeydenian grace at this time. We feed you, we supply you, but we are all living the wrong lives. The only thing that can truly make an attempt at surviving without the other is the human race. If that means that we must shut down, then so be it."

Usually devoid of emotion Flint's facial expressions did take on a hint of sadness at this revelation.

"It will take two days to get to Zeydence, we can arrange transport, but the journey will not be without it's risks. There are colonies of human's who have been able to escape the sector and they run feral in the between roads. But to the best of our ability, we will get you there." Flint stated.

"Two days?" Zack asked, "Will that not be too late for Madoka?"

"No, my friend." Flint replied

"She will be held for one moon before she is to reproduce." Marna added, "Human females bleed for a while every lunar cycle and this hampers their abilities to reproduce. She will be held in a storage cell for this time before any procedure takes place." Zack relaxed a little at the revelation.

"Transport will be here at nightfall." Flint stated, "You should rest up until then. I, Junko and you will be travelling. Marna will wait here for a day and report if we are missed."

"I'm going to catch some sleep then," Junko announced, "Which room shall I head to?"

"There is plenty of room in Zacks room for you to rest." Flint replied, looking at Zack, who looked confused.

"I probably wouldn't be able to find my way back there," Zack said, "It's like a big white maze here."

"I'm sure I can show you the way." Junko replied as he stood up and walked towards the door. Zack followed, but noticed out of the corner of his eye Flint giving him a look he would expect from a big brother, for reasons unknown to him.

Once inside the room that he had just come from Zack settled down onto the bed on which he had slept. Feet on the floor he looked up at Junko who stood still with a thousand-yard stare.

"What's on your mind?" Zack asked. Junko turned to face him with a look as though he hadn't quite understood the question.

"I'm sorry?" Junko replied.

"What are you thinking about?" Zack rephrased his previous question.

"A mixture of things." Junko replied, and turned to face into nothingness again before continuing, "I'm wondering how we've ended up at this moment. I mean, we came to your time to collect you for this, but in such a short space of time we lost hope in it ever happening, and now it is happening, and I don't know what has changed to make it possible. There's a huge feeling of pleasure to finally be taking action, but also of fear. You do know it will probably result in our deaths?" Junko asked as he again turned to face Zack.

"You need to think positively Junko, otherwise that will be a certainty." Zack replied.

"This is all I have thought about for about twenty years Zack, but I'm still a realist."

"Then why are you coming?" Zack asked.

"Because it needs to happen." Junko replied, "I mean, look around you Zack, you've been here for a while now. Is this life?"

"I guess not." Zack replied.

"You should get some sleep." Junko stated as he climbed up onto the top bunk, "It's going to be a long journey and we will need to be alert the whole time."

With that Zack swung his legs up onto the bed and curled up into a foetal position facing the wall. He'd not long woken up and wondered how he would sleep some more so soon. He heard Junko moving around on the bunk above him, and then clap his hands. As he did so the lights in the windowless room switched off and they were thrown into pitch darkness. Zack laid still and thought of Madoka. Where was she right now? What was she doing? Was she accepting her fate or was she being difficult about it? He imagined that, knowing Madoka and how feisty she could be that she was being difficult. That was not a good thought, as Zack had witnessed what happened first-hand to difficult humans. It filled him with fear until he had the thought that Madoka was not stupid, she was a survivor, and she had been through this before. Zack knew that she would know how to present herself to get through this, but it angered him that she would have to. This was akin to slavery in the nineteenth century. He pictured Madoka smiling to try and calm his nerves, and as he did so the darkness of the room, the newfound calm and an image of beauty in his mind enveloped him and pulled him towards slumber.

"Wake up Zack."

There was a gentle nudging of his shoulders and his eyes slowly peeled open to darkness. Out of the corner of his eye he could see some light, and then he realised he was still facing the wall, very closely. As he stretched his limbs out, he slowly rolled onto his back and more light slowly entered his eyes as he did so. He was surprised to see that it was Marna gently trying to wake him. He'd imagined that the voice was male, but then he had just been dreaming about unknown Males at an imaginary location with Madoka immediately before he was woken. As his eyes focused on Marna, he saw her long dark hair was hanging low as she leant over him. He noticed a metallic glint towards the back of her neck that was not covered with skin as her hair fell away from that part of her body.

"How do you grow hair if you are not human?" Zack asked as he started to rise and place his two feet on the floor at the side of the bed.

"That is probably a question best not answered." Marna replied. "Come, it is almost time to leave. They are waiting." She continued as she turned and left the room. Zack stood and looked towards the door that she had left through, and the light that shone in through it. As the door closed behind her Zack was thrown into darkness again. He clapped his hands twice, as he had imagined Junko had done before he slept and was amazed to see the lights slowly start to glow. Much gentler than being hit straight away with the full beam of the lights and it allowed his eyes to adjust to the difference without any pain. Zack had no idea how long he had been asleep and felt a little groggy as he walked towards the door to the room. With a swoosh it opened, and he stepped out into the landing. Still a little disorientated about where he was in this building of identical white rooms, he followed his instincts and soon found the stairs, descending them and arriving at the room where he had earlier eaten. There he saw Flint and Junko sitting at the same table.

"Welcome sleepyhead." Junko greeted as he looked up to see Zack standing in the doorway. Zack walked over to the table and sat down next to Flint.

"Marna has arranged transport and it will be here at the front of the building shortly." Flint started, "I am due to visit Zeydence for a few days in any case for appointments so our visit will not be out of place. But that is all the time that we will have there, a few days. After that there will be one of three outcomes. One, you are successful in whatever you have planned Zack. Two, you will be unsuccessful and will be returning back to Sector sixty-nine. Three, you will be deceased."

"I favour option one." Zack stated, "But, I haven't yet thought of a plan until I see what I am up against."

"Option three it is then." Junko announced pessimistically and rolled his eyes at Zacks announcement.

"I can advise you as we travel as best I can." Flint said, "But once we reach Zeydence, I will be undertaking Zeydenian duties. Junko has visited Zeydence before so he will not be out of place there. I will say that Junko is doing research for me again in the ancient libraries, as he has done previously. But you Zack, you are an unknown, you have a fake identification, and you will raise suspicion fairly quickly, so you will have to enter Zeydence in disguise."

"What would I be disguised as?" Zack asked. As he finished the question the door behind him swooshed open and he turned to see Marna coming into the room holding some familiar looking clothing. "You've got to be kidding me?" He stated as he recognised it to be part of an armoured suit of a Zeydenian soldier.

"This is the only way you will move around Zeydence unhindered." Flint replied. "It's not as uncomfortable as it looks, and you will be somewhat protected by the armour and afforded a weapon to help you."

"Come Zack, I will help you dress." Marna said and nodded towards another door at the far end of the room, opposite the one he had come in from. Marna walked past him towards the door, and he stood up and followed. As they entered the room Zack saw a battery of various pieces of armour and uniform assembled and hanging from hooks, rails, and shelves on the wall. He looked on in awe at the collection and his initial apprehension melted away.

"Wow, this is some collection." He stated.

"The uniforms are usually made for Zeydenians, who are essentially slender machines. These would usually just click right into place. Over time, we have assembled parts and adjusted them to fit humans, preparing for a day such as today so to speak. We've had to strip some parts out as humans are bulkier than Zeydenians, so the level of armour protection would not be as great as if you were machine. But you will be safer than entering Zeydence as you look now." Marna lectured as she swept her hand across the room, stopping at the wall on the right-hand side of her and Zack where he saw a bunch of stocks sticking out of a machine at regular intervals that glowed with a mauve light, "And here we have a small selection of Zey co2 air guns, fully charged. Your normal armoury would be to have two on your person. It will be natural for Flint to carry one as well when travelling the between roads. Junko will not as he will still be classed as in servitude and, although we value him, to the consensus of other Zeydenians his life is worthless. I trust if you come under fire you will supply him with one of your arms?" It was more of an instruction rather than a question.

Zack made his way to the glowing bank of weapons and stroked the butt of one of them.

"How do I even use this?" He asked, looking at the futuristic weapon. He had fired air rifles as a child at tin cans in the fields of Serene, but guns had never really been his thing and he just looked at the Zey Co2's before him in awe and bewilderment.

"Weapons have not really changed much over the ages," Marna replied picking one of the guns from its charging port whose light turned red as it was detached, "You point at the thing you want to kill, and pull this trigger. The weapon will do the rest. Fully charged this is good for approximately one thousand blasts. You will need to keep an eye on the monitor on the turbine which will indicate when the power is getting low." She handed the weapon to Zack who turned it over in his hands looking at it from all angles.

"Is there a safety switch?" Zack asked.

"I'm not sure I know what you mean." Marna replied.

"I mean, is there a switch which prevents it from firing accidentally, you know, stops me from shooting myself?" Zack rephrased his question with an element of humour to it.

"No. Zeydenian guards instinctively know that it is bad to shoot themselves, and you must adopt the same ethos." Marna replied as she took the gun from Zack and replaced it into it's charging port. The light around the port again turned to mauve. "Now. Undress." She ordered.

Zack felt a little uncomfortable getting undressed in front of a female, whatever she was. He pondered how, what were essentially robots, assigned a gender to each other. In the end he resigned to the fact that Marna would think nothing of his nakedness, no feelings of eroticism, he was just a slave to her. There would be nothing there. With this in mind he stripped down until he was naked. Marna urged him to take a shower that she pointed out in the corner of the room. The water had a strange smell to it, almost as if it were mixed with oil to a small degree. As he stepped out of the shower Marna presented him with some towelling material and he dried himself down. He had relaxed sufficiently to allow her to slowly assemble the undergarments and armour of the Zeydenian guard uniform around him. She did not flinch, or acknowledge his penis twitching to life as she knelt before him, inches away from her face, as she assembled armour around his ankles. After about twenty-five minutes he was complete, except for the helmet.

"I'd hate to be caught unaware in an attack if it takes that long to put on." Zack remarked.

"Zeydenian guards can step straight into it if needed." Marna reacted, "Whilst you are in Zeydence you will need to keep this on at all times as you will not be able to assemble it yourself if it was required and you will need to maintain your disguise at all times." Marna placed a Zey $Co2$ gun on either side of the leg harnesses on Zack's outfit, taking them from the charging pods. She indicated for Zack to follow her through the door to where he had left Flint and Junko previously. As the door opened he was surprised to see Diarran standing in the room with them.

"Thank you." Flint stated to Diarran as he was handed what looked like a glowing credit card shaped item. Diarran took a look at Zack, there was no welcome in his eyes, and without saying a word he turned and left by the door at the other end of the room.

"You look passable." Junko said to him.

"It should work." Flint added. "Diarran has just visited Echo to explain the change of plans and has returned with the transport. I think we are ready to leave now."

Marna stepped back into the armoury room and returned with another Zey $Co2$ gun, handing it to Flint. He opened the black bag that was permanently hung around his neck, falling to the left of his legs and placed the weapon inside it.

"Let's go." Simple instructions from Flint as he and Junko stood and walked towards the door at the other side of the room. Zack, carrying his helmet under his arm, followed. There were no emotional goodbyes or any sentiments, it was just another second of another day when no-one would ever know their fate from any other moment. When they arrived at the main door to exit the building Flint stopped them.

"Zack, you should put your helmet on until we are in the vehicle. You may remove it once inside, but better to be careful than sorry. You never know who could be watching." Flint instructed. Zack lifted the helmet onto his head and felt a slight squeeze as the metal of the helmet temporarily fused itself with a ring of metal that surrounded his neck piece, allowing him to move his head from side to side whilst being connected together.

"By the way. You are piloting the transport." Flint added handing the item that Diarran had given him to Zack. Once the disguise was complete Flint opened the door and the three of them stepped out into the open air to the waiting vehicle.

23

Freedom, or so it felt like. Once in the vehicle Zack had removed his helmet and was surprised to learn that vehicles, or cars, had not come a long way in the intervening years. Why did they need to? The Zeydenians weren't interested in the aesthetics of a vehicle, or speed. The Zeydenians had no need for the beauty or roaring sound of Italian supercars. He guessed that that they had no feelings of whether something provided comfort either as he sat on the plastic bucket seats at the front of the vehicle. There certainly was no need for the humans to have access to them either, that would give them a power that the Zeydenians daren't exploit. The vehicle was much more silent than the cars that Zack was used to. Over time, he imagined, oil had become a rarity if it even existed at all. Flint had told him that they had harnessed the power of the sun, some sort of solar power, that would allow the vehicle to move freely for prolonged periods of time. They travelled for what seemed like thirty minutes, until they could no longer see any of the towers that housed the humans. The vehicle was fitted with a navigation system of sorts that kept it to the main road out of the sector, which was just as well as there were very few lights within the darkness of Sector sixty-nine and seeing where he was going was quite difficult. Zack had been told by Flint that if he wore his helmet it would provide night-vision, but sitting as he was in the space that he had, that would be too uncomfortable for any prolonged period, so he opted to use the light of the moon to help guide him, until the helmet was absolutely necessary. They came to a gate surrounded by a high, at least thirty feet, fence. Beside the gate was a small white building that appeared to have windows facing into sector sixty-nine and also to outside of the sector.

"What do I do here?" Zack asked, a panic setting in at the thought of coming across guards as he was trying to leave the sector.

"Just keep moving." Flint instructed. Zack did as he was bade, and the vehicle continued moving towards the gate. With exact precision the gate slid open as the vehicle descended upon it. A guard came out of the hut and stood still as they passed by. As quickly as it opened the gate slid shut behind them.

"To prevent humans escaping through the open gate," Flint

stated, somehow predicting the next question that Zack would ask, "This is a diplomatic vehicle. It has free access and egress into all of the sectors."

If this was a diplomatic vehicle then Zack wondered what depths of uncomfortableness the common variants had. A quick glance over his shoulder to the rear and he saw that Junko did not seem bothered by the seating, or if he did, he was not showing it. Compared to a lifetime in the fields any sitting down must feel comfortable in any case.

"Eyes front." Flint instructed sternly, and Zack snapped back round to look out of the windscreen. "You never know what we will meet on the roads."

"What do you mean?" Zack asked, eyes still facing forwards.

"As much as the Zeydenians rule, there have been breakouts of other sectors in the past. Sometimes they survive. Sometimes they reproduce and become what you would have called Feral. They are wild and they see this vehicle as a source of food." Flint stated in a tone calmer that Zack expected for the topic.

"So, where are we now?" Zack asked, feeling that a conversation would help keep him awake driving this silent vehicle in the dark.

"These are the between roads." Junko joined in the conversation, "Between the sectors."

"There is a great distance between each sector." Flint added, "To stop neighbouring sectors from speaking with each other and conspiring against the rule."

In the darkness Zack could no longer see the wall around sector sixty-nine, and had no hope of seeing the walls of any neighbouring sectors. The road, if indeed there was a made road underneath the wheels felt bumpy which inhibited the speed he could travel at. He focused on the navigation system, pleased to see that obstacles to avoid were marked on the screen as they travelled, assuming that it would show up if any appeared in his path.

"How long will it take us to reach Zeydence?" Zack asked. Desperate to keep the conversation going but feeling as though it were he that was doing all of the leg work on it.

"The sun will rise, and possibly set again, before we arrive." Flint replied. Zack heard snoring coming from behind him where he knew that Junko was sitting. He had lost the conversation battle and just focussed on moving forwards. Looking out of the windows to the front and sides he saw darkness and wondered to himself if he had actually previously covered this land in the twenty-first century on one of his many road trips with Marshall and Jeff. He was fairly certain he'd covered most of the United Kingdom previously, but never felt the fear that he felt at this time, just aimlessly driving through the blackness. Occasionally he saw the distant light of what seemed like a fire burning many miles away and was directed by Flint to steer an alternative course, but that was as far as the communications went. They carried on carrying on.

After what seemed like a few hours, Junko was still snoring in the back of the vehicle and Flint appeared to be unbothered by it. The terrain had undulated as they travelled across it. Zack was feeling a little cramped and had resorted to wearing his Zeydenian guard helmet for the night vision and was pleased to learn that the navigation system could be viewed on the helmet visor too. This novelty helped to keep him awake as the silence encroached upon him. He supposed that Flint had shut down, or whatever it was that the Zeydenians did. His eyes were open, but he had been motionless for the last ninety minutes or so, only reacting when Zack needed to change direction. Zack supposed that the sectors were in perfect squares as the roads seemed to be completely straight in grids. The night vision within the helmet afforded Zack some vision of the road ahead and at some points he was able to see the fence surrounding nearby sectors. Zack had lost all bearings of where he would be within the United Kingdom. It saddened him to think that in Serene there had been listed buildings that had stood for hundreds of years but the landscape was so bleak now that they must all have been razed to the ground. As he continued to move forwards in the vehicle, the navigation system indicated that there would be an obstacle in the road several hundred metres ahead. He looked at out of the windscreen using the night vision and could not yet see anything that may be in the way but noted that the road had become particularly narrow at this point with drainage ditches either side. Looking again at the navigation system it continued to indicate that there was an obstacle that was getting closer as he continued to move. Zack again looked through the windscreen and started to see a bundle of what looked like linen in the road, small at first but getting larger as he approached. It confused him as to why the navigation system would pick up upon some blow-away clothing, until he got closer and saw that it was moving slightly. Zack slowed his vehicle on the final approach and watched as the pile of clothing shuffled closer. As he stared at the bundle a child's head, no more than two years old, popped out from under the clothing and stared directly at the approaching lights of Zacks vehicle. Zack slammed onto the brake within the vehicle bringing it to a sudden halt, mere feet away from the child.

"Shit." He exclaimed as his heart began to beat in his throat. At the sudden lurch of the vehicle, Junko woke up and Flint became more animated.

"Why have you stopped?" Junko asked.

"There's a child in the road," Zack started, pointing towards the child through the windscreen with his left hand whilst his right gripped the door open mechanism.

"No!" Flint shouted, "It's a ...." but he was too late. A dark figure yanked the door open of the vehicle and then four hands reached in and grabbed hold of Zack throwing him with inhuman strength away from the vehicle. Dazed, Zack sat up once he had gathered his senses and saw a dark figure looming towards him. His helmet had come loose, and he had lost the night vision in the dark. He felt the footsteps running towards him and heard the thuds on the dry earth. He heard a scream coming from the vehicle but could not see what had happened.

"Shoot!" Zack heard a shout from the vehicle, it sounded like Flint giving him instruction. It reminded Zack that he had a weapon strapped to the armour on his leg, and he fumbled for it. Removing it from the holster built into his leg armour a green light glowed on the top of it and around the trigger. Whatever it was that had yanked him from the vehicle was still descending upon him. Zack imagined it was some kind of wild animal for he could not make out it's form in the pitch darkness. He pointed towards where the noise was coming from. The thing must have sensed danger and a guttural growl, not unlike a roaring crocodile, came from its direction. Zack gently squeezed the trigger, praying it would fire as he had never tested it before. He might have closed his eyes as he did so and felt a rushing feeling along the length of his arm to his fingertip on the trigger. There was a very brief sound of wind followed by a thud on the ground in front of him. Zack felt a liquid hit his bare cheek on the left side of his face. He had no idea what it was, but it felt warm and thick and he could smell a coppery scent emanating from the left. He lay still and tried not to think about what it could be, but the voice inside his mind kept pressing for the obvious, which was causing bile to rise up in his throat. He could hear his heart beating out of his chest, the strong and rapid pulse rising up the side of his neck into his head. Once the noise subsided a little, he realised that there was silence where there had once been chaos and danger. Braving to stand up onto his feet, not an easy thing to do whilst wearing the armour, he looked towards the beam of the vehicles lights. Unsure of the terrain underfoot Zack made for the direction of the lights, using them as a beacon for travel. He tried not to look down at whatever it was that he had shot at, the idea still uneasy with him and the feeling of the warm liquid running down his face as he had stood up making him want to vomit. As he got closer to the vehicle, he saw a form on the floor in front of the door that he had been pulled from.

"Who's there?" Zack heard Flint shouting from inside the vehicle.

"It's me, Zack." He called back, fearing that he would come to harm if he didn't answer. The rear door of the vehicle opened and with it an interior light came on, shining a small beam of light down onto the form on the floor as Flint and Junko exited the vehicle. Zack saw that it was a woman, wearing just a skirt, breasts exposed and a stream of blood flowing from a hole on the side of her head. Long black hair starting to congeal with the blood. Flint looked down at the female and without looking up at Zack he simply asked, "Why did you stop?"

"There was a child on the road." Zack replied. He had forgotten about the child as he had fought for his life and looked in the direction of the headlights of the vehicle for the mass that had caused him to stop in the first place. Junko and Flint's eyes followed his and there, lit up in the glare of the light beams was a male child, barely two years old and naked apart from the loose clothing that had been wrapped around him to make him appear bulkier in the road.

"You'll have to shoot it." Flint stated, no emotion in his voice. Zack did not immediately register that it was him being spoken to. As the words settled into his brain he blinked and turned towards Flint.

"Excuse me?" Zack asked, believing he had heard incorrectly.

"Shoot it." Flint repeated as he turned to get back into the rear of the vehicle followed by Junko.

"But it's just a child." Zack protested.

"A feral child Zack. No good can come of it. There will be two scenarios if you let it live. One, it will die a slow, lonely, and painful death out here in the between roads if there are no other Ferals about, or two, it will signal to other Ferals that we are nearby if it is found, and we will not be so lucky if a larger herd of them find us. Now shoot it." Flint closed the door of the vehicle behind him after Junko had climbed in. Zack wrenched the door open again.

"You fucking shoot it if you want it dead!" Anger rose in Zack towards Flint for the first time, an anger he could not control. Flint merely looked up at him.

"You are the one in the Zeydenian guard armour. You are the one who wants this mission to be a success. If anyone is watching us from afar and it is anyone else who shoots the child other than you, then your cover would be blown Zack and that would mean your mission is compromised, as is your life. Now pick up your helmet and shoot the bastard. If I need to ask you again, I will leave you here." Flint stated matter of factly as he slammed the door shut again. Zack looked around him and spotted the helmet that he had been wearing had fallen off a metre of so away from the vehicle as he had been thrown clear. He decided to pick it up in the first instance whilst his conscience still wrestled with Flint's command. Putting it on over his head there was a brief pause as his sight went from pitch black to night vision. As his eyes adjusted to being able to see in the darkness, he surveyed his surroundings and saw that he had shot a human male with long matted dreadlocked hair and a huge hole in his back, as he lay face down on the earth. He turned to look at the child in the road. The child was sitting on its backside looking towards the female form on the ground and sucking on its thumb, a look of confusion on its face. Zack pointed his Zey CO_2 gun towards the child, noting the puppy fat around the creases of its legs as it turned to look at him.

"Sorry little fella." Zack whispered as a tear welled in his eyes. He pointed the weapon towards the chest of the child and when he was sure that his aim was on target, he closed his eyes as he pulled the trigger. There was the same silent rushing feeling along his arm as he felt the weapon fire. He opened his eyes again, turning his head to the side so that he could dispel any distressing sight to the corner of his vision if he felt he could not cope. His sight, initially blurry from the tear in his eye, cleared and on the periphery of his vision he saw that the child was now lying on his back, motionless and there was a small puddle of liquid forming nearby. Without looking any further he was confident that he had carried out his instruction and spun two hundred and seventy degrees in the opposite direction in order to be able to be looking at the vehicle without his line of sight taking in the child any further. He strode back towards the open vehicle door and climbed into the bucket seat at the front, pulling the door closed beside him, hoping that the interior of the vehicle gave him sanctuary from the horrors of the exterior, making it all go away. Without looking upwards through the windscreen, he fumbled around for a button for the lights, finding it and switching it off so that darkness washed over the scene in front of him. Looking up he was pleased to see that the night vision did not reveal too much detail of the people outside of the vehicle. He looked behind him into the rear of the vehicle and met Junko's gaze first. Junko simply nodded at him and then upwards nodded as if urging him to move forwards. Zack returned his gaze to the front, trying not to pay attention to the road, and pressed the button to start the vehicle again. Moving off slowly he steered lightly to the left as he felt the road allowed in order to miss any corpses left on the road. Once he was sure that he had left them behind he switched the lights back on and the journey continued.

"At the next junction we will start to head south Zack." Flint stated calmly as if nothing had just happened. "The navigation system will instruct you correctly. No more stopping."

Zack felt a reassuring grip on his shoulder from Junko as he looked forwards and continued driving. There was silence.

24

Zack had been driving through the day, only stopping once at the gate house of sector thirty, a safe environment according to Flint so that he could get a brief power nap and Flint recharged himself. Within three hours they were back on the road again, and Zack struggled to stay awake as the sun started to set to the west of them again. Within no time at all night had fallen and the darkness around them enveloped the vehicle. An hour later Zack was forced to put the Zeydenian guard mask on again in order to take advantage of the night vision capabilities. Very little had been spoken since the encounter with the feral humans in the early hours of the morning. As Zack continued to head south in the darkness it came as a surprise for him to see a thin expanse of light on the horizon, many miles ahead of him. Panicking that they were about to be ambushed again and dreading a repeat of the previous scenario, his mind spun at a million miles an hour, showing him varying images of the child that he had shot, even though he did not watch the actual incident as he pulled the trigger. His breathing became rapid and his heart beat faster as he turned around in his seat. Junko was asleep in the back and it appeared as though Flint had shut himself down again.

"Junko! Junko! Wake up!" Zack called out, the adrenaline clearly audible in his voice. Junko stirred and his eyes opened slowly as he gave a yawn and stretched his arms out. Zack saw Flints eyes become brighter as if lit by a backlight, something that he had not seen before, but couldn't go unmissed in the deep darkness of the vehicle at night.

"What is it Zack?" Junko asked, irritated at being woken.

"What's that ahead?" Zack asked, turning his head to face out of the windscreen again, half expecting for the light to have rushed up towards them at lightning speed and be bearing down on him. He was slightly relieved to see that it was still as far ahead in the distance, but still wary of the fact that he was driving towards it and would eventually meet it. Junko rubbed his eyes and leant forward in his seat until his head was level with Zack and looked out of the windscreen.

"I do believe that is our destination." Junko stated.

"Gentlemen, we are home," Flint added, surprising Zack as he had believed him to be dormant, "Zeydence lies ahead, we should be there within one hour."

Zack did not know whether to be happy that the journey was almost over or apprehensive that he was about to enter the enemy lair under false pretences. Either way, the feeling of exhaustion outweighed any other emotion.

"Is there anything I need to know about driving into Zeydence?" Zack asked.

"You will have no problem driving through there in this vehicle." Flint replied, "Once we are at the city edge, I will give you directions." Flint sat back in his seat and as Zack turned to look at him the light in his eyes dulled.

"Just keep going forwards Zack." Junko added as he too sat back in his seat and relaxed.

Zack drove forwards as the city approached and the lights got brighter and the scene became taller.

Approaching Zeydence was not how Zack had imagined it. He had lived sufficiently long enough in sector sixty-nine, ruled with an iron fist, to expect the security and oppression to be at its height in what was now the capital city of Rebristan. But it wasn't oppressive at all. It was just like driving into any major city in the world in the twentieth century. Zack reminisced about visiting London with Eva in his car when times had been happier. The lights on the buildings of Rebristan reminded him of walking around Leicester square at three am, still abundant with life, noise and hundreds of people going about. And why shouldn't it be like this? After all, he guessed that the humans were all locked up in the various sectors criss-crossing the country now. As he thought of this, he began to get angry inside.

"Is everyone here a Zeydenian?" Zack asked aloud, not quite sure himself who he was directing the question at, and not really expecting an answer.

"Pretty much," Flint replied, no hint of annoyance in his voice or any other emotion, "Some humans live here too but not many."

"How is that so?" Zack asked.

"Some, like Junko here, become trusted among the Zeydenians and are allowed to visit in company with a citizen," Flint started, "Others are brought here for Zeydenian purposes, like Madoka. And the academics of the humans that are identified as being too intelligent for just field work are brought here to programme the applications that keep Zeydenians alive. I would still estimate that less than one percent of the population are humans though."

Zack wondered whether, if he had legitimately been born in Rebristan, he would have been one of the privileged allowed to live in Zeydence programming computers, or whether his life would naturally have been one of misery and enslavement. Other vehicles passed theirs, and there did not seem to be any laws of the road. There was no uniformity of driving on the left or right, you simply drove to avoid, but it worked. The roads appeared to be wide enough to accommodate at least six vehicles abreast. The buildings stood high on either side, lit up like Piccadilly Circus or Times Square, just without the advertisements. Zack chuckled quietly to himself as he imagined still expecting to see a Coca Cola sign lit up somewhere.

"What's funny?" Came the question from behind him. Zack had imagined that Flint was still powered down, asleep, whatever they called it.

"It just reminds me of London." Zack replied.

"Could you die easily in London?" Flint asked.

"You could die easily anywhere." Answered Zack.

"Well then, it's just like London." Flint replied without a hint of emotion. "You will need to head towards the tower."

Zack looked ahead and could see about a mile in the distance, a tall tower that stood above all else. Zack couldn't decide whether it looked more like a tear or a vagina. It stood majestically tall, at least forty stories high, rising to a point. It was actually two towers which started together at the base but separated as it rose and widened out before coming together again at the top, leaving a distinct oval shaped opening in the centre of the structure. In the night sky it gave the impression of glowing with a purplish ultra-violet light. This looked all the more impressive for the neon flashing lights of the much smaller buildings below it. People stopped and stared at the vehicle as they slowly drove by, through the streets of Zeydence. This left Zack feeling uneasy, wondering if they could see him in the vehicle.

"Why is everyone staring?" Zack asked, "There are lots of other vehicles moving around, but they're paying attention to me."

"Worry not Zack," Flint replied, "They cannot see you in here. They stare because this is a diplomatic vehicle. They believe someone of importance is inside."

"I'm not important." Zack half jested. Flint and Junko shared a glance at each other.

"Artificial intelligence, as you humans call it, has come a long way.

The Zeydenians based here in the city enjoy socialising as much as the humans of your time did," Flint began to explain, "and with that comes gossip."

"Gossip?" Zack asked surprisingly, not a word he expected to hear ever again, especially given his recent living arrangements and the destitution that came with it.

"Yes Zack, there is a thriving social circle in Zeydence." Flint started.

"Of which Flint is at the centre." Junko added.

"Hush now Junko," Flint commanded, "Zack has an important mission and should not be distracted by such…. gossip."

The tower loomed closer; the staring did not stop. As he progressed along the street Zack noticed some people running inside nearby buildings as they saw the vehicle approach. He glanced into the back seats and noted that neither Flint nor Junko seemed alarmed by this. Turning his gaze forwards, he continued towards the strange shaped tower. It loomed ever closer and seemed taller than first imagined.

"Best you put the helmet back on now Zack." Flint stated with his usual emotionless voice. Zack reached over to the passenger seat where it had lain for the last few hours of the journey, picking it up with one hand and slipped it over his head with the same skill that he would open a bottle of Pepsi Max whilst steering his old car in Serene. Instantly there was a bright flash as the night vision took in the night lights of Zeydence before automatically adjusting to the light. Zack picked up the same speed that he had previously been driving at as they made the final approach to the foot of Zeydence tower. There was a flurry of activity at the entrance to the tower and a dozen Zeydenian guards emerged. A slight shiver made its way coldly down Zacks spine but he daren't slow down or give himself away. Flint somehow sensed his fear.

"Worry not Zack." Flint calmly stated, "Just stay close to Junko and do as he states, and you will be fine. I will not be able to converse with you too much once the doors are open and we leave the vehicle."

And just like that they pulled up outside Zeydence tower. Zack brought the vehicle to a halt and guards rushed towards it forming a line tunnel either side of the vehicle's rear door between the road and the entrance to Zeydence tower. They turned their back on the path they had created watching the crowds slowly edging closer to get a glimpse at the vehicle as it had stopped. Zack looked out of the window of the vehicle at the steps that ascended to the entrance of Zeydence tower, a majestic display of glass work. As Zack looked, a large dark glass door slid open, easily twenty feet tall to reveal a large chandelier of light in the foyer behind it. As the door slid open a figure rushed to the entrance, silhouetted by the bright lights behind it. By the manner of walking Zack guessed that the figure was male. As the figure approached the vehicle and got closer Zack could see that he appeared panicked by their arrival. It wasn't until he reached the rear door of the vehicle and opened it that Zack could finally see his features in the light emanating from the nearby buildings. The figure was indeed male, a black male, shaved head and of slim build. He appeared to be a more mature person than other Zeydenians that Zack had met, and he guessed his age to be around fifty to fifty-five years old. He wore all dark clothing, all in black, long-sleeved tunic and trousers which had a black chiffon type skirting around it, which flowed freely as he moved, aided by the breeze making its way through the street.

"This is a surprise your Royal Highness." The man stated as he bent into the back of the vehicle.

"Save the pleasantries Rodrock." Flint dismissed with a wave of his hand, "I return most weeks."

"Royal Highness?" Zack asked probably a little louder than he should which caused a glance into the front from Rodrock. Zack looked behind him and saw that Junko had a finger to his lips in a shushing motion.

"Welcome home." Rodrock continued unabated by Flints recent dismissal of his welcome. He gave off a strange presence. On the one hand he gave off an air of importance above that of the Zeydenian guards, but also held an appearance of a man in service. At the same time there was a positive air of excitement about him too, at seeing Flint, that caused his movements to be jerky and jumpy like that of an excited puppy or a child at Christmas. Rodrock stepped backwards allowing room for Flint to alight the vehicle.

"Is there any news of my family?" Rodrock asked excitedly, but also with his head bowed as if he knew he had stepped over a line and was pushing his luck.

"Your family is well." Flint answered, "We stopped at sector twenty-nine en-route. Your mother sends her regards."

"Thank you, your Royal Highness." Rodrock replied, head still bowed in what appeared to be shame.

"Rodrock, Junko has joined me again on this trip. He is to be afforded access to the Royal library as I require some research to be carried out."

"Certainly, your Royal Highness," Rodrock replied, daring to look up at Flint on this occasion, "I shall have a new guard assigned to him immediately."

"There is no need," Flint interrupted, "There is a guard accompanying him already and that will suffice."

"But surely he needs to recharge…."Rodrock began.

"Like I have already intimated Rodrock, we stopped at sector twenty-nine during our voyage and the guard was fully charged during our stay. This guard already has all of my instructions." Flint then turned and walked towards the entrance of Zeydence tower leaving Rodrock to follow behind him. One of the Zeydenian guards glanced into the vehicle and looked Zack and Junko up and down before closing the door on them, leaving them to themselves.

"For Flint's sake we cannot mess this up." Junko stated quietly. "This is the first time I have ever heard of two humans being in Zeydence unaccompanied. If it is ever discovered that he has aided us then, royalty or not, they will tear him apart."

Zack did not know how to answer. The gravity of what he was attempting suddenly hit him, a wave of fear rushed over him and he wished that the ground would open up and make him disappear. Finally, he stated "Where do we go now?"

"Flint has a residence in the north of the city which is where I have stayed on previous missions. He has instructed me to take you there on this occasion and we can get some rest for the night. We should move before Rodrock returns to the vehicle and insists on a guard change. Sometimes he can be a little…. too helpful." Junko stated. At that Zack looked up at the entrance to Zeydence tower and saw Rodrock give a glance back to the vehicle and the remainder of the Zeydenian guards followed him. Zack pulled the vehicle away from the entrance and headed in a direction that he assumed to be north.

"So, what's with the Royal Highness title?" Zack asked when they had driven sufficiently far away enough that he did not believe anyone could overhear him anymore. Yet still the pedestrians stopped and stared as the vehicle made its way through the streets which still made him feel slightly uneasy.

"Flint is part of Zeydenian royalty." Junko replied. "One of the chosen Princes of Lord Dhonos and Lady Zoesis."

"Ok." Zack muttered, "It would have been nice to know."

"Does it make any difference?" Junko replied, "They're all just robots that take our lives for their own at will." A hint of anger had crept into Junko's voice.

"I thought you were friends with Flint?" Zack stated but it sounded more like a question.

"It's complicated." Junko replied to the question, "It's survival. You need to take a right up here."

Zack turned the vehicle to the right as the road came to a crossroads and they continued driving. The further they drove, the thinner the crowds of Zeydenians became that stopped to stare at the vehicle as it passed.

After a time, spent mostly in silence, the pedestrians were few and far between. The road was narrower, and Zack was surprised to see what looked like, in the dark, some lush countryside and hills around him, such was he used to the abject barrenness of the land he had experienced so far. After about fifteen minutes of driving Junko indicated again.

"Right here Zack."

Zack turned the vehicle onto a tree lined road and was surprised to see the remnants of what appeared to be a Georgian Mansion house as he had seen them in his time in the twenty first century.

"What is this?" Asked Zack, mostly to himself but it came out loud enough for Junko to catch too.

"This is the retreat for the Royal Zeydenians." He replied. "Flint has an apartment within the building, away from the hustle and bustle of city life. This is where we will be staying for the next couple of days. Apparently, there is something big going on in the city so this place will be practically empty."

Eventually they reached the building, four stories high and magnificent stonework around all of the windows which appeared darkened and mirror like. There was a sweeping staircase which led up to a huge door, metallic instead of a wooden door that Zack had expected. Zack went to pull up outside the staircase, but Flint stopped him from doing so.

"We're going around the side. There is a storage room for the vehicle there." Junko leant over Zacks shoulder and pointed to the right-hand side of the building. Zack continued to drive and as the rounded the corner he saw a sloping road that went down to a large door that was below ground level. As he descended the door quickly opened and he was blinded by the light that emanated from the garage. Driving in, his eyes soon adjusted, and he saw that there were spaces for about forty vehicles, yet there was only one other parked up inside. He found a suitable place to stop, and actually felt a wave of relief wash over him that he had met his final destination for the day and that, more importantly, he hadn't died.

"There are no recording devices inside the building," Junko started, "But they are everywhere outside of the building. You will need to keep your helmet on until we are in the room."

Taking the advice into account Zack opened the door to the vehicle and stepped out. A massive urge to stretch his muscles out after being sat for so long washed over him, but he thought better of it as a tiny voice in the back of his mind spoke to him and told him that artificial intelligence robots probably didn't have muscles that they needed to stretch. He managed a yawn under his helmet and waited for Junko to alight from the rear of the vehicle. Junko led the way and they made their way to an elevator at the rear of the garage. Only when the doors closed and they started going up, presumably towards Flint's residence, did Zack start to stretch his muscles out and start to relax as fatigue started to take over him.

25

As the sun rose, or maybe it had already risen, but in any case, the photochromic glass of the windows in the room started to let the sunlight through gradually. This took the room that Zack had been sleeping in from darkness to being able to actually see his surroundings. He pondered on the thought at how quickly in this environment a man would get used to just sleeping anywhere, as the tiredness took him and the lack of comforts that one required in respect of security as he would have been brought up to demand if sleeping in the twenty first century in Serene. A few weeks or months in the future world that he now inhabited, and an almost animal instinct took over, to get rest when it was needed, rather than rely on home comforts, and take your chances that nothing bad happens while your eyes are closed. It was better to be fully rested and alert for the rest of the time. Looking around him though as daylight crept into the room, his surroundings did not appear to be too shabby or dangerous. It appeared as though a designer had been tasked with creating a habitat fit for a King and had looked at what was left of historical books on stately homes. It was in stark contrast to the bare rooms he had been used to in Sector Sixty-Nine, which had been functional to live in but also pale and bland. It looked as though he had now awoken in an episode of Downton Abbey, yet the materials used were still not what he was familiar with. The grand four poster bed that he had slept in was not made from wood, but instead some organic composite that was carved and coloured to look like a dark aged wood. The floors were carpeted but it did not feel like any carpet his bare feet had sunk into in the past, and was more akin to the material of which his clothing had been made. The windows had elegant framing around them and yet the glass was more suited to spectacles which changed shade as the sun hit them. Zack sat up in the bed and stretched his arms. As his eyes focussed, he looked around the room. His eyes fell upon the metallic uniform that he knew that he would have to wear, hanging on the wall to the right of him with the emerging sunlight starting to reflect off of it. His mood sank a little at the thought of having to wear it, weighing him down. He had felt an unusual elation the evening previously at taking it off for the first time since his journey to Zeydence had started, and felt as though every pore of his body was able to actually breathe and inhale oxygen once he had been freed from the restraint of it. Part of him longed for some sort of snooze device so that he could sleep a little more and prolong his freedom from the Zeydenian guard uniform. He wanted to slam his head back down onto the bed, pull the cover up over him and disappear for a bit longer. As daylight crept across the room Zack saw Junko starting to stir on the couch opposite. When they turned up the evening previous Junko had turned his nose up at the opulence of a four-poster bed, opting for the (less comfortable in Zacks books) couch that lined the back wall. As Junko's eyes opened Zack realised that there would be no more sleep, as clearly the humans of this age were in no way acquainted with an easy life and comforts of a lie on at a weekend.

"Morning Tiger." Zack announced as Junko started to look in his direction. Junko just stared at him, unaware of what the greeting meant or who it was aimed at. He looked around the room a little to see who else Zack might be addressing before bringing his focus back to Zack. There was an awkward silence.

"So," Zack began again, "what's on the agenda for today?"

"We wait for instructions from Flint." Junko replied. This time, at least, Zack had said something that warranted a response from Junko.

"Ok." Zack answered, feeling none the wiser as to how he was going to progress his mission from that response. "Is there any food around here?"

"We can look. It would be in the servant's quarters if there is any." Junko replied, "Zeydenians only need to re-energise, unlike us that need to consume plants to gain energy."

Zack slipped his feet to the floor at the side of the bed and removed the cover from around his waist. Looking down at his cotton shorts he wondered if it would be decent to walk around the huge building like this without getting dressed up. He had the opinion that he and Junko were alone, at least they had not met anyone the evening before, nor been disturbed by any other noise throughout the night. Standing up, Zack made his way towards the door on the opposite side of the room to him.

"Where are you going like that?" Junko enquired.

"I need a piss." Zack replied still focussing on the door ahead of him. "It's a morning thing."

"Not like that you don't." Junko protested as Zack reached the door. It was a grand wooden effect door with ornate handles, but as Zack had discovered the previous evening, that was all for show and it swooshed across like every other mechanical door he had seen since arriving in Rebristan. He turned to look towards Junko, who had now sat up on the couch, but as his gaze drifted away from the door in front of him, he was surprised to hear the swooshing noise of it coming open. Snapping his gaze back to front he jumped back a little as he saw Diarran standing in front of him. Embarrassed by his own fright he tried not to look Diarran in the eye.

"Where are you going like that?" Diarran asked.

"I was just looking for the boys room." Zack replied, still not looking directly at him.

"Not like that you are not." Diarran retorted, "This may seem like a fun morning to you, but the threat is still the same, even more so now that you are in Zeydence and many humans and Zeydenians are at risk if you are found out." Zack stood there gasping for breath at the length of Diarran's sentence realising that robots or artificial intelligence probably did not have to stop for breath when speaking. The sobering reality of the danger he was in suddenly dawned on him. The temporary safety of the state room he had slept in had lulled him into a false sense of security, and here he was, almost acting the clown as he would have done in Serene, being brought back down to Earth with a thud. Well, a version of Earth anyway. Zack turned to look at the Zeydenian guard uniform hanging on the wall. Diarran followed his gaze.

"Already?" Zack asked with a touch of melancholy in his voice,

"I'm afraid so." Junko replied.

"But I just need a piss." Zack protested, remembering the difficulty of managing to do so on the long journey, especially as the uniform was never designed for species with a penis.

"Flint told me you may need one of these." Diarran added emotionless, holding out a large bottle towards Zack as he turned around. "He has summoned me to bring you to Zeydence Tower. I have brought some food for you both to avoid suspicion and once you have, er, relieved yourself and eaten, you are to clothe, and we leave as soon as possible." Diarran then held out another hand in which he held a metal box presumably containing the food he had mentioned. Zack took the bottle from his right hand with a slight snatch of disgruntlement which went unnoticed and walked away to stand in the corner of the room with his newfound accessory. Zack saw Junko stand and walk towards Diarran, then mid-way through emptying his bladder he heard the door close behind him.

Fully kitted out in his Zeydenian guard uniform Zack was beginning to feel slightly claustrophobic in the helmet. It hadn't bothered him when he first wore it, but now he had become accustomed to the freedom from it overnight and longed for such a moment again. Surprisingly full from the plant-based breakfast that had been supplied, Zack now found himself in the driving seat of the diplomatic vehicle driving towards Zeydence Tower. Without the neon lights of the previous evening the city actually looked quite bland, Tall futuristic buildings scattered the horizon surrounded by much smaller blocks. Zack drove towards them, taking the thirty-minute journey fairly slowly. For reasons unknown he had a sense of dread about stepping out in the Queen Bee's chambers so to speak. Up until now he had interacted with Zeydenians on a much-diluted scale, but this was going to be the first time his feet touched the ground, and he would be acutely in the minority of the enemy. At the back of his mind, he saw the face of Madoka as she was taken by the Zeydenian guards from Sector sixty-nine and this was his impetus to keep going, to embrace the fear but do it anyway. Diarran pointed to Zack alternative directions to the tower.

"We'll take some of the less used roads." Diarran announced as his hand pointed over the shoulder of Zack signalling for him to take a left turn. "We will still reach the tower, but this vehicle stands out far too much. We need to keep you out of view for as long as possible during your visit here Zack."

"Even in uniform?" Zack asked.

"You never know when you will need to, how do you put it? Piss." Diarran replied. "You can't come across as being human, to anyone."

It made sense to Zack, and he wondered how he would succeed in his mission if he felt so inhibited as he continued to follow the directions of Diarran. Junko remained silent and Zack wondered if he was asleep. Another few minutes of driving and the road started to descend into a tunnel.

"This is the way." Diarran reassured Zack as the vehicle headed into the tunnel. If Zack had already been feeling claustrophobic wearing the helmet, this now intensified as the vehicle started to drive around a bend in the tunnel so that he could no longer see natural light behind nor in front of him.

"Where does this come out?" Zack asked, seeking anything to

reassure him it wasn't just a never-ending loop.

"It doesn't." Diarran replied, without emotion.

"What?" Zack asked, a slight hint of panic audible in his voice now.

"This will lead to the terminus." Diarran continued, completely oblivious to the panic his apathy had ignited. "This is where all of the diplomatic vehicles are stored. Below the tower."

Zack continued to drive. Theirs was the only vehicle within the tunnel and he had estimated that they were still at least a mile away from the tower, or so it had seemed as he had taken a last glance towards it before they entered the tunnel. The word terminus always filled Zack with a tinge of anxiety too, but his level head told him there was nothing else he could except go with the flow. There was little speaking as they rumbled on, surprisingly quiet in the tunnel until it eventually started to widen out. Automatic lighting came on and Zack saw that the road opened into a large underground room. The floors were painted red and there were other vehicles parked up along the wall facing him about two hundred metres in the distance.

"Over there." Diarran indicated as he pointed to a space between two other vehicles near a large metallic door. Zack did as he was bade and brought the vehicle to a stop between the others. There was an awkward pause until Junko spoke.

"Don't forget you are supposed to open the doors for us." He stated. Feeling his helmet to ensure that it was on correctly one last time Zack opened the door to the driver's side and stepped out. He then opened the rear door to the vehicle as Diarran emerged from it, quickly followed by Junko. He was startled by a low rumbling sound behind him. Turning, he saw the large metal door opening to a single room containing Rodrock and two other Zeydenian guards.

"Diarran," Rodrock announced as they emerged from the room, "His majesty awaits you on the eighteenth floor. He has asked that your human and guard accompany you." Rodrock cast a glare of disdain towards Junko as though he somehow felt more important than any other human living in the sectors. Junko let the comment slide without reaction, which resulted in a further glare from Rodrock.

"Excellent Rodrock." Diarran exclaimed, "We will go there immediately."

Rodrock turned back towards the room and his thin black skirt flowed as he turned around gracefully. The guards turned with him, neither paying much attention to the new arrivals and Zack stood back to allow Diarran and Junko to go ahead of him. He wasn't completely aware of protocol but assumed that as the guard he should take up the rear, as well as thinking he would follow their lead. They all stepped into the room which seemed to be about fifteen feet by fifteen feet with a plush red velvet couch along the back wall. The wall was lined with faux wooden pointing and rails. As they all ventured into the room Diarran sat on the couch. He indicated for Junko to join him and Rodrock stood to the side. Zack observed the other guards who stood with their backs to the wall observing the door. He took up a similar position and watched the large metallic door slowly close with a low rumble. They stood in silence for a few seconds which caused some confusion within Zack, slightly panicking that he was expected to teleport from the room as he had been shown by his Zeydenian friends in Serene. A wave of relief mixed with slight surprise hit him as the room started to move slightly and he realised he was in an elaborate elevator. The rise was graceful. It wasn't until Zack felt like he was moving sideways as well that he remembered the oval shape of Zeydence tower and realised that the elevator was accommodating for the curves in the building. Everyone remained silent on the ascent, but it seemed dignified within the opulent surroundings. Eventually the elevator drew to a slow halt, there was no jerking movement as it glided to a stop. The door mechanism rumbled again and opened up to a corridor. Diarran rose from the couch and Rodrock led the way out of the elevator followed by Junko and the guards. Zack followed them, watching their mannerisms and how they looked after their important guests. As he stepped out of the elevator he turned left, and saw that the corridor was gleaming white, but not so bright as to hurt the eyes. It took on a strange shape with the external windows slightly angled inwards as if to accommodate the shape of the curve of the building. On the opposite side of the corridor the walls almost stepped down above them to accommodate strip lighting that ran the length of the corridor. There was a bustle as numerous Zeydenians went about their day. Zack tried to imagine what sort of work they would be engaged in. There was a clear disdain for humans from some of them, as some of the glances that even Rodrock received were less than friendly. It shocked Zack that artificial intelligence had come so far that the free thinking had almost taken on an apartheid view among some of them. Zeydenians were everywhere, some walking towards the delegation and some following behind, some deep in conversation with others and some deep in thought. As they made their way along the corridor Zack saw a blonde female coming towards him. The sight of her made him stop in his tracks. It was a face of recognition, one that his mind had tried to bury somewhere deep inside itself. Walking towards him was, Eva. Since arriving in Rebristan, the trauma that his body had been through and the weeks that he had spent asleep had helped him to subconsciously bury his memories of Serene in the twenty first century. Of course, he still sometimes reminisced, it wasn't as though his mind had been wiped, but these thoughts were private, and he could usually sit in private and bury his emotions from the company he was keeping. But, here, now, the person he felt sure he would be accused of murdering and the final convincing reason for him fleeing into the future, was walking towards him. Zack took quick glances either side of him. No-one else seemed bothered by the traffic flow on the eighteenth floor of Zeydence Tower. The other guards were emotionless as expected, simply staring ahead as they walked. His pulse started to race as she got closer, and he could feel his breathing begin to labour. Panic set in as, along with the shock of seeing Eva, Zack realised that Zeydenian guards didn't breathe, they were just complicated robots with intelligence, but no lungs of mammals. As his breathing laboured, he feared his cover would be blown. As they drew closer to each other Eva was completely oblivious to Zack in the Zeydenian guard uniform and was strolling along with another female whom Zack felt he had met before but couldn't place where. This female was tall with long silver hair and dark skin, wearing grey leggings and a black bodice, she was beautiful. Not quite as beautiful as Eva with her long blonde hair flowing loosely behind her, held off of her face with a contrasting black headband. She wore a short, cropped navy blue top with white piping, that exposed her delicate midriff and had a plunging neck line, a matching short skirt and knee high black stockings. As she got closer Zack struggled to focus on the path ahead of him. Junko had sensed that something was wrong and wondered if anyone else would notice. Diarran had noticed but ignored the scene and kept Rodrock deep in conversation as a cover, whilst Junko threw back glares at Zack urging him to pull himself together. The pain that Zack felt in his chest was like nothing before as he had to walk parallel past, and continue without a word, the woman he had once loved so deeply, had crushed him like a vice, had believed that she was dead and he would be held accountable, and had pushed to the recesses of his mind as he had left her six hundred years in the past. It hurt, boy did it hurt, and he had to simply keep walking never knowing if he would ever see her again.

* * *

'Curious.' She had thought as they passed the delegation in the corridor. Kasumi turned as they passed, just in time to see the Zeydenian guard turning back to look forwards, the gate of his walk out of sync with the other guards accompanying the party. She felt a wave of hatred as the favoured human walked along the corridor as if he owned it. As she watched unwatched, she saw the human glaring at the Zeydenian guard who seemed to be all over the place. Her anger at him rose sharply as she wondered how he dared to cast such a look at a Zeydenian. But something about the whole scene was unsettling to her and she couldn't quite put her finger on it just yet. Her gaze from the wall of the corridor as the group moved ever further away was broken by a slight tug on her arm. She turned to see Dove smiling at her.

"Kasumi, this new covering is amazing," Dove enthused, "I can't wait for the Lord's gala. This will be my first time in public for three suns,"

Kasumi smiled down at her younger colleague and as they continued walking, she zoned her hearing sensors out as Dove continued to wax lyrical about the upcoming engagement.

26

"What was that all about?" Junko demanded, as he spun towards Zack once they were in the safety of a state room, away from prying eyes. Zack did not immediately respond, still trying to take in what he had seen, which lead Junko to panic that he had actually spoken to a genuine Zeydenian guard. Taking a look around him to make sure that the coast was clear, and that the door had closed behind himself, Junko and Diarran in the state room, Zack quickly whipped off the helmet that had been suffocating him since he had seen her. Junko breathed a sigh of relief, and Zack just sighed. Long and loud.

"She can't be here Junko, she's dead." Zack eventually exclaimed.

"Who?" Junko asked, confusedly. Zack didn't reply immediately and as the milliseconds passed by feeling like hours Junko continued, "Who's dead Zack?"

Diarran turned to look at the pair of humans slightly behind him.

"Put the helmet back on Zack." Diarran stated apathetically, "You are in safe company now, but should anyone unexpected enter the room your mission is over and there is nothing anyone can do about it."

Zack did as he bade, feeling worse for it. The few seconds he had taken to free himself of it had been long enough for the sweat he had accumulated within it to cool to what felt like a freezing temperature as he slid it in passing the features on his face.

"Eva." Was all the words that Zack could muster before his brain started spinning into a conundrum again that he could neither solve nor understand.

"Who is Eva?" Diarran asked as he looked between Zack and Junko. His curiosity piqued now by any potential hazard to their secrecy. Junko simply shrugged his shoulders. Zack turned his head in his helmet and looked at Diarran, although no-one could see the pain in his eyes.

"I knew her in Serene." Zack solemnly stated. He was met with silence and so he continued "We were a couple in the twenty first century."

As he finished the sentence the door to the state room opened and they all turned to see Flint entering the room, followed by Rodrock.

"Ok, we have a very busy day today." Announced Flint with an air of authority. It almost appeared as if those gathered stood straighter simply by the tone of his voice. "Junko, you shall accompany Diarran to the Zeydence library so that you may continue your studies."

Having been given instructions it was almost second nature for Diarran and Junko to relax a little as their heads dropped in a slight bow.

"And you," Flint continued as he looked towards Zack in his Zeydenian Guard guise, "will accompany me on my tour of Zeydence." Rodrock stepped forward as if to protest the continued usage of the same guard, but a glare from Flint as he did so quashed any idea of disagreement within him. "Rodrock, I want you to remain in my chambers and prepare my transport, for I may have to make an urgent visit to a wayward sector much later in the day."

"As you wish your highness." Rodrock bowed as he spoke and started to walk backwards out of the room, never turning his back on the group. As the door closed and Rodrock was gone, everyone relaxed slightly.

"Are we to visit a sector tonight?" Diarran asked, confused by the sudden change of plans.

"No." Flint replied, "I just needed to keep Rodrock out of the way. He means well, but he is indoctrinated into pleasing us Zeydenians that he will no doubt turn any other humans over, despite their intentions. Until your plan is formulated then it is best to keep him busy elsewhere."

"So, what are our plans for this day?" Asked Diarran.

"Zack is to come with me, we are to visit the birthing tower so that he can see what he is up against. You will take Junko to the library. Something is being planned but I am not privy to the full details, I need research to try and establish if it is a threat to our ideals and Junko is the person to do the research. Diarran, we have a big day tomorrow, so I suggest you get some rest and recharge once you have seen Junko safely to the library."

As Zack and Junko set about preparing to leave the state room, Diarran approached Flint and leant in close to him.

"I fear there may be a slight problem," Diarran started to whisper which Flint heard perfectly clear, "I do not know the full details yet but Zack believes he has seen someone from his time here in Zeydence that he believes to be deceased. I will update you further if I get any more information."

"Noted." Flint simply replied as Diarran turned to Junko and indicated that they should leave the room. Flint beckoned Zack towards him as he made his way to a window on the other side of the room. Zack followed and joined Flint at the window as he heard the familiar swooshing of the door noise behind him indicating that Diarran and Junko had left the room. Zack looked out of the window. The sky was blue with a mauve glow around the edge of the scant clouds that were in the sky. Zeydence in the daytime was not as brightly lit as during the evening but Zack watched as, below him, thousands of people milled around going about their business. Zeydence tower was the tallest building in all of Zeydence and everything else looked small below it as he looked down upon the city. As Zack stood beside Flint, he felt the hand of his artificial intelligence friend touch his shoulder as if to take him under his wing. Flint then pointed ahead to the next tallest building about one mile away from Zeydence tower.

"That, Zack, is our destination. The birthing tower where the human population is controlled and culled." Flint began as Zack turned to look at his face staring forwards before following his gaze back to the tall building, "Inside the tower you will see and experience things that go against your judgement and reasoning, but it is essential that you know the building if you are to stand any chance of helping Madoka and the rest of the humans. You will need to keep your composure and remain as emotionless as any other guard. If you cannot do this tell me now because failure once we are there will most certainly result in the death of yourself, Madoka and many other humans."

Zack nodded his head in affirmation.

"Good, then I shall prepare. We leave in thirty minutes. You will drive." Flint added as he turned from the window and walked away to a side door. Zack continued to stare out of the window at the birthing tower as he was left alone in the room.

* * *

The vehicle came to a stop in front of the birthing tower. Parked at the foot of the tower it looked a lot taller than when he was looking down at it from Zeydence tower. The tower had thirty floors visible from the outside set out into three stacks of ten floors that were encased within a chrome brace either side of the building which then formed a square arch high over the top floor. Each block of ten floors had mirrored windows which complimented the chromework of the braces that ran the height of the building at either side. Between each section of ten floors seemed to be nothing, but although it was clear day it appeared as a dark, unforgiving space. Circumnavigating the entire base of the tower was a transparent wall that appeared to be about twenty feet high. This wall stood out about fifteen feet from the base of the building and within was fire. Dark orange flames leapt about fifteen feet into the air, never quite breaching the top of the clear wall that contained it. Zack wondered if it were just an illusion as the glass did not appear to be scorched at all, and there appeared to be no increase in temperature as he sat within the vehicle mere feet away from it. As if reading his mind Flint spoke from the rear of the vehicle.

"It is true fire Zack."

"Why is it here?" Zack asked, "I mean it looks lovely and all that, but it doesn't seem necessary."

"I did forewarn you that some things you would see today would not sit well with you." Flint began, "This is one of them. The fire serves three purposes. The first is additional security to the building. To prevent escape or invasion from humans. The second is, well you see not everyone who is brought to the tower feel comfortable with the circumstances and some would rather end their lives from the high windows. The fire is to act as a deterrent if they are able to see out of the windows. The third reason is for those who do succeed in leaping from the windows. You humans cause a mighty mess when you land, and it has proven time consuming to clean the footpaths afterwards. Well, the fire takes care of disposing of any waste human parts over a short period of time without the need for cleaning. And like you state, it does add a certain aesthetic value to the building Zack."

"Not after that explanation." Zack retorted.

"You should open the door now." Flint reminded Zack of his position whilst in Zeydence. Zack immediately opened his door to the vehicle and alighted onto the footpath as dignified as he thought a robot guard would be in public, whilst fighting the discomfort of his ill-fitting uniform. Turning to the rear door, he looked around for any danger as he had witnessed other guards doing previously before grasping the handle and pulling it to open. He noticed that there had become a small matter of interest from the people of Zeydence as to who could be in the back of the vehicle. There was certainly something bubbling in the air that made him feel uncomfortable. As the door opened Flint emerged from the rear of the vehicle. There was a hush of gossip as Flint became visible to the public, but he did not seem to notice, merely pointing at a glass box in front of the fire pit as if to indicate to Zack where they were headed. Closing the door behind

Flint, Zack silently turned to face the glass box. It was about the width and height of an old red telephone box but twice the depth. He watched as Flint placed his hand on the glass. There was iridescent light, although through the visor Zack could not work out if that came from the glass or from Flint's hand. A small hum and a further glass box floated upwards graciously into the one at which he stood. Transparent doors slid apart and Flint stepped into the capsule that had just arrived. Without any instruction Zack assumed he should follow his lead and also stepped in behind Flint. There was not much room to move within the capsule, Flint was able to turn around, but in his uniform and armour Zack was not, however he heard the doors closing behind him and then the capsule began to descend. Wondering why they would be going downwards when he had quite clearly seen that the birthing tower was above him Zack said nothing. The darkness was punctuated by strips of LED lights that lit the corners of the square tunnel with which he found himself in. Suddenly the glass capsule came to a halt, just as Zack had lost sight of the street from where he had parked the vehicle. The capsule then started to move backwards, horizontally. Zack looked above him and saw the fire roaring above through the glass ceiling as they passed underneath the fire pit.

"How are we not burning?" Zack dared to ask.

"It is not hot enough to affect anything that it is not directly touching." Flint replied. "The glass on the inside will be scorching hot but to the outside and anything that is not in contact with the flame will remain unharmed."

"How so? It is fire." Zack debated as the capsule continued to slowly move beneath it.

"Many minerals, gases and elements have been discovered since you first lived Zack. Indeed, many have disappeared due to human consumption over the centuries too. This fire is fed by Daflaydian, a gas discovered about two hundred years ago. The flame is intensely hot, but the temperature will drop once it has established that the surface it touches is not consumable by fire."

The capsule stopped moving backwards and Zack saw that they had passed underneath the fire pit and further onwards by about ten feet. The capsule then began to slowly rise upwards through another glass tunnel. As they ascended Zack saw a large, well lit, spacious floor come into view. Daylight seeped through windows at the top of the walls along with an orange glow from the fire outside. There was a desk in the middle of the room with a female stood behind, wearing all white clothing. The capsule came to a halt and glass doors slid open again. Zack stepped backwards out of the glass under passing elevator and Flint followed. There were three other doors on the far side of the room and two Zeydenian guards stood motionless either side of each door. Flint strode towards the desk and the female looked up as he approached.

"Your Royal Highness." She announced as she realised who stood before her. "What brings you here today?"

"I would like to inspect the progress of the birthing program." Flint replied. "I understand that we have had a reduction in successful births, and I have been charged with rectifying this situation."

"Of course, your highness. Do you need accompanying?" Asked the female with as much smile as anyone could possibly have.

"No thank you," Flint came back, "I have my guard with me, that should suffice. This is an unannounced visit so no-one should know that I was coming here."

Without waiting for a reply Flint turned and walked towards the three guarded doors. The guards stood still as stone as he made his way to the door on the far left, swiftly followed by Zack. Zack expected them to stare at him, his anxiety making him feel as though he would be caught out at any minute, but nothing, they simply stared dead ahead. A swooshing noise as the door opened and Zack saw that beyond was another elevator. Flint stepped inside before the doors had fully opened and Zack followed. The doors closed behind them.

"Twenty-one." Flint announced out loud.

"Twenty-one." Came a mechanical voice from a speaker punctuated into the wall of the elevator, and the room began to slowly rise.

"Turn to face the door and look straight ahead." Flint instructed and Zack did as he was bade, leaving Flint standing behind him. The internal doors of the elevator were chromed so Zack could still see Flint in the reflection. "There are cameras in this capsule recording your moves but no audible recording devices. It shall take us a while to reach the twenty first floor in any case.

As Zack watched Flint's reflection in the door he noticed that, although he could hear Flint's voice, he could not see his mouth moving. He guessed that, as robots, they could communicate no matter what, but only moved the lips of their fake human faces to blend in with the humans and appear more authentic and authoritative.

"Each of these capsules goes to a different sector of the tower, representing the three segments that you saw from the outside. This is to avoid any cross contamination between the segments. You can only move from one segment to the other via the ground floor where at least six Zeydenian guards await." Flint began as if he felt Zack needed an explanation.

"Makes sense." Zack mumbled still looking forwards.

"The top sector is where the females are first brought prior to insemination. They are usually detained for up to a month, fed with supplements that will aid their conception, and to ensure that they are not bleeding and ripe to be fertilised." Flint continued.

"You make it sound so sexy." Zack stated with as much sarcasm as he could without shuddering with giggles.

"You believe I do not know what you mean but I do." Flint retorted. "The middle section is for the females who have been inseminated and are awaiting the production of a new human, and the bottom section is for the females who have produced a new human to recover and nurse the child until it is strong enough to be sent to a sector. We are heading to the top as I believe, given the time since she was taken, that that is where we will find Madoka."

At the sound of her name Zack's earlier dash into humour was crushed and everything felt so real all of a sudden. He realised that he did not yet have an idea of how he was to accomplish what he wanted to do, and here he was facing the possibility of seeing Madoka again. Suddenly guilt cruised into his conscious as he recalled seeing Eva too. How was it remotely possible that his dead ex-girlfriend from six hundred years ago was in the same town as the imprisoned female that he was now deeply in love with? As his thoughts rushed around his head into a tightening knot Flint's voice brought him back to reality.

"Remember, if we do see Madoka she will not recognise you. She may well despise you in your current guise. If your identity is discovered, then you are almost certainly dead. I know you humans hate that, but I also know that you sometimes have trouble hiding your emotions, damn things. It's up to you if and when we locate her how you behave and what your outcome will be. I shall walk away from this no matter what." Warned Flint.

"Noted." Zack replied, a sombre note to his voice now. "Why is this elevator so slow compared to others in the sector?" He asked, becoming both frustrated and inquisitive at the same time.

"It is a security feature Zack, if someone should try to escape there will be a long time for staff on the upper floors to alert the security at the base. I'm glad you are taking this in, these are factors you will need to account for if and when you attempt to rescue Madoka."

"You don't believe I can do it, do you?" Zack had noticed an element of doubt in what Flint had said.

"I don't know. I know that you have the courage and the motivation, but the skills are not known yet." Flint replied, "However, you have come further than any previous attempt so let's see how this plays out."

Zack wondered how to respond to Flint's comments but realised his time to speak was coming to an end as the elevator started to slow. He began to feel a popping sensation in his ears which told him that he was quite high up now in the scheme of things. There was no juddering halt to notify him that they had arrived, just the disappearance of his reflection as the chrome doors slid apart at the centre. They opened into a bright white expanse of levels with an open space rising through the middle of all ten floors. The sight before him reminded Zack of the old Victorian prison blocks, just in a pristine bright white instead of the concrete grey he had seen in photographs of the past. Before he could get into the floors there was a glass compartment in which stood another female member of staff and four Zeydenian guards. The glass room served as some sort of security and reception area and was about five metres by five metres in size. The female looked up as Flint stepped forward out of the elevator. Zack slipped straight back into silent guardian mode and swiftly followed behind. Being a subservient security guard was beginning to come a bit more naturally to him now.

"Your highness, what brings you here today?" The female asked as she looked up at him with a smile. The guards remained standing motionless, as they were downstairs, and Zack wondered whether they were just elaborate statues designed to strike fear into anyone thinking of escaping.

"I understand that you have two occupants from sector sixty-nine currently on these floors?" Flint stated rather than asked but still required a confirmation.

"That would be correct. They are both in room 5EH." Came the reply from the female. As he stood closer to her Zack took a time to look at her. Her skin was flawless, and she had thin but long golden blonde hair. She appeared to be about twenty-five years old, and Zack wondered if she were Zeydenian or a human. Dressed all in white she looked at Zack as if she could subconsciously feel his eyes roaming all over her. Zack remained motionless.

"My sources in the Zeydenian tower inform me that they are not behaving in a manner that would be beneficial to our cause, am I correct?"

"You would be correct your highness." The female replied matter of factly.

"As you will be aware, sector sixty-nine is one of the sectors that I hold the royal responsibility for. I shall go and speak with them to see if I cannot curb this behaviour before matters go too far." Flint told the female, rather than asking. "I shall take my guard with me so that there is no reduction in security capability here." He continued, indicating toward where Zack stood.

"As you wish your highness." The female replied but Flint was already walking towards a sliding door within the glass before she had finished her sentence. Zack panicked as he realised that he had waited until she had finished what she was saying before following Flint, and he wondered whether good manners and etiquette was just a human thing. He walked after Flint expecting to hear someone call after him from behind, but as the glass door slid closed behind him, he realised he had gotten away with it. Flint continued to stride along the floor towards another door which was halfway along the hallway that they now found themselves in on the right-hand side. There was quietness all around, even though there seemed to be women looking over the bannisters from each floor all the way to the top. Zack tried to look just by moving his eyes and not by moving his head and neck. He assumed that a Zeydenian guard wouldn't really care about the occupants and being stared at. Flint and Zack strode with purpose until they got to the door. It opened as they approached Zack saw that it was another elevator. They stepped inside and as the door closed behind them Flint spoke.

"Five." He said with the same authority as he had in the elevator from the ground floor. The capsule started to move upwards. "Are you ready for this?" Flint asked.

"Ready for what?" Zack responded.

"We are going to see Madoka." Flint replied. The mention of her name again caused Zacks heart to surge. "I need you to stay focussed on your goal and kill all emotions."

"I understand." Zack replied as the elevator drew to a halt and the doors opened. Flint stepped out and turned to his left with Zack in tow. They walked along a landing about two metres wide that stretched around the whole outside of the floor, leaving a huge drop in the middle whereby Zack could look up to the ceiling five floors above and down to the security office five floors below. Zack saw that there was thin transparent film that ran from the top of the rail to the edge of the ceiling above. Several women stood on the landing, pushing at the film which seemed to expand as they did so but never broke. Some women ran back into their rooms, as if in fear, as Flint and Zack approached. As he walked past their doors he saw that they were sat on their beds with a look of fear on their faces. Some women just stared defiantly as they walked by and others spat at them. This either went unnoticed by Flint or he was not bothered by it. Either way, Zack felt that he had to follow suit and just kept walking, two steps behind Flint until they were almost opposite the elevator on the other side of the landing. Flint seemed to slow as he looked up above one of the doors. 5EH engraved in white on the white wall above the white door. The door was closed. A tear formed in Zacks eye and tickled the side of his face as he was unable to wipe it away with the helmet on. The door took less than a second to open but to Zack it felt like an eternity. Once open Madoka leapt from her bed and rushed at her door with a feral growl. Flint stepped into the room.

"Stop Madoka." Flint commanded. She looked up and saw who had entered and slowed her pace and stood resigned before him. Zacks eyes took her all in as if the vision of her alone was a drug. She was dressed all in white linen, with her long black hair trailing down the front of her shoulders. Her hair was unkempt, and whilst she still looked beautiful, she looked a little wild and insane too. Her eyes were puffy as if she had cried a lot behind closed doors. Zack scanned the room as he stepped inside as well. The room was pristine in white, with beds with white linen and that was basically it. It was total colour deprivation. There was a bed on either side of the room which could not have been any bigger than three metres by three metres. On the opposite bed to where Madoka had leapt from he saw the other female that had been taken from the sector on the morning that Madoka left. She stared catatonically ahead, and he wondered if she even knew they were there.

"Flint." A single word from Madoka, her voice broken, and Zack's eye started to leak again. He stood motionless behind Flint not wanting to see Madoka in this current state but at the same time wanting to absorb every image of her that he possibly could too.

"I hear you are being difficult Madoka." Flint stated matter of factly. Madoka just looked around the room as if in shame but not wanting to be, wanting to rebel still. She did not reply, so Flint continued, "There is only so much rebellion I can supress, you have seen first-hand what happens to those who are a fraction as intolerant to the Zeydenian people."

Madoka span around with anger rising on her face this time.

"I am not going through this again Flint!" She spat, and then appeared to calm a little, "I know you mean well but you cannot have any idea what it feels like to go through this, and then be left empty afterwards." A tear formed in her left eye and started to run down her cheek. This was too much, and Zack stepped forward a step before Flint put his arm out to the side to bid him to remain still. At his movement, in his guise as a Zeydenian guard, Madoka's head span to look at him and she cast him a look of complete contempt and disgust. The look in her eyes bore into Zack's soul and it took all of his power not to whimper. He had never seen this in her before and he hoped that he never would again.

"You are right," Flint began, "I cannot know what you feel as I am incapable, however I see your pain. You must behave to save yourself. Plans are in place, I cannot disclose everything, but please be patient."

Madoka looked at the floor as if a fire had been put out inside of her and there was no energy left in the whole world. She stepped backwards to sit down onto her bed.

"Ok." She mumbled, and then looked up at Flint standing above her, "How is Zack?"

"He's fine Madoka. He's closer than you think. Be patient." At that he turned to leave the room. Zack lingered a second or two longer, not wanting to take his eyes off of her until she glanced back at him with the earlier look of hatred for the guards. At that he turned and followed Flint out of the room. The door slid closed behind him and it felt as heavy as his heart as he realised that he did not know whether that look from her would be the last time he ever saw her.

27

Junko looked up the building before him. Elegant steps, about a dozen or so lead up to the black marble pillars the stood either side of the black glass doors. The two Zeydenian guards stood either side of him, having followed him from Flint's room within Zeydence tower, watching his every move and matching his every step. A few Zeydenians scorned upon him as he walked by, but he expected that. It didn't take a genius, not even an artificially intelligent one, to work out that he was a human being with the entourage that he had. Artificial Intelligence had come so far that the modern age gentry of the Zeydenians were able to form feelings or hatred and disgust for the humans. Taking in the sunshine of freedom in the capital city, for he knew there would be none but artificial once inside the library, Junko tilted his head towards the sky and closed his eyes. There were a few grumbles from passers-by about how dare he take their sunshine, but he ignored this. After the moment had passed and he believed that he had pissed the locals off enough Junko bowed his head forwards again and opened his eyes. He then ascended the steps to the library. As he reached the top the majestic black glass doors slid open for him and he stepped forwards. Walking into the library, the doors closed behind him and his two Zeydenian guards waited outside. There was no need for them to follow his every move. There was only one other exit from the library, and this was accessible only with a data card issued to Zeydenians. For any visiting humans, such as today, there was only one way in or out should there be an emergency, such was the neglect of human life. Junko found himself in a glass vestibule and as the door to the outside world closed behind him, another in front of him began to open. The temperature as he stepped inside rose to seventy degrees Fahrenheit but wasn't uncomfortable as the humidity was kept at the perfect level to preserve the books and papers going back centuries. The artificial lighting inside the library was akin to daylight and for a moment Junko basked in it. He had been here before, but it was still always a novelty to him from the standard lighting of the buildings in the sector.

"Someone said you may pay me a visit today." Came a voice from behind Junko over his left shoulder. A voice that he recognised, husky from years of working in such a controlled dry environment, female, and slightly more aged than it had been the last time he heard it. But still, unmistakably Yioro. Junko turned to his left and there she was. A few more wrinkles than before, but then it had been a couple of years since Junko last set foot inside the Zeydenian library. Yioro's long grey hair was tucked neatly behind her ears, ice blue eyes, and a smile exuding a warmth that defied her eye colour. She was still as tall as Junko, age had not yet started to take her height from her, and incredibly slim. She wore the same immaculate uniform that had been provided to her for her duties, a full length grey trouser suit that was fastened by a double row of buttons and supported by a gold coloured belt and shoulder harness. Junko knew that she had only been given one such uniform but always managed to turn up for her duties immaculately clean and pressed. His smile met hers and he stepped forwards towards Yioro with both arms extended as she walked into his embrace.

"Yioro, it's so nice to see you again." Junko announced.

"And you." She replied as she held him tight, "There have been fewer humans allowed to visit as the months have gone by. It's nice to finally have some company I can enjoy."

There were a couple of Zeydenians within the library who looked up at her comments, but Junko simply laughed. This old girl was never afraid to speak her mind. Junko returned the hug and then stood back to look her up and down.

"You don't look a day older than when I last saw you." Junko announced.

"Now I know you're lying." Yioro smiled again.

"I'm not, you were quite old the last time we met too." Junko stated. Yioro laughed and gave him a nudge in the ribs.

"So, why do I have the honour of your presence today Junko?" Yioro asked.

"It's a very long story, and one saved for more private surroundings, but today I have been asked to come here by Flint to study."

Yioro did not press any further. She hated the fact that she never knew the strength or sensitivity of the hearing devices on each Zeydenian.

"You must come with me for some boiled drink." Yioro said as she took Junko by his arm and gently pulled him towards a convenience room at the back of the library. Junko knew that the room would be airtight and pretty much soundproof in order to stop any food or drink heating or freezing affecting the controlled temperature of the library. They walked in silence until the door closed behind them. Yioro was the first to speak.

"What does Flint know?" She asked.

"I am not too sure at the moment." Junko replied, "He senses a great shifting in the Zeydenians but is uncertain what is being planned. I have been asked to spend time at the library for my own pleasure, but also to see if there is anything I can find out about the current mood of Zeydence."

Yioro turned to take some water from a bottle and place it into two drinking vessels. Upon contact with the inside of the insulated vessel the water began to bubble and boil before settling down. Junko could feel the steam rising to meet his face as Yioro searched a cupboard for another bottle. She then turned and added a few drops of a green liquid to each vessel and the boiled water turned a dark green in colour.

"Is this.......?" Junko started

"Yes," Interrupted Yioro, "It's essence of Trokine. I have a Zeydenian friend who brings me some from time to time. Any chance I get of depriving those sadist robots, for that is what they are if you read the Heinlen files, of the plant that keeps them going.... I take it."

"And from someone who works in the fields to provide it for them, I approve." Junko returned as they both giggled before taking a sip of their drinks. It wasn't the nicest tasting plant that either had tried but it was the defiance of tasting forbidden product, the denial of the product to the Zeydenians that made it so enjoyable. "So, what is new here?" Junko asked.

"Something strange is happening." Yioro replied, "The Zeydenians have started to clear some of the library sectors."

"How so?"

"Each day, a group of intellectuals come to the library in the afternoon with an order from Lord Dhonos himself to remove books in their thousands. They are boxed in the rear corner. I try to tell them to be careful, some of this paper is one thousand years old, but there appears to be an abandon, even from the intellectuals in the care of the books. Lord Dhonos himself has even visited on two occasions."

Junko found this strange and disturbing in equal measures and pondered hard over the direction of the conversation. He took a few more sips from his drink.

"Which books are they taking?" Junko finally asked.

"They seem to be concentrating on the sections about the past, before the bomb, the ancient historical paper works and those books they call the Bible." Yioro replied, "Whole sections of my beloved library are disappearing and there is no talk yet of what will replace it, where they will go, or whether they intend to transfer the texts to automatic download for Zeydenians only. That is my fear that they are restricting the knowledge from the humans."

That wasn't the only fear that Junko was beginning to have, but he couldn't quite place his finger on what was making his skin crawl. The Zeydenians, despite their hatred for humans, had always placed such importance on the library, on the history of the planet that they inhabited. And now the books and papers were being boxed up, for what? Junko didn't like it. Finishing up the last few gulps of his drink as it rapidly cooled, he placed the vessel back on a workspace and walked towards the door.

"I'll let you get on with your work Yioro, I'm off to read." Junko stated, not wanting to make the elderly female concerned about his concerns. Junko opened the door as Yioro finished the last of her drink. "I'll be sitting in the corner, reading. Let me know if you want another drink at any time and I'll be happy to oblige."

Junko walked out of the small resting room and into the library, breathing in again the musky smell of ancient books, and headed to the human history corner. Most Zeydenians were not concerned with human history so he was likely to be undisturbed for longer there, plus he wanted to see for himself if he was right to be concerned about Yioro's announcement. He walked along a shelving rack of computer science books until he got to the end and turned left expecting to see racks of books. Instead, he saw desolation, empty racks in various stages of dismantlement, and a mountain of storage boxes piled high in the corner of the room. Taking a deep breath, he picked up a book from the rack he was about to pass, any book without even looking. It made no difference what it was about, he was hardly going to read today anyway. He sat at a chair in the corner of the emptiness, opened the book, and resolved to just look around at what the Zeydenians were doing instead.

28

Flint was sat in the back of the vehicle as Zack drove in silence. He had been given no directions and so he just drove the streets of Zeydence getting to know his way around. Subconsciously he always kept the birthing tower within view, which wasn't too hard as it was one of the tallest buildings in Zeydence. They had been driving for an hour or so before Flint broke the silence.

"I must recharge soon." Flint stated, "I cannot simply let you loose on the streets, so I have arranged for you to work a shift at the hub."

"The hub?" Zack spoke, asked, with a numbness that drove any emotion from his voice. Madoka still at the forefront of his mind.

"Yes." Flint responded with an equal measure of emotion.

"Where is this hub?" Zack asked, feeling a follow up question would be necessary if his day was to progress any further. He was sure that it wasn't meant personally but the Zeydenians he had encountered became less talkative and sociable as their power began to wane.

"Opposite Zeydence Tower. I shall not be far away." Came the reply from Flint. Zack looked into his mirror into the rear of the vehicle and Flint had become paler, not so much light in his eyes. Zack had never seen him, nor any Zeydenian, like this before and wondered if he was really draining himself to help Zack's cause, Madoka's cause. This helped to pull himself out of his funk. If someone who was not even of his species, and supposed to be the enemy, could try so hard to help then Zack really should not be wasting energy sulking about things that were out of his control. Zack decided that he had asked enough questions for now and that Flint should be allowed to rest until they got to the tower. The next crossroads was broad, three lanes in each direction from each direction. There appeared to be no road markings, but all drivers seemed to be able to pass safely as if driving skills were built into their consciousness. Zack arrived at the crossroads to see a small quantity of traffic slowly seeking their destinations. He looked to his left and could see the birthing tower in the distance along the long straight road. That must mean.... he turned his head to look out of the right front window, and there it was, Zeydence Tower standing majestically halfway along the straight road leading right. As he had been assessing his location there came a point when all other traffic had crossed, and he was free to proceed. Zack moved forwards, turning right with a sigh of relief that no-one was watching him now that he had space to move. Driving the straight lines from Sector sixty-nine to Zeydence had not been a problem, but now that he was in a built-up area, behind enemy lines so to speak, he was always conscious of his driving not being up to par with the standard programmed into Zeydenians. Once he had straightened up, he began the drive towards Zeydence tower. Not too fast, there was no hurry, but fast enough to avoid lengthy gazes towards the diplomatic vehicle from pedestrians. About ten minutes later he pulled up outside Zeydence Tower where he had parked the night previously. As if subconsciously knowing his surroundings Flint became animated and looked out of the windows. Across the road from the tower stood a small squat building. Well, small compared to the tower that loomed over it. It was about four storeys high with a flat roof and made of cold grey stone. It was mainly windowless, a few windows on the first floor, but that was it, the ground floor and upper two floors were barren of any windows, just stone. Zack tried to imagine a more depressing looking building but could think of none.

"Take the vehicle over there, pull up down the left-hand side." Flint commanded. Zack did as he was bade. There was no additional traffic and so it was easy for him to cross straight over. Turning down the left side of the building he discovered that the road sloped downwards sharply and that there were at least two more levels below the street. The building was about eighty metres deep and the road levelled out as Zack approached the far end of it. It was here that he first noticed a door. A metal door with a Zeydenian guard standing either side of it.

"You will need to let me out of the vehicle to follow protocol Zack. You will need to speak with the guards before I emerge and say, 'Be well', do you understand?" Flint spoke

"Yes sir." Zack replied, morphing into the subservient role of a Zeydenian guard. Taking a deep breath before opening the door he wondered if his muscles would be able to function unhindered as he had been sat for so long. Resisting the urge to stretch them out Zack stepped out of the vehicle. Even through the armour that he wore he could feel a breeze going by. The two Zeydenian guards stepped forwards and looked at Zack.

"Be well." Zack bade them both.

"Be well." They both replied in unison before stepping back into position. Was that it? Zack expected more scrutinization but seemed to have gotten away with it. Before he attracted any scrutiny, he turned around and opened the rear door to the vehicle. Flint looked at him before emerging from the vehicle.

"Be well." Flint said to the guards. They appeared unprepared to see him but stood aside either side of the door. Flint stepped forward and the door whooshed open as he approached it. Zack followed. As Flint was level with the guards, they both stated "Be well Sir." Once inside the door closed behind them and they were alone again. Even through the armour Zack felt a chill, a familiar chill of air conditioning throughout the building.

"Jeez, it's cold." Zack spoke to himself. Flint cast him a glare.

"As a Zeydenian you would not feel that, but yes the temperature is lower inside here than in the open, and that sort of comment would get you killed if we were not alone." Flint stated. Zack could not reply, he had let his guard down and felt stupid about it. "Follow me," Flint continued, "I don't have much time left before you are alone, and I need to put you somewhere safe."

Zack did as he was told, following Flint towards an elevator, and climbing inside. They went up and Zack remained silent, still embarrassed by his blunder and afraid to open his mouth for the time being. When they got out of the elevator Zack had no idea how high up they were. He had been lost in his thoughts to count the floors on the way up. They were in a dark corridor, dimly lit by lights within the ceiling. The corridor was about five feet wide, and only about twenty feet long. At the end of it there was a grey metal door. Flint strode towards it with a purpose. Zack was aware that his energy was draining and for a second wondered if the Zeydenians were capable of experiencing panic. The door swooshed open and they entered a large room. Just inside the door stood a single Zeydenian guard.

"Be well." Flint and the guard exchanged pleasantries.

"Be well." Zack joined in, trying not to allow any worry to enter his voice.

"You are relieved." Flint said to the guard.

"I still have time left on my shift Sir." The guard replied.

"You are relieved." Flint stated again, "This guard will take over. You should return immediately to your barracks for an early recharge."

"Yes Sir." replied the guard, who promptly turned and walked through the door. It soon swooshed closed behind him.

"You will remain here until I send for you." Flint stated to Zack before turning to leave himself,

"Yes Sir." Zack stated with a hint of amusement. Flint did not react as the door swooshed open again for him. Within seconds the door swooshed closed again and Zack stood alone. He took some time to look around the room. It was large and appeared to stretch out behind the door, occupying the space behind the walls of corridor he had just come from. It was dark, again dimly lit with a thin window that ran along the top of the far walls that allowed in a little natural light. However, these windows were so dusty and dirty they appeared as if they had never been cleaned since the building had been built. Within the room were rows of walls that were about six feet high that seemed to go on forever. All of these walls had hundreds of small red lights on them, some blinking, some static, and as Zack moved closer to one of them he could feel a great heat being given off by them. Underneath the window in front of him was a desk with what looked like large terminals on it glitching away with various bright colours, and more importantly, a chair. Zack had no idea how long he would be left in this room but didn't relish the idea of standing in his uniform the whole time. He walked over to the chair, slid it out from underneath the desk and sat down. No sooner had the seat of his armour touched down on the chair did he hear a clattering noise from behind him. Turning to his left he saw a strange little man emerging from behind one of the small walls of flashing lights. He only stood about five feet tall which is why Zack had not seen him previously standing behind the wall, they towered above him.

"Well, that's a fucking nuisance." Uttered the little man, surprising Zack that he had a potty mouth. "Now they're making fucking soldiers that sit down on the job. Unbelievable."

Zack hadn't been expecting company and started to curse himself at perhaps making a second mistake in a short space of time. He didn't know whether Zeydenian guards would sit down or not. Why should they? It's not like they had a muscle mass that ached or got tired. He recalled seeing Flint, Diarran and Marna sitting when they visited and spoke with the humans, but maybe they just did that just to be polite or to mirror human customs when in their homes. Who knew? Certainly not Zack but he appeared to have touched a nerve with the person in front of him and it made him feel uncomfortable. He watched as the little man pottered around looking at the red flashing lights, occasionally touching his chest or head as walked back and forth muttering under his breath. Zack could not hear all that the man said but understood a few expletives here and there. The man, despite being quite short, was quite stockily built. Zack would have put him in his late fifties or early sixties in age. Zack assumed he was human rather than Zeydenian due to the amount of unkempt facial hair that was clearly growing on his face. The man's hair was wispy and grey, the same shade as his moustache and beard, but seemed to be receding towards the crown. He had a puffy nose that balanced a large circular pair of spectacles upon them, thin wires linking them behind his ears somewhere under his scruffy hair. Why would a Zeydenian need corrective glasses? This cemented Zacks opinion that the little man was human. He appeared to be wearing blue denim dungarees with a black shirt underneath them and was barefooted. Zack stood up, wondering whether to help push himself up with his arms and waited until the man had his back turned to him. As Zack stood up straight the little man spun around with a speed that surprised him and glared at him.

"That's it!" Yelled the little man, "Just fucking shoot me now and get it over with!"

Zack looked him up and down, still perplexed by his attitude and anger.

"I don't intend to shoot you." Zack replied, a little lost for words. This time it was the little man's turn to look perplexed as he cocked his head to the side to look at Zack. There was a pause before he spoke again.

"You all intend to shoot me. Someday it'll come, once you've fucking finished with me and had all you can out of me."

"Are you......human?" Zack asked, unsure as to whether such a question should be asked. There was yet again another pause.

"Of course I'm fucking human. Seriously? You believe you'd treat one of your own kind like this? Where did they get you from? I didn't see the code come through for retarded stock."

"I don't like your insinuation." Zack retorted, no longer able to bite his tongue with this rude little man. He expected more abuse from him, but the man just stood and stared at him. Zack knew he was thinking and it worried him about what. Finally, the man spoke.

"Who are you?" He asked.

"I'm a Zeydenian guard assigned to this.... room." Zack was thinking on his feet and not very well.

"You're no more Zeydenian than I am." The little man said, his eyes burning towards Zack as he took a step closer.

"I am a Zeydenian guard." Zack repeated, trying to put as much authority into his voice as he could, but failed miserably as the two of them drew closer.

"OK," The little man replied with his head cocked to one side as he stared intently at Zack, "I'm just going to walk out of the room and downstairs. When I meet the guards at the main door, I'll tell them you authorised a code twelve and I'm free to go. You can discuss it with them."

"I have not authorised a code twelve!" Zack retorted, annoyance entering his voice now.

"Hah, that's because there is no such thing as a code twelve." The little man almost jumped for joy as he spoke, "Now, just who the fuck are you?"

Zack was confused. He had been caught out again. He wanted to blame it on being tired, on being emotional about seeing Madoka, but he couldn't blame it on anything, he shouldn't blame it on anything. If you made mistakes here there is a good chance it will get you killed. But his game was up, as far as this little man was concerned. He'd somehow have to just stop him from being able to tell anyone else until Flint turned up again, which could be hours away. He took his chance.

"My name is Zack," He informed the little man as he stepped closer and removed his helmet, "I am a human too." Underneath his armour his legs were shaking. This could go very wrong and could be the end. He waited for a reaction, but all the little man did was stood and stared at him. Zack stepped closer still and as he did so he was relieved to see that the little man did not try and run, shout, and that he didn't actually seem to get any taller or bigger. Eventually Zack was stood in front of him, at least a foot taller. Still, nothing had been said. Then the little man held out his right hand.

"Jackson." Said the little man.

"Excuse me?" Zack replied. It seemed as if both men were as confused by this current situation as each other.

"Jackson. That's my fucking name."

"Oh right," Zack tentatively took his hand with his own, and was surprised at the grip Jackson had. They shook hands, released, and then there was a pause, as neither knew what to say next. Jackson turned around and walked to his flashing lights, looking them up and down leaving Zack stood where he was. It was Jackson who spoke first though.

"So, why are you here?" He asked.

"Erm...I'm here to see someone." Zack replied, not sure how much to give away at this stage.

"And you came here with *his Royal Highness* Flint." Jackson stated with a hint of sarcasm in his voice, "How does that happen?"

"I just know him." Zack replied uncommittedly. Jackson spun around to face him, again his speed surprised Zack, and there was that glare from him again. It didn't take much to light his fuse.

"Listen. If you want to survive in this place, you're gonna have to be a bit more open. At this present time you don't look much like a friend to me, but at the same time you don't much look like a friend to the guards at posted on the doors to the building. And with Flint out of the building you are shit out of people that wouldn't like to see you dead. Now the guard's downstairs, they'd kill you quicker than I could, so I guess it's up to you now who you want to speak to, because trust me, you will be speaking to someone." Jackson lectured Zack with an air of authority that he hadn't yet experienced in a human during his time in Rebristan.

"You wouldn't believe me if I told you in any case." Zack replied.

"Listen buddy, I've spent the best part of forty years in this room," Jackson swept his arm in an arc around the room that they stood in, "My living quarters are on the floor above. I don't get out much, so anything you tell me will be treated with confidence, because I've got no-one to tell, and an open mind."

"OK." Zack started, "I'm from the twenty first century." He paused waiting to be ridiculed.

"Oh, you're a Vanisher." Jackson sighed, "Is that it?"

"You're not surprised?" Zack asked with surprise in his own voice.

"Nah, I've heard of them. Seen them even. Look" Jackson motioned for Zack to follow him behind the wall of flashing lights. Before he got to the end of the wall, he spun around quickly to look at some of the flashing lights, raising a finger up towards them and then pulling it back again quickly before his shoulders shook and he tottered onwards again. Zack followed and saw that there were many rows of the lit-up walls with thousands of flashing lights.

"What exactly are all of these lights for?" Zack asked as they continued their journey to the back of the room.

"It's the Zeydenians." Jackson replied, which took Zack by surprise. He hadn't expected that answer and he hadn't expected Jackson to be so open with him either.

"I don't understand." Zack responded. "What do you mean it's the Zeydenians?"

"It's their heart, their soul, their brain, whatever you want to call it." Jackson stopped walking and stared down one of the corridors of lights. Zack, bringing up the rear, nearly walked straight into him. "You know they're robots, right?"

"Yeah, artificial intelligence." Zack replied

"Well, the intelligence they have is right here in this room." Jackson announced. "These are what you might have called hard drives, each one on this side roughly one exabyte in size, and on the other side of the room they are roughly three hundred petabytes each."

"Wow, I've heard of such memory capability, but never seen so much in action. Why the difference in sizes though? Zack asked.

"This side, the largest of the drives is for the citizens of Zeydence. On the other side of the room the drives are for the Zeydenian guards. You have to work your way up for one of these drives." Jackson chuckled. He could see that Zack was still trying to take in everything that he was saying and felt that there were a few holes that needed filling. "There's one drive for each Zeydenian, and every time they go to recharge their memories are uploaded to their drive. Any important Zeydenian messages can be shared immediately to them all and any updates required in their operating systems are downloaded when they recharge."

"I see." Said Zack, "And what do you do here?"

"You could call me their caretaker." Jackson replied, with not as much enthusiasm in his voice as should be imagined.

"Meaning?" Zack asked. He thought he knew what it meant, but nothing had really been as it seemed since he arrived in Rebristan.

"Meaning, I was raised and educated to a high level, believing I was privileged and special, only to be brought here under threat and all of that education was just to keep these working. If there is a break in power, I am on hand to activate the emergency backup power giving me one day to investigate the initial break. If anyone's drive crashes, the flashing light will go solid, and I am to repair the drive within one hour. I am sent the operating system updates and the emergency messages and I am to distribute them from the server immediately. I came here when I was fifteen years old, and I will leave here after my last breath. Jackson was looking at the floor as he spoke the last few sentences, before looking up and with venom finishing "All for them fucking robots to have the high life."

"It sucks I guess. They'd probably kill you if you refused." Zack muttered, not too loud as he felt embarrassed about the relative freedom he had experienced in the past.

"Not me, I'm too valuable to them." Jackson stated, "I have two surviving sisters and a mother in sector thirty-one. That's who they will take any dissent out on."

"Surviving?"

"Yeah, I refused once before." Was all that Jackson would say on the topic. His eye glassed up a little and he turned to the back of the room again and started walking. "Come."

Zack followed and they got to the last wall of drives. Behind the wall was another desk with a singular chair and a bank of three monitors.

"What am I looking at?" Zack asked.

"This." Jackson indicated with his hand to the desk and monitors. "Flint gave me this to help pass the time in this hellhole. It plays films that had been recorded in the past, some of them are centuries old, but it helps. It's not connected to the main system, it's all mine." He looked like a little boy at Christmas with his one gift he'd ever received in his life.

"So, what do you watch?" Zack asked, curious about the old films and the possibility of a glimpse into the past he had left behind.

"Films, some sports. The news. We really fucked the planet, it's a no wonder these fuckers walked all over us." Jackson replied.

"Do you have a favourite film?" Zack noticed the mood turning negative again and tried to steer it in a more light-hearted direction. It worked, Jackson's face lit up again as he went to the desk and tapped on the keyboard a few times.

"Yeah, this one!" Jackson enthused as the film cover came up on the screen. Zack instantly recognised the cover. Eddie Murphy sitting atop a red Mercedes convertible in his black jacket, white shirt, stonewash blue jeans and white Adidas shoes. A small pang hit Zack. He hadn't expected to be affected by the loss of the past, but just seeing the branding on items he remembered from the past jolted him back there for a split second before he realised again that he was standing in what was effectively a high-tech prison cell in a dystopian future. He composed himself.

"Beverly Hills Cop? It's a classic." Zack stated. "Now I see where you've mastered the art of the English language now."

"Get the fuck out of here." Jackson said and they both laughed together.

"And this is where I see them. The Vanishers. Some of them have turned up in the crowd at sports events, walking in the background during news segments, I recognise them from the sector. I also recognise some of the Zeydenians. It's like they're trying to send me a message."

"And that message is?" Zack asked.

"I don't know. I get angry seeing them enjoying that kind of freedom and my mind gets foggy."

"Well, I'm here to help achieve the freedom goal." Zack replied.

"Many have tried, many have failed. It all ends messy and the Zeydenians make a painful example of any who try. It's impossible. They all get the same messages at the same time instantly. I should know, I have to distribute them. Nothing gets past them." Jackson's voice became melancholic again, but Zack looked around the room, stepped backwards and looked along the length of the walls at the flashing lights and had a lightbulb moment.

"All of these drives are linked to one another?" He asked.

"Yeah, why?" Jackson replied with a question himself.

"Isn't there a shut off switch that would just take them all out?" Zack felt like he was asking a question that should have already been considered centuries ago, and as excited as he was about the question, he still dreaded the answer to bring his idea crashing down.

"That would only work if they were all recharging at the same time." Jackson replied, and there it was, the crushing came down, "Their operating system is only updated when they are recharging which is usually at random times. Any hint that there was anything wrong in the system and I dread to think what would happen to my family. Like the governments of your time, they use fear to control the masses."

Zack had grasped the idea with both hands and Jackson had put an obstacle in the way, but he wasn't about to let go. He had come to Zeydence with a mission, but he didn't have a clue of how to do it. Now, he had a clue, a flawed clue, but it was more than he had when he entered the room. He settled down with Jackson and they spoke for hours on end.

29

Diarran hadn't said much to Zack on the walk back to Zeydence tower. This made Zack feel a little uneasy, but he kept thinking that these Zeydenians were so emotionless that it was nothing to worry about. Once inside Flints quarters the door whooshed shut behind them. A moment later, Flint emerged from the door opposite.

"Diarran, would you excuse us please?" Flint said, more directing than asking. Without a word Diarran turned around and left the room. Zack did not turn around but heard the familiar whoosh noise as it did so. For reasons he couldn't explain Zack felt like a naughty child in a headmaster's office.

"You should take your helmet off when you are in here with me." Flint instructed. Under any other circumstances Zack would be relieved to be rid of it, but he was beginning to feel as if he were under a spotlight, and a feeling of nakedness enveloped him as he took the helmet off. He said nothing but did as he was bade.

"Is there a reason that Jackson believes that you are a human?" Flint asked. So, this is what it was about.

"Erm...He kinda just guessed." Zack stuttered.

"And you confirmed his guess?"

"What was I supposed to do? He wasn't happy with me being a guard and was threatening to tell the other guards. I took a gamble." Zack tried to reason.

"A gamble that could well get you killed and have me banished again, or worse." Flint informed him.

"I had no choice," Zack offered, "Besides, he's cool with it."

"He's what?" The phrase had somehow been lost on Flint.

"I mean. He's with us. He's not going to tell anyone." Zack explained.

"And yet as soon as you left the building with Diarran, he was inputting a message into my operating system to tell me that you're human. Is that the actions of someone who can keep our secret Zack?" Flint continued.

"Look, he knows that you turned up at the building with me. He regards you highly among the Zeydenians. I had to make a choice and I feel I've made the right one." Zack argued.

"Well, let's hope so. For now, we continue as if nothing has happened. We will soon know if the secret has spread any further."

Flint calmed slightly at Zacks reassurance. Zack nodded in approval. "Tonight, there is to be a gala in the penthouse of this building with the rulers of Zeydence. I want you to be there. In guard armour, of course. All Zeydenian guards must recharge once in a while, and people will start to notice that you have been active for too long. Until the gala, you are to remain in the room at the back, out of sight, and I would suggest that you catch up on some of your human sleep." Flint instructed Zack. Without another word Zack looked in the direction that Flint was indicating and saw that the door was open. It was probably the right move to catch up on some sleep for now. Zack made his way to the door. Once it had closed after him Flint turned to the main quarters door and exited too.

* * *

After a quick briefing on how to react to certain situations, he certainly didn't want to make any more mistakes, Zack found himself in an elevator going to the peak of Zeydence tower with Flint. Junko had returned from the library with many questions but not many answers and was instructed to return to the retreat for Royal Zeydenians with Diarran. He felt slightly uncomfortable in his guard's armour. He'd had about three hours sleep but the sweat from wearing it during the earlier hot weather hadn't yet dried out, but had managed to turn an icy damp cold as he put it on.

Eventually the elevator slowed to a halt and the doors slid open. Flint stepped out of it, quickly followed by Zack. He beheld a majestic room that he initially could not believe existed at the peak of the tower, until he noticed the glass ceiling that rose to an apex in the centre. The room was both light and dark at the same time. Lights emitted between the individual windowpanes and there were numerous ochre coloured marble supports that arched upwards to form the point of the top of Zeydence tower. It certainly looked bigger from inside than it did from staring up to the top from outside. Uplights on the marble supports gave further light to the room in contrast to the colour of the supports themselves. On either side of the room were two raised daises, sloping upwards from the floor to be about seven feet off of the ground at the top of the platform. There were further majestic structures hung above each of these which, suspended by steel columns from the ceiling, provided bright white downlights onto the daises and the floor below. Zack looked around in awe at the artwork that the structure seemed to exude.

"Don't be too much in awe." Flint said to Zack over his shoulder, as if sensing Zacks admiration and thoughts, "You realise many humans died to make this statement of opulence?"

Zack hadn't thought of it that way. The grand pillars appeared to him in a different light now. There were only a handful people in the great hall, but ever more seemed to be piling in behind them from the two parallel elevators that were constantly zipping up and down.

"I won't be able to instruct you so much once the room fills up a little more." Flint said to Zack, "Remember what we went through, if there are any alarms you just do what the other guards do, and I will seek you out."

Zack nodded affirmative; he was afraid to speak back in reply as other Zeydenians brushed past him as they emerged from the elevator. This was the most fearful he had felt at being caught. He imagined this is how his great grandfather would have felt during the second world war. He had been a desert rat going behind enemy lines to establish numbers and what was being planned to stay one step ahead. It had cost him a leg, but he was one of the lucky ones.

"Remember." Flint started and paused while a group of people dressed in silk passed them and made their way out of earshot, "There is to be a big announcement tonight. I have not been afforded any advance notice of what it could be, but something is happening. Based on what Junko has told us today too I think it will make your mission all the more important. Now, stay close to me." With that Flint walked on into the hallway to mingle with the dignitaries of Zeydence. Zack always stood close by, silently, watching Flint converse with others. He knew deep down that they were all just robots, with an intelligence all of their own. He tried hard not to think how they had become so advanced and what else was possible. Those sorts of questions, such as where does the universe end, would just rotate in his head until he felt like his mind was blown. As such, he tried not to overhear too much of their conversations. In his own mind he passed the time by playing a game that he, Jeff, and Marshall used to play in the Greasy Dog pub back in Serene. He would watch the lips move of other patrons and they would lip sync absurd conversations between them. Here he was able to imagine the Zeydenians as far less intelligent than they actually were and smile to himself underneath his helmet, but not laugh out loud. It passed the time anyhow that he would have to spend in silence inside the armour. After about half an hour the room had filled almost to capacity. It felt strange to Zack that he appeared to be in the middle of a renaissance royal court banquet and yet no-one held a drink and there was no food. Zeydenians did not need such things, only humans. He then began to realise how outnumbered he was. He knew Zeydence would be different than the sectors but, now more than ever, his ability to play the part of a Zeydenian guard was so important to his survival. As they had almost completed a circuit of the great hall Zack found himself standing beside Flint under one of the great daises as he chatted with other Zeydenians bizarrely about the weather. A noise from atop the dais on the opposite side of the room caught Zacks attention and he looked across to see four minimalist Zeydenian robots being led out to stand on the dais, wearing tuxedos. For the first time since he had arrived in Zeydence, Zack saw musical instruments. It only dawned on him at that moment that music had been stripped from the conscious of the humans and that he had not heard a note since the twenty first century. The four robots appeared to be styled like a string quartet with two on the left holding violins and the third one in holding what looked like a viola. The final player on the far right was seated with a cello held in front of him. Zack saw that these beings had more metallic hands rather than the skin covered ones that the gentry in the room possessed. They could not have been held in such a high regard as the rest of the patrons. There was a sudden silence as if everyone in the room knew that they were there, and within a couple of seconds the quartet launched into a classical piece. Zack strained to listen to it. His mother had been a music teacher at a school so, despite Zacks taste in music later in life, he knew a lot of the old classics. They had been all around him as he had grown up. As he listened it dawned on him that they were playing Smetana's string quartet number one. Within a few seconds the persons assembled in the hall turned to each other and continued their conversations that had been briefly paused by the start of the music. No-one in the room appeared to take in or appreciate the skill that was being used to make such music and Zack realised it was all just a show. The Zeydenians wanted to feel important and emulate the opulence of humans before they lost control. It was a talent going to waste. Flint managed to break away from the circle of Zeydenians he had been engaging with and gave Zack a slight nudge to move with him.

"Won't be long now." Flint stated as soon as they were out of earshot of anyone else, "They always make an entrance just after that racket starts." He continued whilst looking up at the string quartet, who were oblivious to the ignorance of everyone else in the room. Zack was slightly disappointed that Flint couldn't even acknowledge the grace of music, but there had been no malice or frustration in his voice which made it harder for Zack to argue back to him, later. Flint led him to a across the ballroom and turned to look up at the other dais. There seemed to be a flurry of activity around it. Zeydenians in expensive looking glittery clothing walking rapidly up the slopes, large red hats on their heads that were almost triangular in shape. The way they preened and glared at one another reminded Zack of arse kissers in the office but at Aurora Financial Services. Those willing to sell their soul for the favour of their superiors. It was like a guard of honour had been formed on both sides of the dais as the music began to slow and soften, coming to an end. As it did so, a crystal box began to rise out of the floor in the middle of the platform. It was about six feet wide and about the same in depth. The box sparkled at the edges from the downlights and rose slowly. As it rose everyone in the room had become silent. There was literally no sound other than a faint sliding noise of the crystal box. Zack resorted to breathing ever so slightly through his nose to minimise any noise he might make being human. Eventually the top of a tall crystal crown came into view, glittering under the lights. As the box rose ever higher the forms of the leaders of the Zeydenians came into view.

"I present you Lord Dhonos and Lady Zoesis." Flint said quietly. Zack registered what was said but did not answer.

The box stopped ascending, and once it had come to a complete halt, the crystal front of it descended back into the platform, opening it up for Lord Dhonos and Lady Zoesis to step out. They did so hand in hand. Lady Zoesis stunned Zack. She was tall, about five feet ten inches, and extremely slim. The crown perched atop her head looked so fragile, like the wind could shatter it, but she moved without concern. A thin face of hardened looking beauty. She wore dark brown hair which Zack imagined was long but was neatly bound up in a bun beneath the crystal crown. The dress she wore was shoulder less on one side which exposed a bare arm. The other shoulder was covered by the most extravagant chrome shoulder guard that extended upwards towards her ear on her right and down towards her elbow. Below that her arm was wrapped in a mosaic of mirrored pieces that were held together but flexed as she moved. The left side of her dress was a black fabric at the top which covered her breasts. Zack was surprised to think of robots as having breasts, but maybe it was all part of the image that she wanted to portray. The other half of the top was a chrome-coloured breastplate to match the shoulder guard. The dress continued down past her feet but seemed to splay perfectly for about seventy centimetres all around her. It was black, like the top half but shimmered silver between the pleats and was decorated with the most ornate metallic pattern sewn onto the front that sparked with the lights hitting it as she moved. Zack imagined it must weigh too much for any human to be able to carry off, but Lady Zoesis wore it without hindrance. The man standing to her left, Lord Dhonos, had less of an air of Grace about him. He looked serious but more relaxed with hands in his pockets. He was the same height and of a proportionate build, giving the appearance of a male aged around twenty-seven to thirty years old. He had a mop of thick black hair that was brushed back and swept over to the right and a chiselled jawline that any catalogue model would die to have. He wore black trousers and boots, covered with a knee length black leather jacket, double breasted with two distinct lines of chrome buttons running from top to bottom, in line with where Zack imagined he might have nipples. There was a loosely fitted leather belt around the waist and each sleeve was secured with three leather straps on the forearms. Around his neck he wore what appeared to be a snood which gave his upper half a much more bulked out look, and hung as low as the middle of his sternum. The pair of them stepped forwards to the edge of the dais, and the gentry that had lined the dais turned to look directly at them. Lord Dhonos removed his right hand from his pocket, raising it in the air as a static wave to the people gathered below. Zack saw that his hand was also gloved in black leather.

"Be well." Lord Dhonos called out to the gathered throng. He had no microphone, but there was no need. Everyone in the room was in complete silence as if to hang on every word that he uttered, and the acoustics of the room carried his voice to every corner and curve.

"Be well." The entire audience replied in unison and then clapped. An almost metallic tint to the clapping, which ended almost as soon as it began.

"My fellow Zeydenians. This eve, Lady Zoesis and I have an important announcement to make that concerns all Zeydenians and our fellows throughout Rebristan." Lord Dhonos continued. Silence befell the room as everyone awaited his words, "But first, let us be merry with song. I shall make my announcement in thirty minutes."

The band that had stopped playing as Lord Dhonos and Lady Zoesis had arrived continued to play again, this time launching into Pachelbel's canon in D, melancholic at first. The gathered crowd all turned to each other to start talking again, in complete ignorance of the music being played. Those that were standing on the sides of the platform then approached Lord Dhonos and Lady Zoesis Flint stepped away from where he was standing and moved closer to the elevator that had brought them to the ballroom. Zack followed.

"This is big." Flint stated once they were relatively alone and ignored. "We've had gatherings before, but this is twice as many people. I need you to stand over here by the elevator. People are starting to ask why I am followed around by a guard all of the time."

Zack, afraid to speak out loud, simply nodded.

"Whatever happens, I'll meet you back at my quarters after the announcement." Flint instructed as he handed Zack a ceramic looking card that would allow him to get through the door. Flint turned on his heels and walked off into the crowd leaving Zack stood alone on the outskirts of the room. Zack hoped that the announcement would not be a long one. The weight of his armour and his human need to take in a drink and use the toilet were starting to cause problems for him. He watched from the distance as people all mingled together, talking to each other. He marvelled at the way the Zeydenians had almost pulled off a regency party, but the lack of food and drink from the opulence stood out. He also noticed, from the partial conversations that he could overhear, how people spoke to each other about their own achievements but appeared uninterested when someone spoke back to them. So narcissistic. Eventually a wave of stillness seemed to flow through the room. The voices gradually became quieter until there was the same silence as before. Zack looked up to the Dais and noticed that Lord Dhonos was stood at the edge of it with an arm raised in a mock Nazi salute. As Zack looked on Lord Dhonos began to address the crowd.

"Fellow Zeydenians," his voice boomed effortlessly again, "I come to you tonight with some good news. Your peers have been working tirelessly for a cure to the existence that we crave, and I am now pleased to announce that with our colleagues across the water, we have finally found the answer. The Zeydenian people will be able to survive, regenerate, recharge and live without the assistance of the vermin humans that we keep alive."

There were loud cheers around the room, and the metallic clatter of Zeydenian clapping began again briefly. Lord Dhonos raised his arm again and the noise abated.

"Plans have slowly been falling into place," Lord Dhonos continued, "for the eradication of the humans and any trace of their existence from this planet. No longer will we need to keep them, provide for them, give them land to reside, deal with the waste that they produce, deal with their insubordination or the sights that are produced when they die and rot away." More loud cheers from the gathered throng. Zack was open-mouthed in shock underneath his helmet. He could not believe what he was hearing. He scanned the room, and found Flint staring at him. There was no emotion at all in Flint's face, but he ought to know exactly how Zack was feeling hearing this news as the only human in the room but having to remain silent for his own survival.

"How is this possible?" A voice called out from the floor. Lord Dhonos' gaze followed the direction of the call before answering.

"That is a good question Bassol," Lord Dhonos answered, "Our finest engineers have found a patch upgrade for our operating systems that will enable us to be active for ten times longer between charges. That in itself will enable Zeydenians to be more productive and will cause the batteries that we use to last for millennia before we need a complete replace. They will remain cool, and there will no longer be a need for the humans to mine for cobalt to produce new ones or for the Trokine plants to lubricate the cooling systems. We will live forever as Zeydenians, with ample time to develop technology to replace the roles of the humans whenever needed. Luxury, without responsibility for them, is coming and coming soon."

"How soon?" Another voice from the floor called out.

"In one nights time the whole Zeydenian race will go for recharge at the same time. At exactly twenty-five hundred hours everyone here and all the Zeydenians you know, will shut down as the updated patch is sent through the servers to us. When you awake you will be the same person, but you will be forever changed for the better. Then the history of the humans can be eradicated."

"How will we get rid of the humans?" It was the man who had been called Bassol again. He had an eagerness in his voice and Zack imagined that he wanted to use violence in order to eradicate them. Lord Dhonos must have picked up on this as well from the answer that he gave.

"Bassol, my fellow Zeydenian. We will not have to do anything my good fellow." Lord Dhonos announced. People around the room looked at each other, confused by the answer. "Their history in the library, which by the way will be destroyed as soon as they are gone, has shown us that the human species are very adept at getting rid of themselves. All we need to do is stop visiting them. Without our support they will panic. And then.... then, they will turn on each other. They are a feral creature that will fight each other. They have done this throughout their existence leading up to the great bomb that led to Zeydenians taking control, and without food or support they will do it again. They will kill each other. And those that are left will die out on their own when they realise no-one is coming to help them. By the time the winter months are here I predict that there will be no humans left on this land and we can start the process of reclaiming the sectors and the land that we should be enjoying. The final plan is here!"

There was again another loud cheer and clapping. This went on for longer than previously. There was a sense that the announcement had come to an end. Zack looked around the room again. There was a tear forming in the duct of his eyes underneath the helmet. His body moved in short spasms in shock as he looked around, unsure about what to do, but only knowing that he no longer wished to spend an extra second in the room. His gaze found Flint. Flint sensed what was happening from the body language of the twitching Zeydenian guard by the elevator and he gave Zack an upwards nod to indicate that he should leave. Zack did not need bidding twice. He turned towards the elevator and as it opened he stepped inside it, gritting his teeth as the excited voices above him got quieter as he descended through Zeydence tower.

* * *

She watched as the guard turned and made his way to the elevator. From her elevated position atop the right hand dais, she watched the gait of his walk, the speed, and something did not feel right. Her eyes scanned to room below her, and there before the second dais just to the side closest to the elevator she saw him, Flint. Lord Dhonos' creation, once fallen from grace but now one of his favourites again. She followed Flint's gaze and it was straight at the departing guard that she had been so curious about. Curiosity was a strange thing. What was it the humans used to say? Curiosity killed the cat. What did that mean anyway? The decision was made, more information was required to sate this curiosity. With that, Kasumi turned and started to descend the ramp from the dais to the floor, all the while glancing towards Flint in case she lost him in the crowd. He would be a lot harder to locate at ground level than from surveying from above. She reached floor level and started to sashay her way through the crowd in the direction of where she had last seen him. People stepped aside for her with a slight element of fear as she walked unhindered towards the bottom of the opposite dais. As the crowd parted, she noticed that Flint was walking towards her, but looking towards the elevator as if she were invisible, to the point that they almost bumped into each other as she stopped directly in front of him. Flint stopped too and looked Kasumi straight in the eyes.

"Excuse me." Flint said

"Are we going somewhere Flint?" Kasumi asked.

"Excuse me?" Flint replied with a hint of anger in his voice.

"Our Lord Dhonos has just made quite possibly the most important announcement of our existence, and you're leaving the party early."

"It is of no consequence to you where I go or when." Flint retorted.

"Oh, you see it is, when I feel that the existence of the Zeydenians is in danger." Kasumi replied, running a finger up the front of Flint's chest. His eyes did not give her the satisfaction of looking down at it. "And you seem to have become so attached to a particular guard lately." Kasumi continued

"I shall remind of your standing in the Zeydenian people." Flint stated, anger rising in his voice. A few other Zeydenians nearby turned to look at them and Flint lowered his voice as he continued, "You have no right to question me on any aspect of my duties or how I conduct them."

"I am fully aware of my standing," Kasumi replied, "and I have always been trusted on my instincts. What I can't understand Flint is how you, once outcast to destruction, manage to come back and work your way to the top again. Once distrusted, always distrusted I would say."

At that Flint barged passed Kasumi. She turned and watched him as he stormed off towards the elevator, putting an index finger to her bottom lip and allowing herself a smile as he paused for the elevator to arrive. She wasn't sure what he was up to, or if he was up to something at all, but something to Kasumi did not feel right, and when she had these feelings she was not very often wrong. As Flint descended out of view, she turned around to the crowd behind her, smiled and started to mingle. Those who had been staring at her when she had her back turned tried, unconvincingly, to resume with their previous conversations and pretend that they had never been watching.

30

Once inside Flint's quarters Zack took his helmet off, his sweaty warm hair stuck slick to the top of his head and side of his face. He launched the helmet across the room. As soon as it left his grasp, he regretted his actions and prayed silently in that split second that it did not break. Thankfully, it bounced off a wall, with a dull thud and landed on the master bed, appearing to be unharmed. Despite his sudden realisation of clarity at the fact that he would not be able to venture outside of the room if he did not have a helmet to wear, he was still seething inside. This certainly changed the game. He paced back and forth, his brain tying itself into a knot. Zack knew exactly how the humans would react if they were abandoned by the Zeydenians, after all he was one of them, and history portrayed his kind in a poor light. His plan had been to somehow rescue Madoka and make good his escape, whilst trying his hardest to undermine the Zeydenian race to free the humans. But that plan, that he hadn't even thought through yet, needed to be executed with guidance for the humans afterwards, not just leaving them to starve, become desperate and turn on each other. As he paced, he walked to the window. In the night sky he could see the birthing tower lit up in the distance. He looked at it longingly, trying to guess how far up the tower Madoka was, wondering if she was looking out of the window in his direction. He felt so lonely and needed to feel as though he were a part of something loving. A thought occurred to him, if the Zeydenians no longer needed humans to survive then what would happen to the females in the birthing tower already? Bile rose into Zacks throat as he tried to hold back the urge to vomit on an empty stomach. Fear pinched his brain to an almost fainting point that he staggered backwards and had to sit on the bed. He didn't know how long he had been sat there, it could have been minutes, it could have been hours for all he knew as his mind went into a self-preservation mode. He heard the door swoosh open behind him. He couldn't turn his head; the fight had gone out of him. The door closed.

"I wasn't expecting that." Was all the Flint would say. There was a pause, Zack expected more, but it never came. As the pause became uncomfortable Zack slowly turned around. Flint was stood there by the door just staring at Zack as if he had zoned out too. "Is it over?" Flint continued once he had Zack's attention.

"I don't know, you tell me." Zack replied.

"It's only over if you want it to be." Flint stated, "You still have air in your lungs and a desire in your heart. Those are things that Keisa told me when he rescued me all those years ago. It's not something that Zeydenians would understand. but I think you have them Zack." As he spoke, Flint looked up at the window that Zack had originally been standing at before he came in. Zack followed his eyes and knew what he was looking at and why.

"I do." Zack mumbled.

"Do you have a plan yet?" Flint asked.

"Sort of." Zack replied unconvincingly. To be honest thousands of ideas smacked his mind within a split second, but they were all part ideas, and the pain that he felt in his mind at that time simply confused him. He would have loved to have more time to work them out into a flawless plan but for now they disappeared into a sludge that spilled painfully through his mind and made his head feel heavy. He would rather his heart just gave up on him now and he would know nothing about it than to attempt a rushed plan to rescue Madoka and knowingly fail. Flint walked over to the window and stared out into the night. Zack stood and joined him, standing to his left. Neither looked at each other as they spoke, but they could see a reflection of the other in the glass.

"What will happen to them?" Zack asked. Not too much detail but as they both stared at the birthing tower Flint knew exactly what he meant.

"I left before the final plans were announced." Flint replied, "But I can't imagine it will be something positive." Zack had not wanted to hear these words. What he wanted to hear as that all of the women trapped in the birthing tower would be freed into the streets below, Madoka would run into Zacks arms and they would commandeer a vehicle to drive off into the sun and live happily ever after. But reality hit him like a sledgehammer." A tear formed in Zacks eye, but he tried not to let it show to Flint.

"I think I could have a plan together before the abandonment." Zack stated, a quiver in his voice as ideas were carried to his brain on a massive wave of adrenaline.

"It will not be good for me." Flint stated more than asked. Still his head did not turn towards Zack.

"I don't know that yet." Zack replied, another tear welling in his eye and pushing his previous tear for Madoka to run slowly down his cheek.

"It cannot be." Flint replied, "But you have to do what you have to do."

"How can you be so calm about it?" This time Zack turned his head to look at Flint.

Zack remained silent, unsure of what to say. He had ideas, of course he did, but part of the sticking point was how to protect those who had protected him, and that included Flint the Zeydenian.

"Because I am not as foolish as the others. I do not live in the golden bubble that Lord Dhonos and Lady Zoesis live in. They have been shielded from the horrors of the world for all of their existence. But for me, they cast me out of Zeydence for disobeying them once. I was cast into the between roads for a period of three months. In that period my circuits should have shut down from a lack of power. But I made it to sector sixty-nine, with the assistance of a Zeydenian guard who was travelling there to for his tour of duty. Keisa found me close to non-existence. She could have left me where I was, one less Zeydenian in the Rebristan to contend with. But she didn't. She kept me alive, if there is such a thing for my kind. They sacrificed their own energy within their dwellings to keep me charged, barely clinging to existence but at the same time they were without light, heat and warm food and water for close to three months. I was shared between the homes of Keisa, Junko and eventually Vissu. Many feared me, and had I never been cast out by my own kind they would have been right to do so. But in that time, I learned a lot about humanity. I learned a lot about nature. I learned a lot about survival. I learned a lot about giving thanks and sacrifice. The only other Zeydenians to know about this are Diarran and Marna. They have always been aides to me in Zeydence, but once I was gone, they protested and were sent to follow. Through Vissu, they found sanctuary within the company of the humans. After the three months were over, we rode back into Zeydence on the next available transport. I guess our arrival all of those years ago served as the seed sown in Lord Dhonos' head that has led to the announcement tonight. In some respects I feel responsible, but I have never forgotten the compassion of the humans in my hour of need. We have remained close. It is I that taught them to vanish and arrive at some other point in time. To be used in emergencies to further their cause."

"Why doesn't Madoka just vanish out of the birthing tower?" Zack asked, his gaze again turning the tall building in the distance.

"She could. Easily." Flint responded, "But she understands the consequences that would follow. Some Zeydenians believe, but do not know for sure, that there are humans that can vanish. I'm sure there have been others in the past, it's always been an urban legend of sorts among my kind. But she knows that she will then reveal the secret that she needs to keep in order to survive this world. Plus she knows that she would be hunted down. If she disappeared for a couple of days from the fields, like you have done so to come here and as she did to travel into the past to find you, she would return before anyone could establish what had happened. But you have seen the tower, it's impossible to escape alive. If she were to vanish, they may hypothesise as to how she has, but not know for sure, but she would be noticed missing within a short time frame. She would be hunted. And if they did not find her, or should I say if we did not find her, for I am one too, then Echo would suffer for her escape. Keisa would suffer. Zero would suffer. Maybe even killed, until her emotions would flush her back into the arms of the Zeydenians. She is strong. The birthing tower would not ordinarily kill her, but escaping undoubtedly would."

There was a pause as the both of them stared towards the birthing tower. Zack did not dare to ask the question that was on his lips for fear of the answer. He did not like Flint's usage of the word ordinarily when speaking of the safety of the birthing tower. For he and Flint knew that Lord Dhonos' plans for the next few days would turn the ordinary of Rebristan upside down for the humans, and that the intention was that none would survive. Believing that the human race would turn inwards on itself and destroy itself without the support or attention of its slave masters. A kamikaze genocide if you like. Zack knew that if he could get messages back to the humans in all sectors that this is how their captors wished for them to die, then the human spirit could take over, democracy couldn't be too hard to learn and implement, and they would prevail. Of course, there would be hiccups, there always had been throughout time, but the outcome would be far better than just the abandonment of the human race and panic that set in afterwards. He turned away from the window and looked around the extravagant room before him.

"You will sleep here tonight Zack." Flint stated, still looking out of the window, "Tomorrow will start the rest of your life, and I know you will need your rest tonight."

Zack nodded in response, no noise, but he somehow knew that Flint knew. Removing his armour, he let it fall to the floor until he stood in just his white undergarments. He knew that Flint, behind him, would be looking at the mess he had made with his disrobing with disapproval, but nothing was said. The bed in the Royal quarters was higher up than any other beds that Zack had seen in Rebristan so far, so much so that he almost had to clamber up upon it. Exhaustion started to seep through his every muscle as he lay down on the bed, too tired to even lift the covers and clamber underneath them. He lay down on top of the covers and turned to face Flint at the window, laying his head on the pillow. From where he lay, he could see the Birthing Tower out of the window in the distance. He saw Flint reach up to pull a blind down over the window and shut out the outside.

"No," Zack stated quietly with tiredness in his voice, "Please. Leave it open."

"As you wish." Flint replied, turning away from the window and looking towards Zack. "I shall be in the other room. I am going to recharge early. I feel I will need the extra energy tomorrow." Flint then turned without waiting for any response and without looking at Zack and walked through the door into the next room. Soon the lights in the room dimmed and the outside became all the more clearer. Zack stared at the birthing tower. In the darkness he tried to recall his visit there with Flint, tried to walk through the steps and turns they had made to reach Madoka to see if he could establish which side her room would be looking out at. He was unsure if he could succeed, unsure if he would see her again but, wanted to feel some sort of connection between them. As he tried harder to think of her location, he closed his eyes to make it easier for him. His eyelids were heavy, and despite him initially thinking that it would be impossible for him to sleep that night, he soon found himself succumbing to the emotional exhaustion with an image of Madoka on his mind as he slipped into a deep sleep.

31

Awakening with the jolt of re-joining a bad reality, Zack had gotten up and wandered into the next room to find Flint. It seemed strange to see a thing, he had often regarded to be humanoid and had come to class as a friend, in a state of non-animation, just staring blankly ahead, devoid of life. Zack wandered towards him, waving a hand in front of Flints face. Nothing. Zack wandered around the room. From where Flint stood motionless there appeared to be a wireless charging portal that he was leaning slightly back onto, with the charging pad touching the back of his head. In all the time that Zack had seen him animated he had almost come to think of him as a human, but here he stood, as lifeless as a Gerry Anderson puppet between shoots. He strode over to the window and again looked out upon the birthing tower. He knew information that no other human thus knew at this time and was torn between emotions. The pure weight of the information was too heavy for one man to bear, especially as he looked upon the tower opposite and imagined all of the women encased within it struggling through the birthing process in the hope that life would go back to normal for them soon afterwards. But he also felt empowered with being the only human so far to know, that it must be him to stop the looming genocide. As he continued to stare out of the window there was a soft beeping noise behind him. Zack turned to see Flint's arms shuffle slightly and his head turn towards him. As Flint opened his eyelids there was darkness where his eyes should be, followed swiftly by a double flash of LED light before they softened and went a dazzling blue in colour.

"Not a moment to lose." Flint said without emotion as he stepped away from the charging portal.

"How long do we have?" A question Zack had almost been too afraid to ask after last night's announcement.

"Not long." Flint replied, not looking back at Zack as he walked away. "You will need to get changed into your armour. I shall leave you with Jackson again today as I have some diplomatic duties to take care of."

Flint left the room, not looking behind him. Zack looked down at himself in his underclothes. He felt like he needed to shower or bathe, but as that was not something that a humanoid Zeydenian would usually do, resources in the Zeydenian tower were scarce. Zack resolved to try and clean up later and enter the world as his sweaty self for the day. Forging ahead, he stepped into the bedroom in search of his discarded armour.

* * *

As the door drew to a close behind him Zack saw the diminutive Jackson sitting at his desk at the far end of the room. He looked more haggard than he had been before if that was possible. Had he become aware of the Zeydenians plan? He would, after all, be the human that administered the update that render the humans redundant. But is he told of what each update includes or just a glorified IT caretaker? Zack approached him without Jackson looking as he descended upon him.

"Are we alone?" Zack asked. At the recognition of his voice Jackson's head snapped up towards him. Life finally lit in his eyes.

"Zack?" Jackson asked nervously.

"Yes mate." Zack replied, "Is it just the two of us in here?"

"Yeah." Jackson responded, "Something fucking weird is happening, there's been minimal Zeydenian activity in this building since last night."

"I may know something about that." Zack stated as he looked around behind him before removing his helmet. Jackson looked at him anxiously for answers, "And it's not good news." Zack announced.

"What do you mean?" Jackson asked. The life that had been in his eyes previously appeared to drain away at this comment as Zack looked at him without his helmet on.

"I heard an announcement last night. It's fatal for the human race, but...." Zack added the 'but' quickly as it looked as though Jackson's body were about to give up and keel over, "But I think WE can do something about it Jackson. You and I."

"I have family in the fucking sectors." Jackson stated as if he had not heard anything else after the but, looking around at the dusty windows wishing that he could see out of them. Zack grabbed hold of his shoulders with both hands forcing Jackson to look towards him.

"I'm sure they are fine at the moment. Look at me Jackson." Zack said and waited until it looked as though Jacksons eyes had focussed on him. "I said I think that you and I can prevent the extinction of mankind. Wow, it sounds so huge when I put it like that, but if anyone can it's only going to be the two of us."

"How? When? Why? How? Fuck!" Jackson had more questions in

his mind than it could contend with and as he opened his mouth to speak, they all tried to leave at the same time.

"Have a drink Jackson. Take a deep breath and then we'll talk." Zack said, realising he was still gripping Jackson's shoulders. He released his hold on him, fully expecting him to tumble to the floor and was pleasantly surprised when he just wobbled on his chair where he was. Zack straightened up and walked towards a tap that provided Jackson with water to drink in the room. Filling a beaker with water he returned to Jackson, who was now standing and pacing up and down mumbling incoherently to himself. As Zack got closer Jackson spun to look directly at him, this time there was a fire in his eyes.

"How the fuck can just you and I stop a nation of robots from annihilating the human fucking race? It's impossible." Jackson snapped. Anger had started to rise in his voice.

"It's extremely difficult, it's very dangerous, it's not fool proof, but at the same time it's not impossible." Zack stated. He felt glad that he had shared his knowledge with Jackson and that Jackson was worrying about it. That sounded selfish to himself but at the same time it empowered him as being the stronger person. He knew that he could not attempt his plan without Jackson, but feeling more positive than Jackson made him feel more confident that his idea was the way forward.

"But what if we fail?" Jackson asked, his emotions had crashed again, and he was wringing his hands together as he asked.

"Then we fail." Zack replied bluntly, "But the alternative is that we do nothing, and we don't fail because we've done nothing, but the outcome will be the same. At least if we try there's a chance for a different outcome."

Jackson nodded, seemingly taking it all in.

"I need you to focus Jackson," Zack said handing him the beaker of water, "we may not have long to pull this off. Here, drink this and I'll tell you what I have in mind." Jackson sat back down in his chair as he slowly started to sip the water from the beaker whilst Zack walked away behind the walls of hard drives towards Jacksons desk of old computer equipment.

* * *

Junko arrived at the Zeydenian library again. Noticeably there were less people around that he could see, although the library itself seemed to be a hive of activity. He was feeling a little out of joint as he had heard no word from Flint or Zack since the following day. Diarran had arrived to take him to the library but had been incredibly quiet, barely speaking on the journey. Junko hated being left out of the loop. Resentment was beginning to seep into his conscious as to how he had fought for the human's rights pretty much since birth, and Zack just waltzes in from another time and is taken into the bosom of the Zeydenian royalty. He hadn't even come home last night. It was unlikely that he was dead with Flint taking him under his wing, so just where exactly had he been living it up? Junko stood inside the doorway to the library and watched the chaos before him. Scanning the room, he could not see Yioro anywhere and was starting to become concerned for her. Stepping down from the entry he walked through the library looking between the shelves. It appeared as though the room got darker the further he walked into the library, away from the windows at the front of the building. Zeydenian guards were bustling around him carrying boxes towards a door at the back of the library, and the shelves looked even more depleted than they had the last time he had visited.

"Have a seat." a voice behind him commanded. It was a voice he did not instantly recognise but could tell that it was female. Junko slowly turned to see two females standing before him, Zeydenians he guessed. The first was tall, very tall, dark in skin with long silver hair. He believed that she was the one they called Kasumi. He had heard Echo and Madoka speak of her before. He had seen her before at the fields and knew that she was feared among the humans. The second he had not seen before, more petite and rounded than her colleague with long blonde hair. Junko looked both of them up and down.

"Sit I said." The taller of the two commanded again and stepped forwards toward Junko, invading his personal space and causing him to step backwards until the backs of his legs contacted with a chair beside a desk. Junko sat back into the chair and the taller female, who had spoken, loomed even taller over him.

"Do you know who I am?" She asked, as the second female moved silently forwards to stand beside her.

"I can't say I've had the pleasure." Junko replied, deciding not to make life easy for her. The hint of sarcasm was not picked up by the females.

"I am Kasumi." Spoke the taller female, "and this is my colleague, Dove."

"Ok." Junko simply replied, wondering where the conversation was going.

"Do you know what I do?" Kasumi asked.

"Why don't you just tell me?" Junko asked, tired of playing guessing games. He had already established that any contact could not be good news for him, so cut straight to the chase.

"I am a security advisor for Lord Dhonos and all of Zeydence." Kasumi announced proudly.

"Ok." Junko replied. He was unsure if he was to be impressed by this or if anything else were to follow. There was an awkward silence before Kasumi continued.

"Dove here, is my protege, learning the ropes so to speak in protecting the Zeydenians from the parasitic humans we currently share this world with." There was another silence as Kasumi paused to see if Junko had anything else to add. When it was clear that he wasn't going to speak she continued, "And Dove here, has spotted you coming and going from this library at will. She asked me why that would be, and I could not answer her. But it was an excellent opportunity to show her the power that we have in our roles, hence us stopping you today."

"You're only stopping me because I'm human." Junko said.

"Why are you in library today Junko sixty-nine?" Kasumi asked, totally ignoring his previous comment, and getting straight to the point.

"How do you know my name?" Junko asked, surprised. But not as surprised as when Dove stepped forwards and with her left hand slapped him around the face, causing his head to rotate ninety degrees before he realised what had happened.

"We ask the questions, and you have not answered Junko." This time it was Dove who spoke, and her voice sounded considerably softer than he would have imagined having just experienced an outburst of violence from her. Junko slowly turned his head to face the women and flinched a little as his eyes focussed on Dove's raised hand. He relaxed when he saw that it was not about to move towards him. He looked between the two of them, all eyes on him before he answered.

"I'm here at the request of Flint." Junko volunteered.

"That much we know." Kasumi replied, "But what is it that Flint needs to know that he has to use a human to learn it."

Junko was ready for this question. It was a survival mechanism when in the jaws of the enemy that he should be able to think on his feet and have a backstory for any inquisitive Zeydenians should he be asked to explain his actions. He just wished he weren't being asked by someone who had the means to be so aggressive. Of course, Flint could know anything at all with just a simple download, there is nothing that he could learn that he could possibly teach to Flint any faster than he could learn for himself. However, during his previous times in the library he had always thought that Flint was allowing him to gain knowledge to keep the peace within the sector, preventing an uprising so to speak. Learning for himself to pass on to the rest of the sector, so as Flint himself would not have to deal with any problems there.

"It's more for me." Junko began with an air of confidence, "This past winter has been quite dry and there are concerns that when the summer really starts to scorch that there will not be enough water for everyone in the sectors. Flint suggested I may find some prehistoric solutions within the library that would negate the need for Zeydenian assistance and resources. I was looking for the books on er..." Junko looked around him for the area of the library that he knew his get-out story information to be held, "on...er...irrigation." His heart dropped when he saw that the shelves on which he knew the agricultural books to be was empty. He daren't look back at the women in case they could sense the fear on his face. Would they know that the books he was looking for were missing, and may not have been there throughout his current stay in Zeydence? Eventually his pause to look at the shelves became longer than he thought was necessary. It was time to face the music, putting on a poker face he turned to see them both staring at him.

"You can ask Flint." Junko stated with as much courage as he could muster, knowing that he had discussed possible get out conversations with him in the past.

"I know you are up to something Junko Sixty-nine, and you know that I can't just simply ask Flint. I will be watching you." Kasumi stated and then turned and walked away. Dove lingered for a while longer, her hand still raised, which gave Junko grave cause for concern, until she too turned without saying a word and followed after Kasumi.

Afraid he was still being watched he stood up and walked over to the agriculture section, staring at bare shelves. A Zeydenian guard, arms laden with books of all genres walked past him.

"Have you seen the irrigation books?" Junko asked the soldier who continued walking without even acknowledging him. None of these robots were any the wiser.

* * *

"So, fucking humour me." Jackson started as he stood over a hunched down Zack on the floor at the back of the room, "Your plan to overthrow these fucking robots lies in amongst all this old junk from the dark ages?"

"Not the dark ages Jackson," Zack replied without looking up, still frantically scrabbling through the old hardware collection, "my age. Remember I came from the twenty-first century and I can do stuff with this shit if it still works. Aha!!" Zack exclaimed, standing up holding up what looked to be a small piece of plastic to Jackson.

"Pray tell, what the fuck is that?" Jackson asked.

"This, my friend, is a USB drive." Zack proudly announced. "There was a little prank I played on Marshall once," he paused for a second as he mentioned his old friend's name and recalled what had happened before he left Serene, "turning one of these into a USB Killer. He was so pissed when it destroyed his laptop with his porn collection on it." Jackson looked at Zack as if he were speaking another language, and to some degree he was. Zack looked around at the banks of hard drives that filled the room. "We are going to need to adapt what I've done before on an industrial scale. I'm assuming when you do an upgrade that all of the systems are upgraded in one go?"

"No, I pull each fucking drive out and do them one at a time, what do you think?" The sarcasm in Jackson's reply was lost on Zack as he never acknowledged it, causing Jackson to continue, "Of course it's all done at one time. I upload the upgrade to the main terminal that I use at the front, and then as they fucking recharge, their system is updated over the next twenty four hours. Why?"

Zack turned to look at Jackson.

"I may only get one shot at this so I'll need to inflict as much damage as I can with that chance. How do I input into the main frame?"

"There's a wireless plate next to the main frame engine." Jackson started, "I usually get given an update chip with all of the information on to place on the plate and then the data is transferred."

"I'm not sure a wireless plate will work. I need to get into the guts of this system." Zack was looking frantically around him for some inspiration. There was a pause in the conversation before Jackson spoke again.

"So, what is a USB killer?" He asked.

"Back in my time Jackson these drives stored data and were removable to be used between different machines, the input plug on this thing became universal with most electronic devices. It was called a USB memory drive. However, someone came up with the idea to pack into the casing capacitors instead of data memory. When the drive with capacitors on it was plugged into a computer it would immediately send a large electric current back into the machine frying all of the circuits and killing the computer. Completely."

"Tell me more." Jackson's eyes had lit up at the words 'killing the computer'.

"I'll need to get into a motherboard of a main drive that is connected to all of the others..." Zack began.

"Simple. The upload lanes of all of these drives are connected, for the purposes of simplified upgrades. It's the download lanes that are not connected, so that each Zeydenians memories remain exclusive to them." Jackson interrupted.

"Great. Next, I'll need a way to connect this old USB to one of your drives, hopefully I can do that using an old USB input port from one of your old junk computers." Zack continued. Jackson nodded. It didn't sound as difficult and alien as he had first imagined. "Then, I'm not sure that one or two capacitors will suffice for a bank of drives and main frame as big as this. I'm, no, we're going to have to pull as many capacitors out of the old equipment that you have as possible and link them together."

"Great." Jackson said, "What the fuck is a capacitor?"

Looking back at the pile of old computers, there appeared to be thirty of so bundled into a corner behind the last row of hard drives, some definitely from the twenty-first century, a few that looked as though they would run on Windows 98, and some that seemed more advanced than the time at which Zack had left. Zack knelt down beside the equipment and Jackson joined him.

"It's going to be a long day." Zack stated before proceeding to educate Jackson on the parts of the computers from the past that he would need. Between them they remained like that for several hours, scouting the parts that they needed before attempting the build. A true friendship was beginning in the most unfortunate of circumstances.

32

Exhausted, night had fallen before Zack was relieved from the data room. The entire day had been spent pillaging the old computers and hardware for as many capacitors as could be found, linking them all together on a couple of spare motherboards and eventually hardwiring these to the USB input that had been found. Jackson had also found another USB drive and so they had created a backup USB killer so as to have two of them that could be used. Zack had also found some USB inputs and crudely adapted them to what, he hoped, would be able to connect with the insides of the hard drive system. There had been no way for sure of seeing if it would attach as Jackson had warned him that as the seal was broken on one of them an alarm would alert the Zeydenians as to the fact, who would assume sabotage, and that they would have about five minutes to either finish what they had started or they themselves were finished. Jackson had provided Zack with some crude drawings from when they system had been installed and he had hoped for the best. The system that they had devised was as ready to go as it ever would be, however they did not yet know whether it would work or not. Diarran had collected Zack and was silent as he transported him back to Flint's residence at the Royal retreat. Keeping his helmet on until he was fully inside the building, they were met by Junko.

"Where have you been?" Junko asked, a hint of annoyance in his voice. Zack removed his helmet and looked towards him. Diarran still didn't speak. Zack had been asked by Flint not to make mention of his plan to any other Zeydenians, including Diarran and Marna, although he was certain that Diarran would know Lord Dhonos' plans as the Zeydence tower had been rife with the gossip of them.

"Trying to figure out how we can save Madoka and restore some humanity to this planet." Was about all Zack felt he could say in the present company. Junko still looked slightly annoyed, and Zack could not understand why. Before he could say anything else Diarran spoke.

"Flint will be meeting you both here in about one hour. Flint has advised that you both completely update each other on what you have learned. I shall take my leave now." Diarran stated before turning and leaving the room to go back to the transport for Zeydence Tower. Suddenly Zack and Junko found themselves alone in the room staring at each other.

"I suggest we go to the sleeping quarters to speak." Junko said, more of a command than a suggestion, and without waiting for a reply walked off in the direction of Flint's residence within the retreat.

* * *

With the door closed behind them in the bedroom of Flint's residence Junko finally turned to face Zack.

"Had fun at the party, did you?" Junko asked in anger. Zack was too exhausted to argue, and his voice was monotonic in its reply.

"Not particularly. There is lots to tell you and time is running out. I am exhausted." Zack replied.

"Like what?" There was still a snap of aggression in Junko's voice which Zack could not understand. He figured the only way to avoid a confrontation over whatever it was that Junko felt aggrieved by was to tell him the short, sharp truth and not sugar-coat it.

"The Zeydenians are going to wipe out the humans." Zack simply stated, still in his monotone. It had the desired effect, Junko remained silent allowing him to continue, "Or should I say they intend for the humans to wipe out the humans. That's the fun I had at a party Junko. I was dressed up in this fucking tin outfit, sweating my bollocks off, listening to Lord Dhonos announce that the humans are now surplus to requirements and that the Zeydenians are going to abandon us, allowing the humans to turn against each other until none survive." Zack sat down on the bed with his feet on the floor and allowed his body to flop back until he was staring at the ceiling. He could no longer see Junko.

"We wouldn't do that." Junko said, a slight protest in his voice.

"We would Junko," exasperation in Zacks voice as he looked at the ceiling. Turning his head to look at Junko he continued, "Throughout history humans have always tried to annihilate each other. By the Zeydenians you have been controlled and fought a common enemy. Left to yourselves to survive you will become the animals that we are. Just read your books in that library you will see what I mean."

"There are no books." Junko stated. This caused Zack to sit up.

"None?" He asked.

"Well, a few, but they've been busy all day removing boxes of them." Junko replied.

"Why?" Zack asked.

"I don't know. I was going to ask Yioro, she's the main librarian, but she wasn't there today."

"Don't you see? This all makes sense now." Zack stated as he struggled to get to his feet., "Why would the Zeydenians need books, literature or data of the existence of the humans anymore, if they intend to forge ahead as the sole species?" This made Junko think. "Humans are to be erased."

"So, what of Yioro?" Junko asked, the gravity of the situation starting to set in.

"I don't know." Zack sighed, exhausted he sat on a bed knowing that the message had settled into Junko and had taken the wind out of his sails. Junko continued to stare at him for a minute or so, expecting him to have all of the answers. They didn't come.

"So, what are you doing about it?" Junko eventually asked. Zack remained quiet, his head spinning. "I thought you were blazing in to save all of mankind." Junko continued, a hint of disdain starting to creep into his voice causing Zack to look up.

"I'm working on a plan." Zack replied with another sigh.

"What plan?" Junko asked.

"I don't have the energy to try and explain it at the moment."

"Will it work?" Junko's questioning was quick fire.

"I hope so, it's never been tried before on this scale, but in theory.... I hope so." Zack replied.

"Great. The human race is pinning its hopes on a 'hope so.'" Sarcasm crept into Junko's voice, and emotion that took Zack back a little as he had not heard since arriving in his current time. He stood as if to answer back, not willing to take a roasting from Junko for trying his hardest when the door whooshed open behind them. Ceasing any conversation or confrontation that was about to ensue between the two humans, both turned to look towards the door and see Diarran and Marna entering the room.

"Marna brings word from Flint." Diarran announced to them as Marna stepped forward.

"I come from Zeydence Tower at the behest of Flint. I have grave news." Marna stated before pausing, "Lord Dhonos' plans that are spoken of in the tower will commence tonight."

"Ok." Zack replied. Junko looked between Zack and Marna, wondering what was happening.

"All Zeydenians are to go into shut down mode at the start of the next day. They will remain so for three hours." Marna continued.

"Ok." Zack simply stated again. Keeping it brief meant he did not give anything away about his plan.

"Will someone explain what's going on?" Exasperation in Junko's voice starting to seep in. This was largely ignored by the others in the room.

"So, we have five hours before it starts?" Zack asked Marna and Diarran.

"About that." Diarran replied.

"Ok, I'm going to get some sleep, a human recharge so to speak, before it all begins." Zack announced as he sat down on the bed and laid back onto it. Junko stared at him in incredulity.

"You're just going to go to sleep?" Junko asked.

"Yep, it would appear that I am going to have a long night ahead of me, and I'm not going to succeed if I'm as tired as I am now." Zack replied to Junko before turning to face Marna and Diarran again. "I shall be ready an hour before the new day begins. Please could you arrange for transport to take me to the Zeydence Tower at that time?"

"Flint has already made those arrangements for you." Marna replied.

"Thank you Marna, Diarran." Zack stated as he rolled over on the bed to face the other way, ignorant to the stares of disbelief from Junko. Marna and Diarran left the room and Zacks eyes were closed before the door had finished whooshing to a close.

* * *

She looked across at Dove, resting peacefully, getting a little extra charge before night fell and the Zeydenian people entered sleep. Kasumi had already obtained an extra two hours charging for herself in preparation for the big update. She had a feeling something was not right. She couldn't quite understand why. Maybe once everyone was updated, she would have these feelings, as humans do, like a gut reaction, but for now she just felt like something was wrong and it was her duty to put whatever that may be right. She anticipated that she and Dove would have enough additional charge to enable them to start updating two hours after the rest of the population. Until that time would come, and it was near, she would do well to conserve energy as Dove recharged, so she sat down on the bed provided in her chambers within Zeydence Tower, rested back and her eyes glazed over as she drifted into sleep mode.

* * *

Madoka paced in her room, locked in high up in the Birthing Tower. She walked across to the window and stared out. She had no idea which direction she was facing but imagined that fate would have allowed her to be facing towards Sector sixty-nine. She had experienced this before, but it pained her so much more on this occasion. She thought of Zack and that he had awakened something inside her just prior to being taken. The previous time she had been at the birthing tower it had simply been an unfortunate part of life, but all women must go through it at some stage, so she treated it like a very long unwilled duty that would eventually be over. But now she was scared. She had brought a human from the deep past with her to this current time who she felt responsible for. In addition, there was a pain in her chest, a throb in her head and tears welled in her eyes as her mind played tricks with her and told her that Zack would not survive in this time so long without her. She cursed herself. She hadn't cried since she was a small child, as that only showed weakness in Rebristan and that could be fatal. None of the other females she had met during breaks in the tower showed the same feelings, they just continued numbly as she had done so on her first visit. Looking out of the window she could see the flames of the fire at the base of the tower and beyond that the city of Zeydence lit up as always. But the hustle and bustle of the Zeydenians walking around or vehicles moving was not as prominent as usual. Thinking nothing more of it, Madoka wiped a tear from her eye and walked back to her bed. Laying down she stared at the ceiling, as she did every night. Soon the voices would quieten, boredom would encumber her, and she would drift off to sleep to awaken in the morning and do it all over again.

33

Opening his eyes Zack felt well rested. A power nap always made him feel more rested than a ten-hour sleep in a soft bed. There was little light in the room. Beyond the window it was still dark, which came as a slight surprise and a small pang of panic developed in his gut as he believed for a brief second that he had been asleep for too long. He saw that Junko had fallen asleep in a high-backed chair on the other side of the room. Zack decided to leave him that way. Picking up his armour as quietly as he could he carried it into the next room in order to get dressed into it. Twenty minutes later he was resplendent in his armour. All that remained was the helmet. Zack moved to the door to the residence and the weight of what he was about to attempt hit him like a ton of bricks. His legs buckled underneath him, and he sank into a crouch. He wanted to run and hide, wanted to wake up from a terrible dream and be back in Serene, wanted to wake Junko and beg him to do his bidding instead. As these thoughts all raced through his brain in a nano second, he realised that none of these options were going to happen. It was his time, and as much as he hated it, it was up to him to do what had to be done. He stayed there in the crouch for a few seconds more, somehow willing that time would stop and remain still whilst he was in that position and he would have more time to compose himself. However, the sensible part of his brain also told him that this was not going to happen either. With a thought of Madoka, his reason for coming to Zeydence in the first place, he pictured her in the birthing tower getting angry at him when he turned up as a Zeydenian guard, and the burning red of his own anger gave him the energy to stand upright again. As he did so he heard a vehicle arriving outside of the residence which prompted him to put his helmet on. The main door whooshed open and Marna entered the building.
"It's time." She said simply as she looked at him. That was all, she turned on her heels and walked back out towards the waiting transport. Zack followed silently and got into the vehicle alongside her. Looking back at the plush residence, he wondered about Junko who was still sleeping in the bedroom and whether he would see him again. The transport pulled away and they drove mostly in silence on the way to Zeydence tower.

* * *

Dove had awoken, and Kasumi had returned from sleep mode. Something was not right, and Kasumi intended to discover what it was.

"Where should we start?" Dove asked

"I believe we should start with the parasite we bumped into in the library." Kasumi stated coldly. I had him followed and he is staying at the Royal residence on the outskirts of Zeydence. Flint has been acting strangely since coming back this time and it doesn't sit well with me."

"Do you think he knows what is going on?" another question from Dove.

"Flint or the human?"

"Either." Dove continued.

"One way to find out. Get your robes on Dove, we're going out." Kasumi ordered as she in turn proceeded to dress in her black and grey outfit.

* * *

Zack had only known Zeydence for a very short time but even to him this evening seemed exceptionally quiet. There was no traffic on the roads at all. In fact, they had only passed one other vehicle, travelling in the opposite direction, as they approached Zeydence tower. Marna had remained quiet throughout the journey and Zack really didn't know where to begin the conversation. Guilt wracked him as his plan, if successful, would mean that Marna would no longer exist. Did she know this he wondered? She must have some idea that Zack was about to damage the Zeydenians, of which she was a part, in a way that they would never have known before. After all, that is why he was brought here, and she knew it. The vehicle came to a halt outside Zeydence tower. Across the road from the tower Zack could see the memory hub that would be attended to by Jackson. He turned his head back to face Marna and saw that she had followed his previous gaze. Panic struck him again as he thought his plan may have been rumbled, but if she suspected anything dire there was no indication in her gaze. The doors to the vehicle opened automatically and a breeze blew through the vehicle from Marna's side to Zacks.

"Flint bids you good luck and speed Zack." Marna stated, "Be well Zack Sixty-nine."

"Thank you." Zack replied as Marna turned away from him to walk towards the tower, leaving him standing on the road. "Marna, wait." Zack called out, guilt overcoming him, but Marna continued walking up the steps towards the towers entrance door without looking back. Zack felt so alone, stood alone on the street of a capital city with no-one else present at all. The lights of the surrounding buildings were still on, but there was no movement, no-one to cast shadows from the lights. as Marna disappeared from view into Zeydence tower Zack suddenly felt like the only person in the world. Not wanting to be spotted by anyone else he turned to face the memory hub and walked as confidently as he could towards it. Every sense of his was heightened as he expected an attack at any moment, and it seemed to take forever for him to walk down the ramp leading to lower street levels and the entrance door that Flint had shown him on his first day. There was only one guard on the door at this time, and he appeared to be hooked up to a remote charging device, as if awaiting the update. There was no movement from him as Zack approached and was able to open the door and enter without confrontation. The Zeydenians had really dropped their guard at this time, which Zack took as a positive sign as he made his way up to Jacksons workplace. The door whooshed open as he approached, and Zack was surprised to see Jackson awake at this time and bustling around within the room.

"You're up?" Zack stated as a question.

"Yep, I'm up. They're expecting me to deliver this fucking update tonight, just fucking sprung it upon me." Jackson replied

"Then you know that it's time." Zack stated. The door whooshed closed behind him and he removed his helmet. Jackson stopped doing what he was doing and they both stared at each other.

"It's time to shit or get off the fucking pot Zack." Jackson stated. This brought a smile to Zacks face despite the heaviness of the atmosphere.

* * *

Arriving at the Royal residence Kasumi stepped from the transport and looked up at the looming imposing building. Dove stepped out from the driver's side and the vehicle went quiet as the doors whooshed closed. A pang of jealousy rippled through Kasumi's circuits. She had always just been on the periphery of the Royal circle, one of the oldest Zeydenians who had developed the means to understand feelings and emotions over the centuries, but had never quite made it into acceptance that she should have her own quarters here. As such, the emotions and feelings that she had developed were mainly jealousy and hatred. Not towards all Zeydenians but she could not understand how the likes of Flint remained in favour despite being ostracized in the past. Usually, she would require an invitation to visit here, but she was aware that all Zeydenians would most likely be shut down for the night by now. No-one would know where she was or why. She had a feeling that something was amiss and that the answer lay behind the doors in front of her. She would find out what was going on. She would protect the Zeydenians. And she would finally be accepted deeper into the royal circle and be welcome here anytime. Dove stepped up and stood by her side.

"What do we do now?" Dove asked.

"We find that parasite and take his knowledge." Kasumi coldly stated before stepping forwards towards the entrance of the magnificent building.

34

"How long should we leave it?" Jackson asked Zack, sweat furrowing on his brow and nerves starting to kick in. They had worked hard during the day to create two USB computer killers from the ancient components that had been stored at the back of the room for Jacksons entertainment. Hidden away for the afternoon they had now been dragged into the middle of the room, within sight of anyone walking through the door. Zack wanted to leave it an hour or so, to be sure that every Zeydenian was connected to the system. He tried hard to push from his mind that there were some Zeydenians he didn't want connected to the system, but there was no way of telling. Green lights had flickered on the room for the last two hours according to Jackson, and this was an indication that the Zeydenians controlled by that memory bank were connected and shut down. About eighty percent of the lights were green and more were being added to it all of the time.

"Just a little bit longer please." Zack asked as if he were no longer in control of the destiny that awaited them.

"If we leave it much longer then those that logged in first will be disconnecting soon, I'd give it only another thirty minutes or so and we'll start losing green lights. And..... and....what if someone comes in? Fuck that Zack, we're both fucking dead then."

"I know, I know." Zack said, pacing up and down by the door as if he would take on any army that came through it single handed. Sporadically glancing around at the banks of hard drives he watched as the lights changed from red to green rapidly, a new fear growing in him at Jacksons announcement that the earlier green lights might not remain so for much longer. He was not much of a gambler and for once did not know what was best.

"You've seen this sort of update before Jackson?" It was more of a question from Zack than a statement. Jackson nodded in reply. "Then I shall be guided by you. But....I want you to make your judgement on previous knowledge and not fear of being caught."

"Fuck yeah!" Jackson replied, hurriedly looking around at the walls of drives behind each other, rushing across to the other side of the room and doing the same on that side too. "I reckon fifteen more minutes for this side. This is for all of the Zeydenian soldiers. They're running at about ninety percent now, much longer than that and those that went online first will start to awaken. These will be the ones that will be the biggest problem with access to weapons for us if we are discovered. Is that fucking professional enough for you?"

"Ok." Zack replied.

"Great, we're gonna fry these fuckers!" Jackson's rotund body nearly left the floor as the adrenaline surged through him. "This side of the room is the general population, once the other side is dead, they'll be in a panic. They will eventually rise up, but they will be expecting the soldiers to look after them in the first instance."

Zack walked over to the bank of drives that controlled the memories of the Zeydenian soldiers. Knowing the difference between the two made things hard for him still. He was sure that Flint, Diarran and Marna's drives would be on the other side. The Zeydenian soldiers did not look human and therefore it was no different to shutting down an old computer. But the other side took on personalities and human features, mostly evil but some had helped in keeping him alive. Time ticked away and nothing more was said. Zack remained still for the most part, his ears trained for any sound of movement. There was none, but he did not wish to become complacent. The silence was eventually broken by the shuffling feet of Jackson as he wandered across to his desk and fumbled around for a tool to open the bank of drives.

"I think now is the time." Jackson stated.

"Ok." Was all that Zack could say in response.

"But before we do," Jackson was fumbling for something in his pocket and pulled out a folded sheet of paper handing it to Zack, "You'll know what to do." Zack took the piece of paper, staring at it in his hands, before nodding at Jackson and walking over to place it inside his discarded helmet. The Zeydenian soldiers armour wasn't quite equipped with pockets. When he returned to the bank of memory drives Jackson was starting to dismantle the side panel of the main server.

"As soon as this comes off the Zeydenians will be alerted. If there are any guards not recharging or rebooting, then they will be upon us within five minutes or so." Jackson stated.

"There was only one on guard at the entrance when I came in tonight, and he was dead to the world, recharging." Zack replied.

"Great. Let's do this."

Time appeared to stand still for the pair of them as they took a deep breath, then just like a virginity crushing moment, the side panel of the hard drive's server slid to one side, exposing more flashing lights than Zack had ever seen on a piece of computer equipment before. He expected alarms to sound, red lights to spin like a seventies Police car, but there was nothing but the small flashing LED lights on the server. Thousands of them.

"What now? Is that normal?" Zack asked. He had so many questions speeding through his brain but those were the only two that made it to his lips before his mind decided it still wanted silence and he secretly chastised himself for breaking this. He wanted to ask Jackson if he really knew what he was doing but the time to ask this had long passed in the previous few seconds.

"Pass me the receiver you made." Jackson instructed, sweat starting to bead down his face again. Zack handed him a USB female port that he had taken from some old equipment earlier in the afternoon. They had bastardised the wiring at the back so that it would be able to connect to the computer systems of the Zeydenians. Pulling a clip from the server, two wires were exposed and hung down in front of Jackson's face. "Hello my fucking beauties. Come to play with Uncle Jackson have you?" he spoke mainly to himself as he connected the wiring at the rear of the USB receiver to the wires that hung before him. Zack held his breath as it seemed to take forever.

"Are we in?" Zack eventually asked, completing the question on an exhale of breath as he waited for the breath to disappear and silence to resume.

"Your time meets mine." Jackson stated, "Now bring the circuit boards."

Without a word Zack turned to lift one of the circuit boards they had prepared. Jackson joined him and together they heaved to drag it towards the USB receiver. It was quite heavy but more awkward in shape than anything else. The pair that they had made were both in excess of one metre squared. Leaning it against the side of the server Zack fumbled for the wiring containing the USB plug that connected to the circuit board.

"This had better fucking work." Jackson stated as his hand covered Zacks and together they connected the USB drive to the receiver.

There was a loud crack. Jackson and Zack jumped back in surprise. Darkness consumed the room as the walls of red lights for the Zeydenian guards blew and turned to black. There was a smell of smoke coming from the server and a moment of silence.

"I think we fucking did it." Jackson finally broke the silence.

"I'm pretty sure we did." Zack replied as the pair of them stared at the machinery, once illuminated but now cloaked in darkness. Zack then turned his attention to the flashing banks on the opposite side of the room, "No time to celebrate though now, our work is only half done." This broke Jackson from his spell of elation, but didn't break his smile, as the pair then made their way across the room.

* * *

Kasumi had assumed the driver's seat on the way back to Zeydence Tower. Dove sat in the back of the vehicle, beside her a bruised and bleeding Junko. Having been rudely awakened by the two Zeydenians he had been thrown around the room until he gave up information. At one point Dove had pinned him to the bed with one metallic hand around his throat until he had passed out and lost control of his bladder. Awakening soon afterwards, bed soaked and his eyes hurting from the light, the attack had continued. Eventually they had gotten out of him what they could. They now knew that Zack was in Zeydence, that he knew of Lord Dhonos' plan and that Zack had a plan. Fortunately, or unfortunately depending on which way you look at it, Zack had not disclosed what his plan had been. It's probably what had prevented Junko from being killed outright in Flint's bedroom, but also probably what had prolonged the beatings until they were satisfied that he did not know. Now Junko found himself bound in the back seat of a Zeydenian vehicle, Dove running her human looking but metallic feeling fingers up and down his exposed chest, wincing as it crossed any of the many lacerations he had received during the previous half an hour. He realised he was essentially a dead man walking, or at least a dead man travelling in the back of a vehicle at that time, but he had hopes that he would see Madoka, and that together they would save each other. In the time that he was being choked of oxygen he realised what he had felt for Madoka, emotions that no other humans really knew about, just what he had read in old texts in the library over the years. He also realised he had competition in Zack. It had taken a while for him to realise that any chance of survival that he stood relied on him making his own plan, and that he could no longer rely on Zack once he had kept him out of the loop. Eventually he had told Kasumi that Zack was here to rescue Madoka from the birthing tower and that he wished to help them to stop him. That is when the beatings had stopped and he had been dragged unceremoniously by Dove to the vehicle outside, wearing nothing but a pair of shorts.

And that is where he found himself headed at this time. It hadn't taken long to reach the outskirts of the city of Zeydence. The buildings appeared to get taller the closer they drove to the tower. They continued along a straight road with buildings about five stories tall lining the road beside them. Junko knew these to be accommodation for the Zeydenian soldiers, strategically placed should they have to assemble in a hurry for any threat facing the city from the outside. There were similar accommodation placements on all sides of Zeydence. As they drove there was a flickering of light from the buildings around them. Not too much, and barely noticeable to the human eye, but in such darkness it stood out a little. Then the silence. The sound of nothingness as a million lights switched off simultaneously. Thrown into darkness, Kasumi broke suddenly to a halt as the sound of glass smashing from above them to the right was coupled with the bizarre sight of half a dozen or so Zeydenian guards flying from the windows of the nearby buildings to land in the road before them. Headlights of the vehicle being the only light cast at that time showed them to remain motionless. Kasumi turned to look at Dove in the back of the car.

"Are you seeing this?" She asked. It was the first time that Dove had ever seen fear on Kasumi's face as she nodded in response.

"How is this possible?" Dove asked.

"I do not know Dove. I shall continue to the birthing tower. I fear there is an attack on the update, and you must pay Jackson a visit." Kasumi replied as she turned to face forwards again, speeding the vehicle onwards whilst chicaning through the lifeless shells of the fallen guards.

35

With the shock that had ensued following the first USB computer killer, and the sudden dissipation of light on the eyes, Jackson had dropped his tool that was required to open the shell of the servers. With the lights ablaze from only one side of the room now it was nearly impossible to find it in the dark. Jackson scrambled on his hands and knees blindly feeling around for it, without much success. Zack rushed to get his Zeydenian guard helmet on hoping to take advantage of the night vision it afforded him, and ignoring the multiple curses being uttered by Jackson on the floor. As soon as the helmet had settled over his head and contacted the rest of his armour at the shoulders, the room brightened as the visor of the helmet activated into night vision. Zack could see Jackson crawling around and rushed over to where he was. Looking around the floor he spotted something that looked a bit like a screwdriver on the floor about five feet away from where Jackson was feeling. It was placed in the space between the first bank of drives and the second. Without stopping to explain Zack stepped over Jackson and reached down to pick it up.

"Is this it?" Zack asked as he handed the instrument to Jackson. Chubby fingers took a hold of it and Jackson yelped a little.

"It feels like it. Let me see." He said as he got up from the floor and hurried across the room to the side with lights. "Fuck yeah! This is it!"

Zack hurried to his side as he started to manoeuvre the casing from the side of the server on the second wave of hard drives. Together they pulled the casing away, again exposing the flashing LEDs of what was essentially the brains of all of the remaining Zeydenians. Glowing red, the lights gave enough light for Jackson to fiddle around and expose the wiring required to connect the USB receiver. Brimming with confidence from the success of the first try he connected the receiver easily to the server.

"OK, grab me that circuit board, then we're fucking out of here!" Jackson yelled excitedly. Zack stood where he was. For the first time that night he could hear movement that he couldn't attribute to himself of Jackson. "Fucking move it Zack, they'll be upon us soon!"

"Maybe sooner than you think." Zack replied. He could hear the door below them whooshing open and footsteps hurriedly running up the stairs to where they were. Suddenly animated Zack rushed to grab the circuit board which has been placed against the wall beside the door. Jackson joined him and they picked it up together. In what seemed to take forever they rushed it to the end of the server. Positioning it against the side of the server Zack heard footsteps running towards the door to the room. He stepped away from the circuit board leaving Jackson to balance it on his own. Stepping into the middle of the room Zack turned to face the door as the pounding drew closer.

* * *

Dove had gotten out of the vehicle at the hub and run for the entrance door. She heard Kasumi driving off with the human in the back of the vehicle still, headed for the Birthing tower. As she reached the entrance, she saw the guard who had been stationed on the door. It had initially been propped against a charging tower by the look of things, but was now leaning conspicuously to one side, lifeless. She tried to get some response from the guard, but it was no use. The door whooshed open for her and she stepped into the building. Spying the elevator, she was reluctant to trust it, given the mysterious electrical anomalies she had witnessed recently. Taking the stairs would be just as quick for her and she started to climb them with speed, metallic feet pounding down on the concrete as she went. Eventually she reached the floor that housed the hard drives and beyond that hoped to find Jackson in a compromising position. Running the length of the corridor towards the door she was upon it within seconds. Placing her hand beside the frame, the door whooshed open. Before Dove stood a Zeydenian guard, not what she had expected. They stared at each other for a second or two before she heard the other voice calling for her destruction.

* * *

Zack stared at the female who had come through the door, as she stared back at him. He had his hand on his Zey $CO2$ gun. He had been prepared to use it but was momentarily stunned at the view before him. He had supressed thoughts of Eva since seeing the bloodied mess on her bed in a completely different time and place. He had imagined he'd seen her in passing since being in Rebristan but put those moments down to hallucinations. Yet here she stood, staring at him with her blue doe eyes, her long blonde hair swept back with the draught of the door whooshing open. A lot of strange things had happened this evening, and Zack believed that that was all par for the course but seeing his dead girlfriend from six hundred years in the past took him off guard. She was every bit as beautiful as he remembered and if any moment at all during his time in Rebristan was going to make him feel like he was in one big comatose nightmare and could wake up from it, then this moment was it. He opened his mouth to utter her name, but other voices came first.

"Just fucking shoot it!" It was Jackson, struggling with the circuit board on the opposite side of the room. Zack could not take his eyes off of the female stood before him and noticed her eyes dart in the direction of Jackson. He saw an anger in those eyes that he had never experienced in Serene with his Eva. She reached behind her back with a perfectly pale arm, and just as quickly brought the same arm back to the fore only this time she too had a Zey CO_2 gun. It was pointed towards Jackson in an instant.

"Eva, No!" Zack shouted out, but her gaze never moved towards him. He did not see any projectile, just a slight kickback ripple along her arm. He heard a thud behind him and a gasp for air. Pulling his own Zey CO_2 up in front of him, he pointed it towards the female in front of him. Quick as a flash she turned to face him. She looked like Eva but there was nothing in her eyes that showed any hint of human emotion. Zack closed his eyes, not bearing to look, and squeezed the trigger of his gun. Only a slight whooshing sound was emitted, and he felt the kickback for himself as his Zey CO_2 fired a hard bolt of air forwards. He expected that to be the last sound he ever heard. Nano seconds seemed like hours as he expected the world to turn dark and numb. He certainly didn't expect to hear a clattering of metal in front of him. Slowly opening his eyes, he saw that Eva, or at least the figure that had portrayed her splayed on the floor, back against the closed door. Where Eva's beautiful face had once been there was metal, tiny flashing lights and a large dent in the centre of it. The skin that had once covered the face was split into two with eyes where ears should be. The long blonde hair he had once cherished swung wildly behind her like a tent that had lost its pegs. There was no blood, and it took a second for the flashbacks of Serene to sew themselves to the present in Zacks mind as he began to understand what had happened.

"What did you do to Eva!?" Zack yelled at the top of his lungs, no longer afraid of being heard. The thing began to raise an arm and pull its weapon towards Zack again, flailing around as if it could no longer see him. Without the same hesitation as before Zack pulled back on the trigger of his gun, watching the shoulder of the robot in front of him smash backwards against the wall, knocking the weapon from its hands. Stepping closer Zack kicked the weapon away from the reach of the Zeydenian. Anger coursed through his veins, for a while his vision appeared to be red, and he pulled back on the trigger again, again, again, and again. As fast as he was pulling the Zey CO_2 was sucking in more air from around him to propel out of the weapon at a deadly speed. There were no bullets, just compressed air hitting the thing as hard as it could. There was a screaming noise, but Zack paid no heed, in the madness he believed that it was probably coming from himself in any case. Over and over again he fired air at the Zeydenian until the clothes that it had worn, as alluring as anything Eva would have worn, had been ripped to small pieces and blown away from the body, pieces of fabric being picked up with each blast of air and spun around the room like confetti. He had been so consumed in a rage that he had not noticed the lights within the unit switching to darkness, had not noticed when the limbs had come away from the torso and no longer posed a danger to him, he had not noticed until at least ten seconds afterwards that there was a gaping hole straight through the chest of the torso and out the back allowing him to see right through. His trigger finger began to ache, and he slowed down. Looking down at his hand through tear blurred eyes he saw that his finger was bleeding, and the skin was worn where he had tried to maintain his grip on the trigger, his aim on the enemy and fighting the continual kickbacks. As his breathing suppressed to a normal level, he could hear rasping behind him. He turned to see Jackson on his backside, propped against the wall beside the server, clutching desperately to the circuit board that they had assembled together earlier that same day. Zack rushed to Jackson, fearing the worst. There was blood coming from his mouth which he spat out with venom. Looking lower Zack noticed that there was a hole that had been torn through Jacksons abdomen, but very little blood as if the air had seared the skin shut as it passed through his insides.

"Hang on there Jackson." Zack begged, looking into Jacksons eyes, but he simply shook his head wincing with the pain of the movement.

"Finish." Jackson uttered between laboured breaths as his eyes turned to look at the USB receiver in his hand. Zack understood perfectly what he meant and took hold of Jacksons hand in his own.

"Together buddy." Zack said as he moved Jacksons hand towards the circuit board to connect the two.

"Fuck............The...............Machines." Jackson grinned through bloodied teeth and rasps as the circuit board connected to the USB receiver. There was another large electrical crack and what felt like a sonic boom that threw Jackson and Zack apart from each other, plunging the room into darkness as the lights on the hard drives dissipated. It took a few seconds for Zack to gather his thoughts, forcing out the exhaustion that wanted to consume his body and allow him to curl up in a ball where he sat. He turned his head towards Jackson who was still sat with his back against the wall. Grinning from ear to ear, eyes wide open, but even Zack could see that there was no longer any life behind them.

"I'm sorry buddy," Zack stated choking up as he said the words, leaning across to Jackson he drew his fingers up to his eyes and gently brought them to a close. "I'll finish what WE started." He continued. Picking up his discarded Zey CO_2, along with the additional weapon that he had relieved Eva of, he stood up and walked towards the door. As it whooshed open, he broke into a sprint towards the stairs.

Next stop, the birthing tower.

36

Kasumi brought the vehicle to a hard stop outside the birthing tower which slammed Junko from his position on the back seat into the rear of the front seats, knocking the wind out of his already pain-wracked body. Opening her door in a hurry Kasumi got out of the vehicle spinning immediately to the door for the back of the vehicle. Pulling it open she reached inside and found Junko's fleshy shoulder. She gripped it with hands stronger than their appearance and pulled him from the vehicle with little effort. Junko tried to let out a yelp of pain, but he was still recovering from having the wind knocked out of him seconds before. Instead, his protest was more inward and heard within his own mind. The internal sound that he made sounded like a thousand screams and he tried to curl up into the foetal position, but that just brought more pain as his weight shifted to his feet pulling him down harder on Kasumi's grip.

"Come parasite." Kasumi simply stated with a degree of hatred in her voice that was rarely heard in Zeydenians. Barely conscious it took all of his energy for him to be led to the glass elevator in front of the firepit at the base of the tower. Kasumi placed her hand on the glass and the doors opened for them both to enter. Junko didn't really notice the fire that passed above them as the elevator slid its way into the heart of the tower before rising. As they got out of the elevator the reception area was in darkness, only lit by the flickering glow of the flames from the firepit. Kasumi surveyed the reception and stood still as she took in the lifeless forms of the Zeydenian guards that were propped against charging stands behind the reception, leaning precariously to one side. The pause gave Junko enough time to get his breath back.

"Why are we here?" Junko asked. His reply was a hard slap across the left side of his face from Kasumi that caused him to sprawl across the floor in the direction of the reception desk. Kasumi strode towards him, grasping his arm before he could get back to his feet and yanking him up. She then continued to pull him towards the elevators behind the desk. As they reached the elevators, they both heard the noise. The feral sounds of a thousand women howling, yelping, screaming, chanting, and cheering. The elevator door opened, and the volume increased as the additional layer of soundproofing had separated. Yanking Flint into the elevator Kasumi turned to face the control panel.

"Twenty-one." She stated clearly and louder than would usually be necessary to be heard over the din that was spinning around the landings of the birthing tower. Junko leant his naked torso against the cold glass as the elevator ascended slowly, ever so slowly. Eventually it stopped and the doors opened to a cacophony of sound.

"SILENCE!" Kasumi shouted to no avail, "YOU WILL BE QUIET!" The noise continued. Kasumi turned her attention to Junko, "Where is she?"

"I don't know." Was all that he could reply. He wanted to inflict sarcasm or hatred into his sentence, but he did not have the energy. Kasumi grabbed his face by the jaw and squeezed forcing him to look directly into her eyes.

"Who is she?" Kasumi demanded.

"Who?" Junko uttered and then cursed himself for wasting energy on the word when he clearly knew that his interrogation was far from over.

"The one who yourself and your friend seek." Kasumi replied. Just a thought of Madoka brought a surge of energy to Junko. He had always watched her and cared for her from afar. Learning of the ancient human emotion of love from the books that he had read during previous visits to the library he had hoped to introduce Madoka one day to the same feelings. That was until Zack had been forced to return with them. He again watched from afar, but this time at someone with experience of that emotion encouraging Madoka ever further from him. He again felt another emotion, this one more negative, at Kasumi's suggestion that he and Zack were friends. He had considered him a convenience and had been using him in order to locate Madoka. He had hoped to remain in the shadows of the Zeydenians. As he looked around himself, he couldn't believe how wrong he had been about that, but he felt some consolation that he was at least closer to Madoka now, although he tried to suppress any thoughts of how the day would end.

"WHO IS SHE?!" Kasumi yelled it this time breaking the train of thought that Junko had been riding and brought his focus back to her.

"Madoka. Section sixty-nine." He replied. Guilt struck him that he had given her name up so easily, but he had also thought that if he had not replied then he would be killed before he saw her again.

Kasumi spun to an electrical board on the wall detailing the names of all of the occupants in this section of the tower. Her eyes scanned the data on it far quicker than Junko could ever read it, and she spun back around grasping him by his arm.

"Whoa!" Junko protested. Kasumi's head span around to glare at him, seemingly without her shoulders moving too, "Where am I gonna go? You don't have to yank me around everywhere. Just tell me where we're going, and I'll go."

"We're going up." Kasumi replied, slightly relieved that she could keep her hands free and that her prisoner had resigned himself to his fate, "Five more floors in the other elevator and you'll be reunited with your old friend. Now move!" She continued by giving Junko a shove in the direction of the internal elevator. The noise all around them had subsided a little as it had started to be noticed that Kasumi was in attendance. Junko looked up at the walkways that circumnavigated the void running through the centre of the tower. There were female faces looking down upon them. The noise picked up again as he and Kasumi entered the elevator to go even higher. As it rose slowly Junko could feel as if two hundred eyes were all focused hard on where he was. As they emerged from the elevator on the fifth floor a female dressed all in white rushed towards them.

"Die machines!" The female yelled as she ran, throwing herself at Kasumi. Several other women had started to step forward towards them, spurred on by the first females rage and bravery. Kasumi grabbed the female by the throat, as she descended upon them, and lifted her high into the air with little effort. With her feet off of the ground, Junko watched as the bravado in the female's eyes turned to panic and her face blushed red with her feet flailing and kicking around seeking anything to take a hold of. The rail that went all around the edge of the walkway was about one metre high and Kasumi grinned as she started to push the female over the rail. The transparent membrane that prevented anyone from leaping over the barrier extended outwards as Kasumi pushed the female against it. Blood vessels were starting to appear within the whites of the female's eyes as Kasumi reached her right hand out towards the membrane. As she touched it, the transparent rubber started to smoke as her finger seared a hole into it. With the pressure on the membrane broken it started to split and open up, tearing in a long line around the top of the barrier. Without a second glance Kasumi guided the form of the female through the membrane to be dangling five stories above the floor below her. She then released the female who disappeared immediately from sight with arms flailing above her. She tried to give a scream, but her throat had been so compressed within Kasumi's grip that it did not recover enough to make a discernible sound before the thud of her body hit the floor far below. Junko felt physically sick at the sound he heard and dared not look over the barrier. Walking towards the other females that had gathered, who had made the decision to step slowly backwards away from Kasumi towards their rooms, she kept her finger within the tear in the membrane that she had created and continued to rip it throughout the walk around the walkway. Junko followed. He daren't do anything else. They seemed to walk slowly in an anti-clockwise direction, which seemed to induce more fear on the faces that had emerged from their rooms. The constant sound of the membrane tearing as they walked became a loud hiss as the rest of the noise subsided to be replaced by supressed sobs of fear. Kasumi's presence on the floor was intimidating. Eventually they arrived at a closed door. Junko read the number and letters engraved onto the door itself. 5EH. Kasumi stood before the door and placed her hand on the receptor beside it. A whirring mechanism as if the door were trying to open whined, but the door remained closed. Kasumi then placed her hand against the door itself and pushed. Her strength buckled the metal of the door so that it folded at the middle before giving way and falling inside the room. Junko was still standing to the right of the entrance, until Kasumi reached out with her hand grasping him by the shoulder, dragging him along and propelling him into the room. He slammed against the wall at the back of the room, smacking the back of his head against the wall at the same time, with such force that his legs gave way and he slid down onto his buttocks on the floor. As the pain subsided in his head, he looked around himself, blinking away the red blurs that danced across his eyes, and slowly looked up to his right. There he saw Madoka. Sitting on her bed in a white gown with her back against the side wall, her knees tucked under her chin being held tight there by her arms. She had tears in her eyes, which also held a look of anger, and her long dark hair flowed down to her bare feet in the position she was in.

"Where is he?" Kasumi asked as they both turned their heads to stare at her.

* * *

Running in a Zeydenian guard outfit was not easy. The additional weight of the armour was slowing Zack considerably. He did not encounter anyone else as he exited the building onto the streets of

Zeydence, which was a relief, but there was still a nagging doubt at the back of his mind that kept teasing him and telling him that not all Zeydenians had been permanently destroyed. It was these thoughts that spurred him to continue running towards the birthing tower. It was also these thoughts that were telling him that he would surely be shot at any time as he envisioned that he must be running a lot slower than a true Zeydenian guard would in their armour. He had thought about throwing the armour to the ground and continuing as he was, but as quick as the thoughts came, the fears of being spotted came. It was so that his journey to the birthing tower seemed to never end. Even though he knew that he would know nothing about it his mind tormented him with the thought that at any time the lights could go out and he would be no more, feel no more, ever, but would also have failed Madoka and the humans that populated Rebristan. Eventually he came to the foot of the birthing tower, illuminated by the Daflaydian flames that surrounded the base. He saw a Zeydenian vehicle parked up on the road and approached it with caution. After establishing that it was empty, he approached the glass door that he had used previously with Flint. Summoning the elevator to his location the glass doors slid open and he stepped inside. Passing underneath the flames whilst the rest of the world outside was dark made Zack feel like he was taking a trip into what he imagined Hell to be like. Eventually rising into the reception area of the tower he braced himself for an attack. None came, it was a relief to see that Zeydenians present within the building were lifeless, that his plan had, as far as he had seen, succeeded. With his confidence lifted by every lifeless Zeydenian that he saw he made his way quickly to the elevator that he knew would take him to the area he had last seen Madoka. He hoped that she would still be there. He recalled that the ascendence had been slow the previous time he had been there, and this occasion was no different. With the thought of seeing Madoka again the ride seemed painfully slow this time. There was noise coming from the top segment of the tower that Zack had not expected, like a wailing or sobbing, some anger. He had run with only thoughts of Madoka, oblivious to the fact that there would be other humans within the tower facing the same fate as she. He wondered how they had known about the Zeydenians being no more, and then wondered why they did not sound happier at the fact. Something was wrong, but he couldn't quite place his mind on what it could be. As the elevator glided into the top segment of the tower the doors opened and he stepped out, dashing into a nearby shadow to catch his breath and figure out the scenarios. The noise seemed louder as the door opened and he breathed deeply safe in the knowledge that he would not be heard by anyone above the din around him. He recalled looking around the walkway when he had visited with Flint and memorised the location of the elevators in respect of the location of Madoka's room. Taking a glance from where he was, he could see that the landing around the fifth floor had something flapping in the breeze, but he could not make out what, there was just movement that he couldn't focus on. As he looked away from the fifth floor to focus on his current level his eyes spied a form on the floor. As he focused on it he saw that it was a human, unmoving, and as his mind registered the amount of blood around it he understood that they were probably dead. Glancing back at the fifth floor for any signs of danger as his brain put the flapping membrane and the body together his heart started to race. Was it a coincidence that the body had come from the same floor as Madoka? Did something know that it was himself who had caused such devastation to the Zeydenian people this evening and his connections to Madoka? Anything was possible in this land that he still struggled to comprehend. If he took the elevator to the fifth floor, he would surely be a sitting duck, especially at the speeds that they moved. With the night vision on his helmet he could see a door directly in front of him on the opposite side of the tower, which he hoped would lead to stairs. Walking within the shadows of the overhead walkways he stuck as closely to the wall as possible as he circumnavigated the tower. He stayed on the same side of the tower that he knew Madoka's room to be on for fear of being seen from above on the other side. As he made his way around, he saw that the crumpled human body on the floor was female, eyes wide open with a look of anger and defiance in them as well as pain. He stopped for a moment, unsure if she was still alive, and waved a hand out to his side to see if the eyes registered the movement. Nothing. He then continued his journey until he reached the door. There was still enough noise coming from the other floors for him to open the door without being noticed. Then, as he stepped through, a sound he had not wished to hear echoed through the chamber.

"Guard!" It was a female voice, high pitched full of fear and anger at the same time. Then other voices shouting, "Guard!" "Guard!" "Guard!"

He turned to look through the door, imagining that he was about to be under attack from Zeydenian guards himself, until he saw that several women had left their rooms on the second and third floors and were pointing angrily in his direction. He had been wearing his armour so long that it felt like a part of him and had not paid much heed to its appearance being that of the enemy for the very people he had wished to protect. He quickly removed his helmet to show those that could see that he was human. The noise subsided a little but there were others who could not see that continued. Holding his helmet under his arm he raced up the steps of the tower until he reached what he believed to be the fifth floor by his counting. Completely out of breath Zack wondered how he was still moving forwards and whether adrenaline ever ran out. He stood behind the unopened door trying to take some deep breaths and cursing the six months in Serene when he had tried to play it cool for an ex-girlfriend and was smoking daily with her. When he felt that he would fall over if he did not get moving and find something else as scary to fill him with adrenaline, he stood up straight and bade the door to open. With a whoosh he stepped out onto the landing. This was it. He could now be seen at any moment by whatever was up here, but that was inevitable if he were to get any closer. With his helmet under his left arm and his right hand on the Zey CO_2 in its holster on his right he strode towards the room that he had last seen Madoka in. When he was about twenty feet from the door he saw Junko, a much battered half naked Junko, emerge hobbling from the room. He stopped where he stood as his mind tried to compute why Junko would be here. There was no time for him to generate an answer before the female emerged too. He had seen her before, the tall, slender, silver haired but exotically dark-skinned female, he had seen her in Serene before he ever came here. Thoughts of Eva filled his mind as it raced to understand why he would see Eva here and this female there in Serene, and concluded that she must have played a part in the bloodied mess he had found on Eva's bed. This was the wakeup call he needed to pump him full of energy and he felt his body rise to rush at her. Junko turned his head towards Zack and the female's eyes followed. Laying sight on Zack as he was starting to rush towards her, he was throwing his helmet down and his Zey CO_2 was being raised. She grabbed Junko around the throat and started to raise him off of the floor. There was a guttural growl emitted from Zack as he ran towards her and squeezed the trigger. No projectile was seen but there was a thud on the right shoulder of the Zeydenian and she released her grip on Junko, causing him to fall to the walkway floor, as she spun around three hundred and sixty degrees, loosing balance, and landing on her backside. Slowing down, Zack passed the bedroom door, eyes angrily focussed on the, quite frankly beautiful but evil, Zeydenian on the floor as she tried to get back to her feet. Firing again at the same arm he caused her to again sprawl backwards until she was lain prone on the floor. Anger flashed in her eyes, which Zack had not expected, and she appeared damaged but not giving up. Zack paused as he took aim at her throat, intending to sever any connections between the body and the head.

"If there is a hell for you machines, I hope you fucking rust in it." Zack stated through gritted teeth as he pulled the trigger. Nothing happened. He pulled again and again as she was starting to get up and get to her feet. He threw the gun to one side and ran at the female kicking her square in the chest causing her to fall back again hoping to buy himself some time while he came up with a plan Z. As he stood up straight, he felt a thud from behind him and realised that something was grabbing at him around the shoulders and throat. A bare arm had him in a headlock. He could sense that it was human as he could feel breath on his ear.

"You can't have her, she's mine." Junko spat venom in his voice, resentment at Zacks relationship with Madoka coming out in a blast of words.

"Junko." Zack gasped for breath as the headlock tightened, "What are you doing?"

"I'm going to finish this without you." Junko replied as he pulled Zack closer to the rail of the fifth-floor landing. As he was being pulled backwards Zack watched helplessly as the female Zeydenian stood up, her right arm a little mangled but still as dangerous looking as before.

"Let me go Junko." Zack gasped, "We need to finish this."

"I'll finish it." Junko stated, but he didn't get the chance as a hand grabbed him around the throat. The female Zeydenian was upon them. As the grip tightened on his throat Junko released his grip from Zack as both of his hands reached to grab the mechanical arm that was attached to him. Zack crouched down, noticing that her right arm hung limp at her side and tried to push her away from Junko and him. It was futile, he could not move the female as they proceeded towards the barrier with Junko elevated from the ground. Zack stepped out between them and swung a punch at the female's head, striking her in the face. Despite being human looking his hand cracked as if he had struck a steel block. Pain shot up his arm like a shockwave and he slumped to the floor. He did not see Junko being flung over the edge but heard the very brief scream and a thud. His eyes were clenched shut with the pain in his hand from punching the enemy. He felt the sudden grasp upon his armour though and being dragged along the landing to the railings. He tried to open his eyes, but he was still reeling from the pain. As his eyes parted slowly the world was blurred with the moistness of tears of pain. Through the blur he saw a figure rushing towards them. He could only make out that it was dressed in white and humanoid in shape through the tears and that was it, and then he felt a sudden yank, he was propelled closer to the edge but had a sense that it was not through the actions of the female that he had been fighting. Movement seemed to stop momentarily, although the grip upon him remained, as he heard a thud of metal upon metal. His eyes clearing, he could make out that the newest addition to the party had long black hair flowing down the white outfit.

"Madoka." Zack whispered but there was no reply. Just a struggle between the two females. With her good arm holding onto Zack and her right arm useless the Zeydenian female was being pushed towards the barrier, unable to defend herself from another attacker. Zack heard the footsteps of other people running along the hallway and could make out a group of females dressed in white running from their rooms towards them. They were carrying whatever they could from their rooms to be used as makeshift weapons. There was a lot of clattering and clanging going on above him, that he couldn't see due to being held down. He was sometimes struck in the melee himself, but the pain soon subsided as he heard Madoka's voice screaming "No!" Suddenly he was pulled tight against the railings in a sitting position as he saw the Zeydenian female's legs and torso being lifted by the many women up and over the rail. He was stuck on the safe side whilst she floundered in the air on the other. Essentially, he was the ballast that was keeping her from falling to the ground below. As the women struck at her arm to release her grip, he could feel himself being pulled upwards, as the grip was not loosening and the blows being rained upon her only served to assist gravity. Then it stopped.

"Move out of the way!" A female voice shouted and the claustrophobia of flailing bodies around Zack eased as they stepped aside. Zack saw a female, again dressed all in white, standing about five feet away. She was pointing a Zey Co2 gun in his direction. Where she had got it from he had not seen. It could have been his own that was discarded for being useless, or another from any of the lifeless guards that were in the building. Either way it was not a sight he was enjoying.

"I'm not a real guard!" Zack shouted nervously, "I come in peace."

As he shouted the words there was a blast of air that he felt above him, causing his hair to ripple followed by a metallic thwack noise. At the sound of the initial strike, he was yanked upwards but then the hand that had a grasp on his shoulder was released. Gravity took care of both him and the Zeydenian female. Zack slid down the railings onto his buttocks on the landing. As he landed he heard the metallic crash of the Zeydenian hit the surface five floors below. The noise echoed throughout the tower, followed by the whoops and yelps of a hundred women or more from every floor. Exhausted he pulled himself to his feet with his arms on the rail. Peering over the top of the rail he saw the sprawled broken body of Junko with limbs at unnatural angles and a pool of blood forming around his head. To the left of him lay what remained of the Zeydenian female he had been fighting, the one he had seen at the top of the cliffs in Serene too. Her head had come away from the rest of the torso upon impact, the skin that was covering it split revealing a chromed interior. The torso had wires coming out of the neck laid on the floor. He watched as Junko's blood pooled and ran to touch the wiring. There was a spark and a puff of smoke but no movement. He had seen enough. Holding onto the rails with both hands he steadied himself to turn around. As if in a dream he saw her face before him, she looked beautiful in white with her long black hair contrasting as much as possible against it. Tears ran from her beautiful blue eyes and her lips looked puffy and full.

"Madoka." Zack said. And then it all went black.

37

Sunlight flowed through the window hitting Zacks closed eyes as he began to stir. Slowly opening his eyes, he discovered that he was laid flat on a bed in a small room that he partly recognised. Leaning up onto his elbows every muscle in his body ached, feeling like he had gone ten rounds with a heavyweight boxer. He saw her. Sitting on the end of the bed, never taking her eyes off of him was Madoka.

"Morning." Zack said, as calmly as he could. He still wasn't sure if his plan had been one hundred percent successful but the fact that he and Madoka were both alive was a good sign. Surely any Zeydenians left would have brought the battle to the birthing tower, the only place in Zeydence with a huge population of humans.

"How are you feeling Zack?" Madoka asked, unable to hide the concern in her voice.

"I'll be honest, I've been better." He replied, trying not to make her worry. Concern remained in her eyes. She did not know of the feeling that was taking over her body, making her eyes water. She had known loss, she had known fear and she had known hardship, but this feeling ran so deep inside her soul, causing a throbbing in her chest. Seeing the pain in her eyes Zack tried to make her feel better stating "I think it's all over now."

"What is?" Madoka asked, still unsure of what had exactly happened the previous night.

"The Zeydenian rule. I believe they are all gone." Zack replied with as much of a smile as he could muster through the aches and pain.

"All of them?" Madoka asked with a hint of concern. Zacks smile dropped as well as he realised what she meant. Thoughts of Flint, Diarran and Marna rushed into his mind.

"It was the only way." He replied nodding solemnly. "You were all to die. I couldn't let that happen." Madoka leant forwards and placed her index finger on Zacks lips.

"You do not have to explain." She said, "I know you did what you thought was best."

Zack groaned as he tried to sit up straight, and Madoka rushed in closer to him at the sound of his pain.

"Lay down still, you need to recover still." She instructed.

"There is too much to do." Zack protested.

"If what you tell me is true then we have all the time in the world to do it." Madoka replied, "Now tell me where it hurts the most?" She laid her hands on Zacks shoulders and he instantly felt as though the muscle pain was being evaporated from his body. He recalled his first waking day in Rebristan and how she had made him feel better with her touch, with Zero excitedly telling him 'Maddie is a healer'. Within a few minutes of being rubbed all over his body felt as supple as it ever had done in the past, but the energy had left him too.

"Just a little bit longer." Zack stated more than asked, as his eyes began to slowly close. He felt Madoka kiss him on the forehead, as one would do to a sleeping child to wish them sweet dreams, and then she laid down beside him, placed an arm across him and held him close. A feeling he had not felt for such a long time. He had no idea that he had missed the warmth of a hug or intimacy until he drifted off to sleep with a tear falling from his closed eyes and a feeling of his soul being lifted.

* * *

They had slept for only a few more hours. The noises within the birthing tower, as the realisation of a new future unfolding settled in, made it hard to sleep in any case. Zack awoke and saw that he was dressed in one of the white gowns that had been worn by the women of the tower.

"Really?" Zack exclaimed.

"You can't go out looking like you did." Madoka stated, "You would cause a scare upon first glance."

It made sense and Zack nodded in a semi-approval, although the idea of wearing female clothing still didn't sit right with him. They stood to leave the room and as they reached the door, he witnessed an exodus of women making their way along their respective landings towards the exit elevator.

"Where will they go?" Zack asked realising he hadn't given any thought until that moment of the humans in Zeydence.

"Every one of them would have formulated an escape plan during their time in the tower, in case the moment arose. You brought them that moment. Do not worry about them." Madoka replied.

Leaving the building hand in hand they stepped out of the glass elevator on the other side of the firepit. Madoka took a deep breath as other women passed by the side of them from behind.

"The air from outside." She sighed as it filled her lungs. Zack looked towards the Zeydence tower as it loomed silently in the distance.

"I have something to do before we return to the sector." Zack stated. Whilst maintaining his hold on Madoka's hand he turned in the direction of Zeydence tower and started to walk in its direction. Madoka did not question his decision.

* * *

Standing at the base of Zeydence tower and looking up the steps to the entrance, Madoka and Zack were still hand in hand, never letting go of each other on the short walk from the birthing tower. Zack had found a discarded Zey CO_2 gun and held onto it tightly in the other hand. Just in case. As they started to climb the steps to Zeydence tower a figure emerged from the entrance. Tightening his grip on the weapon Zack began to raise his hand until he recognised the figure. Blustering about in a state of confusion was Rodrock, the human servant Zack had seen upon his arrival in Zeydence. Not quite relaxing his grip on the gun Zack called out to him.

"Rodrock!"

"You know me?" Rodrock asked as he stopped scurrying around in confusion and focused on the two people ascending the steps towards him.

"We've met." Zack replied, which clearly didn't end Rodrock's confusion. "How are things inside?"

"I don't know what's happened." Pure panic registered in Rodrock's voice, "Everyone's still."

"Everyone?" Madoka asked.

"I haven't found one master yet that will move. They are all so...."

"Lifeless?" Zack finished the sentence for him with a question.

"Exactly." Rodrock replied.

"Rodrock," Zack caught his attention again and looked him square in the eyes, "today you are a free man. The Zeydenians are no more."

"But....they are my masters." Rodrock began to protest his freedom.

"They were." Zack corrected, "But they intended to kill you, and all humans." Rodrock stood stunned into silence. Years of obedience counted for nothing and a tear leaked from his eye.

"But where will I live?" Rodrock finally asked.

"Anywhere you like Rodrock." Zack answered. "You are a free man now. Stay here if you like. You are the only human in this tower, I think, so call it yours."

All three of them looked up at the height of the tower, shining in the setting sun for a moment.

"If you'll excuse us, I have something I need to do before we leave." Zack stated as he motioned for Madoka to follow him. Stepping past Rodrock, who was still staring up at the tower they entered the reception area.

"I hate looking up at tall buildings from the floor. Makes me feel sick." Zack stated as they made their way to the elevators. Apprehension filled Madoka, she had never been into Zeydence tower before. Despite knowing what she knew about the previous night it still felt like she was stepping into the lair of the enemy. Sensing her anxiety Zack simply said "Relax, I've got this." Feeling her body relax as he held her hand, he led her to the elevators and they stepped inside. This elevator was much quicker than those of the birthing tower and when the door eventually opened the long, pristine white corridor opened up in front of them. Doors along the corridor were open, as if Rodrock had truly checked in on every room, and looking inside as they passed Zack saw various Zeydenians in a state of malfunction, some exploded and some simply flung across the room. All lifeless. As he approached the entrance to Flint's room, he dreaded what he would find. His work had been essential, and this visit was essential, but he didn't want to see the devastation to something that he had come to consider a friend. Walking through the door into Flint's quarters Zack headed for the bedroom. Upon entering he saw the lifeless form of Flint, Diarran and Marna laid side by side on the bed without any damage. There was no response from them, but they were not in the same state of disrepair that he had witnessed to other Zeydenians. Madoka joined him at his shoulder as he stared upon the sight before him.

"They didn't log in for the update." Zack stated.

"What update?" Madoka asked. Zack turned to face her.

"Lord Dhonos had a plan to update all Zeydenians in such a way that they would no longer need to use humans as slaves for them to function and survive." Zack began, "All Zeydenians were to connect to the main servers last night at the same time whilst they recharged to receive the update. Then they were going to abandon the humans. Without the supplies from the Zeydenians the human race would either die or kill each other for that last slither of survival."

"So, what's different now?" Madoka asked.

"There are no Zeydenians to kill any humans that wished to overthrow them in their quest for survival anymore, and with the exodus from the birthing tower word of freedom should reach the sectors before desperation and selfishness set in. Everyone is free, not just abandoned within a fence." He tried to make it sound as heroic as he could but still envisioned problems as the human race became accustomed to freedom. "So, I attacked the update in a way that all of the Zeydenians would never be able to function again."

"They look just like they're sleeping." Madoka said as she looked at the three figures side by side on the bed.

"Essentially they are." Zack replied, "They just ran their energy down together, but they can never be recharged as there is nothing now for them. I didn't want it this way, but it was all or nothing."

Madoka's gaze scanned the room and she saw on a desk an envelope. Walking over to it she picked it up.

"Zack. This has your name on it." She announced. Zack joined her and took the envelope from her. Printed across the front was the words 'TO ZACK'. Opening the envelope there was a piece of folded paper inside. Opening it he saw a printed letter that was addressed to himself.

Zack,

If you are reading this then your plan must have been successful. Humans taught humanity to me, Diarran and Marna that the other Zeydenians could not comprehend. I imagined your plan would involve some degree of destruction, how could it not? I had not instructed anyone to veer from Lord Dhonos' schedule other than Diarran and Marna. We will simply stay functional until our batteries expire. In truth I had not expected your plan to be so successful, given the time frame you had to plan it, but you did good. I guess. We managed to function for about two hours after the plan had been executed. I wandered the halls of the tower. I saw that Lord Dhonos and Lady Zoesis were no more. That made me the most senior Zeydenian, albeit briefly. I can assure you that I would have run this place differently. Do not feel guilt. There was no other way. Before I run down and cease to exist, I must tell you, as I am now the most senior Zeydenian, that the city of Zeydence and all the buildings within it are yours. You have liberated your people and therefore are rewarded by a supportive Zeydenian, myself. I imagine you would want to get out of Zeydence in the first instance though. In the basement of this building are numerous vehicles of all sizes. They are yours too. I expect you will see fit to distribute them fairly for the human race to thrive in peace. I would hate for the sacrifice I have made for the humans to actually behave as Lord Dhonos predicted. In the drawer below this letter is a glove. This glove, when worn will be all you need to press against the sensors at any gate, building or door to gain entry. Use it wisely to free your people Zack. I wish you all the best.

Sincerely
Flint.

Tears had formed in the corner of Zacks eyes as he read the letter, even though it eased his feelings of guilt. He looked across to the bed at the three still figures.
"We can't leave them here." Zack stated.
"What do you mean?" Madoka asked.
"Last night, it was hurried. Rushed. We had little time. But they are not destroyed like the others, just inactive. With time I could find a way to bring them back. But if I leave them here, humans will come in victory and they may harm their current state." He could not believe that he was using the words 'humans' and 'harm' so soon after liberation, but he was realistic. "We'll take them with us."
Opening the drawers upon which the letter had sat Zack pulled out a black glove, fine wiring ran through the fingers and the tips had a sheen of a million microscopic lights. Zack pulled it onto his right hand. He took Madoka's hand with his left and lead her to the entrance of the room.
"Let's go find ourselves some wheels." He said as the two stepped into the corridor.

38

They had driven through the night and sun was just coming up when they arrived at the gates.

"This should be it." Madoka said as Zack came to a stop before the gate. All sectors had seemed the same as they passed but they had followed the navigation system and found themselves at what should be sector thirty-one.

As they had finished moving Flint, Marna and Diarran to the transport they had chosen for their journey Zack chose some alternative clothing from Flint's wardrobe, leaving behind the female robes he had on. At that time Madoka handed him the piece of paper that she had found wedged in his discarded helmet. The letter from Jackson.

Zack stepped down from the vehicle which resembled a futuristic tank, all in chrome, and approached the gate. Placing his gloved hand against a sensor to the right the gate slowly opened. He walked back and climbed into the cabin of the vehicle, urging it forwards as soon as he was behind the wheel. They drove for what seemed like another thirty minutes until they saw what appeared to be residential buildings. Unlike the tall towers in sector sixty-nine the buildings here seemed more nomadic. Wooden structures a maximum of three stories high built on stilts. This sector sat close by to a river with no flood defence. As they drove closer people came to look out of the hut doors briefly before darting back in. As they approached the closest hut a short stubby man about sixty years old with long hair and a long grey beard emerged. Despite his diminutive size he looked as though he commanded respect as he raised his hand for the vehicle to halt. Zack obeyed bringing it to a standstill, then exited and climbed down to speak with the man.

"Who are you?" Asked the man gruffly.

"I am Zack from sector sixty-nine." Zack replied, "I come in peace with my friend Madoka. I bring news from Zeydence. Who are you?"

"I am Canna of sector thirty-one." Replied the man, "What news do you bring?"

"The humans of all sectors are now free people. The Zeydenians are no more."

"How can that be?" Asked Canna

"They all ceased to exist in the early hours of yesterday morning. One of the former residents of this sector played a major part in securing freedom for the humans and that is why I am here." Zack replied.

"Freedom?" The word hadn't quite sunk in for Canna as he stared blankly ahead as if looking straight through Zack towards the horizon.

"Yes." Zack didn't want to elaborate any more, time was of the essence and he had things that he needed to do. "Do you know of Erinna, mother of Jackson if she is still with us?"

"Aye." Canna replied, snapping back to reality.

"I must speak with her." Zack stated before Canna could drift off into thought again.

"She resides along the back row with the others too infirm to toil." Canna stated, looking behind himself. He turned his gaze back to Zack. "If you will allow me to ride with you, I can take you there."

"Of course." Zack replied.

Helping the older man into the vehicle, Zack climbed aboard and moved off. They drove for another twenty minutes before Canna indicated a hut about two hundred metres ahead of them near to the sector fencing. It was only two stories high and stood on stilts in one of the boggier areas of the sector.

"There she is." Canna stated pointing ahead of him. Zack followed the line of his finger, as crooked as it may be, to find that he wasn't pointing exactly to the hut but to fencing just behind the hut. There he saw an elderly lady, quite rotund with long grey hair cascading down the back of a grey dress, which was muddied at the bottom. "Erinna. She waits there every day for a glimpse of Jackson coming home."

Madoka looked fearful at the task that lay ahead, but stood anyway. Zack touched her on the arm.

"It's ok. I've got this." He stated, "You keep Canna company, I won't be long." As the vehicle came to a stop, Zack climbed down out of it and approached the lone female stood by the fence until he was about ten feet away from her.

"Erinna?" Zack asked. She continued to look forwards through the fence into the wilderness beyond.

"Do you know Jackson?" Erinna asked without looking around.

"I know him." Zack replied.

"Tell me." she commanded more than asked.

"Erinna, Jackson will not be coming home." As he said this, he witnessed the muscles relax in Erinna as she went from being a rigid and upright elderly lady to one sunken into her own body with a deep breath. She turned around to face Zack.

"And you know this how?" Erinna asked.

"I was with him as he died." Zack answered, desperately looking for a way to make the situation better, and then he added, "Saving all of the humans of Rebristan and giving them their freedom."

Erinna's head tilted to one side as she looked Zack up and down. She took a couple of steps towards him.

"You should come inside." She said as she proceeded to walk past Zack towards the hut at a pace that surprised him. He turned to follow and saw that Canna and Madoka were both watching him intently from the vehicle. Following Erinna up the steps to the ground floor of the hut he walked into the wooden building as she had simply swung the door open. Inside was just as sparse with a few wooden pieces of furniture and wooden walls. There were no carpets, just bare floor, and a couple of wooden beds all in one room. A curtain was drawn across one side and Zack imagined that would be where the bathroom and toilet were as he could not see them anywhere else within the room.

"When did this happen?" Erinna asked.

"Early hours of yesterday morning." Zack replied, "I came as soon as I could."

"How?"

"We devised a plan to destroy all of the Zeydenians. We were attacked halfway through, and he was shot. He hung on though long enough to complete the plan, and he destroyed all Zeydenians. Humans now have their freedom because of Jackson. Your son died a hero."

"Was he in pain?" She asked.

"If he was, he didn't make it known." Zack replied, and as he reflected on these words, he realised there was truth to them, and that they weren't just some rubbish that he was making up to soften the blow. "Erinna, before we started the plan Jackson gave me some papers he had written. One was a letter to me and the other was addressed to yourself." Zack held out his hand with a piece of paper in it. Erinna stepped forwards and took it from him.

"Is there anything else you need to know?" Zack asked her.

"No, I'm sure my Jackson will tell me everything in here. Thank you." She replied as she sat down on the edge of a bed with the letter in her hand. Zack decided that she should have her privacy to read her letter so backed out of the hut away from her.

"I am sorry Erinna." He said as he stood at the door. She did not look up and so he closed her door for her and turned to walk back to the vehicle. Madoka and Canna were now stood by the side of it.

"Look after her please Canna. Jackson isn't coming home." Zack implored.

"So your lady friend here has told me." Canna indicated towards Madoka. Zack sighed with relief that he hoped he would not have to break any more bad news in the sector.

"I see you as one of the elders of the sector Canna." Zack stated.

"Aye, that I am, a small sector we are though." Canna replied.

"Can I entrust you to bring the people together, to grow your own crops for yourselves and to live in peace and harmony?"

"I have dreamt of nothing else for these last sixty years." Canna replied with a smile creeping through the thick facial hair.

"Then be well Canna. You are free." Zack told him.

"Thank you young man." Canna praised as Zack and Madoka climbed up to enter the vehicle. Stopping before he got in Zack turned to look at Canna.

"No, give thanks for Jackson of Sector Thirty-One. He made this happen. Do you need a ride back Canna?"

"No thank you. I'm going to see how Erinna is." Canna stated and gave a wave with a calloused hand before turning to walk towards the hut that Zack had just exited. With that Zack swung himself into the driver's seat of the transport vehicle, smiled at Madoka sitting beside him and they moved off towards the entrance for the sector.

39

It was nightfall again as they finally made it to the gates of sector sixty-nine. Zack opened them and they drove through, continuing for another thirty minutes mostly in silence knowing what was to happen. They arrived at the building where Zack had been held overnight having been taken out of tower fourteen, which seemed like an eternity ago. Madoka jumped out of the vehicle as it came to a standstill, stretching her body after the drive. Zack stepped out as well and looked up at the building. Holding onto his salvaged Zey CO_2 he silently bade Madoka to wait in the vehicle. She was having none of it and followed him to the door, standing behind him as she did so. Opening the door, they stepped in. The place was just as Zack remembered and silent as a tomb. Walking towards the room where he had first received his Zeydenian guard uniform from Marna, he saw that shattered remains of a Zeydenian guard who had no doubt stopped at the building to recharge and receive the update. This gave a swell in Zacks confidence that his plan had truly stretched beyond the city of Zeydence alone. Madoka picked up the guards discarded weapon and they proceeded to the next room. Another thirty minutes and they had checked every room in the building. It was clear.

"We'll put them in the room with beds on the ground floor." Zack suggested.

"Ok." Madoka replied. It was a sombre mood that hung in the air. They both left the building and walked back to the vehicle opening up a rear compartment. Inside lay the lifeless remains of Flint, Diarran and Marna, resting on gurneys that Madoka and Zack had managed to move them onto at the Zeydence Tower. Slowly and silently, they pulled each gurney out of the vehicle and wheeled them into the room they had decided upon. Once it was completed, they both stared at their robotic friends lying motionless in the room for a few minutes. Zack had never been a religious person, that was pretty much an impossibility with his taste of music back home, and he doubted that Madoka even knew what religion was. He had considered uttering some sort of prayer as if he were attending a funeral, but he realised that essentially they were robots and not generally regarded to have any religious influences anyway. Looking at Madoka, they both knew that it was time to leave. Closing the door with a promise to return soon, they walked away from the building to begin the drive back to their friends and family.

* * *

Arriving at the foot of the towers in the Zeydenian vehicle caused quite a stir. Despite the darkness of the night people came out of the towers to see what was happening. There was a buzz of fear in the air. Obviously there had been no transport arrive during the day to take them to the fields for work, or the previous day, and the majority of the population believed that there must be some consequences to follow. Zack stopped outside Tower fourteen.

"You're home Madoka." He stated.

"We're home Zack." She corrected him.

Looking up through the windshield of the vehicle Zack saw some familiar figures walking towards him from Tower ten. Vissu and Echo took long strides towards the vehicle, looks of defiance and concern on both faces.

"We come in peace!" Zack shouted out as he opened the door to the Zeydenian vehicle, unaware that Madoka had opened the door on her side too.

"Echo!" She shouted with joy in her voice which caused the two men to stop dead in their tracks. Zack then felt confident enough to pop his head outside of the vehicle, and the jaws dropped on everyone around as he and Madoka emerged and dropped to the ground. Echo ran towards his sister and grabbed her in a big bear hug swinging her around whilst Vissu remained rooted to the spot in shock.

"Good evening Vissu." Zack said as he walked towards the elder man, "We're back."

"What have you brought back with you?" Vissu asked with a hint of anger as he pointed towards the Zeydenian armoured vehicle they had travelled in.

"What?" Zack asked, turning towards the vehicle, "You didn't expect us to walk back from Zeydence did you?"

"They will come." There was now a hint of panic in Vissu's voice, "You have condemned the whole sector."

"No, no, no, calm down old man." Zack interrupted, turning back to face Vissu. "They're all gone."

"Gone?" Vissu asked.

"Yes. You are free now." Zack replied.

"All?"

"Yes. All."

"Flint?" Vissu asked.

"All are gone." Zack simply replied not wishing to elaborate on the loss of his friends any further.

"What do we do now?" Vissu asked. This question from the old man took Zack by surprise.

"Well, whatever it is you planned at you many meetings for when you achieved freedom. I told you I would do it." Zack replied. Echo and Madoka had walked over to join Zack and Vissu.

"I think for now Zack and I need a shower after the journey we've had." Madoka interjected.

"Yeah, I could do with a shower too." Echo responded.

"You know, it gets kinda cramped in there when there's three of us." Zack stated, Madoka smiled, "Let's maybe keep it to a maximum of two and you can go after we've relieved our aching muscles Echo."

"Sounds fair." Echo replied.

"Sleep now Vissu, you are free," Zack started, "Tomorrow is a new day and we can plan life with the whole sector and how to move forward in peace."

Taking their leave Zack and Madoka walked hand in hand towards the entrance for tower fourteen.

Reaching the apartment Madoka gestured for the door to open. With a familiar whoosh it slid open and she stepped inside.

"Mama, I'm home." She called out as she walked into the living room area.

"Maddie!!!!!" Zero was on his feet within a nano second and rushed towards Madoka with his arms wide for a hug. Zack saw that Keisa had stood up from the chair she had been sitting in. She had a tear in her eye but a smile on her face as she mouthed "Thank you" to him.

EPILOGUE

They had been back in the sector for about two months. Zack had had daily meetings with Vissu and never once mentioned that he had been awarded the city of Zeydence. The people of sector sixty-nine had pulled together well after a couple of days rest and were now successfully growing crops for food from seeds within the food supplied that they already had, on land that had previously laid barren. There were those, mainly the older population, who had remained scared for a week or two that the Zeydenians would come back to punish them, but by now everyone was relaxed and at peace. Used to the idea that the artificial intelligence that had governed their every waking move since birth were truly gone. Keisa had passed away three weeks after they had returned. Peacefully in her sleep, and with a smile on her face. Zack believed that she would have hung on forever as a slave to finally see the day that her children would be free, and now she was at peace with the world she felt like she could let go. She was the first human being for nearly six hundred years to have a proper burial within the land that she had inhabited rather than just being taken away for disposal by the Zeydenians. There wasn't nearly the same amount of wailing or mourning that Zack had expected but he guessed that the people of Rebristan were used to loss and sadness. The weather was beginning to get warmer for the time of the year and the people were getting excited about cutting their first crops. Zack stood on the balcony of the apartment watching the sun set.

"Are you ok Zack?" Madoka asked as she came to join him and rested her arms around his shoulders, taking in the view.

"Yeah." Zack replied unconvincingly.

"Tell me what's bothering you?" Madoka persisted, not believing Zacks previous response.

"The weather." He offered.

"The weather? Why?" She asked resting her head on his shoulder as the sun started to dip below the horizon.

"It's warm." Zack responded, "It's summer, I guess." He didn't want her to become frustrated with his off the cuff answers, so he continued, "My parents were born a day apart. every year they would have a joint garden party at our house. It was always the happiest day of the year. The weather was always fine, there was never a party that I can recall where the weather was rubbish. And....and I'll never see them again. The weather just made me miss them." He replied as a memory rolled down his cheek from his eye in the form of a tear.

"Ok." Madoka simply replied, her mind digesting what Zack had said.

"In this timeline," Zack continued, "they're long passed away. I don't know when, where how or why. It's just an emptiness not knowing." He was starting to think that he must be sounding ungrateful and saying too much now. Madoka pulled on his shoulders forcing him to turn around and face her.

"You can go back Zack. Remember how we met, I jumped through time. You jumped through time to get here. It's possible." She stated.

"But...you're here. I don't want to leave you." Zack stammered at the thought of losing Madoka again. This caused her to smile.

"Don't be silly Zack. I, how do you say it, love you. Wherever you go is where I will be."

Zacks eyes narrowed as he tried to comprehend what she was telling him.

"You'd really leave here?" Zack asked.

"Of course, if that's what you wanted. It's not like I could never come back is it?" she replied. A smile crept onto Zacks face at the prospect she was offering but was then quickly crushed as he thought further.

"You know, things happened before I left. They will believe I killed someone." His heart became heavy as he uttered the words.

"They?"

"Erm...the Police, the authorities. My friends." Zack replied.

"Did you?" Madoka asked as she wrapped her arms around him to hug him.

"No, of course not, no." Zack replied. "I think it must have been that female that I fought with in the birthing tower. I saw her in Serene at the same time that you were there."

"Then you tell everyone that you didn't do it." Madoka suggested.

"It's really not as simple as that." Zack responded.

"I'll tell you what is not simple Zack." Madoka started with a hint of frustration in her voice, "It's sneaking into a city controlled by superior beings, formulating a plan to eradicate them, and saving the human race from extinction, with just three days to prepare for it. That's not simple. I've watched as you selflessly lead these people with compassion, fairness, and peace since you returned. No-one can believe that you have killed anyone in Serene and the risk should not prevent you from missing out on happiness. Besides, you'll have me by your side."

"You have a life here Madoka." Zack felt he was losing the battle.

"What life? I have family. Females do not toil so long, the males are doing the hard work. Echo takes Zero with him every day and I just sit here alone most of the time. Besides, I can always come back at any time and no-one will have missed me." she countered, and Zack felt that he had finally run out of reasons not to return to Serene in the twenty first century.

"When should we prepare to go?" he asked.

"What prepare? The beauty of time hopping is that you can do it at any time, there are no preparations required." Madoka replied.

"I was quite ill the last time...." A final reasoned argument that Zack had pulled from the periphery of his brain.

"I know." Madoka interrupted before he could give it too much thought. "Second time is always easier. We leave now."

Taking his hand, she led him to the door of the apartment and they made their way to ground level in the elevator. As they emerged from the tower the sun had set and there was darkness around them. Nothing more was said as Madoka lead Zack to the alcove where they had shared their first kiss behind the tower. Feeling his way in the dark Zack could not see a thing.

"What do we do now?" He asked, still gripping hold of Madoka's hand in the darkness. She did not reply. There was a flash of light that spun in a wide circle, enveloping them both, getting tighter and glowing a fire orange as it did so. Eventually with a pop, it flashed and disappeared and the pair of them had simply.... Vanished.

AUTHOR'S NOTE

Well, there you have it. My first novel to be printed. I would love to hear any feedback about it, whether positive or negative. This is the first of, hopefully, many and I need to respect and learn from negative feedback as much as wallow in the positive. I would ask all readers to please consider leaving a review on Good Reads or Amazon. If you would rather contact me directly you can do so at
tmthomasauthor@gmail.com
Thank you

Follow me:
Facebook - @tmthomasauthor
Twitter - @TMThomasauthor
Instagram - @tmthomasauthor